REAP THE WHIRLWIND

'You're a beautiful woman, Laura. If only you'd let me help with your demons, you would be even lovelier.'

She felt his lips warm against her cheek and swayed against him. She needed his understanding and strength, but how could she tell him about her demons? How to explain the terrible lie she had told him and risk destroying what they had together?

There had been other men she'd trusted with the full horror of what had happened all those years ago. She had learned to stay silent, to cover up the truth . . .

'Don't shut me out Laura. Nothing could be that bad.'

Laura snatched up her bag and headed for the door. If only that was true, she thought as she raced down the stairs and slammed her way out of the building. Even in his worst nightmare, Ben could never imagine how wrong he was . . .

About the author

Born and raised in Tasmania, Tamara Lee was eventually adopted by her grandmother and brought to England. Two marriages, three children and a chequered business career followed. She now lives on the south coast and writes full-time.

Reap the Whirlwind

Tamara Lee

CORONET BOOKS
Hodder and Stoughton

Copyright © 1996 by Tamara Lee

The right of Tamara Lee to be identified as the Author of
the Work has been asserted by her in accordance with the
Copyright, Designs and Patents Act 1988.

First published in Great Britain in 1996 by Hodder and Stoughton
A division of Hodder Headline PLC
First published in paperback in 1996 by Hodder and Stoughton
A Coronet Paperback

10 9 8 7 6 5 4 3 2 1

All rights reserved. No part of this publication may be
reproduced, stored in a retrieval system, or transmitted,
in any form or by any means without the prior written
permission of the publisher, nor be otherwise circulated
in any form of binding or cover other than that in which
it is published and without a similar condition being
imposed on the subsequent purchaser.

All characters in this publication are fictitious
and any resemblance to real persons, living or dead,
is purely coincidental.

A CIP catalogue record for this title is available from the British Library

ISBN 0 340 67246 3

Printed and bound in Great Britain by
Cox & Wyman Ltd, Reading, Berkshire

Hodder and Stoughton
A division of Hodder Headline PLC
338 Euston Road
London NW1 3BH

I dedicate this book to my mother, Dareen Eva Liefchild McKinley, who has always been my greatest inspiration.
I would like to acknowledge the encouragement and enthusiasm given by my agent, Teresa Chris, and thank my friends, Sharon Searle and Valerie Harris for their love and support through a difficult year.

They have sown the wind,
And they shall reap the whirlwind.

                Hosea 8:7

Like one that on a lonesome road
Doth walk in fear and dread.
And having once turned round walks on,
And turns no more his head;
Because he knows, a frightful friend
Doth close behind him tread.

S.T. Coleridge
The Rime of the Ancient Mariner

1

A goods train clattered by as he walked from the bus stop into the deserted street. Number 29 Station Villas was at the end of the small parade of houses which stood like decaying molars in the debris of rubble that had once been a thriving community. The shunting yards and warehouses huddled on the edge of the wastelands, and the new tower blocks cast deep shadows across the overgrown plots that had once been gardens. His world was changing – soon there would be nothing left.

Malcolm Squires stood for a moment and listened to the sound of the wheels on the tracks. Their voices were the only constant in his life. The only mantra that made any sense.

'The time is right. The time is right. Do it now. Do it now.'

An urgency took hold of him and made his fingers clumsy as he unlocked the door. Stepping into the hall, he took off his glasses and rubbed the bridge of his nose. He could smell the grease from the hotel kitchen on his hands and feel the sweat itch his skin where it had dried on his shirt. Yet none of that mattered. Only the voices of the wheels were important.

His mouth twitched in a fleeting smile, but there was no humour in him. That had been quenched long ago.

'That you, Malcolm? What are you doing down there?'

Malcolm started at the sound of Lillian's voice.

'Nothing, Mother. I was just about to get supper.'

'I heard the postman. Bring up my letters.' Lillian's voice

was loud and it echoed down the stairs and through the dimly lit hallway.

Malcolm took a deep breath and tried to shut out the sound of her demanding voice. He didn't want to hear it, he wanted to listen to the wheels. They were soft in their demands, mesmerising in their repetitiveness.

'Malcolm!'

Malcolm picked up the letters. After a quick glance, he found the fat brown envelopes he knew his mother was waiting for and threw the rest on the hall table. Then he loosened his tie and began the long climb up the stairs. A dread weighed heavy on his shoulders and made his feet hesitant. He hated coming home and if it wasn't for the wheels, he would have left long ago.

'About time. What have you been doing down there? Not the Lord's work, I'll be bound.'

Malcolm edged into the room and squinted in the harsh light of the bare bulb. The floor was naked, scrubbed boards, the windows shuttered with blinds and the walls painted white. The only decoration was a massive crucifix that dominated the wall above the headboard.

He glanced at the grossly obese woman who leaned against the crumpled pillows, and looked away. The thin, grey remains of Lillian's hair poked from her pink scalp in jagged tufts. Her arms were folded against her heavy breasts and her eyes were gimlet sharp in the pale, fleshy face.

'Sorry, Mother.'

Lillian stretched out an arm that was white and bloated. 'Have they sent them?' Her jowls trembled as her small, mean lips rubbed together in moist anticipation. She had caught sight of the letters in his hand.

Malcolm crossed the floor to the heavy oak bed and put them on the grubby quilt that was littered with sweet wrappers and cake crumbs. Lillian had been eating chocolate and it was smeared on her chin and down her cotton nightdress. The sight of her sickened him, yet, at the same time, he was terrified.

Lillian grasped his hand with the lightning strike of a snake and the strength of a Goliath. She brought her face close to him and hissed, 'Kiss the feet of Christ and ask him to forgive you your sins. I can see you've been having those thoughts again. Ask the Lord to wipe them away and cleanse you of evil.'

Malcolm looked away from the snarling lips and chocolate-stained teeth, and up at the tortured figure of Christ. He closed his eyes to avoid the steadfast gaze and dripping blood on that painted face, and leaned across Lillian to kiss the nailed feet that hung inches above his mother's head. The plaster was cold, and veined with age, and Malcolm had the strongest urge to wipe away the feel of it on his mouth. Yet he didn't dare. Lillian would punish him.

'Forgive me, Lord,' he intoned.

Lillian clutched his collar and pulled him down until they were inches apart, and Malcolm could smell the sourness of her breath.

'The mark of Satan is on you, Malcolm. The fires of hell are waiting to consume you. Repent before it's too late.'

Malcolm touched the puckered flesh on his cheek and nodded as the fear of retribution swept through him.

'I repent, Mother. I repent. Forgive me Lord, for I have sinned.' His breath was ragged as his heart thudded against his ribs and the sweat trickled down his back. It wasn't the fear of God that made him tremble. It was the fear of Lillian.

She nodded. 'Good. Now take your pills.'

Malcolm opened his mouth and Lillian shoved three tablets down his throat. The invasion of her fingers made him gag. He could taste the chocolate and the dirt beneath her nails. Could smell her flesh, rancid and aged. He grasped the tumbler and drank deeply of the cold water until it ran down his chin and dampened his shirt.

'Forgive this sinner, Lord. Wash away the evil that is in him and cleanse his soul.' Lillian clutched her Bible, her eyes tightly shut as she muttered. Then her demeanour rapidly changed and she pushed him away. 'Now, cook the supper. I'm hungry.'

He stumbled away from the bed and raced down the stairs.

With Lillian occupied by her religious tracts from America,

the house was silent and still behind the barricaded windows. It was waiting for him. Waiting to embrace him and draw him into its shadows. He breathed in the familiar smell of dust and decay and felt a semblance of peace. Lillian couldn't invade this stillness, this silence. She'd taken to her bed years ago, and left it rarely.

As he crossed the hall, he saw the letter. It had dropped from the table and now lay at his feet, the whiteness of the envelope gleaming in the shadows. It brought back a half-forgotten memory of another glimmer of white in another time, but it was elusive, and as it appeared to hold no importance, he was able to dismiss it.

The letter was typewritten and looked official. A brief scan of the closely written pages told him it was another eviction notice. He shredded it and cast the pieces to the floor. They couldn't make him leave, he had the voices of the wheels on his side.

A shiver goosed his skin as their whispers returned.

'Revenge is mine. Revenge is mine. Revenge is mine.'

The familiar warmth took the chill from his bones and he listened for a while. It was a sound he'd grown to welcome over the years. The power he'd been given was not to be denied. He needed to use it, to feel it in his hands and in his head. Only then, could the voices be appeased.

The restlessness grew and he pulled off his jacket and shirt, and stripped to his underwear. Moving into the kitchen he poured cold water from a pitcher into a bowl and cleansed himself. It was all a part of the ritual he would act out tonight, and the shiver that ran through him was not because of the cold – it was in anticipation.

As the stink of the Hastings Metropole kitchens was erased by the soap, he grimaced. He knew how others saw him, quiet, polite, barely noticeable amongst the peacock displays of the chefs and waiters. He was a non-entity, a colourless drone to be scorned or ignored as he stood day after day at the hotel kitchen sink.

How surprised they would be, he thought with a thrill, if

they knew the truth. How their attitude would change, how in awe of him they would be.

The gathering excitement made his heart beat faster, and he could hear the rasp of his breath, loud in the silence. He thought of the humiliation they meted out. A kitchen porter was the lowest life-form as far as the other dining-room staff were concerned. He thought of the chef's pompous voice and the dismissive attitude of the waitresses. Saw again the insidious sneers of the waiters and hotel managers.

He sniggered into the darkness. They were unimportant – dust beneath his heel. They didn't possess the power, couldn't hear the voices.

Malcolm pulled on clean clothes and began to cook supper. Every moment delayed the orgasmic pleasure which was to come. Yet he knew it was better to prolong that delay. Experience had taught him that.

*

Laura Kingsley tried to ease her shoulder muscles, but the pain merely shifted to her spine, then lodged in her hip and finally cramped her thigh.

'For Christ's sake, will you sit still!' Ben's Texan twang was an explosion in the silence between them.

Laura pulled the silk kimono around her and swung off the chaise-longue. 'I've had enough,' she said. 'Anyway, it's time to collect Cass.'

Ben ran his paint-smeared hands through his dark hair, bringing chaos where there had been merely disorder. His brown eyes glared at her over the canvas.

'How am I expected to finish this portrait, if you keep chasing after Cassandra? She's a big girl, now, Laura. Surely she can make her own way home?'

They glowered at one another, but it was Laura who broke the tension by looking away. She couldn't answer him.

Staring into the flames of the gas fire that barely heated the attic studio, she pulled the belt on the kimono into a tighter knot. How could she explain the anxiety that swept through her every time Cassandra was out of sight? To Ben it seemed irrational, but then she hadn't told him the complete truth about the reason behind that fear.

Ben gave an exasperated sigh and furiously began to clean his brushes. 'You have to let her go, Laura. She's not Melissa, and doesn't need you as much as she did.'

Laura turned abruptly from the fire. 'She needs me more than ever.' She jerked an arm towards the windows that gave a wide panorama of Brighton. Dusk was settling on the Downs and the lights were pin-pricks in the shadows. 'It's dangerous out there. I have to protect her,' she muttered finally.

She stopped, afraid of having said too much. Yet, she wondered, why not tell him the truth about Melissa. Why not share the secret she'd hidden for so long? The need to speak, to unburden the weight she'd carried all these years was growing stronger. The words she needed were formed in her brain, ready on her tongue. She and Ben had been lovers for two years. Surely she could trust him not to judge too harshly?

The silence between them was tangible, as though he knew she wanted to speak – understood something of the turmoil she was going through. She looked into his face, saw the stillness in him, and was tempted. Yet the doubts crowded in, muffling the words, reminding her, always reminding her. I made the mistake of trusting someone before, she thought. I won't do it again.

'I have to go,' she muttered as she picked up her clothes and began to dress. 'I've got a party of twenty booked in for the weekend and I need to speak to Chef. He's been hitting the bottle again and I daren't risk a fiasco in the kitchen.'

Ben made a noise in his throat and she heard the clatter of his brushes as he stuffed them into jars. A glance over her shoulder confirmed that he was watching her. Arms folded across his paint-spattered shirt, lean hips nonchalant against the wall, his dark hair fell to his shoulders, partly shielding the amusement in his eyes. The plains of his face were as rugged as the Texan landscape he'd left behind, and she had to tear her gaze away from the sensuous mouth and determined chin. It was late, Cass would be waiting.

'Between the twins and the Harbour Lights Hotel, I seem to come a poor third.' Ben's southern drawl was soft, with a hint of sadness.

'That's nonsense and you know it,' she snapped. Laura yanked up her jeans, fastened the belt and slipped the sweater over her head. She achieved this with a speed and dexterity she used in everything. Emerging from the loose cowl collar, she caught the speculative gleam in Ben's dark eyes and felt her own answering heat. Yet she had to ignore it. There were things to be done at the Harbour Lights which couldn't wait.

Ben padded barefoot across the studio floor and took her coat from her. Throwing it to one side, he wrapped her, protesting, in his arms and pulled her close. He brought with him the smell of turpentine and oil paint, the heat of his arousal, and a solidity and strength.

Her resolve faltered. Resting her head against his chest, she listened to the rapid drum of his heart and closed her eyes. The need to tell him was stronger now, the words almost spoken.

She lifted her chin. But he silenced her with a kiss that smothered all reasonable thought. Her arms reached up and she buried her hands in his hair as she gave herself up to the pleasurable sensations that temporarily shut out the world. Yet the knowledge that Cass would be waiting, and the chef still had to be dealt with took the edge off her pleasure, and the moment was gone almost before it had begun.

'Why is it,' he murmured against her mouth, 'that you can sit over there naked and I hardly notice, but the minute you dress I get the biggest boner this side of the Atlantic?' His hands ran over her rump, drawing her closer, making her acknowledge his need.

Laura felt herself respond, and knew she must stop before it was too late.

'You don't notice, because you're concentrating on other

things,' she said more sharply than she intended. She pulled away. 'I have to go.'

Ben dug his hand into the pockets of his jeans and fished out a battered pack of Marlboros. Flicking his thumbnail over the head of a match, he lit the cigarette and inhaled deeply. Then he watched the smoke drift to the ceiling before speaking again. When he did, his voice was low, the sadness more profound.

'Is it always going to be like this, Laura? You employ staff to look after the hotel. Can't you at least stay with me tonight?'

Laura jammed her feet into shoes. 'It's impossible, Ben. I promised Cass I'd pick her up, and the guests this weekend are the first from an Anglo-French consortium of businessmen. I had to pull a lot of strings to get them here, and if all goes well, it will mean a regular booking. Times are hard enough as it is, I can't afford to leave it to the staff.'

She brushed back her hair and looked up at him; at five feet three, she barely reached his chest. 'Another night? I promise.' The words sounded hollow, they'd been uttered before.

'Don't you want to look at my masterpiece before you go? It's almost finished.' Ben's voice had a resigned edge to it and Laura knew he had capitulated. She felt a pang of regret, but she had no other choice. Cassandra would always come first.

With a surreptitious glance at the clock, she approached the canvas.

'It's the best thing I've done in a long while. I hope you approve,' he murmured.

She was aware of Ben watching her as she approached the portrait, and knew that the sensual gleam in his eyes had turned to professional pride, but she wasn't prepared for the stunning image he'd created.

Laura looked into her own blue eyes, and the breath caught in her throat as she realised how Ben saw her. He had given her an ethereal quality that her mirror had never reflected. He had enhanced her eyes with a hazy, languid desire and coaxed her wiry auburn curls into a Raphaelite tumble that shone like polished copper in the light of the tiffany lamp.

The attic studio faded as a rush of jumbled emotions took hold. It was as if she was alone with Ben's image of her, and there, in the bright studio lights, she was faced with the depths of his feelings, and the insight he'd had of her inner self. He had seen her as a woman in love, a woman with a wanton side that she'd never known she'd possessed. Yet, he'd also seen the child in her, hinted at it in the delicate brushwork of skin tone and soft mouth. There was a vulnerability there that she'd thought she'd hidden, a wistfulness she had never dared acknowledge. Until now.

Laura swallowed the lump in her throat. What else had he seen in her, that he hadn't included in the painting? She hadn't realised how deep their relationship had become, and it made her uneasy.

The rasp of denim against the wall made her suddenly aware of Ben's expectant silence. She would have to say something, have to face him, knowing her soul had been bared. To take the edge off any criticism, she forced a lightness into her voice.

'I don't look like that!' she said. 'I've got freckles, my nose is a blob, and I'm sure you've managed to lose several pounds in weight, especially around the hips.' Yet she couldn't turn away from the portrait, couldn't face him.

'Yes you do,' he whispered as he folded his arms around her waist and pulled her close. 'You're a beautiful woman, Laura. If only you'd let me help with your demons, you would be even lovelier.'

She felt his lips warm against her cheek, and swayed against him. She needed his understanding and strength, but how could she tell him about her demons. How to explain the terrible lie she had told him and risk destroying what they had together? There had been other men she'd trusted with the full horror of what had happened all those years ago. She had learned to stay silent, to cover up the truth – the hurt of their betrayal had been a harsh lesson.

He turned her to face him and she steeled herself to meet his gaze.

'Trust me, Laura. Tell me what it is I see behind those lovely eyes. Let me share the secret that makes you sad.'

'I can't. I'm sorry.' She bowed her head and pulled away, her vision blurred with tears as she slipped on her coat. 'I trusted someone once and they let me down. I can't let that happen between us. I love you too much.'

There, she thought. It was said. Her voice cracked and she angrily knuckled away the tears. 'I'm thirty-five, Ben. I have a history. Let's just leave it at that.'

Ben hooked his fingers into his belt and watched her, his dark eyes troubled. Then he shrugged. 'Okay. But don't shut me out, Laura. Nothing could be that bad.'

Laura snatched up her bag and headed for the door. If only that was true, she thought as she raced down the stairs and slammed her way out of the building. Even in his worst nightmare, Ben could never imagine how wrong he was.

*

The man who called himself Paul Galloway looked out of the window and felt the anticipation knot in his stomach as the 747 circled Heathrow. It seemed a long time since his last visit to England, but in reality, it had only been three months. There was no place on earth that compared with it, but it could no longer be called home. And that made him angry – very angry. The knot tightened in a white heat of vengeful rage and his hand shook as he drained the last of the whisky.

'Are you not feeling well, sir?' asked the hostess as she collected the last of the glasses and tidied away the table. 'Can I get you something?'

Paul shook his head and abruptly turned away. He didn't want to see her powdered face and preened hair. Didn't wish to converse with someone who probably opened her legs for the price of an expensive dinner.

All women are bitches, he thought as he ground his teeth. Lying, scheming, conniving bitches. There's only one way of dealing with them, a way that makes them crawl. A way that

Reap the Whirlwind

bends them to my will, subjugates them and brings them down to the level where they really belong. Beneath my heel.

Just the thought of it made him feel good.

The muscles in his face relaxed as calm settled over him. His business would be completed in a matter of hours, then he would be free to do as he pleased. His masters were generous, they could afford to be, and as long as he clinched the deal, they wouldn't question his expenses.

He leaned back in the seat and stared out of the window. Yet he barely noticed the landscape sprawled beneath him. His mind was running over the plans he'd made for this visit. Excitement caught him up in a wave of euphoria as the sun sank behind the terminal buildings and the plane landed with a thud on the runway. The last visit to London had been most satisfactory. Shame about the girl though, things had got a little out of hand.

Still, he mused, I'm not planning to stay long, or to visit the same haunts, so it won't be a problem.

The plane taxied and came to a halt at the terminal. Paul waited impatiently as the other passengers scurried to leave. He had a score to settle, and what better place to do that, than England. Living in Saudi had meant he couldn't risk indulging his fantasies, but he was back now, and the anticipation was pleasurable. The planning was over, now for the final execution.

Paul Galloway drew his lips into a grimace that barely passed as a smile, as he thought of the malicious twist to his usual plan. This time he would drive south, to Sussex.

*

As Malcolm cleared away the last of the supper dishes, he noticed the remains of the letter he'd discarded earlier. They reminded him of how it used to be, when the street had been alive with the sound of voices and the heavy tramp of boots on the cracked pavements. Doors slamming, the cry of children and the shouts of the women as they gossiped on doorsteps. The men worked in the factory or the shunting yards and railway, it had been a lively place, a place where everyone knew your name . . . and your business.

It was almost all gone now. Destroyed by the bulldozers, taken away and packed neatly into the tower blocks of concrete where they became anonymous. Solitary beings, little lives in little boxes, unremarkable in their dullness. Like rats in a trap, existing only to procreate and become fodder for the factories and warehouses of the rich.

He shook his head, but felt no sorrow for what had been. Merely a determination to remain apart – different from the rest.

'They won't parcel me up and put me in a box,' he muttered. 'I'll leave when I'm ready, and not before.'

He stared at the boarded up window. Only the voices of the wheels and the urgency they brought with them were important. The need had become a living thing, squirming in his belly, itching to be released. Yet he stamped down on that need, putting it off until there was no denying it. It was better that way, more satisfying.

Malcolm finally left the kitchen and stood at the bottom of the stairs, his hand lightly touching the newel post as the whispers of the wheels made his heart hammer. He cocked his head as he peered into the gloom and resisted the tremor of anticipation. Lillian was snoring. There would be no interruption of the ritual that needed to be performed before he capitulated to the voices.

The door leading into the attic space was low and narrow, hidden by a heavy chest of drawers. Secreted from Lillian's surreptitious forays into his room when her curiosity burned and she left her bed. He knew she came into his room, because she always left evidence of her visit. A brush out of place, a shirt not quite squared up with the others.

He sniggered as the door swung open on well oiled hinges. He was too clever for Lillian, she thought she knew everything about him, but she was wrong. She would never know about the wheels and the voices and the location of his secret place of ritual.

He lifted the candle and watched the flame throw trembling

shadows against the walls as he breathed in the familiar musty smell of his special place. The breath hissed through his teeth as he fought to control his emotions. What would happen when the men came to tear it down? How would he complete his ritual then?

The thoughts ran helter-skelter through his mind, twisting and turning, bringing heat to his skin, touching icy fingers to the raw edges of his confusion. He would have to find a way. Have to rebuild this shrine in another place. But would it be the same? He doubted it, and that frightened him. The wheels were demanding, but could they be fooled? Would they simply desert him, once the house was gone?

He sighed and the flame flickered as his hand trembled. He couldn't think about that now. There were things to be done, a mission to carry out before the end of the night.

Malcolm's footsteps were silent on the mouldering scrap of carpet as he approached the dressing table. It had taken years to collect these precious things. Things Lillian now regarded as sinful.

His heart thudded as he thought of the woman he had unwillingly come to hate. Her presence filled the attic room, bringing with it memories that would not be banished. He thought he could hear her voice, shrill and demanding when she was roused. Whining and petulant as she grew old and fat. He shook off those memories and concentrated on the voices of the wheels.

'The time is right. The time is right. The time is right.'

He sat down on the padded stool and looked in the mirror. The yearning for the impossible was etched on his face and he looked away. Would he never find peace?

'Listen to me,' whispered the wheels. 'Go back, go back. Perform the rites. Listen to me.'

The blonde wig glistened in the electric light and he carefully took it off the shop mannequin and placed it on his head. Then he watched his reflection in the candlelight as he stroked the tarnished hairbrush through the long tresses.

The voices were softer now. 'Go back, go back. Remember, remember.'

He closed his eyes as the brush swept through the hair. The voices were a lullaby. A siren's song that had never escaped from his mother's lips.

Years ago, he remembered, before the voices and before the crucifix, Lillian had allowed him to brush her hair. It was fair then, like his, but long and thick, reaching almost to her waist. He smiled, as once again, he saw himself as a small boy standing on a stool behind her, the brush sweeping through that honey-coloured hair that smelled of flowers.

The memory of her voice ripped away the pleasure. 'Mind what you're doing, you stupid child. Can't you do anything right?'

He was five again, confused and awkward as he faced her temper. The brush was snatched from him and he was snared by her angry glower in the mirror.

'You're as bad as your father. Both of you are useless,' she sneered. 'Go on, get out. I'm sick of looking at your ugly, sinful face.'

The smile faded and he returned to the present. There had been too few moments of happiness. Too many painful memories. He didn't wish to dwell on them now, but the ritual demanded it.

He replaced the brush and looked at the collection of bottles and boxes on the dressing table. His memory conjured up her face as it once had been. She was beautiful then, and young. But the bitterness had already soured that beauty, bringing a harshness to the voice, and a twist of malice to the mouth.

'I waited years for a child and the Lord saw fit to punish me by sending you,' she spat as she clutched her Bible. 'The Devil placed his hoof on your face, marking you with the sign of sin.'

Malcolm cowered and touched his face, feeling the puckered skin beneath his fingers.

'Cleanliness is next to godliness. I will burn away the mark of Satan.' Lillian poured the bleach onto his face and began to scrub.

Malcolm felt the agony renewed by the memory as Lillian ignored his screams and scrubbed harder. Once again, he could see her face, red with anger, lips tight, eyes crazed with fervour as the heat seared his flesh. Now he could hear her voice, strident and powerful. 'Wash clean in the blood of the Lord. Only the pure can enter Heaven.'

He shuddered. No wonder Lillian had never loved him. He was a freak. A freak with the bloodstain of a cloven hoof on his cheek.

'Pay her back,' whispered the wheels. 'Pay her back and show her she was wrong.'

Malcolm lit the remains of the candle stubs and their light brought little warmth to the cold inside him. It was easy for the wheels to demand vengeance, they didn't have to face Lillian day after day.

He lifted the lid of the powder box. The musk of roses drifted into the room and he picked up the delicate powder puff and feathered it over his face. He closed his eyes and imagined that it was her hand caressing his cheek, her softness touching his soul.

His eyes snapped open. That was not how it had been. She had never caressed him, never shown him any sign of the affection he craved.

Dropping the powder puff, he picked up the lipstick. Dark red, with the imprint of her mouth on the soft tube of colour, it was almost finished. He touched it to his lips, watching as he traced the outline, remembering – always remembering. Her lips had been full, like his. The skin pale and flawless.

He stared into the mirror. Saw the pale eyes that peered myopically back at him from behind the thick glasses and the blemish on his cheek that could never be disguised. The mark had been small and almost invisible before the bleach. Now it was red and obscene, the skin around it, tortured.

With an angry swipe, he smeared the back of his hand over his mouth. The lipstick and powder made the hatred burn. Brought the pain back to the surface, the rejection by Lillian sharp in his memory. Like a fat white spider, she had wrapped him in her sticky web of malice and kept him prisoner as she fed from him.

Malcolm tasted the bitterness in his throat as he remembered the slam of the front door as his father left home for the last time. He hadn't even bothered to say goodbye, or to ask if Malcolm wanted to leave with him. The loneliness descended on him in a pall of grey. It was on his fourteenth birthday, he remembered. The day he first heard the voices. They had become his only friend, his comforter. The one thing he could rely on to never let him down. All he had to do was obey them.

The laughter bubbled deep inside him and he buried his face in his hands to muffle the sound. 'I have a secret,' he whispered. 'A delicious secret.' He took a trembling breath. 'Don't you want to share it, Mother?'

The silence seemed to mock him and he bunched his fists. 'It's time to show you how clever I am, Mother dearest,' he hissed. 'I'll make you see how wrong you are to dismiss me.'

The perspiration was cold on his skin and his pulse raced. He waited until the nausea and the anger drained away. The wheels were right, they always had been. Now it was time to obey them again.

The suitcase was in the cupboard, beneath the faded colour of her dresses. The buckles were tarnished, the leather straps worn, but it was the contents that were important. He lifted out the dark clothes and heavy boots, and dressed quickly.

There was only one item left, and it was the most important. He picked it up and felt its familiar contours. Then with a tremble of pleasure, he surveyed his reflection in the mirror.

It was time to fulfil the last part of the ritual. Time to go hunting.

2

The apartment formed a rear annexe to the main building of the hotel. Built during the first year of their ownership, it had been designed to blend with the rest of the Victorian façade.

Laura slammed the car door and ran across the gravel carpark at the back of the hotel, and made her way down the narrow alleyway to her private side door. It had begun to rain and the short journey from the car had left her wet and bedraggled. She threw the keys onto the hall table and dragged off her sodden coat. A pile of mail waited for her and after a quick glance, she put it aside. More circulars, a few bills, nothing that couldn't wait. She sighed and dredged up the last of her energy. The pleasurable afternoon with Ben was a distant memory, now she had to deal with Cassandra.

'You are not going, and that's final,' she said sharply, carrying on the conversation that had begun on their journey home.

'Typical!' shouted Cassandra as she slammed the door, then unlaced her Doc Martens and threw them aside. 'You don't like me having any fun. Just because you're stuck in this dump, doesn't mean I have to be.' She glared back at her mother, her face a storm, her pupils brittle shards of blue.

The anger in those eyes made Laura falter and she watched Cassie wrench off the long black coat to reveal a baggy sweater and black leggings.

'You know as well as I do, the reason for us coming here,' she said quietly. She wanted to say more, to reach out and take Cassandra in her arms and quell the anguish which ran through her child. But words couldn't heal the pain. Nothing could. For it was mirrored in her own heart.

'Don't do that, Mum. Don't lay the guilt on me. It's not my fault we had to come here.' Cassandra's face was red with anger, but her gaze shifted away as Laura reached for her. 'And don't smother me! I'm not Melissa.'

Laura swallowed the frustration. The last few days had been the worst, and there seemed to be no way out of the tunnel of despair through which they both travelled. It was said that time was a healer, yet she'd no evidence of it. For her, it was merely a reminder of what might have been. Each passing year an anniversary, a memorial. Bringing back the pain.

'I know you're not, darling. But I still want to protect you. I know what's best for you. I'm your mother.' Laura stopped abruptly. She hadn't meant to sound patronising, but how else could she make Cass understand the real fear that haunted her. Melissa was as safe as she ever would be. But it hadn't always been so.

Cassandra flung her coat over a chair and picked up her bag.

'You can't stop me from doing whatever I want,' she said defiantly. 'I'm nearly seventeen. I don't need you any more.'

Laura struggled to keep her temper, this was an old battleground, familiar to both of them. 'I don't care how sophisticated you think you are, you are not going to the rave.' A headache was looming and Laura hastily glanced at the clock. This argument had been going on since she'd picked Cass up from Sixth form college. The hotel was full and she still had to talk to Chef.

'I don't want you exposed to drugs, Cass. Those raves are just an excuse to hook young girls like you.' She reached out to touch Cassie's shoulder, but her hand was shrugged away and Laura knew the argument wasn't over.

Cassie flicked back the long fair hair which had been streaked with red and purple dye. 'God! You're so predictable,' she shrieked. 'I don't do drugs. That's not what raving's about.' She whirled away and slammed into the tiny kitchen which they rarely used. 'Everyone else is going. I'm sick of being treated like a child,' she shouted as the door swung behind her.

Laura hesitated. Is that what she was doing? She was still young enough to remember her own teenage years, and the frustration of being thought of as a child when her hormones were telling her otherwise. Yet it was different now. Teenagers were being forced to grow up too soon. Forced to face the reality of the dole queue, their futures unpredictable because of the recession, their ambitions fuelled by the slick marketing of the media. And then there were the drugs. An easy way to forget the uncertainties, a balming influence in the stormy sea of adolescence. A forbidden fruit to be tasted in defiance of rules and restrictions. Troubled children like Cassie were easy prey.

She shivered as the thoughts whirled through her mind. Drugs were not the only dangers. Melissa was proof of that.

Yet the past had not brought them closer. It had merely widened the chasm between them as the years sped by. Cassie had become a stranger. A virago that stormed through the house and through her life like a whirlwind. Where had she gone wrong?

Laura sighed as she hung up their coats and picked up Cass's boots. If only David had been a different kind of husband, maybe, just maybe, things might have been different.

'That's nonsense, and you know it,' she muttered to herself crossly. 'We're better off without him.'

She followed Cassie into the kitchen and filled the kettle. With a concerted effort, she ignored the slamming of cupboards and heavy sighs coming from the other side of the room. It's going to be a long night, she thought ruefully, as she swallowed a couple of Paracetamol and shoved her feet into slippers.

'Dinner's in an hour. Can't you wait?' she said.

Cassie turned, her cheek bulging with a sandwich. 'I'm meeting my friends,' she mumbled sullenly.

Laura lit a cigarette and tried to keep her hand from

shaking. Ben might see her as a fiery redhead, but a powerful temper went with the territory and she knew that if she lost control it would only make things worse.

'You have homework,' she said firmly. 'As for these so-called friends ...' She took a deep breath. 'They're trouble, Cass. I forbid you to leave this house tonight.' She waited for the inevitable storm. Why did life have to be like this, she wondered. I'm battle-scarred enough.

Cassie slammed the remains of the sandwich onto the kitchen table and stood with her hands on her skinny hips. 'This isn't a house, or a home. It's a bloody great mausoleum of a hotel in the middle of nowhere-land. I'll see who I like, when I like and where I like. No wonder Dad left if you nagged him the way you nag me.' She paused to draw breath, her pale eyes lit with malice.

She reminds me of her father. The thought shook Laura as she watched her daughter's transformation. She has that narrow, spiteful look he had when he couldn't get his own way. Inherited both our tempers, too, she admitted silently. Yet there was a frailty in her daughter's anger, a confusion of hate and bewilderment, fear and conviction. Laura ached to ease that confusion, but knew Cassandra would reject all attempts to pacify. She hadn't finished her tirade.

'You're a bloody hypocrite, Mum. You're sleeping with an ageing hippy who hasn't got two pennies to rub together and you have the nerve to object to Snake and his friends. And what's that in your mouth? Tobacco's a drug. Just as difficult to give up as heroin. So don't fucking preach!'

Laura's hand connected with Cassie's face in a stinging slap.

The shock of what she'd done stunned them both into momentary silence.

'I'm sorry, Cass. I ...'

Cass tore away from her and crashed out of the room. 'I hate you! I hate this hotel and I hate Saxonbridge. I wish Dad had taken me with him.'

Laura was left with the sound of her daughter's feet pounding up the hallway. There was a slam of a door, followed by the repetitive, bass thud of music.

'Damn, damn, damn!' Laura leaned against the sink and stared out of the window onto the rain-soaked carpark. Her heart was racing and she gripped the sink until her knuckles showed white. She had never hit Cass before, and was stunned by the intensity of her reaction to the child's foul language. She had lost the argument by losing control, and that was something she had always vowed she would never do. She of all people had first-hand proof that violence never solved anything.

Laura ground the cigarette out, took a deep breath and went to change her clothes in preparation for the evening ahead. It seemed that no matter what she did, Cassie would always blame her for David's leaving. Yet how could she damage the image her daughter had of the errant father who sent expensive presents when and if he remembered? Cassandra adored him, looked up to him as a hero. It wouldn't be fair to tell her the truth.

Her rage ebbed and flowed as she tugged viciously at the zip on her black cocktail dress. David could walk in and out of their lives when it suited him, and even after all these years apart, she could still be hurt by him. He filled Cassandra's head with highly imaginative stories of the famous people he met and the places he'd been to. But he never went to the hospital. Never visited Melissa. It was a burden he refused to share and she tasted the bitterness at the thought. He was too weak for that, too spineless. As far as David was concerned, it was in the past, put away and forgotten, a shameful episode in their lives that was never to be shown the light of day.

'Bastard,' she hissed as she savagely slammed the bedroom door and headed up the stairs to the main reception area of the hotel.

As she reached the heavy door that divided the hotel from their apartment, the anger cooled into bitter reality. This was no time to wallow in self-pity. Cassie was out of control and she had no idea how to handle it, but tears and recriminations were not the answer.

*

Cassandra flicked the switch on the stereo, turned up the volume and threw herself onto the bed and stared at the ceiling. The anger she had felt was merely a forewarning of what was to come. Now there was an awareness in her, a clarity of vision that came stealthily and uninvited during these times of extraordinary perception. It washed away the rage, and smothered the tension that had built during the day. She could see the smallest vein in the plaster on the ceiling, the prism of light in the tiniest drop of rain on the window and hear the roll of the sea in the distant harbour.

Her heart raced and desperation surged at fever pitch. She had to escape the visions that would come. Had to find a way to deal with what was happening in her head. The fear was palpable, and she wondered for an instant if she was going mad.

She turned on her side and brought her knees to her chest as she squeezed her eyes shut and tried to quell the thoughts that rampaged through her mind. She wished she could be with her twin. But Melissa was far away in the hospital, out of reach, distanced by her silence. Was this how Melissa felt? Did she too, have these pictures flashing before her?

'I wish you were here, Mel. I miss you,' she whispered. 'I shouldn't have said those things to Mum.' She buried her face in the pillow. 'She doesn't understand what's happening to me. Can't possibly know how it feels.'

Her hand crept to her face and she cupped her cheek. She could still feel the heat of her mother's slap, but the hurt was more than skin deep, and the shock of Laura's reaction made her ashamed of her behaviour.

As the minutes ticked away and the music filled the room, she was tormented by the silent parade of images that came into her head. In a last desperate struggle to banish them, she leaped from the bed and stood at the window. Sometimes it helped to find something else to focus on.

The hills and valleys of the Sussex port were spread before her. The rows of terraced houses, with their pin-pricks of light, huddled alongside the twisting, downland roads of Saxonbridge. The winter sky was tinged with the sulphurous yellow lights of distant Brighton and the ancient copse of trees on the far hill stood out in silhouette against it. Saxonbridge had taken its name from the burial mounds that dotted the surrounding hills. It was a timeless place, despite the new housing estates that had blossomed in the last ten years.

'God, I hate it here,' she moaned as the emotions gathered force and the other images jostled for her attention. The feeling of entrapment closed in, powerful in its strength, smothering in it's intensity.

She closed her eyes and prayed for release. Yet she knew it was impossible. There could be no escape from the power of the visions that filled her head. No release from the restrictions that power forced on her life. She was different to the others, and although that difference was invisible, it set her apart.

Cassandra turned away and slumped onto the bed as she gave herself up to the heavy bass of the music. It whirled in her head, throbbed in her veins and drew her down into the maelstrom of sound. She could lose herself in the layers of notes, switch off the outside world and become one with the rhythm. Yet it could not halt the familiar parade which passed behind her eyes.

Faces of strangers, their features blurred, their voices muted, raced before her. Landscapes in technicolour brilliance, uncharted in her world, yet real. Whispers in the canyons of her mind, unintelligible, yet foreboding.

She whimpered and buried her face in her pillow. She had thought it was over. Thought that her mind had succeeded in its fight to banish the horror. Yet it was happening again. The evil had re-surfaced. Only this time it was closer than before and the force of its breath was rancid as it carried a foreshadowing of what was to come.

With a growing sense of despair, she realised she no longer possessed the power to control the forces that descended on her. Closing her eyes and burying her head in the pillow she began the titanic struggle to overcome the malevolence that battled for her sanity.

At the brink of her resistance, on the ebb tide of her strength, the visions faded, then were gone. Yet she knew they would return, demanding to be acknowledged, lucid in their intensity. They always did.

Cassandra felt the emptiness follow. Soon the migraine would blot out all feeling, all emotion. It was a familiar pattern, one she had accepted many years before as natural. Only now, as the years had passed and her knowledge had grown, did she realise that this was not so. She was the possessor of a demonic gift. One she would have gladly relinquished if it was at all possible. That gift had grown over the years, and now these latest images held a force which made her blood chill and her hackles rise. There was a darkness about them, an evil which could not be explained. The tentacles of their malice were entwined in her mind and refused to loosen their hold.

For the fourth time in sixteen years, Cassandra was forced to face the demons that stalked the dark corridors of her past.

*

Paul Galloway stood at the basin in the seedy bar's washroom and smoothed back his blond hair as he viewed his reflection in the age-spotted mirror. What he saw, pleased him. He was almost forty, but his fair hair was still thick and in good condition, his face tanned from the desert sun. Long sessions in the gym had kept his figure trim and in the black leather jacket and denim jeans, he could have passed for thirty.

'Want some company?'

Paul was startled from his thoughts as the soft voice penetrated his senses. He glared at the skinny youth with the razored scalp and artfully painted face. 'What makes you think I could possibly wish to spend time in your company?' he sneered coldly.

The youth backed away and Paul experienced a sharp thrill

Reap the Whirlwind

of pleasure as the wariness of fear crept into those heavily shadowed eyes.

'Sorry mate. My mistake,' muttered the youth, his hands held up in surrender as he stumbled against the urinal in his haste to leave.

Paul swiftly covered the space between them and the boy whimpered as his shirt was grasped in a stranglehold and he was pushed against the cold green tiles.

The sound of dripping water echoed in the murky walls and cracked porcelain. The heavy bass thud of the jukebox rock and roll rattled the rusting mesh over the window.

'They should castrate animals like you,' whispered Paul. 'You're a perversion.' He saw the fear, felt the tremble in the boy's torso – and liked it. This was power, this was strength, this was what made him a real man.

As the timeless silence stretched between them, he decided, almost with regret, to leave it there. There were more important things on the agenda tonight than a sweating little poof.

He gave the boy a shove that sent him sprawling in the drain beneath the urinals. 'That's about your level. Stay there and don't bother decent people again,' he hissed.

The door slammed behind him and the coldness of his anger made him tremble. He needed a drink.

Leaving the bar, he crossed the road and walked through the Brighton Lanes until he came to a pub that he'd visited before. No nasty surprises in here, they had ways of dealing with queers in the Stag's Head.

He sipped his whisky and let his gaze roam over the other drinkers. Like Brighton, the pub had seen better days. The old whore was showing her age, he thought as the memory of childhood holidays and a cleaner, more sparkling Brighton sprang to mind. But it was the kind of place he liked. The music was loud, the lights dim, the clientele mixed, but heterosexual. Leather and rags seemed to be the appropriate dress and both sexes wore jewellery in their ears and noses. The pungent aroma of hash hung like a pall from the ceiling, but it didn't seem to matter very much.

No-one asked questions in a place like this. No-one noticed a stranger.

The door was flung open and Paul flinched against the bar as a group of bikers pushed their way through the packed bar. A brightly coloured flyer was pressed into his hand and he was about to close his fist over it, when he had second thoughts.

He looked at it again. The paper was cheap and brightly printed with signs of the zodiac. In the centre of the red pentacle was the face of a wolf, its bared teeth and slavering jaws surrounded the legend, 'Rave.'

A slow smile touched his mouth as he realised he knew the location of the rave. Wolves Farm – why not? It was as good a place as any to find what he was looking for.

*

Laura faced Edward the chef, and not for the first time, wished she was at least five inches taller. Tall women were taken seriously. Tall women had a presence.

'This is your last warning, Edward. If you can't stay off the booze, then you'll get your cards.'

The chef towered over her, his whites gleaming in the bright, noisy kitchen. 'Have there been complaints from the customers, Mrs Kingsley? I think not,' he sneered, his eyes not quite settling in her direction. 'I'm an artist, and a little drink merely inspires me to greater things.'

Piss artist, more like, thought Laura sagely. 'That's not the point, Edward. You've been late twice over the last two weeks and there have been complaints from the other staff. They don't appreciate having to cover for you when you're too drunk to be left in charge of a sharp knife.'

They glared at one another as the noise in the kitchen grew around them. Dinner would be served in an hour and the pace was hotting up.

'If you and the staff find my presence so uncomfortable, then I will look elsewhere. My talents would be appreciated at the Grand.' Edward's chin had lifted, and there was an angry flush in his cheeks.

Laure moved closer and spoke quietly, aware of prying ears and eyes all around them. 'With no recent references, I doubt whether the Grand would look on you kindly, Edward. Your reputation as a drunk goes before you, and getting fired from that London hotel did you no favours.'

She paused to let the full impact of what she'd said sink in. 'Now do we have an understanding? Or do I look for a new chef?'

As she waited for his reply, she was only partially certain of his decision. If he left, she would be in deep trouble, the second chef was good, but not in Edward's league.

Edward yanked the tea towel from his waist band and cleaned his hands. 'There's work to be done. If there's nothing else,' he said coldly.

'Have you kept to the menu I prepared? I don't want any more cock-ups. Tonight's important.' Laura moved around the kitchen, lifting lids, tasting, sniffing. Edward was right, he was an artist, and she was relieved he was staying. If only he'd restrict his drinking to after hours.

'Everything to your satisfaction, Mrs Kingsley?'

Laura swallowed the delicious morsel of wild salmon and dill sauce. 'I have no complaints about your cooking, Edward. It's wonderful as usual. Just stay sober.' She shot him a warning look, then hurried through the kitchen and out into the dining-room.

It was a large room that overlooked the front garden and the harbour. Each table was draped in pristine damask, and the silver and glass glittered in the light of the chandeliers. Moving from table to table, she watched the serving staff finish their preparations for the evening. With a word to one of the waiters about the cleanliness of his shirt, she sent him off to housekeeping for a replacement, then looked at her watch. There was just time to check on Cass before the evening got under way.

Laura heard the door-bell as she hurried back to the apartment, and when she looked through the frosted glass, she took a deep breath, pulled back the chain and opened the door. After the confrontation with Cass and the delicate sensibilities of the chef, she was in no mood to be polite.

'Cassandra's busy. She's not going out.'

Snake looked down at her, his hands loosely tucked into the belt of his baggy trousers. A tattoo slithered its way up his forearm and disappeared beneath the rolled cuffs of his baseball jacket. As he flexed his arm, the snake seemed to come alive and Laura was almost mesmerised by it.

'Hello, Cass. You ready?' Snake looked over Laura's head, his matted dreadlocks dripping rain onto his cavernous face.

Laura whirled round. Cassandra was still wearing black, but now her eyes were heavily lined with kohl, and silver jewellery adorned her ears and fingers. She looked a mess.

'Get indoors, Cassandra. You are not going.' She turned to shut the door, but found Snake's size eleven Doc Martens in the way. There was an angry edge to her voice. 'Let me shut the door. Leave now and there won't be any trouble.'

'For God's sake, Mum. Do you have to show me up like this?' Defiance and fear were a cocktail in her eyes. Belligerence in the set of her shoulders. Cassandra pushed past Laura and stepped out into the rain. 'I'm going. See you sometime tomorrow.' She turned swiftly and ran down the alley to the carpark.

Snake grinned, showing an expanse of rotten teeth as he filled the doorway. 'Yea. Chill out, Mamacita. See ya.' He moved his foot and the light from the hallway shone on the stud in his nose before he turned away.

'Cassandra, come back here. I won't have you disobey me like this.' Laura's furious shout was lost in the darkness of the alleyway and all she could hear was the clump of heavy boots and the snigger of laughter.

'Cassie!' Laura ran down the alley and into the carpark.

The souped up, rusting hulk of a Fiesta stood in the gateway, its engine growling beneath the heavy thud of techno music. There were three other youths inside, each dirtier and rougher than the other. Laura was perplexed.

Reap the Whirlwind

What did Cassie see in this Neanderthal. Was he a part of her defiance? Cassandra climbed into the car and slammed the door.

Laura tried to grab the handle. 'Cassandra, get out of there – now!'

Cassandra turned her head away as Snake floored the accelerator. The tyres spat gravel and the car roared through the gate and down the road.

Laura clenched her fists as the blast of the car horn echoed in the stillness. Her thwarted attempts to control Cassandra had brought back a frustrated helplessness.

As the Fiesta turned the corner, Laura swore loudly into the rain.

*

He melted into the darkness, as silent and ethereal as the shadows themselves. The euphoria was still on him, still pounding his pulse and filling his senses. It was a need that returned ever more frequently, since the first time he'd obeyed the voices.

Malcolm grinned in the darkness. He'd easily fooled them all those years ago. They'd never caught him. Not that time, or the next, or the ones after that. They wouldn't catch him this time either. He was too clever for them.

The trek across the fields led him away from the farm track towards the ring of trees and the Saxon burial ground. From the shelter of those trees, he had a clear view of Wolves Farm and the site of the rave.

The barn was in darkness, but now and again he saw a glare of light as someone opened the door. Yet Malcolm didn't need to get any closer. There was plenty to watch from here. Formless shadows moving in the darkness, the flair of a match, a snatch of conversation, the grunts and groans of those who coupled in the darkness, thinking they were alone.

It was three in the morning, and the rave was at its peak. The bass rythm echoed the beat of his heart as he crouched in the bushes. The adrenalin surged. It was almost time. And he was prepared.

Something stilled his hands and he lifted his head to scent the air. Someone was watching him. Someone close and silent in the shadows. Yet that someone had no form. It was merely a presence. As he listened to the pulse of the music, he closed his eyes and willed the presence to draw near. He felt it reach out to him and touch icy fingers to the core of his being. Intrigued, but wary, he searched the darkness for a face. He needed to know his intruder.

With a sigh of regret, Malcolm felt his concentration break as the mysterious inquisitor pulled away. Yet he knew they would meet again when the tenuous link was strengthened. Whoever it was, was still uncertain of their power. But it would return. Those probing fingers were too curious. The mind behind the presence too determined.

The flicker of a smile touched his mouth, then was gone. The knowledge that he was no longer isolated was double-edged. With it came the fear of discovery, but also the excitement of vindication. There were others like him. And it made this particular hunt even more enthralling.

*

Cassandra stood in the centre of the vast barn as the shadows crept into her mind. The strobe lights flickered over the dancers, throwing their features into surreal relief against the darkness of their surroundings. The music throbbed in the walls and in the floor beneath her feet, touching her skin, filling her head. Yet the images in her mind were too strong to ignore.

She could almost see him. Could almost reach out and touch him. But he was hidden by a barrier that she wasn't strong enough to breach. The certainty that the time would come for her to cross that bridge made her afraid. More afraid than she had ever been.

The coldness of his menace touched her and she tried to draw back. But he held her there, mesmerised, and at his mercy as he probed the darkness between them. He was searching for her, willing her to come to him. She felt her resistance weaken, and her mind edge towards him.

Who was he? What did he want of her?

Trees loomed over her in that imaginary world he brought with him. Their bare branches twisted and grotesque like arthritic fingers. Then she was drawn to the shadows of the briars, to the wet grass and mud-stained feet.

'Cass! What the fuck's the matter?'

His voice was distant and ghostly in the kaleidoscope that flashed in her head. She turned towards him as though she had no will of her own. His face looked familiar, and there appeared to be no evil there. It was not the face in her head.

Hands gripped her, forcing her to look into his grey eyes, drawing her away from the surreal world in her mind.

'Snake?' The name felt strange on her lips, the sound of her voice robotic beneath the pulsating music. The emptiness was returning, blotting out the images. 'I have to go,' she muttered.

His fingers tightened in a steel bracelet around her wrists and she looked down at them as though watching from outside her earthly body.

'We only just got here,' he shouted above the music, his mouth close to her ear. 'What the fuck's the matter with you, Cass?'

She swayed towards him. The emptiness was taking over, filling her with its silence, pulling her away from reality and towards the evil in the darkness. She was tired. So tired.

Cassandra was vaguely aware of falling. Could feel Snake's arms around her as he dragged her through the crush of gyrating bodies and off the floor. She looked up at him, confused and frightened. She needed Snake's strength to help her fight the demon that lured her into his darkness, yet she doubted he had the capability.

'Here, take one of these and you'll feel better.' Snake held out a tiny white capsule and a can of Coke, then peered into her face. 'Or have you already scored? You look weird.'

Cassandra drew back from him, but nothing seemed real any more. Something was wrong. What he was asking her to do didn't feel right.

Snake jammed the capsule into her mouth and she was too confused to resist. Chasing it down with a slug of Coke, she closed her eyes and let the music wash over her. Perhaps the Ecstasy would obliterate the menace, take away the fear and the darkness. She had to trust him, there was no other way to banish the horror.

White lights pulsated above her, the heat of those around her embraced the chill on her skin. Reality was beautiful, she thought in awe as the tab began to do its work. I can feel the blood coursing through my veins, see the tiny imperfections on my skin, hear each minute sound that mingles beneath the overpowering music. Yet that perception didn't hide any visionary shadows or predatory eyes of evil. It brought warmth to her soul and love for Snake and the others who basked in the strobe lights and repetitious music.

Energy returned and she began to dance. This was what she needed. This was the way to fight the probing fingers in her mind and strengthen the barrier that separated her from the malevolence that haunted.

Snake danced with her, his slender body moving against her, his hands touching her, bringing a desire she had never known. She looked into his eyes, saw the fire dancing in the charcoal irises, and the lightning white lasers flicker on his skin. He was beautiful and at that moment, she loved him.

He took her hand and she went with him into the night. Yet as he drew her down into the long grass behind the barn, she felt the coldness of the rain on her face, and it melted the fever, bringing her sharply back to reality.

She looked up at him and saw with clarity, the slackness of his mouth, and the vacancy in his eyes. The feel of his lips made her flinch and she tried to push him away as his hands moved down to remove her leggings.

'No!' Cassandra struggled, but the tab had made her limbs heavy, her mind sluggish. 'I can't. I don't want to. Not like this. I'm still a virgin.'

Snake pinned her beneath him and brought his face within inches of her. 'Shut up and keep still,' he hissed.

Cassandra could smell the hashish and beer on his breath, and the sweat on his clothes. Yet more frightening was his intention, now clear in those dilated pupils. With a swiftness born of fear, she jabbed her fingers in his throat and brought up her knee.

Winded, Snake gasped and doubled over.

Cassandra wriggled out from beneath him and stumbled into a halting run. Her breath was a sob, her mind confused by the dazzling images that ran headlong in a carousel of meaningless colour and form. She had to get away. Had to find somewhere to hide. The emptiness was coming, descending on her like a frosted veil. Its companion was pain, and she knew it made her vulnerable.

She looked out into the darkness and saw the ancient ring of trees that surrounded the burial mound. It seemed to be calling her, offering her shelter; and she went willingly towards it.

3

The reception desk was busy that Saturday morning. People leaving, people arriving, people arguing over their bill, or in search of luggage and keys. Taking advantage of a late morning lull, Laura left the desk to the trainee and went to check on the housekeeping staff. The chambermaids cut corners if she wasn't around to check hand-towels and the dust on the windowsills.

As she climbed the staircase that had been restored to its former elegance, she decided she would have to speak to Martin, her assistant, about replacing the YTS girl. She was useless in reception even when she did turn up. And it cost nothing to smile at the guests, surely she didn't have to be quite so sullen?

Her thoughts progressed from one scowling teenager to another, and she looked at her watch. There was still no sign of Cass.

Laura quickened her pace and tried to put Cassandra to the back of her mind. She'd turn up when she was ready.

'I just hope she's in a better mood,' she muttered as she reached the first floor. The night had been a long one, and even though she was exhausted when she finally climbed into bed at two o'clock, she had leaped from a troubled sleep at every sound. The last thing she needed was a moody teenager giving her grief. It was too nice a day for that.

A quick word with the housekeeper and an inspection of the vacated rooms took longer than she expected, and it was almost lunch-time when she finally returned to the apartment.

The silence in the annexe brought back the unease. This wasn't the first time Cassandra had stayed out all night in defiance. But she was always home by ten thirty. Painful images of Cass hurt, or unable to reach home, were conjured up as she stood there indecisively next to the phone. Then an image of something else came to haunt her and she snatched up the receiver.

'Not that,' she whispered as she began to dial. 'Please, God, not that.' She listened to the ringing tone. It wouldn't hurt to check with some of Cass's friends, she convinced herself. At least I'll know she's all right.

An hour later, Laura's unease had grown. Her college friends hadn't seen her since the start of the rave. None of them would admit to knowing Snake or his friends and she had no idea what his real name was, so couldn't trace him.

She tried to plaster over her doubts with a thin veneer of common sense. 'She'll be at Mum's,' she muttered as she dialled once more. 'I'm just getting in a panic over nothing.'

Laura impatiently lit a cigarette as she waited for Clara to answer. Cass often stayed with her during her infrequent visits from California. Clara's third marriage to the wealthy Tom Bartlett meant she spent a good deal of her time travelling. Cass was in awe of her glamorous grandmother and the two of them got on well considering the generation gap.

The telephone rang unanswered for several moments before she put the receiver down. There was no-one else to call. A fleeting thought that she should contact the police, was instantly dismissed. Cassandra had stormed out, but she'd said she'd be home today. Though Cass might be many things, she acknowledged silently, she wasn't in the habit of lying.

'Probably sulking,' she muttered, trying to convince herself. But if she wasn't at Clara's, where on earth could she be?

Laura stared at the telephone, willing it to ring. Was Cassandra merely being defiant, or was there a more sinister reason for her not returning home? Those youths last night looked a rough lot.

'I mustn't think the worst,' she scolded as she turned

away. 'Never that. She's probably lurking somewhere with that awful Snake. I'll give her hell when she comes back.'

Checking on the time, she changed into jeans and a sweater, and scraped her auburn curls into an untidy knot on top of her head. There was an hour before she had to be in the dining-room and the apartment needed cleaning.

The doorbell brought a halt to her frantic attempts to occupy her thoughts with the mundane, and she hurried to answer it. Cass must have forgotten her key.

Hope turned to disappointment as she saw her mother was alone.

'Hello, darling. I'm on my way to a late lunch and bridge. So I thought I'd drop in and see you both.'

The bright, musical voice was as delightful as the sunshine which streamed in behind her. Clara was as usual, carefully made-up and beautifully dressed. A cashmere overcoat was slung over her shoulders, and underneath was an expensive tailored suit. Long slender legs were sheathed in fine hose and her feet were shod in high-heeled black court shoes. Clara could have passed for an American socialite at least ten years younger than she really was, and not for the first time, Laura wondered vaguely whether she'd succumbed to the lure of the plastic surgeon.

'Cass isn't with you then?' Laura kissed the proffered cheek absently and looked over her mother's shoulder.

Clara drew back, her green eyes startled. 'Should she be?'

Laura followed her mother into the apartment. 'Cass and I had a row last night. She went off with a Neanderthal called Snake and I haven't seen her since.'

Clara smoothed her thick bob of hair that had lost none of its fiery colour, and smiled. 'She'll come back when she's ready. It's her hormones.'

Laura turned from the window and stared at her mother. It never ceased to amaze her how calm she could be. Clara, despite the red hair and green eyes was the most laid-back person she had ever known. In all their years together, she could never remember her raising her voice. But, she reminded herself coldly, Clara was also supremely selfish.

If things didn't directly concern her own welfare, they held little importance.

'You wouldn't have said that if I'd done something similar,' Laura retorted.

Clara looked at her and smiled indulgently. 'You never had the inclination for adventure, darling. Cassandra obviously takes after me.' She shrugged and studied her reflection in her powder compact. 'Let her have her freedom, Laura. She has to learn. You can't protect her all your life.'

Laura bunched her fists. 'I'm sick of people telling me to stop protecting her. She's only sixteen, for heaven's sake. Look what happened to Melissa.' She bit her lip as the words hung between them, and turned away.

Clara snapped her handbag shut and stood up. 'You won't do yourself or Cassandra any favours by imagining the worst. Come on darling. You need a drink.'

'I need to know my daughter's all right, Mother. Not a shot of alcohol.'

Clara didn't appear to be listening. She handed Laura a tumbler of gin and tonic and poured one for herself. 'Why don't you have more faith in Cassandra? She's not a child any more. She's bright and lively, and needs to find her own way in life.' Clara settled herself against the cushions and sipped her drink. 'What happened to Melissa was a tragedy. But it's in the past. Cassandra has to be allowed to make mistakes. You must learn to let go.'

Laura felt the frustration burn, but deep down, she knew Clara was right and that she was making a big deal out of nothing. She nodded reluctantly and sank down onto the couch beside her. 'I can't seem to get through to Cass. And when I think of what happened to Melissa . . .'

'That's enough, you're wallowing in self-pity.' Clara put down her glass with a thud. Her green eyes flashed and she gripped Laura's arms in hands that were strong despite the long delicate fingers and painted nails.

'We all make mistakes, look at me and your father, and then that disastrous eighteen months with Edgar.' She shuddered delicately. 'But I learned, and now I'm happy with Tom. What

Reap the Whirlwind

happened to Melissa was out of your control. You must purge yourself of this guilt, Laura. It will destroy you.'

The weariness and anxiety overcame her, and Laura clung to her mother, the tears hot and ready to fall. She wanted to feel like a child again. Wanted to be comforted by Clara's warmth, shielded from the outside world and all its terrors in a cocoon of safety and Chanel No. 5.

Clara eased away, then handed Laura a delicate handkerchief. 'Do be careful darling. This is an Yves St Laurent.'

Laura felt the sting of those words and they brought her sharply to her senses. Clara never changed, nothing seemed to touch her.

'That's better,' said Clara briskly as Laura downed the gin and composed herself. 'It's time we talked. There's more to this than Melissa and Cassandra, and it will do my figure no harm to miss lunch.'

Laura looked at her hands. The polish on her nails needed attention and the knuckles were white. Her jeans were grubby, and she knew her hair looked a fright. She felt shabby and worn out next to the elegant Clara, but then she had little time to spend on beauty treatments. Despite everything, she knew it didn't matter. She needed to talk, to share some of the burden. Cass was a minor problem compared to the many others she had to cope with.

'The bank's threatening to foreclose. The only reason they haven't, is because they know they won't get their money back if they sell the hotel for brick and mortar value. The bookings are up this year because I've finally managed to persuade some Anglo-European companies to use my hotel for their representatives. I've also snared two conferences away from Brighton, not the big ones, but big enough.'

She fell silent for a moment, and watched her fingers twist the handkerchief. 'But I can't get rid of the debts David left behind. I think I'm almost there, then I have to find the VAT money and I'm back to square one. If I don't keep up with that, they'll close me down for sure.'

Laura took a tremulous breath. 'Cass isn't the easiest person to get on with at the moment, and between her and the worries over the hotel, I'm worn out.'

'I didn't realise things were so bad. But I did warn you. David was never reliable.' Clara sighed. 'But then, you wouldn't listen to my advice. Perhaps there is more of you in Cassandra than you dare acknowledge.'

Clara raised a finely pencilled eyebrow, her pupils shards of caustic emerald. 'After all, darling, you do share the same awful temper. Up one minute, down the next. She'll be all right, you didn't turn out so bad.' The pale hands drifted across the Yves St Laurent skirt. 'You should have kept an eye on what David was up to, though. I thought you had more sense than to mortgage yourself up to the hilt.'

'We needed the original mortgage to refurbish, and that was well within our budget. It wasn't until he'd left I discovered what he'd done. The building society lent him the money and he forged my signature on the loan agreement.'

Laura gave a harsh cough of laughter that held no humour. 'He looked after most of the paperwork so it left me free to run the hotel,' she added bitterly. It had been over nine years, but the memory of his betrayal was still raw.

'I always wondered why you bought this place. It wasn't the kind of life I wanted for my only daughter. I had such dreams for you, Laura.' Clara sighed and took a sip from her drink.

Laura looked across at her mother, but she couldn't quite meet her steady gaze. 'We had to get away after . . . It seemed like a good idea at the time,' she finished in a rush.

Clara's gaze remained steady as she waited for Laura to go on.

'I thought that if we could start again and I could help David have a stake in something for our future, everything would be all right. How was I supposed to know it would end the way it did? He certainly got his revenge, didn't he?'

Clara was silent, seemingly caught up in her own thoughts, and Laura wondered if, for once, her mother understood some of the pain she had gone through – was still going through. But her next words were to shatter the illusion.

Reap the Whirlwind

'Go and shower and do something with your hair. I'm meeting Tom at the Grand in Brighton. It will do you good to get out of this place.' Clara looked around her, her expression speculative. 'You should have told me sooner about the money problems. I'm sure Tom and I can help financially. I'll get him to talk to the bank.' Clara's voice was firm, her face set.

Laura gave a sigh. She knew Clara meant well, but for her mother, money was the answer to everything. Poor Tom had his work cut out keeping track of her clothing allowance and extravagant ideas about interior decorating. But then Clara had known poverty as a child. Now she was merely making up for lost time.

Laura stared into the past. She could only vaguely remember her father as a quiet, thoughtful man who wore a grey suit and travelled on the train to London every day. He'd died of a heart attack when Laura was ten, and she could remember Clara vowing on the day of his funeral, that they would never be poor again. She had duly followed up this pronouncement by marrying her first millionaire four years later. She divorced him soon after, when she found him in bed with a boy half his age, but the settlement was large enough for her to mix in the appropriate circles, and she met and married Tom five years later.

The touch of Clara's hand brought her back to the present, and she forced a smile.

'I can't come, I'm sorry. There's the dinner dance tonight and I have too much to do.'

'Stuff and nonsense,' retorted Clara. 'You have staff, an assistant manager. It won't hurt to leave them to their own devices for a couple of hours. I realise you think you're indispensable, but the hotel won't fall apart if you aren't here.'

Laura thought of all the things she should be doing, realised Clara was right, and finally capitulated. Lunch-time could be handled by her assistant manager and there didn't seem to be any disasters looming in the kitchens.

'I'll have to check with Martin first,' she said firmly. 'But I must be back before three.' Laura grasped Clara's hand.

'I want you to promise not to say anything to Tom about my finances. This is my mess and I'll deal with it. I've worked too long and too hard, put too much into the business to let the bank take it away without a fight. I'll beat them somehow.' They were brave words, but the dread of losing everything gave them a sharpness she hadn't planned.

Clara kissed the air above Laura's ear and drew her to her feet. 'That sounds more like the old Laura. Come on. I'll help pick out something nice for you to wear and after lunch, we'll go shopping. Why don't you telephone the delicious Ben and ask him to join us?'

Laura tried to show some enthusiasm. She hated shopping with Clara. Their tastes were so different, and she had no desire to be consoled with new clothes she would probably never wear, but she understood Clara's need to give in the only way she knew how. It couldn't be avoided. Perhaps, by the time she got back, Cassandra would be home.

'Ben's tied up in a staff meeting at the University. Besides, he's a man of simple tastes. The Grand would merely bring out the socialist radical in him.'

Clara threw up her hands as she laughed. 'Ben Farraday? You obviously don't know the man.' Her voice dropped to a conspiratorial murmur. 'Tom and I bumped into his parents in Antigua. Stewart Farraday owns half of Texas, with a couple of islands in the Indian Ocean thrown in.'

She must have noticed Laura's stunned expression. 'He didn't tell you?' She shrugged eloquent shoulders, hooked her hand in the crook of Laura's arm and steered her towards the bedroom.

'I'm not really surprised. According to the gossip, Ben's the black sheep. Mad, bad and dangerous to know, as they say. His father cut him off when he refused to follow him into the oil business.' She winked. 'Still, he is rather scrumptious, and quite a catch if he can make it up with his father. You should talk to him, Laura. See if you can't persuade him to mend a few fences, so to speak. It could be to your advantage.'

Laura couldn't take in what she was hearing. Ben's political leanings were far left. He scorned the pomposity of wealth and the privileges it brought. They'd argued about it many times and had come to the understanding that neither of them would change their opinions, so it was best left out of conversation. When she'd asked about his family, he'd merely told her his father lived in New York and did a lot of travelling. She'd assumed he was just an ordinary businessman.

She tried to picture Ben moving in the same exalted circles as Clara, but the idea was preposterous. Her mother had always tried to bully her into marrying for money, and she had deliberately avoided the suitors that were brought out at regular intervals when Clara was in match-making mood. It was the reason she'd married David. The reason she couldn't believe what Clara was telling her.

Laura dismissed the whole idea as absurd. It had to be another Ben Farraday. Mother's antennae for wealth, usually so accurate, were picking up the wrong signals.

*

Paul Galloway was one of the eight punters who isolated themselves in the darkened cinema and watched the screen. Each looked furtive, and by the sound of it, they were all jacking off. Paul ignored them, his attention was fixed on the screen.

The black actor was standing over the girl, his oiled torso gleaming in the bars of sunlight which came through the cell windows, his erection massive. The girl was a little mature for Paul's taste, about twenty. She was naked but for a pair of gold stiletto sandals, and was manacled to the rough prison bed, her legs and arms spread wide.

Paul shifted his coat on his lap and began to stroke himself. The actor was an arrogant son of a bitch, hung like a horse. He reminded Paul of his inadequacy and he found it more comfortable to ignore him. It was the look of fear on the girl's face that gave him a pleasurable excitement, and he watched in fascinated expectation as the actor unfurled a cat-o'-nine-tails. She was squirming now, just like the bitch last night. Calling out, pleading for mercy.

He began to stroke harder, coaxing his reluctant flesh to maintain an erection. Her screams as the strips of leather bit into her writhing flanks made his balls harden and his penis stir. It had only been a few hours since he'd heard another woman's screams. Only a few hours since he'd subjugated and dominated another half-naked, writhing whore.

The girl's face was in close up. Paul could see the beads of sweat on her forehead, could almost taste those full red lips that opened in a pleasureable gasp as the actor thrust himself between her legs and brought her to orgasm. She'd been tamed, was submissive and almost silent.

Paul closed his eyes as his hand moved in rhythmic frustration over his still flaccid penis. In real life they didn't submit quite so easily. In real life they fought back with their talons. Perhaps he should tie the next one up. It might make it more exciting, might stir his unwilling flesh into life.

He drifted into his own fantasy, his hand still pumping in his trousers. The anger remaining, the need just as urgent. Last night had merely been the hors d'œuvre.

The bright, blinding sunlight made his eyes water as he left the porn theatre and hurried back to the hotel. He would sleep for a while, then see what the coming night would bring before he returned to the Middle East tomorrow. Whatever it was, it would have to be exceptionally satisfying. It could be a long time before he had such freedom again, and some bitch somewhere had to pay for the damage to his face.

The hotel bed was soft and comfortable and when the jangling telephone rudely interrupted his sleep, it seemed that only minutes had passed since he'd climbed beneath the duvet. Paul snatched up the receiver, and with one bleary eye, glanced at the bedside clock. It was one o'clock on Saturday afternoon. He'd had less than five hours sleep.

'Yeah,' he mumbled. His mouth tasted foul, the scratches on his face stung, and the fifth of Bourbon he'd drunk the night before had brought an army of drummers to pound a tattoo behind his eyes.

'Where have you been, Paul? Surely the negotiations didn't take all night?'

At the sound of the heavily accented voice of Sheik Mohammad, Paul attempted to pull his concentration into focus.

'The negotiations went well. The men and the machinery will be in place on the first of December.'

'And the terms?'

Paul grinned and sat up. He regretted it immediately. The sharp movement encouraged the drummers in his head.

'Better than we expected. Business is slow over here, they were only too delighted to take a cut in profit when they saw the colour of the money.'

The Arab chuckled at the other end of the line. 'Good. You've done well, Paul.'

'My flight leaves early tomorrow morning. I'll see you around five p.m. and we can go over the contracts. Then, if everything is to your satisfaction, I'll call Zurich.'

There was silence for a moment and Paul heard the click of the worry beads threading through the Arab's fingers. As the silence became pronounced, he began to fret. Something was going on in that devious Arab mind and he didn't like the feel of it. There was one final payment to be deposited in the Zurich bank, and he didn't trust the old bastard.

'You are to stay in London. There's a friend of mine that I want you to meet. He should be with you in a couple of days.'

'I have appointments that I can't cancel at such short notice, Sheik Mohammad.' The drummers had finally been silenced by the cold drench of fear that ran over him.

'You will remember who pays you, Mr Galloway,' said the emotionless voice in his ear. 'Or do you wish me to discuss your little problem with the authorities. I'm sure they'd be most interested.'

Paul gripped the receiver. 'Who is he, and when is he expected? Any negotiations will be made at my usual charges of course. But I cannot agree to anything until I have confirmation of your final deposit from Zurich.' He tried to sound confident and aggressive, but knew he failed on both counts.

'You will be paid handsomely for your trouble, Mr Galloway,' snapped the Sheik. 'My instructions will be sent, as usual, by diplomatic courier. See that you do not leave the hotel.'

The line was abruptly cut and it was several seconds before Paul was capable of replacing the receiver. The perspiration was cold on his face and his hand shook as he picked up a cheroot and tried to light it.

England was the last place he wanted to be for any length of time – especially after what had happened in Sussex the night before.

*

Laura finally persuaded the old blue Ford to start and headed out of town. There were three hours until she had to be back at the hotel for the evening session, and Martin had assured her that the arrangements for the cabaret act and dinner dance were well in hand. The shopping trip and lunch had taken longer than she had expected, but she felt better for it. Clara had been right, she had to get out more, let go and start to live a little.

As the town gave way to the rolling downs, Laura opened the window and let her cigarette smoke drift out of the car. Why hadn't she thought of this before, she wondered. Cassandra always came with her to the clinic on Saturdays. She must have gone on her own. The twins were close, despite Melissa's handicap, and Cassandra never missed a visit.

She turned off the main road and drove between the impressive stone pillars and up the wide, gravelled drive. The clinic had once been a manor house, and its grandeur could still be seen behind the ivy-clad walls and gleaming columns. It was outrageously expensive, but Clara had insisted on paying and for that Laura would always be grateful. Yet that didn't make the guilt easier to bear. Laura felt it every time she came here. She had given up her child to others and her failure to cope never ceased to be painful.

Parking the car, she ran up the steps and into the reception hall. The floor was chequer-board marble, the walls covered in priceless paintings. It looked more like an expensive hotel that a psychiatric clinic.

Laura greeted the receptionist and made her way through the maze of corridors and flights of stairs to the recreation room. A sharp disappointment made her hesitate in the doorway as she realised Melissa wasn't there. And that could mean only one thing. She had taken a turn for the worse.

She turned and headed down the corridor. It was as familiar as her own home, yet she still felt like an intruder.

The door to Melissa's room was closed, and Laura peered through the window, knowing what she would see, but dreading it anyway.

The walls were padded, so was the floor. Melissa sat in the corner as she always did, her knees up to her chest, her long hair trailing over her shoulders. The doll was clasped to her heart and she rocked incessantly. The only sound in the room was her tuneless humming.

Laura kicked off her high heels and pushed open the door. The nurse smiled up at her from her low chair.

'We were beginning to think you weren't coming, Laura. Melissa's been waiting for you.' Her eyes flickered to the door. 'No Cassandra?'

Laura shook her head. 'She hasn't been here at all?'

The nurse frowned. 'No.'

Laura bit down on the panic. She daren't transmit her fear to Melissa.

'How is she?' she asked as she sat on the floor next to her daughter. The sight of her brought a deep ache. She was so like Cassandra. The same hair, same eyes, the same dimple in the chin. But Melissa's eyes were vacant, staring into some distant world that only she could comprehend. Her mouth was pinched shut and her skin was pale and untouched by the elements.

Laura put her arms around her and kissed her hair. She

should have been going to parties, falling in love for the first time, enjoying being young. But, although she was sixteen, she had the damaged mind of a six-year-old.

'Oh, Melissa. My little love,' she whispered.

Melissa stared into space as she rocked back and forth. The tuneless humming never faltering as she clutched the rag doll.

'She's no better, Laura. I'm sorry.' The nurse got up. 'I'll leave you for a while. Press the bell if you need me.'

Laura nodded and turned back to Melissa. The child had ceased to rock and was staring at her. For a hopeful moment she wondered if Melissa was more aware than they thought. There was something in her eyes, something that resembled a need to communicate. Hope died as the eyes resumed their vacancy and she went back to rocking her doll.

Laura kissed her, and stroked back the long hair, feeling the silken fineness of it in her fingers. 'I'd give anything to have you back my darling. Anything,' she murmured.

Melissa stiffened in Laura's arms and she dropped the doll. 'Cassie. Cassie. Cassie.' The screams grew louder as her hands beat the air.

Laura tried to hold her, to soothe and comfort, but Melissa's spine went rigid as her arms and legs flailed and the screaming became a monotonous drone. 'Cassie. Cassie. I want Cassie.' Her eyes rolled back in her head and her limbs went into jerking spasms.

The nurse appeared and took Melissa into her arms.

Laura sat there, helpless, desperate to be able to calm the trauma that Melissa was going through. Yet it was impossible. Melissa didn't want her. Apart from Cassandra, this nurse, this stranger, was the only one Melissa responded to; and the knowledge made her bitter.

'Doctor Baines would like to see you, Laura,' shouted the nurse above Melissa's screams. 'It's best if you leave now. It could take some time to calm her.'

She reluctantly left the room and stood for a moment in the hallway. She could hear Melissa's screams and the sound of them barbed her heart. The marble floor was cold under her bare feet, but not as cold as the ice that lodged deep inside her.

'Hello, Laura. Come and have a cup of coffee. Nurse Hall will look after Melissa.'

Laura sniffed back the frustration as she slipped on her shoes and looked up at the man who had become a friend over the long years of Melissa's illness.

'I feel so bloody useless.'

Simon Baines took off his steel-rimmed spectacles and pinched the bridge of his nose. He looked tired, and older than forty-five. 'We all feel useless at times. You're not alone.' He smiled and his face was transformed, giving her a glimpse of the younger, carefree man he must have once been. 'Let's have that coffee. I could do with it.'

Laura followed him into his office suite. It was comfortably furnished and there was a thick carpet on the floor. She sank into a deep leather couch and lit a cigarette.

'You smoke too much, but I suppose you won't listen to reason,' he said with a weary smile as he handed her a cup of coffee and pushed an ashtray across the table.

Laura shook her head. 'Smoking's the least of my worries. Why wasn't Melissa in association with the others?'

Simon took a moment to drink his coffee, his gaze fixed on the floor.

'She's causing concern,' he said finally. 'Her behaviour over the past few days has disturbed the other patients and we thought it best to isolate her.' He paused, his eyes misted with thought. 'Her mental state has deteriorated. She's become more agitated, more violent. The epileptic attacks have grown stronger and now there is damage to the heart.'

'What about an operation? Surely there's something you can do?' Laura stabbed out her cigarette and lit another one barely realising what she was doing.

Simon shook his head. 'She couldn't take the anaesthetic, Laura. It's gone too far for that. And a transplant isn't even an option.'

Laura stared into space. She had lost Melissa a long time ago. The real Melissa, not the shell of the child back in that awful, padded room. Yet surely something could be done for her? Life couldn't be so cruel as to take her away completely. Could it?

'I was hoping to see Cassandra, today. Melissa benefits so much from her visits.'

Simon's voice interrupted the whirl of thoughts and emotions, and Laura forced herself to concentrate.

'She's been getting more fractious, calling out for Cassandra, demanding to see her. I nearly called once or twice, but I know how busy you are.'

'I'm never too busy for Melissa. How dare you suggest otherwise,' she snapped.

Simon held up his hands. 'Sorry. I didn't express myself very well. Usually we can calm her down and it would be a wasted journey. She'd be sedated by the time you got here.'

He shot his cuffs and the light of the lamp winked on the gold cuff-links as he steepled his fingers and pursed his mouth. 'These latest attacks have us worried. Her demands to see Cassandra are so violent, so urgent. And she wakes up screaming as though she has nightmares. This in turn, brings on an epileptic fit. But it's the drawings that really baffle us.'

'Drawings?' Laura's concentration was brought sharply into focus.

Simon pulled open a drawer. He took out a wad of paper and laid it on his desk. 'We encourage the children to draw. It gives us an insight to their feelings and thoughts. We can learn a lot from them. But these are puzzling. She's never done anything similar before.'

Laura crossed the space between them and looked at the brightly coloured, childish scrawl. The artwork, though primitive, was unmistakable and chilling.

Melissa had drawn page after page and row upon row of blood-filled, lupine eyes. Beneath them, was the lopsided figure six.

'I don't understand,' she murmured.

'Neither do we. These are what she drew last night. She worked in a frenzy for over an hour, and when we tried to take away the crayons, she began to scream about a fox. It was confused and hysterical and we had great difficulty in calming her. But it was as if she thought this fox was chasing Cassandra. We couldn't make sense of any of it, but I thought you should know.'

'Can I use your telephone?'

Laura picked up the receiver before he could reply. She dialled the apartment and waited, her gaze drawn repeatedly to the garish pictures that had come from Melissa's troubled mind. The thought that it was all starting up again was too awful to contemplate. There had to be a logical explanation.

There was no reply at the apartment, and yet it was after five. She tried Martin. There were no messages at reception.

Replacing the receiver, she hugged her waist. She could feel her legs trembling, and the dreadful fear she'd tried so hard to banish had come alive.

'I haven't seen, or heard from Cassandra since six o'clock yesterday evening.' She licked parched lips before uttering the words that would confirm the awful dread. 'These drawings are too similar for them to be a coincidence. The same kind of thing happened ten years ago, only then, it was Cassandra who drew the pictures.'

Her gaze flickered to Simon's and held it. 'I think Melissa's trying to tell us that her twin is in danger.'

4

The train travelled east as dusk settled on the hills and a mist of rain softened the outlines of factories that huddled beside the railway tracks.

Malcolm closed his eyes, but found it impossible to relax. Were the other passengers watching? Could they read his thoughts? Turning away from the curious glances of the man opposite, he nudged his glasses over the bridge of his nose and stared out of the window. Yet it wasn't the landscape that interested him, it was the memory of what had gone before. He could see it laid out in front of him in the gathering gloom.

Malcolm felt a thrill of excitement and clasped his hands between his knees as he savoured the memory. His knuckles showed white as he bit down on the chuckle of glee and turned his shoulder to the other passengers. He had a secret. A wonderful secret.

As the train neared its destination, Malcolm felt the elation drain away, to be replaced by a nagging doubt. He touched the scar on his face, needing the assurance of reality. Yet as the train slowed on the final bend into the station, he knew he couldn't ignore the truth.

A fifth dimension had been added to this latest adventure. A presence that watched from somewhere in the darkness. One that made him clumsy, and carelessly hasty. A silent witness that had followed him onto the train and was looking over his shoulder, even now.

Malcolm sank his chin into his chest as a shiver feathered spiny fingers down his back. He had come close to being discovered, and it was the presence that had almost betrayed him.

The staccato slam of the train doors was a ghostly echo beneath the gathering force of the voices of the wheels. The ritual had not silenced them this time, neither had it quenched the desire for vengeance.

Malcolm felt dazed by the revelation. He looked around him, momentarily confused by the jostle of the other passengers as they left the train. He stood up and leaned on the door frame. His limbs felt heavy, his head full of images and sounds. But as he reached into his coat pocket and found the souvenir of his night's adventure, he knew it had not been imagination playing tricks on him. The reassurance calmed him, but it was several moments before he could summon the strength to leave the train.

Hastings was deserted. The shop windows stared blindly back at him as he trudged through the rain soaked streets, and the echo of his shoes made a lonely sound as they struck the pavement. He began the long climb up the hill. He would soon be home.

A whisper in the rain made him stumble and he turned fearfully to glance over his shoulder. But the locked doors and shuttered windows seemed to mock him, barring him from the warmth and light he knew they offered.

He pulled his coat tighter, and tried to convince himself he was alone. Yet he couldn't ignore the fear that rippled up his spine. Couldn't dismiss the touch of those icy fingers in his mind, curious, probing, ever restless.

A car sped past, its tyres throwing a spume of water from the flooded gutter beside him. Malcolm paused, the surprise of that cold shower momentarily wiping out the fear. He looked up at the houses that lined the hill, and felt a dread that weighed heavy. In half an hour he would reach the crumbling terrace that was home. He'd been away for over twenty-four hours, and Lillian would be angry. He hadn't taken his medication.

He slowed, then stopped, as he thought of his mother and their nightly ritual of the pills. The voices of the wheels whispered in his head and gnawed at his senses as he replayed the scene in his mind.

With a clarity that was startling, he realised why Lillian made him take his pills. They forced the voices of the wheels into silence, and took away his power. Bringing with them the unseen presence in the ether to witness his secret adventures.

Malcolm watched the tail-lights of a motor-bike disappear around the corner. The roar of the bike hadn't muffled the sound of the train wheels. They were talking to him again, whispering, soothing, luring him into their hypnotic world.

'The pills and Lillian. The pills and Lillian. The pills and Lillian.'

He sank his chin into his coat, and retraced his footsteps as the rain stung his face. He wouldn't go home tonight.

*

Laura had tried to concentrate on the guests, but having checked that things were running smoothly at the dinner dance, she left them to it. Now she paced the apartment floor, her thumbnail bitten to the quick. The past was coming back in all its cruel intensity. She was re-enacting a scene that had been well rehearsed and she knew the awful climax. Yet there was no escape, no absolution. Helplessness had her in a manic grip and she could not banish the memories.

'What are they doing? Why don't they ring?' she said for what felt like the hundredth time in as many minutes. It had been four hours since she had reported Cassandra missing, and now it was almost midnight. She shivered as she thought of Cassandra out there in the dark. Anything could have happened to her.

Ben struck a match with his fingernail and lit a cigarette. 'Wearing the carpet out isn't going to make them any more efficient, Laura,' he drawled. 'Sit down and try to get some rest.'

He propped his booted foot on his knee and peered at her through the cigarette smoke. 'The cops know what they're doing. Cass isn't the first kid to stay out all night.'

Laura jammed her hands in her trouser pockets. 'The police had the same attitude,' she snapped. 'I had to insist before they would even take her details. Seems a missing teenager is low on their priorities. Cass has to disappear for more than twenty-four hours before they even begin to take it seriously.'

She let out a sharp sigh of frustration. 'I feel so useless. Shouldn't we take the car and try and find this Snake? He's got her somewhere, I know it.'

Ben pulled her onto his lap. But Laura was so tense, she flinched away from him and refused to be comforted.

'The cops said to stay home. They seem pretty confident she'll turn up.' He stroked her hair from her eyes and kissed her forehead. 'I'll stay with you, Laura. Doesn't matter how long it takes.'

She gave the shadow of a smile in reply, but her face muscles felt tight and her head buzzed with conflicting thoughts. Wearily scrubbing her face, she dragged back her thick, unruly hair into a bunch and fastened it with clips. She realised Ben was making light of Cass's disappearance for her sake, but it didn't help.

Thinking back, her visit to the police station had merely endorsed the hopelessness of her situation. The duty sergeant had been kind, but she'd seen by his expression that he thought she was overreacting. Especially after she'd told him about their argument.

The memory of the previous night brought an almost unbearable guilt and she sagged against Ben, finally giving in to the need for consolation.

'I shouldn't have slapped her,' she muttered. 'This is my punishment.'

Ben shifted on the couch, and Laura could feel the tension in him as he gave an exasperated snort.

'By the sound of things, Cass deserved it. You spoil her, Laura, and she's the one who's doing the punishing. I wouldn't mind betting she's off somewhere without a care in the world.

Reap the Whirlwind

After all, it is Saturday night – party time. She'll turn up, try not to worry.'

'Easy to say,' Laura snapped as she left his knee and curled up in the furthermost corner of the couch. 'She's not your daughter.'

She closed down on the electricity of frustration that burned for release. Stifled the anguish that made her skin crawl and her heart thud. Ben wasn't a mother. He couldn't possibly understand what she was going through. Yet she regretted having spoken so sharply when he was merely trying to be a comfort.

Ben stabbed out his cigarette, eased his long legs and stood up. 'Well, I care about what happens to you.' He swept back his dark hair and hooked it behind his ears. 'We were all teenagers once. I bet you went off without a thought for anyone, then swanned in when you were good and ready.'

He grimaced and tucked his thumbs behind the heavy silver belt buckle. 'I know I did. I was a pain in the ass.' He came and squatted in front of her, his fingers buried in her hair, cupping her face. 'Cass is just reacting. She'll come home when her pride's intact.'

Laura looked into his face and wanted to believe him. Yet the urgency, and the knowledge that Cass was in danger, could not be dismissed. How could she tell him about the drawings, and make him understand? It was a feeling, an intangible acceptance of Melissa's warning she was trying to cope with. The certainty of past experience that the twins had a special gift of foresight, a fifth dimension, which they could tune into. If she tried to explain it, she would only confirm Ben's belief that she was imagining things.

'You sound like Mother,' she mumbled around the cigarette she was attempting to light.

Ben took the cigarette and lighter away, and caught her hands. 'You don't need that. You've had too many already.'

Laura's angry retort was smothered by his kiss, and she leaned against him, savouring the warmth it offered. Yet the images of Cass still haunted, put a honed edge to her restlessness. She clung to him, willing him to make everything all right.

'Want me to call your mom?' he said finally. His voice was low and she could feel his breath on her face as he held her.

Laura shook her head. 'There'd be no point. Like everyone else, Mother refuses to take Cassandra's disappearance seriously.' She shrugged. 'She's gone to London anyway, and I don't know where she's staying.'

She tried unsuccessfully to blot out the images of the past. Clara hadn't been around then, either.

Laura took a deep breath, letting it out slowly in an attempt to quell the rising tension. 'Mother thinks Cass is being adventurous. Quite admires her for it, in fact. Regards her as a chip off the old block.' She gave a tentative smile to hide the pain of her mother's indifference. 'Mother would be absolutely no use right now. Panic is not a word she would recognise.'

Ben shrugged, his gaze steady as he regarded her. 'I tend to agree with her. I think you're overreacting. You seem determined to look on the dark side of things.' He sighed as he ran his fingers through his hair. 'Hell, Laura. You're letting your imagination run away with you.'

Laura heard the exasperation and chewed on her nail to smother the angry defence. Ben didn't know the reason behind her dread. And now was not the time to tell him. 'Just let me handle this my way Ben,' she snapped.

'Whatever you want.'

Ben's eyes held questions she couldn't answer. At least, not tonight.

'I want my daughter,' she said, her words muffled by lips that had grown numb. 'You and Mother say she'll come back. I'm not so sure she will.'

*

Knowing his appearance would provoke comment, Paul Galloway had stayed in his hotel suite all day. It was an inconvenience, but under the circumstances, one he was prepared to withstand. Room service had provided meals, the adult channel his entertainment, and the well stocked courtesy bar supplied the whisky. Now, as he looked in the bathroom mirror, his reflection came back to him in a blur, and the pleasant haze of alcohol dwindled as he examined the damage.

He touched the purple swelling around his eye and flinched. That could just possibly be explained away, he thought as he ran the tap and doused his face with cold water. But the three long, jagged scratches on his cheek were self-explanatory. The bitch had left her signature for all to see.

A short foray into the bathroom cabinets supplied a tube of antiseptic cream and some cotton wool. God knows what infection she's left in there, he thought as he dabbed at his face.

He leaned over the marble basin and looked more closely, turning his head to catch the light. The cuts were deep – her nails had been long – and he wondered if they would leave a scar. It would be a shame, he'd always been rather proud of his looks.

Turning away from the bathroom he crossed to the bed and slumped against the pillows. With his hands behind his head, he stared sightlessly at the ornate ceiling. She'd been a fighter, that one, and the memory of their encounter gave him a pleasant tingle in his crotch, which rapidly faded at the thought of what had happened next.

The cold seeped into him despite the overheated hotel bedroom, and he pulled the silk dressing-gown closer to his chest. He needed to get away, couldn't risk the new life he'd made for himself by hanging around. This was supposed to be a flying visit, and it had gone badly wrong. The phone call he'd made after speaking to Mohammad had confirmed the absence of the last payment, and without the Sheik's money, he was stuck.

He had no illusions about the situation he'd found himself entangled in. The Sheik was not a man to cross, and he had no choice but to wait for the courier and the mysterious visitor.

He looked at the expensive watch on his wrist. It was almost two in the morning, but he didn't feel the need for sleep. His cool, clinical mind weighed up the dilemma, putting it into sharp focus, examining the smallest detail under razor bright scrutiny until he was satisfied he'd thought of everything.

Another day or two would make no difference. No-one but the Sheik knew who he was or where he was staying. The events in Sussex couldn't be traced to him – he'd made very sure of that.

He checked the watch again. No-one would call at this time of night, and a restless energy after the day's inactivity made him leave the bed and dress.

If I'm stuck in London, I might as well use the time profitably, he thought as he tugged down the homberg hat until it shadowed his face. If there's another job in the pipeline, I might not get a chance again. Grabbing his keys, he left.

Soho never slept, at least, not until dawn. The pavements were jammed with people all out for a good time. It was Saturday night and London was in full swing. Paul checked his appearance in a shop window. Satisfied, he began to stroll down Dean Street, allowing the flow of pedestrians to carry him along.

It was almost an hour later when he found himself in the narrow alleyway off Piccadilly. Neon lights flashed and hummed on either side of him and litter blew around his feet. He was assaulted by the heavy beat of music coming from the different strip joints and seedy bars, but it was here that he felt most comfortable.

He ignored the tout who tried to pull him into the strip joint with the lurid photographs plastered over the windows, and watched the girl swing towards him. Her legs were long and shapely in the fish-net stockings and red high heels. She carried a red vanity case in one hand and a cigarette in the other. The black plastic coat was tightly belted and Paul had a suspicion that she wore very little beneath it.

His gaze travelled up the face and the pleasant tingle returned. She was young, very young, despite the mask of make-up and tangled beehive of peroxided hair.

Reap the Whirlwind

Her gaze swept over him and moved on.

Paul experienced a twinge of anger. It was as if he didn't exist. Arrogant cunt. They were all the same. Yet he couldn't ignore her, and he turned to watch her progress. The high heels struck the pavement in a confident tattoo, making her slender hips swing beneath the coat. His breath was trapped in his chest as he thought of that tight little arse squirming on a bed, and those long legs thrashing at the bindings he would tie her with.

The girl threw away the cigarette and turned into a brightly lit doorway.

Paul approached on the other side of the street and grimaced. The Paradise Club was a narrow building jammed between two others. The façade was peeling, the doorman oriental. He crossed the street and peered at the photographs in the window.

I was right, he thought. She's just what I'm looking for. His gaze trawled the black and white photograph. She was on her knees, the pert backside lifted in invitation above the spiky shoes. Her heavy breasts only partly shielded by her hands. Her mouth was open and he could imagine how it would feel around his cock, wet, warm and all-encompassing.

Barely acknowledging the oriental, he handed over his money and climbed the stairs.

The sight of the bouncers made him adjust his plans, and as he sat down, he decided to cool things a bit. There was no sense in courting trouble, he was too conspicuous, but the fantasy he could weave around her over the next few days would serve to put an edge to the pleasures to come. He knew where she was now, and as he would be here for longer than planned, he could afford to wait.

5

Laura opened her eyes and for a moment, wondered where she was. As the cataracts of sleep cleared from her mind, she felt the cold weight of reality. It was Monday. Cass had been missing for three nights. She dragged herself up from the couch and rubbed her neck. It wasn't the most comfortable place to sleep.

'Drink this, honey.' Ben stood over her with a steaming cup of black coffee.

Laura threw off the blanket Ben must have put over her during the night, and massaged her face. 'You should have woken me,' she muttered as she cradled the cup in her cold hands.

Ben shrugged and hooked his thumbs in his belt. 'You needed the rest, and I didn't like to disturb you. I snatched a few zees on the chair.'

A lowering cloud of uncertainty blotted out the sunlight. Would today bring back Cass? Or would it merely stretch endlessly into another night of waiting?

'Have the police . . .?'

He shook his head. 'Drink your coffee. I'm fixing breakfast – French toast and bacon.'

Laura drained the last of the coffee and began to tidy up. 'I'm not hungry, but thanks anyway.'

Ben stilled her. 'You've got to eat, Laura. You haven't touched a thing since Saturday.' He put his hand under her chin, forcing her to look into his face. 'You won't do Cass or Melissa any favours by making yourself ill.'

She regarded him solemnly. He hadn't shaved and his hair was still tangled from his night in the chair. 'You don't look so hot yourself,' she teased, putting a lighter touch to the words than she felt.

Ben planted a kiss on her nose. 'Neither do you, lady. But being a mad artist, does give me an excuse. Go shower, then we'll work out a plan of action over breakfast. I know there's a lot to do in the hotel, but in the state you're in, I doubt if you'll be of much use.'

Laura pulled away. He was right, there were things to see to upstairs, and although they masked the worry and kept her occupied, she wanted to be out looking for Cass. Yet what if she came home and found the apartment deserted? What if the police tried to contact her while she was out?

The muscles tensed in the back of her neck as she went to shower and dress. There were too many permutations to the equation, and her befuddled mind just couldn't cope with them. Only once before in her life had she ever felt so helplessly trapped.

The hot water sloughed the last scales of weariness, and Laura stepped out of the shower feeling more positive. To be anything else was a betrayal of Cass. With a towel over her wet hair, she went into the kitchen to find Ben fussing over grilled bacon.

'Sit, eat,' he ordered as he served up breakfast with a flourish.

Laura looked at the plate of food and realised she was hungry. Yet the crisp bacon and French toast tasted of nothing. Her senses were numb.

She picked up the stack of mail and sifted through it. Bills, bills and yet more bills. There was also a reminder that she had to meet the bank manager. It was the end of the month and she had to give a progress report.

Putting the letters aside, she sipped her coffee. At least there was a glimmer of hope in one aspect of her life. Bookings were up and if she could maintain that level of business, he would have no cause for complaint.

'I see you don't appreciate my cooking,' said Ben wryly as he picked up her plate.

'Just not very hungry. But it looked lovely.' She sat in silence as she watched him move around her kitchen. It was unfair not to tell him everything, she thought. Then swiftly dismissed the idea. Why burden him with things that didn't concern him? The past was something she had to deal with on her own. She'd done it before. She could do it again.

'I have a full day at the University unfortunately, but I'll come back as soon as I can. The final year students have made excellent headway on their exhibition and exam pieces, so I'm planning to use the time between tutorials to finish my lecture notes. What with my own exhibition coming up and the worry over you and Cassandra, I've fallen behind schedule.'

He tucked his hair behind his ears and took something out of a plastic bag and dumped it on the table. 'I went home after you fell asleep, and picked this up. Thought it might come in handy.'

Laura eyed the answerphone.

'I'll set it up and tape a message. If someone needs to contact you urgently, I'll put the number for this on there.' He held out a small portable phone and eyed her quizzically. 'That okay?'

Laura tugged his shirt and brought him closer so she could kiss him. 'You think of everything, Ben. What would I do without you?'

'Starve to death,' he said, then grinned. 'I'll sort this out, then I have to go.' He looked at her, concern darkening his eyes. 'You will be all right, won't you? I could always try and cancel the tutorials.'

'I'll be fine,' she lied, as the day stretched before her.

'I should be back by five. If you leave the hotel and look for Snake, then I want you to promise to be careful. Don't approach him, don't even speak to him.'

He must have noticed her gaze shift away, for he tilted her chin towards him and looked deep into her eyes. 'Don't take risks, Laura. It's what the cops are paid for. Keep yourself busy in the hotel until you have to go to the bank. Then if there's no news by the time I get back, I'll drive you round. There are a few hang-outs I know of from my students. Someone, somewhere must know who Snake really is.'

*

Paul Galloway stepped out of the bath and towelled dry. He resisted the temptation to shave, although the two days growth was irritating and made him feel unclean. If he was to remain in London for another few days, then it would thicken enough to do a fairly good camouflage job and he thought he could put up with the inconvenience. It was a small price to pay if it kept him anonymous.

Striding into the bedroom, he picked up his suit that had just been returned from the cleaners, and dressed quickly.

The knock on the door came just as he was straightening his tie, and although the courier's message had said very little, he felt his stomach execute a slow roll. The reputation of Abbas Hussein had gone before him and despite the Arab's education at Eton and Sandhurst, men with far greater courage than Paul had found him to be a dangerous adversary.

A hasty glance at his reflection in the mirror assured him that he appeared well groomed, calm and in control, and he opened the door with a confident flourish.

Abbas Hussein was tall and thin, with dark hair and eyes and a long, hooked nose which swooped over a full-lipped mouth and black moustache. He was dressed in an Armani suit and silk shirt and his fingers glittered with heavy gold rings. Power and wealth emanated from him like a heady cologne. This was a man used to having his own way – at any price.

'Salaam, Alikhum.' Paul's voice didn't betray his nervousness as he sketched a bow and stood aside for the Arab to enter.

Abbas Hussein strode into the room in silence, the only sign that he'd heard Paul's welcome was the flicker of a cold dark eye.

'I hope you are well and that your family is well. I pray that Allah will bless you with many sons, and . . .'

Reap the Whirlwind

'Enough.' Hussein waved a dismissive hand and sank into an overstuffed chair. 'We are not in my country. You do not need to follow our customs.'

Paul hovered under the Arab's penetrating gaze and wondered what to do next. He was used to Arabs and their meticulous attention to custom and ritual. Business meetings could go on for days before the true purpose was broached, and even then, it was in such an obtuse manner, it was like trying to find one's way through a contorted maze. Paul was proud of his ability to speak their language and follow their ways. It had earned him money, if not respect. Now, in just a couple of sentences, Hussein had taken charge of the meeting and reduced Paul to silence.

Hussein opened the briefcase and pulled out a roll of paper. Using the heavy marble ashtray and lighter, he spread out the engineering drawings and pinned them to the glass coffee table. He then sat back in the chair, lit a cigarette with a wafer thin lighter, and carefully adjusted the crease in his trousers.

Paul sat opposite him. He swallowed, but his mouth was dry and his heart beat so rapidly, he found it difficult to breathe.

'You understand what these drawings mean, Galloway?' Hussein's voice cracked the silence.

Paul nodded. 'I've seen something like this before – but much smaller.'

Hussein's lips twitched beneath the thick moustache, but to have called it a smile would have been an exaggeration.

'Sheik Mohammad tells me that you are an astute negotiator, Galloway. I would like to make a proposition to you.'

The spittle was gone from Paul's mouth and he masked his nervousness by lighting a cheroot and unbuttoning his jacket. The room suddenly felt very small, the air thick, like treacle. 'How can I be of service, Mr Hussein?'

'My brother-in-law is most interested in finding someone to make this for him. He has granted me the honour of entrusting me with these most secret of plans and he would not be pleased if something should go wrong.'

Hussein held Paul's gaze with eyes that were as cold and unemotional as beach pebbles.

'There will be problems, Mr Hussein.' Paul slicked his tongue over his lips as he searched for the most diplomatic way to turn down the Arab's proposal. This was dangerous territory.

Hussein raised one laconic eyebrow, but remained silent as he smoked his cigarette.

Paul cleared his throat and began again. 'My government does not have the foresight or the wisdom to remain on good terms with your brother-in-law, Mr Hussein. It is regretted that after the débâcle of a similar order a few years ago, things have been made almost impossible.'

Hussein dropped the cigarette into the marble ashtray and left it to burn. He sat forward, his hands resting lightly on his knees. 'Almost impossible, Mr Galloway. But not entirely so. Sheik Mohammad assures me that you are the man to find the right manufacturer for this project. Both he and my brother-in-law would be most distressed if you should let them down.'

The sweat was running in cold rills down his back, but Paul knew he had to maintain his composure as well as eye contact with the Arab.

'I do not wish to cause distress to anyone, but no manufacturer in this country would make this up. It's obvious to an engineer what these drawings are for, and should the origin of these plans come to light, there would be hell to pay.'

'I think not, Mr Galloway.' The Arab lit another cigarette and filled the room with the sweet pungency of hashish. 'You will find a way. You have contacts, people who can be persuaded to do as they are told without asking questions. It would not be wise to refuse my request, Mr Galloway.'

Paul heard the emphasis on his name and knew Sheik Mohammad had told Hussein more about him than he would have wished.

'The people you speak of are being watched, Mr Hussein. They cannot do what you suggest without incurring the wrath of the government. I'm sorry, but I cannot comply.'

'You can and you will, Galloway.' His voice was a pistol crack in the silent apartment and Paul flinched.

'You too are under surveillance, and if you do not comply with my brother-in-law's wishes, then you will be exposed to the authorities.'

Paul sat opposite the Arab, as mesmerised as a rabbit in the headlights of an oncoming car.

Hussein nodded slowly as the curl of smoke drifted from his nostrils. His eyes were heavy-lidded, but penetrating.

'We know who you are, and what you are, Paul Galloway. We have seen you hunting in the filth that London offers – and we know what happened in Sussex.' He clucked his tongue. 'Such carelessness, such rage. Who would think a man like you could sink to such depths?'

He leaned forward and Paul could see the sprinkling of fine white hairs in the Arab's moustache. 'But then this wasn't the first time, was it?'

The silence between them lay heavy as they regarded one another and Paul forgot to breathe.

'I should think very carefully before refusing, Mr Paul Galloway. You have already lost so much. It would be a tragedy to lose your freedom . . . or your life.'

*

The reservations for the coming few weeks had been confirmed, the account books were in order, Chef was sober and busy with the grocery suppliers, and Martin was dealing with the plumbers. Three of the lavatories had packed up during the night, and there was a blockage somewhere in the basement. Luckily it had been discovered quickly, so there was no damage.

Laura eased the stiffness in her neck and left the small office that backed the reception desk. The morning had been a relatively quiet one and she knew there was really nothing much to occupy her until this evening. A restlessness took her over and she left everyone to it.

For almost an hour she drove back and forth through

Saxonbridge, hoping to see Snake's Ford Fiesta. Then she widened the circle and began her search in Brighton. Up and down the hills, through the town centre, along the seafront, then in and out of the twisting narrow streets that wormed along the Downs behind the town. She trawled the sprawling council estates, drove through the campus of both universities, then tried Hove.

Several times she thought she saw him, but as she pulled alongside, she realised her mistake. So many youths wore their hair long and unkempt, and they all seemed to wear the uniform of baseball cap, jeans, rags or black leather. He had to be local, she convinced herself. Somewhere, in a back street, or outside a pub, she would find him.

Three hours later, Laura parked on the seafront and rested her head on her hands. It was an impossible task and she had to concede defeat. She stared out at the few hardy souls that walked on the windswept promenade and sniffed back the tears. This bewildering, emotional turmoil was unbearable. What had she done to deserve such punishment? She gazed, unseeing out of the window. Cassandra was out there, somewhere. But would she ever see her again?

'Stop it,' she scolded. 'Of course she'll come back. She's just being selfish and thoughtless, like teenagers always are. Little cow, I'll give her hell!' With an angry swipe at the tears, she switched on the portable phone and called the apartment, willing Cassandra to pick up the receiver, to be at home, to be safe and whole.

There were no messages, and she switched off the receiver as the tears blurred her vision.

'Oh, Cass,' she whispered as the anger melted and she closed her eyes. 'Where are you?'

Laura climbed back into the car and headed home. She had found it almost impossible to concentrate on the pages of figures the bank manager had insisted she discuss, and the meeting had come to a premature conclusion when they both realised they were getting nowhere.

Hope seared through the fog of weariness. Perhaps Cass

had come home? She tried the telephone again, but there was still no reply, and hope died.

She lit a cigarette as she waited in a traffic queue. At least the hotel could still be called home for another few months. She glanced across to the passenger seat at the wad of papers the bank manager had given her. The forecasts and rows of figures seemed daunting, but finally there was a glimmer of hope. All the work and energy she'd put in over the past eight years were beginning to bear fruit. But that small victory seemed hollow in the circumstances, and she felt little pleasure at her achievements.

Saxonbridge looked fresh and laundered by the recent rain. The new harbour walls gleamed in the late afternoon glow and the sea reflected the pale grey of the sky. Gulls wheeled over the fishing boats and the cross-Channel ferry looked very grand in its new company livery of green and white.

Laura parked the car and sat for a moment looking up at the Harbour Lights Hotel. It was a large, Victorian building that had once been the home of a wealthy London solicitor, before a thirties entrepreneur had turned it into an hotel. Set back from the main road by a low wall and sweeping driveway, it looked down on the harbour. It gleamed dull cream against the backdrop of the Downs, and in the fading light, the brass handrail and miniature conifers at the top of the steps gave it an air of gentility. Automatic switches turned on the lights in the landscaped garden and Laura felt a thrill of pride as the hotel took on an aura of magic.

The feeling didn't last as she thought of her present predicament, and she drove past the grand façade and into the rear carpark.

She and David had bought the Harbour Lights ten years ago. It was going to be their salvation, a new start to the next chapter of their lives, with plans to bring Melissa home and give her a semblance of family life. But the hotel needed so much money spent on it and it had soon become evident that it would take years to build up a regular clientele. They never seemed to have enough money to afford around-the-clock care for Melissa. And David had merely exacerbated the problem by his deceit.

'I should never have trusted him,' she muttered as she collected her things. 'Men like him don't change.'

The telephone was ringing as she opened the apartment door and she rushed to answer it. It was only the housekeeper.

'I caught one of the chambermaids pilfering. Luckily, I managed to replace the things before the guest discovered they were missing. What do you want me to do about it?'

'Give her what we owe her and instant dismissal. I'll leave it up to you to advertise for someone else,' Laura said firmly. 'I want to be in on any interview, and all references have to be checked. This has happened before, Mrs Harris. It's not good enough.'

Shrugging off her coat, she rewound the tape on the answerphone. There was still nothing from Cassandra, and she wandered into the tiny kitchen to make coffee. Turning on the television for company, she waited for the kettle to boil.

When the telephone rang again, she snatched it up.

'Laura? I don't want to alarm you, but do you think you and Cassandra could come to the clinic?'

Laura swallowed. 'What's happened?'

There was silence for a moment, and Laura realised Simon Baines was choosing his words carefully, like a man picking his way across stepping stones in a raging river. When he finally spoke, his voice was sombre.

'Melissa's been inconsolable. She screams for her twin and during association today she attacked one of the male nurses. She's been drawing the eyes again and when he tried to take the crayons from her she went into a violent rage. She needs to see Cassandra. We have to convince her that her twin is safe and that there isn't a fox tracking her down.'

'A fox?' Laura almost dropped the telephone as ice clutched her heart.

'It has something to do with those drawings, Laura. It would help if you could stay with her for a while.'

'I'll come immediately.'

Laura put down the telephone. Her hands stilled on the remote control as her gaze fixed on the television screen and the breath caught in her throat.

'The police statement earlier today has confirmed that the unidentified body of a girl was found in Saxon Woods on Saturday night. She is thought to be about sixteen, and to have attended the rave at Wolves Farm on Friday. Police are anxious to interview everyone who was there. No further details have been released, but the death was suspicious and the police are mounting a full-scale murder inquiry. We will of course bring you more news when it is available.'

Laura dropped the remote control and covered her mouth with her fingers. She stared at the screen, unblinking and frozen. The dragon of terror reared its head and she felt its searing breath worm through her.

'Laura!'

Ben crashed into the room and scooped her into his arms. 'Oh Christ! I didn't want you to find out like this. I'm sorry. So sorry.'

'Nooooooo!'

The scream echoed in her head, bounced off the ceiling and shattered the wall of resilience she'd constructed so carefully. Her world splintered into shards of steel, fragmenting thought, piercing soft flesh beneath flimsy layers of hope.

Then she was falling, floating, sinking ever deeper into the darkness and away from cruel reality.

6

The body had been found, like most bodies, by someone walking their dog. The hysterical woman had telephoned the police, and within hours the area was swarming with the various agencies that had the gruesome job of examining, and photographing the evidence whilst closing off the area from the usual gaggle of onlookers. East Sussex CID co-ordinated this seemingly chaotic gathering, and the man in charge of the inquiry was Chief Superintendent Chapman. His DCI was Jack Stoneham.

Chapman sat back in the leather swivel chair and steepled his fingers. The inquiry was already a day and a half old, and things had a habit of slipping away if they weren't dealt with immediately. It was surprising how quickly the leads went cold.

'I don't want the press getting wind of our suspicions yet, Jack.'

'They already know something's up. The desk sergeant's been fielding calls all morning.' Jack yawned and tried to find a more comfortable section of the wooden chair. There had been little sleep for any of them, and even Chapman had dark circles under his eyes.

'I've given the press as little as possible, but that won't satisfy them for long. Forensics are still up there and I don't want the gutter press getting their size twelves all over the scene.'

'Yellow tape and police vans aren't exactly inconspicuous, Chapman. I wouldn't mind betting the place is swarming by now.'

'That's as maybe. No point going off half-cocked.'

DCI Stoneham's expression was grim. 'Touch of the déjà vu, sir?'

'We had a safe conviction,' barked Chapman. 'Are you questioning my judgement, Stoneham?'

DCI Stoneham backed off. Policing was like soldiering, it didn't do to argue with a superior, even if he was in the wrong. Just his luck to have this arsehole in charge – especially after what happened the last time they worked together.

'I still think we got the wrong man last time, sir,' he mumbled. 'There was nothing to prove Miller was the murderer. Nothing at all. Now this. It's too much like the others for it to be a coincidence.' He thrust back his chair. 'I have work to do,' he muttered as he headed for the door.

'Stoneham. You're not dismissed.' Chapman stood up and tugged at the hem of his jacket. His face was grim. 'I had the best criminal psychologist in the country on that case. Miller fitted the profile, he admitted to being in the park, and had no alibi for the previous two murders. A judge and jury found him guilty. Case closed.'

He rested his knuckles on the desk and leaned over to emphasise his words. 'This is a copy-cat killing, Stoneham. And if I hear a whisper from anyone that you've been saying otherwise, I'll have your balls.'

Jack paused. The contempt in the other man's eyes was clear, but in his demeanour was a shade of doubt. This was an old bone of contention between them, but the DCI knew better than to argue. Keeping his voice pitched to a steady level he maintained eye contact with his newly promoted boss.

'This last murder bears hallmarks of the others that were never revealed to the public. And I don't believe in coincidence. I worked on that case for a year, and I know this bastard's MO. The mask he left behind was his signature.'

The two men had reached an impasse and they knew it.

'I just don't like seeing innocent men banged up because it makes things easier and tidies up the conviction numbers. That poor bastard Miller didn't stand a chance once that trick cyclist got his hooks into him. Miller was sick. Confused, lonely, frightened, and conveniently without an alibi. But he was not a sadistic killer.'

Chapman opened a file on his desk, his eyes downcast, his tone dismissive. 'You said something about having work to do, Stoneham. I suggest you get on with it.'

The DCI left the office and resisted an urge to slam the door. They were all tired and on edge, and he still had the image of that girl imprinted in technicolour brilliance in his mind. Visiting a scene of crime at five thirty in the morning was not his favourite way of starting the day.

A wall of noise greeted him as he swung through the doors of the incident room. East Sussex CID was in full swing.

'We've re-interviewed the overnight prisoners out on bail and come up with nothing.' Detective Sergeant Ramona Knight added an overflowing folder to the ones already piled before him. 'Most of them were in here when the murder was committed. But we still have Darren Smith and his mates to round up. Seems they weren't arrested until the early hours of the morning after. They should be here soon. I sent a patrol car.'

The DCI grunted as his second in command shuffled through the files.

'Smith was arrested near the scene, Guv. Charged with possession, suspicion of dealing and causing an affray. Got six previous and two convictions. All drug related except for an ABH which his brief managed to quash.'

Her hands stilled for a moment and she looked thoughtful. 'I interviewed him when he was brought in. He was very jumpy. Seemed anxious to make a statement and get out. Refused to say much, which surprised me. He usually shouts police brutality and demands his lawyer.'

'Darren Smith's a regular visitor, Ramona. But he lacks the imagination to be a serial killer.'

WDS Knight grinned. 'Want a coffee? Looks like you could do with one. Chapman cutting up rough?'

'You could say that,' he replied grimly. 'Coffee sounds like a good idea, but I expect I'll regret it.'

He began to read the arrest sheet for Smith and his cronies and was startled when a plastic cup filled with what appeared to be ancient dishwater was placed in front of him. He hadn't heard her leave the room.

'How are things going?' He sipped the drink, grimaced and added four spoons of sugar. The station house coffee was getting worse if that was at all possible.

'The patrols are out picking up the usual collection of perverts and nutters. All the snouts have been contacted as far as possible, and told to keep their eyes and ears open.'

She paused for breath, her eyes glazed in thought. 'Someone must know who this guy is, and if there's a whisper on the street, we'll get to hear it. We've also sent out a call to round up the travellers. They couldn't have got far, so it shouldn't be long before they catch up with them. The drug squad are involved because of the rave and the Yardie connection. They're using their snouts to spread the net to London. Should start to get feedback soon.'

'Any news from pathology?' They'd both attended the initial examination of the body, but the police surgeon hadn't been able to do much but state the obvious.

'Time of death around three a.m. Saturday morning. Last meal several hours before. She'd taken Ecstasy, traces of it still in her blood. But she wasn't a heavy user. No needle marks. Her clothes were cut with a knife blade, too jagged for scissors. As for the mask . . .' She paused. 'It's unusual, and probably from old stock, but we're checking on it now. There seems no doubt that death was caused by attempted decapitation. The other wounds came after.'

She opened a file and laid it in front of him. 'Forensics sent these,' she said grimly.

The two police officers stared down at the photographs. Time and experience hadn't dulled them to the horror of a brutal murder. There in graphic detail was the nightmare end of a young girl's life. Somehow, seeing her like this, was worse than their first sighting of her beneath the dripping trees in Saxon Woods. There was a childlike vulnerability about her, a stark brutality in the pale limbs and dark bruising that lay obscenely exposed on the autopsy table.

'Do we know who she is yet?'

Ramona Knight shook her head. 'I contacted missing persons. They're looking through the local files first, but missing teenagers aren't always reported, and there are so many kids on the streets today, it's difficult to track them down.'

He slammed the folder shut and stood up. 'We have to catch this bastard before he kills again, Ramona. Get on to records and see if there's anything local we can pick up on. Then ask Ryan to put the details of this murder through the Central Computer. I'm going to retrieve the Miller files. I reckon we have a serial killer on our hands.'

Ramona stilled, alert yet wary. 'What do you know that we don't, Guv?'

In a few sentences, he told her about the two previous murders and Chapman's major role in the arrest of Miller.

'So what happened?' Ramona's gaze was brown and steady.

'I was hauled up before an inquiry, and threatened with demotion. They didn't like my attitude – disruptive and insubordinate, they said. I wrote a statement at the time and put my doubts on file. It was all I could do. Chapman was working his way up the ranks and it was his judgement against mine. Hell, I was only a DI. He was acting Superintendent. Miller was found guilty, Chapman got a result and I ended up at the bottom of the heap for promotion.'

'That was tough. Christ, I don't envy you now Chapman's here in Brighton.'

The two police officers regarded one another. They went back a long way, and in their line of work trust was forged in the melting pot of man's inhumanity to man. They both knew this conversation would go no further.

'I was right to doubt that conviction, Ramona. That's what really sickens me. We have to find the real culprit, and this time, put him away for good.'

'Chapman won't like it.'

'Bugger Chapman,' retorted her DCI.

They shared a conspiratorial smile, then the phone rang and DS Knight listened for a moment before hanging up.

'They've got Smith and the others downstairs. Want me to deal with them?'

DCI Stoneham looked at the files on his desk, then stood up. 'I need to get out of here. You get onto records for me and find the files for these two cases.' He wrote down the appropriate names on his pad and handed the page to her.

'You'll have to contact London. Ask for Sergeant Hills. They call him Print-Out. What he doesn't know about previous cases could be put on a pin-head. Photographic memory.'

DS Knight left the room, and grabbing his jacket, her boss followed her out.

The youths had been placed in separate cells, and Stoneham decided to begin with the youngest and most impressionable of the four. Lennie Bates was seventeen and none too bright, but he had a built-in sense of self-preservation and if there was anything to be learned, he was the most likely to spill his guts.

The interview room was small and apart from a desk, four chairs, a table and a tape recorder, featureless. Lenny was exploring his nasal cavities as the DCI and the duty sergeant walked in, and he guiltily rammed his hands into his pockets.

'Looking for your brains, Lennie?' Jack Stoneham dropped the file on the table between them and sat down. 'Want to be careful, me old son. You stick your finger up much further and you'll lose the few you got left.'

Lennie blushed and fidgeted on the hard wooden chair. He was an uninspiring sight. The acne cratered his skin, his hair was long and unkempt beneath the baseball cap, and there was a sour smell coming from his clothes. Probably hadn't washed for days.

'Right Lennie, just a few questions, then you can go.'

'I done a statement.' The boy's tone was surly.

Reap the Whirlwind

The DCI ignored him, went through the ritual of declaring the people present and the time of questioning to the tape recorder and opened the file. 'I want to talk about the night of the rave, Lennie.'

'Done that on the statement.'

The DCI maintained what he hoped was a friendly expression. No point in putting the wind up the little shit just yet.

'I know that, Lennie. It's just a couple of details I need that weren't covered before.'

Lennie scratched idly at his acne and stared back, his muddy brown eyes void of interest. 'So?'

'You were with Darren, Peter and Gavin. That right?'

Lennie shrugged. 'So what?'

'No-one else? No girlfriends or other mates?'

The youth shrugged again and studied the wall.

'Do I take that as a yes, or a no?'

'What ya want to know for?'

'I ask the questions, sunshine. And if I don't get any answers, then I'll have to assume you're hiding something.'

They held one another's gaze. Interrogator and detainee locked in silent battle.

'There was a couple of slappers with Gavin and Darren. What's that got to do with anything?' There was confusion in his eyes, but his expression was still sullen.

'What's their names, Lennie?'

'Dunno. Tarts is trouble. I told Darren. But he wouldn't listen.'

'So you didn't want them along, but Darren insisted. That right?' DCI Stoneham had perfected the art of watching for signs of duplicity, but there were none in Lennie's face. 'Come on, Lennie. The girls were there because Darren insisted.'

'Yeah.' Lennie sat up and leaned his arms on the table. 'It was supposed to be just the lads, but when Darren gets an idea, it's best to go along with it, see. So I didn't say nothing.'

The policeman nodded. 'Where did Darren and Gavin meet the girls? At the rave, or before?'

'What's all this about?'

'Just answer the question, there's a good lad. The sooner you do, the sooner you can leave.'

Stoneham watched the expressions flit across the youth's face. There were conflicting emotions there, but none of them hinted at fear. Perhaps, after all, there was nothing more to find out and he was wasting his time.

Lennie slumped back in his chair and folded his arms. 'They was in the car when he picked me up.'

'Lookers, were they? Bit of all right?'

Lennie shrugged again.

'Well?' It was a bark in the silence between them.

'They was tarts, that's all. A Goth and a Sharon.'

'Was that her name – Sharon?'

Lennie laughed. 'Naagh. Sharon, you know, Essex girl and all that. Blimey, you coppers don't know much, do ya?' he sniggered.

'So the girl you called a Goth – that means she was dressed in black?'

'Course. What else?' Lennie studied the ceiling as though he was dealing with the demented.

'Describe her.'

Lennie regarded him for a moment, his murky gaze drifting between the silent duty officer and the DCI, as though trying to decide where this was leading. He shrugged again and lit a cigarette.

'Blonde, bit skinny, about sixteen, dressed in black, lots of silver jewellery and black eye make-up. Not the kinda slapper Darren usually likes.'

'What was her name?' Stoneham's voice was low and cajoling. That description could have fitted hundreds of girls at the rave, but it also fitted the victim.

'Can't remember. Don't think she said much and Darren ain't one for the chit chat.'

'The girls weren't with you when you were arrested. What happened to them?'

Lennie dragged on his cigarette and peered at his inquisitor through the smoke. 'We was sorting out the Yardies. No place for tarts. 'Spect they was still in the barn.'

'When was the last time you saw the blonde girl, Lennie? Think hard, son. I won't repeat anything to Darren. This is between you and me.'

'Did something happen? You think Darren's in trouble 'cos of her?'

The DCI knew he had to handle the next few moments with care. He didn't want Lennie to clam up, but on the other hand, he needed to know as much as possible, as soon as possible. Other witnesses had seen the girls with Lennie and Darren, and he needed to put names to them.

'I want you to tell me what happened that night, Lennie, so I can get Darren out of trouble. Tell me what you know, and you and your mates can leave here.'

Lennie screwed up his eyes and looked down his nose at the DCI, then took the cigarette from his mouth and stubbed it out.

'Last time I saw them together was a couple of hours before we was picked up by your lot. She and Darren left the barn. Going to get his leg over, probably. She looked up for it. All over him she was.' He sniggered and swiped the back of his hand beneath his nose.

'How long were they gone? When did you see Darren again?'

'I dunno! What you think I am – a fucking pervert?'

The detective ignored that and changed tack again. 'Tell me about the run-in with the Yardies.'

'What's there to tell? They was muscling in on our patch and we had to sort them out.'

'Did you go into the woods that night?'

'Na. Didn't need to. Why?'

'Did you see anyone hanging about the woods? Someone who looked suspicious, or out of place?'

Lennie regarded him for a moment, his gaze dancing over Stoneham's face as he attempted to read his thoughts. Then he shook his head. 'We was too busy sorting out them black bastards to be looking at the scenery.' He tugged at the baseball cap, his gaze slipping away.

'So you didn't go near the woods until the fight?'

Lennie shook his head, but there was something in his demeanour that told the detective he was hiding something.

'Did you see a girl near the woods, Lennie? A young girl, about sixteen with long blonde hair?'

'I told you – NO! I ain't saying nothing more. You can't make me.' Lennie was giving off waves of fear. It was in his eyes, his face and in the trembling of his hands as he shook a cigarette out of the packet.

The DCI leaned forward. There was a charge of electricity between them and he was almost afraid to break it.

'What did you see that night to make you so jumpy, Lennie? Come on, tell me. It won't go any further.'

'I ain't saying nothing. I want my brief.'

Lennie's mouth shut like a steel trap and Jack Stoneham knew he would get no further until Lennie had stewed for a while. He pushed back from the table and stood up.

'I'll get someone to bring you a cuppa. Be back in a while.'

The door closed on Lennie's protests and the two policemen interviewed the other youths before heading for Darren Smith. They hadn't told the DCI much more than he already knew, but he now had a name for one of the girls and confirmation that a young, blonde girl had gone to the rave with Darren Smith. That girl fitted the description of the victim, and although the evidence was flimsy, Stoneham was too old and too wise not to know that all three youths were hiding something.

He nodded to the duty officer, and the door to the interview swung open.

'You got no right keeping me here. I been waiting more than an hour. This is police harassment.' Darren Smith leaned against the wall and glared belligerently through his dreadlocks as he rolled a cigarette.

'What you afraid of, Smith? I merely want to ask you some questions.' Stoneham laid the arrest sheet on the table and sat down.

'I ain't afraid of nothing.' Darren lit the cigarette with deliberate nonchalance, and watched the smoke curl to the ceiling.

Reap the Whirlwind

Being hauled in for questioning was a natural event in Smith's life, but there was a tension about the youth, a wariness that the experienced detective could almost touch. It had been the same with Gavin and Paul, and Stoneham felt a tingle at the nape of his neck.

He introduced himself and the duty officer, informed Smith of his rights and switched on the tape recorder. He looked at the youth who now slouched in the chair opposite and felt his lip curl with disgust. Darren Smith was typical of the yobs who came in here. His ears and nose had been pierced, and he was unkempt, street-wise and surly. Like his mates, he came from a rough family on an even rougher side of town. With a sigh, the detective acknowledged that he could think of better ways to pass a Monday afternoon.

'You were arrested at the rave the other night.' It was a statement more than a question.

'Yeah. So what?'

Stoneham eyed the snake tattoo that ran up Darren's arm and disappeared beneath the cuff of his jacket. Snake was Darren's nickname. It suited him.

'Were you there all night?'

Snake leaned on the desk, his eyes narrowed as he regarded the policeman who sat so still on the other side. 'Yeah.'

'You didn't leave the barn until you were arrested?'

Snake eyed him closely, suspicion in every drug-ravaged plane of his face. 'Had to take a leak, that's all.'

'Had to do a bit of business as well, didn't you Darren? You and the others were arrested just outside Saxon Woods.' He looked up from the file and caught the wariness in Snake's eyes. 'Had a bit of bother, did we?'

Snake shrugged. 'Just a little disagreement with the soul brothers. Nothing we couldn't have handled if your lot hadn't interfered.'

He stabbed out his cigarette, and the tattoo on his forearm seemed to come alive as he flexed his fingers.

'We been through all this shit. I done a statement. You got no right holding me here. I got bail.'

'I'm trying to find a girl, Darren. About sixteen, blonde,

slim, dressed in black with lots of silver jewellery.' The detective was waiting for a reaction.

He wasn't disappointed. Darren looked away, but there had been the flicker of something that resembled guilt, before the shutters came down.

'Don't know what you're talking about.'

'Did you see a girl like that, Darren? At the rave? Did you know her?' Snake was afraid of something – the confirmation of that fear was in his wary demeanour.

'Might a done. Tarts all look the same in the dark.' Snake dragged back his dreadlocks and tipped his chair away from the table.

'You'd remember this one,' said Stoneham softly. 'She was pretty, with long blonde hair and blue eyes. I have witnesses who say you were with a girl like that. Brought her to the rave.'

'Then they're lying. I told you. I was with me mates. Don't have time for tarts.' Snake was shouting, his face tinged with colour, his hands balled into fists on the table. Yet his gaze flickered uneasily and refused to meet the detective's determined glower.

'You were seen with her, Darren. She arrived at Wolves Farm in your car. Who was she? What was her name? Why don't you want us to know about her?'

Snake recovered the squall of temper and lolled back in his chair, his hands jammed into the pockets of his tight, black jeans as his gaze slid away. 'Like I said. They all look the same. I ain't saying nothing more till my brief gets here.'

'Don't waste my time, Smith. We know you took this girl to the rave. We know you went outside with her. We know she wasn't with you when you were arrested. Who was she? Where did you pick her up? And where is she now?' Stoneham's voice had risen to an angry bellow.

Darren Smith tipped back and forth on his chair, a sarcastic smirk plastered over his face. 'I want my brief,' was all he said.

The DCI picked up his papers, then turned to the duty

officer. 'Put him in the holding cells until his brief arrives. Then book the lot of them on suspicion of murder.'

The chair came down with a thud. Snake's fists hit the table. 'I hardly touched the bitch! You can't stitch me up with fucking murder.'

Stoneham turned with the speed of a striking cobra. 'Hardly touched who, Darren? Who was she and what was her name?'

Darren thrust away from the table, grabbed the chair, and threw it across the room. 'I want my brief. Now!'

The two police officers finally managed to wrestle him to the ground and handcuff him. Darren was still struggling and shouting as he was led away.

'Let him stew for a while, and keep him away from the others. I want to know the minute his brief arrives. That little shit knows more than he's letting on.'

*

Malcolm pulled open the great jaws of the industrial dishwasher and stepped back as the steam made his clothes cling and the sweat sting his eyes. Yet none of this concerned him as much as what was going on around him.

The Hastings Metropole Hotel had a vast kitchen, but space during the rush hour of meal times was at a premium. The crash of pans, the shouts of the chefs, the barked orders of the waiters and slapping of swing doors, all came together in a cacophony of sound that jarred in his head and stifled the voices of the wheels. He needed silence. Yearned for the solitude of his secret room and the familiar ritual.

'Move yourself, Squires. I need those dishes.' The chef de partie glared at him as he threw yet more basins into the sink.

Malcolm kept silent as he hurriedly pulled the red hot plates from the dishwasher. He almost dropped them as they burned his hands, but determination to escape the chef's wrath saw them safely onto the plate racks. He turned back to the sink and plunged his hands into the greasy water. There was still a mountain of copper cooking pans to wash and he was very tired after a restless night in the small staff bedroom in the basement. It was right next to the boiler room and although it was warm, it was very noisy. The boilers fired up and the pipes clanked as they fed the vast central heating system which was left on constantly.

'Clean up this fucking mess, Squires. Jesus. Where do you come from? A pig sty?' It was the head chef, a wiry little cockney with a short fuse and foul mouth.

Malcolm left the sink to bag up the kitchen refuse, and as he bent to pick up a stray tomato, he felt a knee in his back that almost sent him toppling to the floor. He whirled round, humiliation burning his face as he clenched his fists.

'Don't do that!'

'Ooh. It speaks. Fuck me, Squires. Thought you was dumb as well as daft.' The chef turned to smirk at the others and there was a gaggle of sniggers as all eyes fixed on Malcolm.

The frustration was alive in him, but he knew that any battle he fought with the chef would only result in humiliating defeat.

'I'll show you,' he muttered as he heaved the refuse sacks out of the kitchen and into the yard behind the hotel. 'One of these days you'll find out who I am, and what I know. Then I'm going to make you sorry you ever set eyes on me.'

Two hours later, the kitchen was scrubbed and silent. Malcolm switched off the lights and closed the door behind him. The rest of the staff had gone to the pub or to their rooms. No-one had given him a moment's thought. Yet he didn't mind their rejection, he preferred his own company.

He sat on a dustbin and stared up at the night sky. The rain was soft on his face, cool and soothing. The whisper of the wheels came with the rain, gentle, teasing and calming. The night shift was over, but he wouldn't be returning to the staff quarters. It was time to go home and face Lillian.

He dragged on his rumpled jacket and wrinkled his nose at the sourness of his shirt. He'd been wearing the same clothes for two days. Lillian had taught him that cleanliness was next to godliness, and he didn't like the feel of the dirty clothes against his sweat-stained skin.

The thought of Lillian made him shiver, but he knew he had to return home. His most precious things were there. The voices of the wheels were closer there. And he had the gnawing hope that the unknown presence that still watched him could not follow him into the house.

The walk along the seafront to the bus stop gave him a chance to assemble his thoughts. The short journey on the bus through Hastings helped to clarify those thoughts. And as he approached the house, he knew what he had to do.

With a trembling hand, he unlocked the door.

'Where have you been?' The voice was thunderous in the stillness of the house.

Malcolm looked up the short flight of stairs and saw Lillian. The light from the bedroom behind her cast shadows in the craters of her eye sockets, and made a demonic halo of the wispy hair. A filthy nightdress, that had once been white, ballooned down to her bare feet, and the outline of her grotesque figure could be seen through the thin cotton.

Malcolm swallowed. The fear of her was a squirming, living thing in his gut.

'I stayed at the hotel. I just came back to pack my things. I'm moving out.' The timbre of his voice was weak, his mouth dry, his lips parched. It was the first time he'd dared to defy her.

Silence fell between them like a heavy velvet wall and Malcolm's resolve began to falter despite the whispering of the wheels in his head.

'Come here, Malcolm. Let me look at you.' Lillian's demeanour had changed, now her voice was soft and wheedling, as she gestured for him to climb the stairs.

Malcolm hesitated. To disobey her would rouse her anger, and he didn't want to part with bad feeling between them. But could he trust her?

He listened to the wheels, but their chatter was unintelligible, and they offered no advice. Looking up, he was startled to see that Lillian was smiling. Perhaps she had missed him. After all, he reasoned, he looked after her, she must have been lonely these past two days.

Malcom experienced a sudden knife of guilt, and it shamed him. She was his mother, he should have taken care of her, not left her to fend for herself. She was old and helpless and she must have been frightened on her own. Perhaps he should change his mind about the move to the hotel. He didn't really like it there. He didn't fit in, and he knew they talked about him behind their closed doors.

With hope in his soul, he began to climb the stairs. He was twenty-four, and she was the only family he had. The people in the hotel weren't friends, merely shifting, sniping protagonists. Perhaps his disappearance had made her realise that she needed him. Perhaps now, she could finally learn to love him?

'Come, Malcolm. Come into the light and let me look at you.' Lillian's voice was a caress in the stillness.

Malcolm reached the top of the stairs as Lillian stepped back into her room. With an eagerness he despised, he followed her. He knew he was being weak and malleable, but if Lillian could learn to love him, it didn't matter. He had longed for this moment. Spent most of his life waiting for her to accept him with all his faults. Perhaps now she would offer the haven of peace he yearned for. Show him the mercy that her unforgiving God had denied him.

Lillian's hand shot out and there was a crack of flesh on flesh as she swiped his face.

'Spawn of the Devil. Cast out the sin. I see it in your eyes, smell it on your clothes.'

She hit him again: then again and again.

Malcolm was frozen with terror and the euphoria melted like ice in a furnace as his spectacles spun across the floor.

Lillian put her hands on his shoulders and forced him to his knees. 'Pray for forgiveness, devil child. Pray that your sins be washed in the blood of the Lord. Cast out Lucifer, cleanse your body and soul of your wickedness.'

Malcolm began to cry. Lillian hadn't changed. This house,

this place called home was a prison. 'Don't do this, Mamma. Please don't hurt me,' he sobbed.

Lillian's fingers pinched his chin as she forced him to look up at her. He could smell the sourness of her and feel the heat of her passion like a burning aura which surrounded her. Her faded eyes were wide, and filled with a fanatic light. Her face trembled with emotion.

'Look at Jesus on his cross and tell him you have not sinned. Dare to perjure yourself in the sight of the Lord. For I can see the wickedness in you. It's written in your eyes, burning in that mark of Lucifer,' she screamed.

Malcolm tried to pull away, but Lillian had him in a vice.

'No, Mamma. No.' He was moaning now, writhing to escape from her, scuffling on his hands and knees to find a dark corner, a refuge. But there was no lessening of her fervour, no remission in her grip.

'They'll take you away again, Malcolm. Put you in that place and throw away the key.' Her voice was a hiss and he felt the warmth of her spittle on his face.

Fear was sharp. It slipped like a blade through his intestines. 'I won't go back. You can't make me.' His voice broke as the tears choked in his throat.

'Yes I can, Malcolm. The Lord has told me it is the right thing to do.'

In a frenzy born of terror, he tore at her fingers. 'You can't send me back. I won't go.'

The hazy images of locked doors and white uniforms, of needles pricking his arms and pills that made him dull and useless, tormented him. The echoes of screams in the night, of staring eyes and dulled senses brought it all back. It was over five years since he last saw the inside of that place. He'd vowed then he would never return.

'All it takes is a telephone call, Malcolm. The will of the Lord must be obeyed. Trust in the Lord and he will give you salvation.'

'I won't go back,' he screamed. He ripped away her hands and held her wrists. The fear of that place made him strong – stronger than he had ever been. He couldn't allow them to take him back. Couldn't let them distance him from the voices and the ritual.

The sound of the wheels grew louder until they were a thunder in his head. 'Take you away. Take you away. Take you away.'

'I won't go!' He pushed Lillian from him and stumbled to his feet.

Lillian sagged onto the bed, her head thudding against the nailed feet on the vast crucifix.

'I have to do the Lord's bidding,' she gasped. 'Satan has found a dwelling place in your soul. You must be cleansed.' Lillian put out her hand, searching for something to push against so she could get off the bed.

Malcolm's breath was ragged as the fires raged through him and the wheels screamed their mantra. He had to stop her. Had to find a way to silence her before she sent him to that place again.

Lillian pushed herself up the wall, her shoulder jolting the crucifix, making it sway.

'Wash clean, Malcolm. Wash clean in the blood of the Lord.' She inched forward, her nightdress riding up her fleshy thighs as she clawed the air between them.

His glazed vision travelled to the wall behind Lillian's head. Without his glasses, he couldn't be sure if it was only in his imagination, but the crucifix seemed to move. He stared in horrified fascination at the plaster face that regarded him with hooded, pain-filled eyes.

Jesus Christ on his cross was tilting, sliding, slowly descending in a graceful arc towards Lillian.

'Take you away. Take you away. Take you away,' screamed the wheels as they thundered through the echoing tunnels of his mind.

The crucifix thudded into the back of Lillian's head. Her skull splintered like a cracked walnut and splattered the wall. She gave a grunt as she slumped beneath the crashing weight, then toppled slowly onto her side. The crucifix came to rest across her inert, silent body. The plaster face of Jesus was buried deep in her skull.

Reap the Whirlwind

Malcolm began to tremble as that silence stretched into endless seconds. He watched the ponderous descent of viscid tissue on the wall. There was blood on the sheets. Dark, sticky red blossoms that had been seeded and sown by Lillian. The bloody flowers bloomed and spread like a macabre harvest over the bed beneath her. Yet, still she didn't move.

'Mamma?' His voice was a whisper as conflicting emotions jostled for attention. She couldn't be dead, not Lillian.

Yet the evidence was clear before him, and he experienced a sharp thrill of excitement. Never again would she chastise him, or make him take his pills. Never again would he have to hide from her, or play out his rituals in secret. He was free.

The euphoria was swept away on a wave of fear and guilt. Punishment was inevitable. Lillian would reach out from her grave and find him. She would watch him, follow him, haunt his every move until she had him once more in her snare of malice. It was because of him she was dead. Because of him that the crucifix had nailed her to the bed. Lillian had God on her side – there would be no escape.

He began to tremble and his voice was a whimper. 'I'm sorry, Mamma. I didn't mean it.' The tears were hot as he fell to his knees beside the bed and plucked at her nightdress.

Her silence mocked him, bringing with it the enforced dread of retribution. Her eyes stared blindly back at him, but he knew she could see him.

'Forgive me, Mamma. Please say you'll forgive me.'

'Gone away. Gone away. Gone away,' the train wheels murmured.

The tears became choking sobs as weariness finally descended. He rested his burning face on the cool, naked floor and closed his eyes.

The wheels whispered a lullaby. 'Free at last. Free at last. Free at last.'

Malcom heard them, gave into them with a sigh of pleasure and smiled. He would sleep for a while.

7

Detective Stoneham looked up as Ramona Knight tapped on his door and entered the room. It was after ten and he was about to call it a night.

'We got a call from Saxonbridge, Guv. The desk sergeant there saw our notice about missing persons and thought we should handle this.'

'What?' DS Knight's intrusion wasn't welcome. He'd escaped to the relative sanity of his office to get away from the chaos of the incident room and to catch a few moments' rest. His eyes felt scratchy and the fatigue had finally doused the adrenalin buzz that had kept him going until now.

'A Mrs Kingsley rang about her missing daughter.'

'So have a dozen other mothers. Let missing persons deal with it, I've got the co-ordination of the house-to-house to contend with.' He gave a vast yawn and pushed the thin report away.

She pushed it back. 'I think you'll want to talk to her, Guv. She says her daughter went to the rave, and she wasn't alone.'

'Spit it out, Ramona. This isn't bloody *Crimewatch*!'

She folded her arms, the humour evident in her eyes. 'Cassandra Kingsley went to the rave with Darren "Snake" Smith. She hasn't been seen since.'

The detective leaped from his desk, all thought of sleep dismissed, the tiredness forgotten. 'We have to be absolutely positive about this, Ramona. I don't want any cock-ups. Where's Smith now?'

'In the holding cells. His brief's been tied up in court all day and has only just arrived.'

Stoneham looked at his watch and grunted. 'Plenty of time before he starts screaming habeas corpus. Let me see that.'

The two police officers stared down into the face of Cassandra Kingsley. 'How long ago was this photo taken?'

DS Knight ran her finger down the page. 'Two years ago. Mrs Kingsley didn't have a more recent one.'

'She's the right age, but I'm not sure. Kids change so much in two years, and our little girl's face was such a mess.'

They studied the wide blue eyes and dimpled chin, following the line of her long blonde hair before returning to the eyes again.

'This could be her,' Stoneham muttered.

Looking past his Detective Sergeant, he caught sight of the photographs on the wall of the incident room. Was that broken, battered girl Mrs Kingsley's daughter? He sighed. She was someone's daughter, and it would be his onerous task to inform the distraught parents. This was the time when he hated police work. The victims and their families were the ones who were punished – sometimes for the rest of their lives – whilst the murderers and thugs spent a few years in prison only to be released to do it all again. The whole system was a frustrating joke.

DS Knight's voice interrupted his thoughts. 'She has all the right credentials, Guv. I think we ought to see the mother.'

'First, I want to interview Darren Smith again. It's time the little bastard earned his keep. You'd better come with me.'

*

Laura's hands were clammy and she was shivering despite the heat from the gas fire. Snatches of memory paraded like ghostly video tape and refused to be dismissed. She closed her eyes willing them to leave her, but they were insistent and sharp.

A quiet street, the sound of children at play. The brightness of the sky, the spring warmth and the impertinent yellow of

Reap the Whirlwind

forsythia. Then came the emotions, the cold fear and clutching panic. Faces of people, snatches of conversation, the melting, mesmerising terror as time stood still and the hands on the clock never moved past midnight.

The doorbell fragmented the ghostly parade and she leaped from the chair.

'I'll go.' Ben squeezed her hands and left the room.

Laura watched the door, listening to the deep voices that came from the hall, dreading the moment she had no choice but to face.

'Please God, don't let it be Cassandra. Please, I beg you.' It was a prayer from the deepest part of her, and as the footsteps approached, she hoped God was listening.

'Mrs Kingsley? Detective Chief Inspector Stoneham and this is DS Knight.'

Laura barely gave their identity cards a glance, and allowed Ben to pull her onto the couch beside him.

'I know this is a distressing time for you, Mrs Kingsley, so I won't drag this out longer than neccessary. You've reported your daughter missing. What makes you think she could be the girl we found in Saxon Woods?'

Laura watched as his face swam in and out of focus. His voice seemed to be coming from far away.

'We had an argument,' she said, surprised at how calm she sounded, when inside, she was in turmoil. 'Cassandra went off to the rave with Snake and I haven't seen her since.' She took a breath, marshalled her strength, and carried on. 'I've looked everywhere. None of her friends remember her leaving the rave and she didn't turn up for college this morning.'

'Has she ever done something like this before?'

'No. She wouldn't do that, not willingly. Not after . . .' Laura bit down on the words, her gaze flying, unbidden, to the snapshot on the mantelpiece.

'After what, Mrs Kingsley?' DCI Stoneham had edged forward in his chair, and Laura realised he'd followed her fleeting glance at the photograph.

She dug her nails into her palm. 'Nothing. I just meant she would never leave home for three nights without telling me first.' She tried a weak smile. 'It was about the only rule she obeyed with grace.' Her gaze drifted back to the photograph of the twins.

The silence grew heavy and Laura turned back to Stoneham to find that he too, was staring at the photograph.

'That was taken over ten years ago,' she said. 'Cassandra and Melissa are twins.'

'Is your other daugher at home? Teenagers often confide in each other, rather than their parents. She may know something.' The detective was making notes.

'Melissa was involved in a nasty car wreck ten years ago. She's in a sanitarium for the mentally impaired, Detective.' Ben's American twang momentarily alleviated the tension. 'We've just spoken to her doctor and she's been heavily sedated. She has no knowledge of Cassandra's disappearance.'

'I'm sorry, Mrs Kingsley.'

Laura remained silent. Ben's explanation would suffice. What had really happened to Melissa was none of this Detective's business. It certainly couldn't help to find Cassandra.

DCI Stoneham's face was grim. He cleared his throat, glanced once more at the photograph of the twins, then turned to face her.

'We have made inquiries and spoken to her college teachers and her friends. No joy, I'm afraid. The youth, Darren "Snake" Smith, is in custody. So are his mates. They were arrested in the early hours following the rave. An unconnected arrest that does not need to concern you. My men are searching their homes at this moment, and we have statements to confirm that he was seen with your daughter at the start of the rave.'

Laura was still. Fear was a bird pecking at her insides.

'I have a problem.' Detective Stoneham shifted in his chair and shot a look at his colleague. 'Darren Smith has admitted to being with Cassandra. Has even admitted to having an altercation with her. But he and his friends swear she was alive when they last saw her.'

'Well they would, wouldn't they?' Laura said coldly. 'You have to make them tell the truth.'

Stoneham must have found her steady gaze unnerving, for he gave a sigh and looked away. 'Darren's refused to say any more on the advice of his solicitor. It's his right, Mrs Kingsley.'

Laura jumped from the couch and stood over the detectives with her hands knotted into fists. 'Rights! What about Cassandra? What rights is she entitled to?'

Stoneham stood before her, awkwardly clasping his hands in front of him. 'We haven't yet established that it's your daughter, Mrs Kingsley. For now, we have to assume that she's merely missing. Please try and stay calm.'

'Calm!' she spat. 'Would you keep calm if it was your daughter?'

'Laura, hon. Take it easy. The guy's only doing his job.' Ben went to put a protective arm around her shoulder, but Laura shook it off. She was blazing with the injustice, fearful of the outcome to this interview. It was only the detective's voice that brought her back to the sharpness of reality.

'Could you describe what she was wearing that night? I understand she liked silver jewellery. Do you remember if she was wearing any?'

Laura closed her eyes and tried to remember. She could see Cassandra, angry, defiant, standing with her jacket slung over her shoulder.

'She was dressed in black, as usual.' She could hear the falter in her voice, but there was an eerie calm settling over her. It was as though the world had gone into slow motion and she was on the outside looking in. 'Leggings, long sweater, Doc Martens and an old leather jacket. I think she had silver hoops in her ears and she always wore several rings on both hands and lots of bracelets.'

She looked back at the detective, her chin up, her face set. 'It's not very clear, I'm sorry. I was concentrating on Snake more than Cassandra the last time I saw them. I was trying to make him leave. Alone.'

Stoneham looked thoughtful and Laura caught the silent look that darted between him and the policewoman.

'What is it? Does the description match the girl you found?'

Detective Stoneham opened a briefcase and pulled out a

small plastic evidence bag. 'Do you recognise anything in here, Mrs Kingsley?' He tipped the contents onto the coffee table. 'Take your time. We need to be certain,' he said gruffly.

The pathetic array of silver jewellery seemed tawdry, sitting there on that cold, glass table. There were rings, a number of bracelets and a pair of hooped earrings, but nothing that looked familiar. Nothing that screamed Cassandra. A surge of hope made her tremble.

'I don't recognise anything, but Cassandra was always buying new things.'

The detective nodded. 'They are pretty common pieces. All of them can be picked up for a few quid in Brighton. We were hoping you would recognise this. It's fairly distinctive compared to the rest.'

He prodded a silver ring with a grinning skull. 'Do you remember her wearing anything like this?'

Laura looked at the ring until it blurred and became a speck of light. The grinning mouth wavered and the blind eyes stared back at her. She felt hope dwindle.

'Cass had a lot of stuff like this. Skulls and crucifixes are popular with the kids these days . . . or so I'm told.'

The policeman gathered the jewellery up and put it back in the evidence bag. 'Is there anything different about Cassandra that would help in identifying her? A birthmark, a tattoo, pierced body parts, or a scar?'

Laura shook her head. Cassandra's scars were internal. Damage caused a long time ago, and not on display.

'What size shoe does she take?'

'A five and a half, but the boots are a six so she can wear thick socks with them.' Laura saw the confirmation in his eyes and the panic began to gather strength.

'What happens now, Detective?' Ben's quiet voice broke the tension.

'The statement from Smith confirms he was with Cassandra that night, but denies murder. All four youths are keeping things tight to their chests, and no-one can confirm a sighting of Cassandra between the time she and Darren left the barn, and Darren's arrest several hours later.'

He paused and the silence was ominous. 'It is possible that the girl we found is your daughter.'

Laura froze. She was vaguely aware of Ben's arms tightening around her waist, but her attention was fixed on the detective's face. She watched his mouth move, and his words seemed to come to her wrapped in fog. Slowly and inexorably they reached her, muffled by the crashing thunder of her pulse, penetrating the numbness with the power of a sledge hammer.

'It will be necessary for someone to make a formal indentification, Mrs Kingsley.'

The dam of control crumbled as stone by delicate stone it tumbled away. 'Not Cassie. Please God, not Cass.'

'I'll do it,' said Ben, his voice unsteady as he held on to Laura.

Stoneham nodded. 'It might be for the best. I'll make the arrangements. A car will come to collect you in the morning.'

'NO!' Laura emerged from behind her hands which she'd thrown up as a barrier to ward off the horror of what was happening. 'I have to see her, believe it's really her. I need to know what that bastard did.'

'It would be better if you let your friend do the identification, Mrs Kingsley.' Stoneham's face was ashen, the lines of age deeply etched around his mouth. 'It is sometimes best to remember them as they were. She was badly beaten, and you would find it too distressing.'

Laura shook her head – in control – cold – determined. 'She's my child. It's only right I should be with her.'

'What about this Snake character?' Ben's voice rumbled as he maintained his grip on Laura.

'He isn't going anywhere.' Stoneham's tone was grim. 'Would you like DS Knight to stay with you for a while, Mrs Kingsley?'

Laura shook her head. 'My mother's on her way. I'd prefer it if you left.'

*

Malcolm opened his eyes and stumbled into wakefulness. Disorientated and confused, he stared myopically at the floor-boards and watched a spider skitter into a crack in the wainscotting. He was cold and stiff and there was a strange smell in the room. As the final wisps of sleep departed, he realised what it was, and knew he hadn't been dreaming. It was the smell of Lillian's blood.

He slowly turned towards the bed, fearful that she had somehow recovered. But she was still there beneath the crucifix, her mouth open in a perfect circle, her eyes already shrouded in death beneath the bright light of the naked bulb.

He scrambled for his glasses, then knelt beside the bed, his hands fluttering over her inert form, touching, pecking, stroking.

'I didn't mean to do it, Mamma,' he whispered. 'But you made me. You shouldn't have threatened me with that place. You shouldn't have done that.' The last words were lost in a sob.

Lillian lay silent, her milky gaze fixed on some distant vista that only the dead could see.

Malcolm ran his sleeve under his nose and blinked back the tears. He would clean mother up and put her to bed. Then he would go to his secret room and listen to the voices. They would tell him what to do next.

The crucifix was heavy and he had to tug at it to pull it away from Lillian's head. Now there was blood, real blood crowning His head, and grey matter clung to the plaster face.

Malcolm stared into the painted eyes and felt a shudder of apprehension. It was as if they were silently accusing him. He felt his skin crawl and he dragged the crucifix off the bed and leaned it against the wall. Jesus could stare at the plaster, he decided. He'd seen enough, and it was none of his business.

Lillian was heavy when she was alive. Dead – she was like a beached whale, and he struggled to strip the bed. The blood had dried into rusty blooms and rivers and he didn't like the smell of it.

'Soon get you comfortable, Mother,' he whispered as he hurried to get Lillian settled.

The sweat was cold on his back as he worked feverishly to clean things up. Yet there was now an elation inside him. An elation that told him things could only get better now the old bitch was out of the way. He would have the freedom to come and go as he pleased. The freedom to listen to the voices and to perform the rites.

Lillian couldn't hurt him now. He was finally rid of her.

An hour later he turned in the doorway and took a last look at the woman he'd come to despise. She was lying in a clean bed, with the blankets tucked up to her chin. The long blonde wig from his secret hiding place was arranged artfully around her face. It spread its glittering harvest of gold on the pillow, making her suddenly youthful and almost attractive. Her hands were folded piously on her chest and her eyes were closed.

Malcolm gave a tremulous sigh. This was the way things should always have been. Lillian silenced. Lillian still. Lillian young and almost beautiful.

He turned off the light and closed the door.

*

Laura climbed out of the car and tugged her coat up to her chin. It was cold, the early morning lost in a haze of low cloud. She felt Ben's hand on her arm. There were no words that could describe her emotions. No form of communication between them that would take away the dread.

'I'll do it for you, darling.' Clara's gentle voice drifted into Laura's consciousness. 'You've been through enough.'

Laura turned to her mother and gripped her hand. Clara suddenly looked older. Her skin was translucent in the dawn light, her green eyes huge in her elfin face.

'I must do this thing myself, but . . .' There was nothing more to be said, and the silent hug of gratitude was the most she was capable of.

'If you're ready, Mrs Kingsley?' WDS Knight shifted her bag from one shoulder to another and tightened the belt on her coat. She looked ill at ease.

Laura nodded. Would she ever be ready? What was the right time to identify the body of your child? Even the experiences of the past hadn't been enough to prepare her for this.

Like an automaton she allowed them to lead the way up the steps into the Borough Morgue. She heard the echo of her footsteps on the highly polished floor. Smelled the cloying scent of formaldehyde that was mingled with another, darker aroma. One of body fluids and flesh – the secret smell of death.

She took a breath and stared ahead as they walked down the endless corridors. This cold, impersonal building, with its echoing walls and dark pervasive scent, was Cass's last resting place. And the thought of it was almost too much to contemplate.

The detective was waiting for them. He nodded to his colleague, then stepped forward to clasp Laura's cold hands.

'You don't have to. Mr Farraday . . .'

Laura pulled her hands away and tucked them into her pockets. 'Yes I do, Detective. I have to know.' Her voice sounded dull, too calm, yet her mind was in jagged revolt.

Stoneham pushed open the door.

Laura closed her eyes for an instant and tried to marshal her strength, but her heart hammered and the cloying, sweet smell seemed to pervade her every sense. She left the others, and stepped into the room.

It was as if she was alone, isolated in a sea of misery, abandoned to the clinical symmetry of this island of the dead. The banks of cold white perspex which lined the walls looked like a giant's frozen storehouse.

The dread encircled her, closed in in ever tighter bonds as she saw the still, shrouded body waiting to be identified.

WDS Knight came to stand beside her, yet Laura was

hardly aware of her. Stoneham nodded and the attendant pulled back the corner of the crisp, white sheet.

Laura glaced at DS Knight, then at Stoneham, but her gaze was drawn in an inexorable downward spiral to the figure that lay beneath the sheet.

The girl's flesh was greenish-grey in the blinding lights, her long hair a drift of ragged gold about what was left of her face. Angry welts and bruises darkened the skin around her eyes, her nose had been broken and rammed into her skull and her childish mouth was split and swollen.

The teenager had died violently and alone, and Laura felt the nausea hit her throat. This child, this poor dead child looked just like her own. But she was not Cassandra.

8

Paul Galloway had paced the hotel suite for over an hour after the Arab left. The restlessness had grown until he could no longer contain it, and the room began to close in on him, making the need to escape more urgent. With an angry curse, he snatched the keys and left. They could watch all they wanted, he hadn't spent all these years ducking and diving without learning to cover his tracks. Soho was calling. He had things to do.

It was cold on the streets tonight, a damp, bone-chilling cold that made him pull up his coat collar and bury his hands in his pockets. Yet it suited his purpose. On such a night he was anonymous, just another man sheltering from the wind, eyes downcast, busy with his own thoughts as he tried to keep warm.

A snatched glimpse of his reflection in a shop window reassured, the hat shadowed his face and the collar masked the ragged scars. He smiled to himself, the Arab thought he could frighten him with his threats – well, he didn't know the real Paul Galloway – the man he'd kept hidden for all these years – the man who had fooled so many and still kept his freedom. Still, it would be wise not to take risks.

As he walked through the crowded streets that buzzed and flickered with neon, he kept watch for a face, a shadow following him. Turning abruptly down alley ways and through jostling video game arcades, he was soon fairly certain he'd shaken off any watchers.

The blast of music came at him from all sides as the clubs

and bars tempted him in, but he knew where he was going and pushed quickly past the snatching hands and hectoring voices of the touts until he reached the peep-show. He checked his watch, she should be there by now, she had been on time both of the previous nights.

Paul handed over the money and descended the stairs to the vast cellar. His senses were assaulted by the smell, the heat and the noise, but there was an excitement here, a pleasurable erotic filth that made his pulse race. He walked along the row of curtained cubicles until he found one empty, then settled in the uncomfortable chair and put his money in the slot.

A metal flap lifted to reveal a window the size of a large letter box and Paul bent forward eagerly, suddenly able to ignore the discarded, used tissues on the floor and the sounds of the men on either side slapping their meat. There she was, long legs glistening with oil, red stilettos flashing as she strutted across the small floor. Her breasts jutted arrogantly as she turned towards him and simulated masturbation within inches of the grimy glass. Paul watched her rotating hips, saw how the G-string bit into the swell of her arse as she bent over to give him a better view. He could feel the sweat bead his lip, could imagine how it would be to have her tied beneath him, the arrogant sneer wiped off her mouth, the strutting peacock insolence replaced by fear.

He touched himself and shuddered. Oh yes, she would do just fine.

The metal flap clanged shut and he hastily fed in the coins, but it was over too soon, suddenly she was gone, to be replaced by a suet dumpling of a woman who had seen better days. The sight of her made him turn away and leave. The girl would be out of the building, he would have to hurry if he was to follow her.

The cold hit him like a cleaver and he shrugged further into his coat. He waited in a doorway until he saw her, but the knife of disappointment was sharp. She had a man with her, a great bull with no neck and a cheap suit which stretched over bulging muscles. Their eyes met for an instant and Paul melted into the shadows. He would have to find someone else.

* * *

Reap the Whirlwind

It was almost four in the morning, the streets were quieter now, the strip joints and clubs winding down. Paul hurried along the dark alley until he came to the lighted entry with the row of doorbells and faded names behind murky plastic. With a glance snatched over his shoulder he pressed the one marked Jade.

'Yeah?' The voice was thick with sleep.

'Let me in. I got a pocket full of money, this could be your lucky night.'

'Piss off.' The connection was cut.

Paul bunched his fists and controlled the urge to break down the door. Instead, he pressed another button and waited impatiently.

'Sabrina, want some loving?' The voice was warm as honey, inviting.

'How much?' Paul didn't really care, but it was the way these negotiations had to be handled. The frustrated anger burned, and it seemed an age before the buzzer went and the door creaked open.

She stood in the doorway of her room, naked but for a G-string and diaphanous nightdress. 'Fifty quid straight, seventy-five blow, hundred anal, and anything else two hundred.' The honeyed voice was sharper now, the face behind the voice sagging with tiredness, the pupils dilated from the joint she'd been smoking.

Paul could smell her, but it made it more exciting to think of all the men she'd fucked that night. This pink quilted, over-ornate room was perfect for what he planned, the girl's appearance and age no longer mattered. He had to release some of this anger before he blew a fuse.

He shoved four fifties into her palm. 'Let's get going,' he snarled.

She turned away from him, tucking the money into a wall safe and twisting the combination lock. Smart cookie, he thought as he stripped off his clothes and folded them neatly over a chair. Yet not smart enough to know her punters, there wasn't any fear in those dreamy eyes, not yet, anyway. He bunched his tie in his fist. He would need it in the next few minutes.

''Ere, watch it, no need to tear me clothes off. What you want anyway, you didn't say?' Her mouth became a tight white line as she shed her clothes and posed on the bed. 'Bit of S and M, by the looks. Just don't mark me face, I gotta work tomorrow.'

Paul knelt astride her, his erect cock nudging her lips.

'Suck it bitch, and don't bite.'

He felt her mouth surround him, shuddered as the moist, lapping tongue flicked over him, but she was too compliant, too easy. Ramming his groin in her face until she had no choice but to take the full length of him in her mouth, he reached out and picked up the gossamer scarves that were draped over the cheap bedside lamps. In a swift, easy movement, he had her wrists tied together and firmly anchored to the brass bedstead. He felt her squirm beneath him as she fought to breathe, her knees pummelling his back as her teeth bit into his rapidly dwindling erection.

Paul pulled away from her, hit her once, twice, rocking her head on the pillow. His hands were around her neck, squeezing. 'You need to be taught a lesson, cunt.'

The prostitute's eyes were clearer now, and there was fear shadowing her face. This was excitement, this was what he wanted. If only he could maintain his hard-on.

'What you planning?' She sounded young, vulnerable and it made him shiver. If he closed his eyes he could imagine she was the other one. Blonde, leggy, barely passed her teens.

'That's for me to know and you to find out. Now shut the fuck up.'

She opened her mouth to scream, her legs pumping on the bed beneath him as she tried to fight him off.

Paul gagged her with his tie, then hurried to lash her ankles to the bedposts. Her eyes were wider now, alert and sharp with fear as he stood in front of her. She fought against her bonds, her head rolling on the pillow as she tried to rid her mouth of the tie. Paul watched her as he stroked himself. It was different this time, but it still couldn't rouse him.

Reap the Whirlwind

He curled his fist and punched her in the soft swell of her stomach. Then as the breath sobbed from her gagged mouth, he felt the release of all that anger, and as he punched and slapped and squeezed, he saw her as all the women who'd let him down. All the women who had turned their backs on him, scorned him, made him look a fool because he couldn't get it up.

The prostitute was quiet now, her chin slumped to her shoulder. She no longer cried out behind the gag, no longer struggled.

Paul climbed off her, grasped the empty Coke bottle from amongst the jumble of rubbish on the floor, and rammed it inside her until only the thick end of double glass could be seen.

'That should give her something to think about,' he murmured. Then he sniggered. It was probably the biggest thing she'd had up there in a long while.

He took his time to wash in the small curtained-off lavatory. He was drenched in sweat, and there were spots of blood on his fist where he'd split her lip and busted her nose. It would have to do, to go further would be dangerous. But he knew now, that it was better to tie them up, they couldn't brand him like the one in Brighton. Couldn't kick and bite and claw. He was master of the situation, dominant. He was omnipotent.

When he had dressed and checked his appearance in the mirror, he turned to the girl. She was breathing sonorously through her broken nose, but she lay very still. He took back his tie and shoved it in his pocket. It would have to be thrown away, it was covered in blood and saliva. With one last check to make sure he'd forgotten nothing, he left.

Paul had slept well, the bottle of Bourbon finishing off the successful night. He had given no further thought to the girl, it was as if he'd merely dreamed the episode in that tart's sickly pink bedroom. Now, as the noon sun streamed into the hotel suite, he screwed up his eyes and gulped down the coffee. It was hot, sweet and black, just the way he liked it.

He looked down at the crisp white napkin and delicate

china that had been laid out on the bed-tray. He approved of things when they were neat and clean, ordered and in harmony with his day. The omelette was done to perfection, and the croissant was fresh. Suddenly he was hungry and eager to begin the Arab's challenge. He could turn things to his advantage. He was clever enough, knew the right people. By the end of the week he would have Abbas Hussein where he wanted him.

Drenching the croissant in honey, he savoured the taste of it and licked his fingers. The plans for the day began to take shape and when the last of the croissant was swallowed and the coffee had lost its heat, Paul leaped from the bed and headed for the shower.

Standing under the invigorating jet of water, he thought about the man he'd known before he'd become Paul Galloway. It was a risk, but he didn't think Bill would care too much about what had happened so long ago. Not when he heard what Paul had to say.

Bill Boniface had started out with a small lock-up on an industrial estate in Crawley. He hadn't been afraid to trample on competitors, and some of his methods were questionable, but he always managed to slip and slide around the law and had finally made the big time. During the boom of the eighties he'd floated the company on the stock exchange. His reputation was impeccable, his status well respected.

Paul stepped out of the shower and began to dress, a tuneless whistle hissing between his teeth. Bill Boniface was in trouble according to the rumours. He had a wife who'd grown fond of the finer things in life, a mansion in Bedfordshire, an apartment in Portugal, and three children at private school. Two of his factories had closed and his shares had tumbled. Bill was close to bankruptcy, and a man in that position could be persuaded to bend the rules. And he, Paul Galloway, was just the person to do the persuading.

Paul smiled as he picked up the slim gold chain and fastened it around his neck. There were a few things about good old Bill Boniface that had never been made public. If Bill cut up rough, then Paul would threaten to use them. But he doubted he'd have to. Bill wasn't that stupid.

As he bent to pick up his overcoat, Paul caught sight of the newspaper. He'd been so busy planning the day, that he hadn't noticed it. Reaching down, he plucked it off the bed. It might be a good idea to look at the stock market prices before he had the meeting with Boniface.

After a quick glance, he folded it neatly and was about to leave it on the tray, when he caught sight of the screaming headline on the front page.

SUSSEX MURDER

Paul dropped the paper. His hands began to tremble and the rapid thud of his heart threatened to smother him. The light went out of the day and time stood still. All thoughts of Bill Boniface and Abbas Hussein fled from the pursuit of other, darker, more terrifying thoughts, and it was endless moments before he could summon up the courage to pick up the paper and read the report.

*

Malcolm hurried away from the hotel to catch the bus. The morning had seemed endless, and his mind was preoccupied by what had happened the night before. He hadn't liked leaving Lillian, but to break his routine might have caused suspicion. He'd never missed a day's work before and he couldn't afford to lose his job, regardless of how much he hated it.

Now, as he got down from the bus and turned the corner into Station Road Villas, he felt a shiver of apprehension. Was Lillian really dead? He hadn't checked before leaving for work, because the tightly closed door to her bedroom had been too daunting.

Letting himself into number 29, he braced himself for the sound of her raucous shout.

Silence greeted him. The house closed in around him, familiar and comforting. A breath of relief escaped him and he slumped against the front door. She was gone – silenced for ever.

He looked up the stairs at the closed door of Lillian's bedroom, his pale blue eyes blinking rapidly behind the thick lenses as his breath hissed through his teeth. The stillness that had settled over the house was eerie. Even the wheels on the tracks were sinister whispers that darted out from the shadows to pluck at the raw edges of his newly found confidence.

Slowly climbing the stairs, he went into his mother's bedroom. A quick glance confirmed that Lillian was truly dead, but the odour that drifted up to him made him gag and he hurried to open the window. Gulping in the cold fresh air, he stared out at the ravaged landscape. A line of bulldozers were standing idle beneath the shadows of the tower blocks, and the glow of a brazier illuminated the men who stood round it drinking from thick white mugs.

A flicker of movement at the very edge of his vision made him turn. Old Mr Hodges at number 27, was in his garden. Fleeting eye contact was made before Malcolm slammed the window shut and drew the curtains. Nosy old git. Why hadn't he left with all the rest?

Turning away from the window, he rested against the sill and regarded the woman on the bed. Curiosity drew him across the room. She no longer represented anything to be afraid of and he had no qualms at pulling back the blanket and studying her.

Lillian's mouth had dropped open and her head had rolled to one side, making the wig slip over one dead eye. He looked at the cavernous mouth and ill-fitting dentures that had dropped over her bottom lip. With clinical precision, he extracted the teeth and dropped them onto the bed. Then, with emotionless curiosity, he let his gaze travel slowly over her bloated form. The dirty nightdress was stained with rusty smears, and the sharp stench of urine rose from the sheet beneath her.

He began to giggle at the thought of Lillian lying in her own filth. This was punishment on a grand scale and he was enjoying it.

Reap the Whirlwind

Stepping closer, he reached out and touched her. The feel of that cold, marbled arm made the anger well up inside him. The touch became a prod. Then another and another until the prods became a barrage of punches. His breath became ragged as he relished the sound they made, drawing satisfaction from the way his fist sank into that yielding, bloated flesh.

'This is for all the times you hit me,' he hissed.

Lillian's head rolled on the pillow as the gases escaped from her mouth in a rasping snore.

Malcolm leaped away, his eyes snared by her milky gaze and gaping mouth. His courage faltered then crumbled. Could she still see him? Was she still capable of shrieking at him?

He huddled in the corner, suddenly wary of the power of the dead, afraid that he would see a rise and fall of that monstrous chest, before she climbed off the bed and reached out for him.

He didn't know how long he cowered there, but his terrified gaze never left the bed. Finally, as the light faded and his courage returned, he reached out and pulled up the blanket until it covered her face. She really was dead.

He drew back his lips and sniggered as he touched the puckered skin on his face. She couldn't hurt him any more. Couldn't make him do anything he didn't want to. She was never going to force him to take his pills again.

At the thought of the pills, he picked up the bottle which always stood on the bedside table. He watched the tablets dance and judder as he shook them. Then he opened the lid and emptied them into his hand. They appeared harmless, laying there in a heap of yellow, but he knew what they did to his head. They stopped the wheels from talking to him, blurred the edges of reality and made him dull and stupid.

He began to chuckle and the sheer delight of knowing he was finally free from Lillian turned the chuckle into a full-bellied laugh.

When he had finally quietened, he tipped the pills back into the bottle. Now there was only cold, clinical determination.

'No more, Mother. No more,' he whispered as he put the bottle in his pocket.

'Mr Squires! Are you there! Hello!'

Malcolm whirled round, his heart thudding wildly as he looked down the stairs to the front door. It was open and a woman was standing there. He was finding it difficult to swallow and the sharp knife of fear plunged ever deeper until it reached the soft, delicate tissue of his intestines. For just an instant, he'd thought Lillian had played a trick on him and was standing on the doorstep.

'Oh, there you are. Sorry to burst in like this, but I did knock and the door was open.' The woman stepped into the hall.

Fear brought an adrenalin rush and Malcolm acted quickly and decisively. He closed the bedroom door and hurried down the stairs to forestall the woman's advancement.

'Please be quiet. My mother is asleep.'

The woman was fat and dressed in heavy tweeds. Her feet were shod in sensible brown brogues and she carried a battered leather briefcase. She looked about fifty, Malcolm decided as he rapidly appraised her, and had the eyes and nose of a ferret. Whoever she was, she was going to be difficult to shift.

'Mrs Phillips from the Housing Department. My card.'

Malcolm took the card, but barely glanced at it. His whole attention was on barring her from entering any further. He stood too close, invading her space, attempting to make her retreat.

But Mrs Phillips stood her ground, glaring back at him.

'What do you want?' he said with all the meekness he could dredge up. The woman was making him angry, but he knew he couldn't let it show.

'We have been trying to contact you for the last six months, Mr Squires. Haven't you received our letters?' Her gaze darted round the hall and fell on the pile of mail that was stacked on the table. She took in a sharp snap of air, clenched her lips and hitched up her bra strap.

Malcolm caught a glimpse of age-freckled flesh and white underwear beneath the severely cut blouse and suit jacket.

Her hazel eyes bored into him with ill-humour and her

blue-rinsed hair flopped over one shaggy brow. 'It would save so much time, if people opened their mail.'

'I'm a busy man,' Malcolm replied quietly. 'I have my mother to look after as well as going to work. What is it you want?'

Mrs Phillips glared at him, then looked away and riffled through her briefcase.

Malcolm hadn't missed the revulsion in her eyes as her gaze swept over the mark on his face. She was like all the rest. Bitch.

'As a council tenant, we are obliged to rehouse you and your mother, Mr Squires. I need you to sign these papers today, or you will forfeit the right. If you refuse to sign, then your mother will be taken into care and you will have to find your own accommodation.' She waved a sheaf of paper under his nose.

Malcolm barely looked at the typewritten pages as he signed where she indicated. The irony of his situation wasn't lost on him, and the hard core of anger congealed in his gut. If only he'd waited one more day before returning home.

He glanced up the stairs before handing back the papers. How Lillian must be laughing, he thought bitterly. Now I'm stuck with her.

Mrs Phillips followed Malcolm's anxious glance before taking back the signed documents. 'Are the new housing arrangements going to be a problem for your mother? I understand she finds it difficult to get about, but I made sure the flat was on the ground floor.'

Malcolm smiled, drawing his lips back from his teeth and maintaining eye contact. It was becoming increasingly difficult to hold back the rage. 'She won't have any problems.'

The papers disappeared into the briefcase, and the bra strap was once more adjusted. 'You have four days before demolition takes place. You must make your own arrangements about the removal of your effects, of course, but the caretaker will meet you at the flat with a key. Try and be there by two o'clock at the latest.'

Malcolm stared at her as her words washed over him. He

hadn't realised how short his time was, and the thought made him shiver. What about Lillian? How could he find a way of hiding her before the men came to tear down the house? Cold perspiration beaded his forehead as he felt the colour leave his face.

'Are you all right, Mr Squires?'

Her abrasive voice brought him back to the present and the flash of anger was quickly smothered in a nod.

'Here is your copy of the tenancy agreement. The address is at the top. If you need to speak to me, my number is on the card.' She threw him an anxious glance. 'Everything is all right here, isn't it? You seem a little . . . out of sorts.'

Watery blue eyes held gimlet hazel as they regarded one another.

Malcolm wanted her gone, out of his house and out of his life. He stared at the fat red mouth in the fat red face and wondered how it would feel to sink his fist into it. To smash it to a pulp and feel the bones crack. This old bag was bloated like Lillian. It would be like punching a pillow, yet at the same time, it would be very satisfying.

Mrs Phillips hovered uneasily, her gaze darting away from him and up the stairs as her confidence dwindled. Malcolm took a step nearer, his hands crushing the tenancy agreement, his face set.

She backed out of the door, clumsy in her haste. 'See you in four days' time. Such a shame these old houses are being pulled down. Still, that's progress, I suppose.' She was gabbling and her feet stumbled over the cracked concrete path as she retreated.

Malcolm slammed the door on her mindless chatter. His heart was hammering and the rage was returning. There were other Lillians out there. Other mean-minded, sneering, domineering women who looked at him with disdain.

The wheels were turning, turning. Talking, whispering, chiding him into making the next move. It was time for him to search for the prying eyes and restless fingers that probed the deepest recesses of his mind. He would come face to face with the shadow in the darkness. Seek out the eyes behind that inquisitive mind and pluck them out. Only then would he really be free.

9

Laura knew she appeared calm and in control as she shook the hand of DCI Stoneham, but inside she was quaking. If it wasn't for Ben's steadying hand at her elbow, she felt sure she would stumble in the slender-heeled brown sling-backs she had chosen to wear with the autumnal ochre suit.

She had dressed carefully that morning, setting her mind to occupy itself on the unimportant things. Reality was too frightening. She wore no jewellery and very little make-up, but her pale complexion and sapphire eyes needed meagre enhancement according to Ben – yet she could see the pulse that beat erratically in her neck and the shadows beneath her eyes when she'd looked in the mirror – and they betrayed the weight of her situation.

'They're waiting, Mrs Kingsley,' Detective Stoneham said softly. 'Are you sure you want to do this? I can speak for you, if you'd prefer.'

She looked up at him and caught her reflection in his eyes. Her face was almost drained of colour, but Ben's hand on her arm was giving her strength. 'No. Thanks anyway.' She took a breath and squared her shoulders, pulling down on the short jacket and smoothing her skirt. 'It's better if I do it. Cassandra could be watching.'

Stoneham led the way, and for just an instant, Laura leaned on Ben, drawing on his strength and replenishing her fortitude. Then she was in control again and moving forward with purpose.

The line of chairs had been set up in front of a dark blue

screen in the police conference hall. A long table separated them from the media who jostled for position beneath the canopy of lights and sound equipment. Cigarette smoke lay heavy in the heated air and the noise increased by several decibels as Laura and Ben appeared with DCI Stoneham.

Flashlights popped and Laura flinched.

'Have you got a name for the victim, Jack?'

'Is this the girl's mother?'

'Any leads on the killer?'

Stoneham put up his hands for silence, his lips tight, his eyes frosty as he surveyed the reporters. It was several moments before the noise petered out and the press stilled.

'I called you here today, to ask for your help. There is a missing teenager, who was last seen at Wolves Farm on Friday last, the night of the rave.'

A chorus of questions greeted this statement, and Stoneham had difficulty in bringing the interview back to order.

'As far as we can ascertain, Cassandra Kingsley has no connection with the murder committed that night, and it has already been established that she is not the victim.'

'How do you know the killer hasn't made off with her? He could be holding her somewhere.' A young reporter with a flashy suit and ponytail shouted the question from the back of the hall.

Laura closed her eyes as unforgiving images tore through her mind. She dipped her chin to her chest and firmed her grip on Ben's hand as he grew increasingly restless beside her. This was far worse than she'd expected.

'That is pure supposition, and I won't have Mrs Kingsley tormented like this,' roared Stoneham. 'She's come here to make a plea for her daughter's return, and I expected a little respect from the "gentlemen" of the press.'

His words seemed to have had an effect, for the room settled into an uneasy hush, and he turned to Laura and nodded.

Laura sat forward and rested her hands on the table. She stared into the television cameras, frozen for a moment before she began to speak. When she did, her voice was steady and clear.

Reap the Whirlwind

'Cassandra is sixteen and has not come home for almost a week. If anyone saw her at the rave, or knows where she is, please tell someone.'

She held up a photograph, her hands trembling.

'Cassandra, if you're watching, please come home. Melissa and I need you. We love you and want to know you're safe. Whatever reasons you have for staying away can be resolved. Call me – write, anything. We just need to know you're all right. Someone out there must know where she is. Please – I beg you – pick up the telephone. The worst part of all this, is the not knowing.'

Unnoticed by Laura, the detective leaned back and watched her, stilled by a frozen memory shrouded in time. There it was again, the feeling of déjà vu, the cold certainty of having witnessed this small scene in another time, another place – but where, and why? And how did the photograph of the twins fit into all this? There was more to Laura Kingsley, much more. And in that moment of clarity, he made the decision to find out what it was.

*

As the sun rose slowly on its morning arc, the first dusty fingers of light pierced the cracks in the boarded-up window of the kitchen and touched Malcolm on the face.

He opened his eyes and slowly emerged from the heavy sleep he'd finally drifted into after a night's pacing. Weariness was still heavy in his limbs and his head throbbed with the sound of the different voices that whispered and seduced him to obedience.

He fumbled for his spectacles and put them on, then sat quietly for a moment, slumped across the kitchen table, his arms pillowing his head. It was time for him to leave for work, but the hotel seemed to exist in another time and another place, and he had no desire to return to it.

Dust motes danced on the pale shafts of light that streamed into the grey gloom of the kitchen and he watched them for a while, with childish pleasure.

When he was small, he'd thought the motes were fairies, and had sat on the floor and tried to catch them. He knew that if he did, they would have to grant him a wish, and his greatest hope, even then, was that they would make Lillian love him.

Malcolm sighed at his naivety as he sat there the morning after the fat woman from the social had called. Yet, there was a sadness in him today that he couldn't explain. A longing for a time when anything was possible, a time when there could still be hope for a miracle. He'd never caught a fairy, never got his wish. Now it was too late.

The babel of noise clamoured in his head and the roar of the train wheels thundered across the points and swept beneath the bridges that took him from the kitchen into their world of hot oil and shining metal. Whispering, cajoling, drawing together to become a monstrous chorus, the voices demanded to be heard.

He put his hands over his ears, closed his eyes and tried to shut them out. They no longer brought peace, they confused him, made his head ache and his flesh creep with cold.

'They'll find you out. Got to hide. Take her away, take her away.'

'I hear you!' he screamed. 'Leave me alone.'

'They're coming to get you. Put you away. Coming to get you. Put you away,' roared the wheels as they gathered speed and raced along the tracks of his mind.

'NO!' Malcolm thrust himself from the table, knocking the chair, making it spin across the room. The anger spiralled into a vortex of rage, and he picked up the table and flung it against the wall.

'Put you away,' whispered the wheels as they gathered pace. 'Lock you up and leave you there. Got to run. Got to hide. They're on their way, on their way, on their way.'

Malcolm ran from the kitchen and stumbled up the stairs. He had to talk to Lillian. Had to tell her to stop the voices.

Flinging open the door to Lillian's room, he came to an abrupt halt. The smell was warm and secret, bitter and pervasive, it stuck in his throat and made his stomach shrivel into a fist. He put his hand over his mouth and turned away, banging the door behind him. Lillian wouldn't be able to help any more.

'Have to hide. Have to run. Take her away. Take her away,' hissed the wheels.

Malcolm knew they were right, but the thought of touching her, of smelling that overripe flesh was more than he could bear. He pushed his glasses up his nose as the first tears ran down his face.

'How?' he whispered. 'Where can we go? There's nowhere to hide.'

The wheels muttered and clattered and disappeared into the distance, but they had no answer for him.

Malcolm leaned against the wall and cried. Never before had he felt so helpless, or so alone.

*

The recreation room was bright and cheerful in its coat of yellow paint and chintz curtains. Toys spilled from shelves and lay abandoned on the floor, and there was a hum of noise from the other children which overrode the sound of the television.

Melissa was sitting on a low chair at a broad, highly coloured table. Crayons and paper and a collection of building bricks were strewn in front of her, but the child seemed unaware of them. The rag doll was tightly gripped against her chest, and there was a stillness in her, a rigidity in her spine that made Laura wonder what was going on behind those staring eyes which looked out on a world that only Melissa could understand.

Laura tentatively reached out and touched her before slipping an arm around her and drawing her close. There was no response, no softening in her slight frame or acknowledgement of their presence. Laura kissed her hair and felt a deep ache for which there was no cure.

She looked across at Clara and tried to smile, but she knew her mother hadn't been fooled. It had been a traumatic week for all of them, and even after this morning's television interview, there was little relief from the tension.

'What do you think causes these sudden mood swings, Laura? What has the doctor said?' Clara shifted on the uncomfortable plastic chair and tugged the hem of her skirt down to cover her knees.

'Simon believes it's another manifestation of her brain damage. In a way, this silence is a relief. The hysteria and fitting weren't doing her heart any good.' Laura rested her cheek on the immobile head that lay uneasily against her. 'At least she seems peaceful.'

Clara nodded as her cool green eyes swept over the other children in the room, before they returned to Melissa.

Mother's looking tired, Laura realised. And there was a delicacy in her features that she'd never noticed before, a luminosity in her skin that showed her age and her weariness.

Laura's tight rein of control on her emotions nearly snapped. Poor Clara, she was trying so hard to do the right thing. If only she would unbend a little, or show some emotion behind that icy façade.

'It all makes one feel so helpless,' sighed Clara, fiddling with her rings. 'I wish we could understand more of what's happening in Melissa's head. She was such a lively, intelligent child. It all seems such a waste.'

Laura didn't have the energy to contradict. At least she still had Melissa, even though she wasn't perfect. And that had to be better than the alternative. Melissa gone. Melissa dead and buried.

The sharp image of the girl on the mortuary slab came back and she thrust it away.

Looking down at the fine, pale hair she thought of how her child had been all those years ago. Tiny fingers and toes, trusting eyes, blonde curls and an impish grin. Melissa hadn't been afraid of anything. She was the naughty twin. The one that led Cassandra to climb trees, skin her knees and tear her dresses. She'd been so full of life and sunshine, so loving and noisy.

Laura closed her eyes and breathed in the smell of Melissa's hair. Cassandra had been just as pretty, just as adventurous, but quieter, more insular and thoughtful. Now she too was in trouble.

'Don't torture yourself, Laura. I know it's been rough, but we have to keep faith.' Clara's voice tore through the veil of misery that Laura was sinking beneath.

'You're right.' Laura dragged herself back onto an even keel. 'Life must go on. But I can't help wondering if I'd been older when I had the twins, whether any of this would have happened. I didn't see the dangers back then, didn't watch out quite so carefully.' She gave a derisive laugh. 'And I'm still making the same mistakes, that's what's so hard to take.'

Clara briskly shook her head and brushed lint from her skirt. 'There's no point in dredging up the past, and even less point in punishing yourself over Cassandra. You might think I'm cold and unfeeling, but what good would it do to lose control, or give in to the welter of emotions that I know are swirling around inside you? It won't bring Cassie back, won't make Melissa whole.'

Clara gave a sigh. 'It's hard being a mother. I should know. But none of us are given instruction manuals when our children are born. We just have to muddle through the best we can.'

Laura stared at her mother. 'You really have no idea what I'm going through, have you?' she said in cold wonder.

Clara leaned forward and grasped Laura's chin in her long firm fingers until she was forced to look at her. 'I can only guess. You never trusted me enough to tell me very much.'

Laura experienced a rush of hostility at the unfairness of that remark and jerked her head away.

'How could I, when you were never around? It's difficult to trust someone who sends you away to boarding school, then spends the rest of their life on the other side of the world.'

The words came out in a rush, regretted the moment they were uttered, but Laura knew she couldn't take them back. They were, after all, the accumulation of years of resentment.

'This must be quite an experience for you, Mother. When was the last time we spent more than a few hours in each other's company?' The bitterness could not be disguised as she held Clara's gaze for uncounted seconds.

Clara's manicured hands fluttered before settling in her lap. When she finally spoke, her voice was low and there was a tremor underlying the words.

'I understand your bitterness, your fear for your children and the strain this is putting on you. But it's not right you should blame me entirely for our lack of communication.'

She lifted her chin and studied Laura's face. 'Did you never question the reason why I left you to get on with your life?' There was silence for a breath of weariness. 'I think it's about time you did, don't you?'

The confusion swirled in Laura as she looked into those green eyes that were bright with tears and saw the yearning there. Was this the same Clara who always seemed so in control? The same Clara who had never encouraged emotional closeness, who scorned tears and lack of courage? Suddenly there was doubt seeded in her mind and it made her uncomfortable.

'You left me to get on with my life because you had better things to do – places to go, people to see – far more exciting than bringing up a daughter,' Laura muttered defensively.

'You were never the kind of mother who gave kisses and cuddles on the spur of the moment. Never the soft shoulder to cry on or the comforting lap to snuggle into. You were always off somewhere, too busy to bother about what I was doing. I don't see why you're so surprised we don't communicate. You forced me to become like you – strong and independent – when you sent me away at seven years old. I can't be blamed for that.'

Clara gave an exasperated sigh and thrust herself back into the chair. 'Independent and strong? Me? You don't know how wrong you are.' A frown creased her brow and her voice dropped to almost a whisper. 'I really screwed up in the motherhood stakes, didn't I?'

Laura regarded her mother with unease. The seed of doubt

was growing, flourishing, taking over the barren wastelands she'd come to regard as their relationship. The confusion made her sharp with her retort. 'Like mother, like daughter.'

Clara shook her head. 'You're a good mother, Laura, because you find it easy to be tactile. Sometimes I think you tend to smother the girls with your affection, and I regret not having had the same rapport with you.' She took a breath, the green eyes swimming with unshed tears. 'I've never found it easy to hold someone close and give them warmth, but that doesn't mean I don't love you. I do, and I'm proud of you, always have been.'

'Then how come you were never there when I needed you?' Laura was aware she sounded like a petulant child, but there had been too many years and too many tragedies for them to be swept away in a moment's sentimentality.

'How was I supposed to know if you never told me?' Clara's gaze was steady. 'I was never more than a telephone call away. I could have come to you, shared the problems you had with David in the early years. But you never called and I thought you didn't want me, so I stayed out of it.'

Laura's grip on Melissa faltered. 'You knew? And you never said anything? But why?' she breathed.

'The last thing I wanted to be accused of was being an interfering mother-in-law, but I could see what he was doing to you and that made me very angry. Think back, Laura. Remember all the times I tried to talk to you about it?' Her gaze was direct and piercing. 'You just shrugged it off, made excuses and changed the subject. What could I do when you obviously couldn't – or wouldn't – confide in me?'

Clara looked down at her rings as she twisted them round her fingers. 'There was many a time when I almost called the police, but you were so adamant, I knew it wouldn't get anywhere. You would only have defended him.'

Laura was stung into silence. The truth of her mother's words was a bitter reminder of how things had been all those years ago, but the regret for the loss of her mother's understanding and support made the bitterness even sharper. How many nights had she sat in the darkness, terrified and hurting, wanting to pick up the phone, needing to hear her voice?

'Children break your heart. They can twist the knife with such exquisite carelessness that you're left wondering why you still love them.' The sigh came from deep within Clara and she faltered before carrying on.

'This terrible business with Cassandra reminds me of when you were her age. There's a great deal of you in your daughter, Laura. Probably more than you would care to admit. I can remember the arguments when you wanted to go out with some obnoxious boy whose only attraction was his unsuitability. And the temper tantrums when you couldn't get your own way. Even when you were small, you had very set ideas on what you would wear and what toys you would play with.'

Clara's face was illuminated by a sad, weary smile. 'Your sixth birthday was a prime example. I'd worked for hours preparing the food and making you a special cake, then you decided at the last minute that you didn't want a party. You locked yourself in the bedroom and refused to come out until everyone had gone home.'

Laura felt a stab of anguish as she recognised the hurt that small defiance must have inflicted. 'God, I remember that. Was I really such a brat?'

'Yes, you were,' replied Clara shortly. 'I never really understood you, still don't if the truth be told. We're so different in our tastes, so at odds in the way we deal with things. I needed to make amends for my inability to make physical contact, to shower you in the kisses and hugs you so clearly wanted. So I gave you parties and pretty clothes, designed you a bedroom fit for a princess and made sure you had all the things you could possibly wish for. But you scorned anything feminine, anything soft and pink and pretty. It was as if you deliberately set out to antagonise me.'

Laura wanted to defend herself, needed to put into words the emotions that jostled for attention. 'I didn't want things,' she said quietly. 'All I wanted was for you to hold me.'

Clara's eyes were emerald shards of pain, and her voice

dropped to a murmur. 'You certainly knew how to punish me for my lack of affection. I remember the parents' meetings and sports days you deliberately forgot to tell me about. The swimming galas and netball matches I wasn't encouraged to watch. It was as if you were ashamed of me, didn't want to be seen in my company. And although I didn't say anything at the time, those little acts of thoughtlessness hurt me very much.'

Clara sat up straight, her small chin lifted in defiance. 'But I never stopped loving you. Just as you'll never stop loving your children regardless of how they treat you.'

Laura felt the heat redden her face and experienced a sinking, fathomless shame. Why had it taken so long for her to examine her own attitude to Clara? The years that had been lost between them could never be resurrected, and all because she'd been too quick to pass judgement.

'I'm so sorry, Mum. I didn't realise. The hurt I caused you must have been unbearable.'

The words felt inadequate and the emotions that swelled inside her were far too overwhelming for expression. She began to rock Melissa in her arms, seeking comfort and forgiveness, attempting to give solace and find the words that would heal the rift between her and Clara.

'Looking back, I suppose I was trying to punish you for not being the mother I wanted you to be. After Daddy died, I thought we would become closer, but it never turned out that way. Boarding school to me was just a punishment, a way for you to be free to get on with your life. But I was never ashamed of you, merely too young and stupid to realise that having such a beautifully dressed, sophisticated mother didn't make me dull by comparison. I remember feeling something shrivel inside when people remarked on how much we looked alike. I knew they couldn't be telling the truth, because I could never have been as beautiful as you.'

Clara blinked away the tears that were blurring her vision. 'God, how we hurt each other. And for what? We both missed out on so much, didn't we?'

Laura watched the sorrow darken Clara's eyes and thought

back to the way things had been when she was small. Shyness had ruled her, making her dread being the centre of attention, always wary of the new men in Clara's life. That's why she'd steered away from parties. As for the clothes and the frilly bedroom – well, Clara was always so glamorous, so in charge of her life, that Laura had felt like a usurper, a paler shadow of what she thought her mother wanted her to be. Looking back on those years made her realise that she was like her father. She felt she couldn't compete, so she didn't even try.

'I was always afraid you were disappointed in me,' she said finally. 'So I hid behind a veneer of independence, and I suppose the habit stuck.'

Clara grasped her hand and pressed it to her cheek. 'I was never disappointed in you, my darling. Just a little wary. You've always been so strong, so capable. I still find you daunting, but I'm proud of you. You've proved you're not afraid to go it alone. Proved that no matter what, you have the strength to fight. And I never really had that strength. I always needed a man to lean on who would take away the responsibility of making decisions. That, and the inability to show affection, was my weakness.'

Laura pulled Clara nearer and kissed the soft, damp cheek that smelt of Chanel No. 5 and face powder. The knowledge that their relationship could only grow stronger from this moment on, brought an inner peace that soothed the turmoil of the past years.

Clara stroked back the heavy copper curls. 'You've had a rough time of it. I just wish there was something more I could do to ease the burden.'

Laura leaned her cheek against her mother's and closed her eyes. 'You help by being here, Mum. I don't know how I would have coped without you and Ben.' A memory flash took her back to the morgue and she hastily blanked it out.

'Ben has certainly been a rock over the past week,' replied Clara softly. 'That man has depths I never dreamed of. I wonder why his father is so against him?'

Laura eased away from Clara but didn't release the grip

on her hand. She was reluctant to break the needed contact, the warmth, the bond that had been newly forged.

She gave a wry smile. 'Who knows? Mothers and daughters, fathers and sons – their relationships are so complex that even those involved can't find a way to explain them.'

They regarded each other in a moment of silence. Each drawing strength from the other, building the bridges that had come so close to demolition, strengthening the ties that would always bind.

'We've had our differences, but I reckon I was lucky to have a mother like you.'

Clara flushed with pleasure. 'Darling, that's the nicest thing you ever said to me.'

The moment was shattered by Melissa who suddenly broke from her trance and grasped a crayon off the table. As the two women watched, she began to draw. Within moments she had covered the sheet of paper with pairs of eyes. Lupine eyes. Eyes that were yellow and red and slashed with wicked black pupils.

Laura held her breath as Melissa's frantic explosion of energy flagged. The child flopped back into her arms and stared off into space, the doll once more clutched to her chest. There was no expression on her face and no intelligence to brighten her eyes. She appeared as lifeless as that poor dead child in the morgue.

Then Laura caught Clara's horrified gaze and as they looked down at the drawing, they knew that Melissa was trying to communicate with them. There had been something added to the drawing.

*

Detective Chief Inspector Stoneham took the folders and pressed the call button for the lift. Bill Ryan had come up trumps on the Central Computer. Now, at last, they had something to go on.

'Enter.' Chapman's voice was muffled by the thickness of his office door.

Stoneham approached his chief's heavy, oak desk and hovered. 'I think you should see these, sir.'

'What are they?' Chapman lifted the corner of the top file with a pencil, then let it drop. His attention returned to his computer.

Stoneham opened the files one by one and laid out the photographs on the desk. 'We've got a lead, sir.'

'If you've got something to say, then spit it out.' Chapman's voice was arctic as his gaze skidded over the photographs and returned to his DCI.

Stoneham swallowed his impatience and struggled to remain calm. He stabbed a finger at the first photograph.

'Karen Walker, Crawley. Only twelve, but she looked older. She was beaten and strangled in 1985. No sign of sexual activity, but her clothes had been cut neatly into two and carefully turned back to expose her nakedness.'

Stoneham's finger stabbed the next photograph.

'Patricia Riley, Southampton. Thirteen, blonde, dead. Strangled in 1986, left in woodland with her clothes neatly cut, her badly beaten body exposed to the elements. Again, no sexual activity. Both girls were persistent runaways.'

He took a breath before going on to the next one.

'Lesley Moore, Dover. Fifteen, blonde, dead. Strangled in 1987, left in a derelict warehouse. This time he didn't use his hands, he used a wire garotte. Her outer clothing was intact, but the coroner discovered that her underwear had been neatly cut in half and an attempt at sexual intercourse had been made – probably after death. No semen was found on the victim, so we have to assume that he isn't capable.'

There was still no reaction from Chapman, but Stoneham knew the man was listening. He might be a prat, but he was a consummate police officer and nothing much passed him by.

'1989 was the year Tanya Van Hauer went missing from her job as an au pair in Reigate. She was found a year later, dumped in bushes behind a golf course. She was sixteen, blonde and dead. Strangled by a wire noose, her underwear cut neatly into two. She was raped, not by our killer, but by a wooden stake after she was dead. A mask had been placed over her face.'

Chapman had steepled his fingers to his mouth and was benefiting his subordinate with his full attention.

'Then we come to Finsbury Park, November 1990, and Gina Pirelli. She was fourteen, blonde, pretty and very dead when we were called in, remember? She put up one hell of a fight, but she too was strangled with a wire noose. She must have died in agony, because the stake was shoved inside her before she took her last breath. The only clue to the murderer was the mask he placed over her face. Similar to the one found on the latest victim. Our killer was getting more confident – and more violent.'

Chapman pushed his chair away from the desk and stood up. He turned towards the window and stared out at the Brighton skyline. 'Go on.'

Jack looked down at the latest victim, and picked up the photograph. '1995. Blonde, pretty, about sixteen, identity unknown. Strangled by a wire noose, beaten almost to a pulp, clothing cut in half and raped with a wooden stake. I think he was interrupted this time, because the mask wasn't covering her face. He simply pinned it down onto her chest with her arm.'

Chapman remained at the window. He was silent.

'I want to open this up nationwide. We have a serial killer on our hands, and it's not the poor bastard doing time in Broadmoor for the Pirelli and Van Hauer murders.' Stoneham took a breath. 'This latest one has all the hallmarks of a progressively violent psychopath. I wouldn't mind betting that when we finally track him down, we'll find he's been involved in assaults that we know nothing of. Maybe he even murdered before 1985.'

Chapman's torso was rigid, and only the sinking of his chin to his chest indicated that he was listening.

Jack Stoneham riffled through the files for the forensic reports.

'He left his calling card each time, but because we didn't have the technology, we failed to pick up on it. The mask is just another addition to his twisted sense of perversion.' He laid the reports out on the desk. 'Please sir, you have to let me follow this up.'

Chapman turned from the window and sat down, suddenly businesslike and eager. After he'd read the reports he gave a nod of approval. 'Well done, Jack. So you were right after all.'

Stoneham wisely kept his mouth shut.

'Have copies of these files sent to me. I'll get on to the DPP and put the wheels in motion for a full-scale murder inquiry. This will mean co-ordinating the entire country's network. Quite a task, so we'd better get on with it.'

DCI Stoneham gathered the files and left the room. He closed the door quietly and gave a deep sigh. The work was only just beginning, but first, he had to find out why Laura Kingsley and the photograph of the twins bothered him. As he made his way down in the lift, he had a nasty premonition that the Central Computer would soon tell him.

10

Paul Galloway watched as the porter collected the expensive luggage and loaded it onto a trolley. It had taken him more than twenty-four hours, but the panic had subsided and now he could think clearly. It was tempting providence to stay here. Hussein wouldn't like his abrupt disappearance, but as long as he clinched the deal, he would have nothing to complain about. It was better to be on the move. Better to carry on negotiating for the Arab and get his money, then he could leave England for good. Things had changed in ten years, the police methods were more sophisticated, and he didn't like the way things were shaping up in Sussex.

The hotel lobby was almost deserted, being so early in the day, and Paul followed the porter to the desk and paid the bill.

'Your hire car is outside, Mr Galloway. I have made sure there is a telephone connected for you.'

Paul curtly nodded and took the keys from the receptionist. He didn't like the curiosity in the man's eyes. He turned from the desk and followed the porter out of the door and down the steps.

He was imagining things, he told himself silently. Hundreds of people must change their minds about their bookings and suddenly decide to leave early in the morning. He'd merely been rattled by the things he'd read in the paper. The claw marks had healed much quicker than anticipated and were now almost imperceptible, so this morning, he'd finally managed to shave off the worrisome beard. There was nothing to worry about, nothing at all.

The BMW was top of the range and a sleek metallic grey. Paul slid into the comfortable leather seat and switched on the ignition. Within minutes the porter and the hotel were forgotten as the car purred its way through the sleepy, almost deserted streets of London. Turning onto the motorway, Paul put his foot down and the car responded with a smooth gliding speed that ate up the miles. He would make Bedfordshire in plenty of time to catch Boniface.

The house was set back from the road behind a high stone wall and ornately worked iron gates which had been left open. The early morning sun tinted the white façade a delicate pink and the double row of lead-paned windows glittered like diamonds in an exotic setting. Dark green trees made a perfect backdrop and the verdant expanse of lawn that ran either side of the gravel driveway was planted with beds of shrubs.

At the turning circle in front of the wide, shallow steps leading to the front door, was a raised flower bed surrounded by a low stone wall which was draped with ivy. A lichen-covered statue of Pan stood in the centre, water flowing from his magic pipes into the pond at his feet.

Paul let the engine idle for a moment as he took in the opulence of his surroundings. His heart beat a faster tattoo and everything else was forgotten in those moments of confirmation. Bill had done well for himself, and if he was the man he thought he was, there would be no difficulty in persuading him to take on the Arab's proposal. Boniface was a man with too much to lose.

Turning through the gates, Paul drove the car up to the steps and killed the engine. Stepping out, he buttoned his jacket and swept another appreciative glance over the house. The envy was a sharp tug in his solar plexus. He could have had a house like this if he'd been allowed to do things the way he wanted.

A swift kaleidoscope of memories made him shiver, then they were gone and he climbed the steps and rang the bell. A lot of things had changed since those early years, it would serve no purpose to resurrect them now.

The heavy oak door with the shiny brass fittings was opened

Reap the Whirlwind

by a small, dumpy woman who had the dark hair and olive skin of southern Europe. 'Si?'

'I wish to speak with Mr Boniface. My card.' Paul handed her the white embossed business card and the maid closed the door. Several moments later, she returned and handed it back.

'Mr Boniface not receiving visitors. Sorry. Please call office for appointment.'

Paul hastily scribbled something on the back and returned it. 'Give him this. He will want to see me, I assure you.'

The dumpy little maid looked apprehensive and once again closed the door on him.

Paul clasped his hands behind his back and began to whistle tunelessly. He was confident Bill would want to see him, and was prepared to be patient.

He didn't have to wait long.

The door was thrust open and Bill Boniface stood before him. Despite the early hour, he was already immaculately dressed in a suit, with highly polished black brogues on his feet. His thick, white hair was brushed back from his forehead and reached the collar of his linen shirt, but his face was tinged an angry red and his mouth was set in a grim line. He glared at Paul from beneath shaggy eyebrows.

'What do you want?' he barked.

Paul felt none of the intimidation that was surely Bill's intention, and he smiled confidently as he took a step forward.

'Is that the way to greet someone after all these years, Bill? And I took such trouble to look you up.'

Bill Boniface filled the doorway with his substantial figure and Paul could almost feel the aura of power and command that surrounded the man.

'I'd hoped I'd seen the last of you. Why are you here?' The furious glare hadn't diminished, and the voice remained just as bluff.

Paul returned Bill's glare. 'I have a business proposition. But I don't think the doorstep is the place for discussion.'

There was a flicker of something in Bill's eyes which

Tamara Lee

made Paul uncomfortable. And as the silence grew and the small white business card was repeatedly turned in those age-spotted, manicured hands, Paul's unease grew.

'I don't do business with people who use false names. What do you call yourself now?' The card was turned over for the last time. 'Paul Galloway. Never heard of you. Good morning.'

Paul jammed his foot in the narrowing gap between door and frame, and hissed, 'Remember the Asian contract, Bill?'

Boniface lost some of his bluffness, but his face had become suffused with rage and the bulbous hazel eyes glowered.

Paul leaned forward as the door opened a fraction wider. The two men were now only inches apart. Go for the kill, hook him with the snare, then reel him in like the great wily old salmon he always was.

'I know about the way you bribed your way into the right boardrooms, and paid kickbacks to the right people. You did well out of that, didn't you? But what about the men you laid off, the union rules you broke when you hired cheap, unskilled labour to fulfil that contract? What about the inquiry into dangerous workmanship you covered up? The missing parts? Cheap materials and sub-standard workmanship could have ruined you. It still could if it ever got out. I don't think a man in your position can afford to let those old skeletons out of the cupboard. Not now. Not when you're in such deep, deep trouble.'

Bill seemed to grow taller, wider, more daunting. 'You might have changed your name, but you're still the same little weasel you always were. Now leave before I call the police.'

Paul had a instant's hesitation, then dismissed it. Bill was merely calling his bluff, he'd forgotten how clever the man was. After all, it had been Bill who taught him how to negotiate. Bill who'd been his mentor and guide in those early years.

'Doesn't our friendship over the years amount to anything? I've come to offer you the chance to redeem something of the mess you're in. A contract for the Middle East, which would ease your circumstances and give you breathing space to pick up the pieces.' Paul spoke with rapid precision, attempting to blast his way through Bill's anger and get to the core of the man.

Bill Boniface remained a solid, awe-inspiring presence between Paul and the inner sanctum of his hallway. When he finally spoke, his voice was sombre and there was more than a hint of revulsion in his eyes.

'Our friendship came to an end when I found out what kind of man you really are. The mistake I made was to believe you would do the decent thing and emigrate. I have nothing to say to you. Please leave.'

The knowledge that Bill had slipped away from him made Paul break out in a cold sweat. He needed the old bastard because there was no-one else. The rage clenched a fist into his throat and he swallowed it with difficulty. He couldn't afford to shatter the calm illusion. He had to make Bill see sense.

'This proposition is above-board and guaranteed to make us both a lot of money,' he said quickly. 'I have the plans in my briefcase, and the fee is open to negotiation.' He ran the tip of his tongue over his top lip and tasted the salt of his desperation. 'Fifteen minutes, ten. That's all the time I'm asking for.'

'If this contract is an honest one, why come to me? You don't owe me anything, and your attempts at blackmail have merely provided me with the proof that you are as crooked a little shyster as you ever were.'

'There was no proof, Bill. I was merely a scapegoat. I did leave the country, but my contacts are here and my employers respect my ability to negotiate.' He plastered on a smile. 'I owe you a great deal, Bill. You taught me everything I know. Without you, I wouldn't be the man I am today.'

Boniface snorted. 'You might have a glib tongue and a knowledge of your work – but don't saddle me with the credit for what you turned into.' Paul scrabbled in his briefcase and pulled out the rolls of plans. 'Just take a moment to look, Bill. What I'm offering you could change things around. The deal's worth at least seven figures.'

The expression of the older man was arctic as his gaze bored into Paul's face. 'I'd have thought you had better things to do, than spend time pestering me. Why aren't you occupied with Her Majesty's Police down in Sussex?'

Paul's stomach lurched and a pain knifed his groin. Surely the old bastard hadn't put two and two together? He couldn't have, it was impossible.

His tongue dried and his mouth opened and shut in the effort to speak. When he did, his voice was a rasp.

'Sussex? Why should I be in Sussex? What's all this about the police?'

Bill began to speak, and when he'd finished, Paul knew the colour had been bleached from his face. The door slammed and he was left alone on the doorstep. Things were going from bad to worse, and he had a nasty feeling there was more to come.

*

Laura turned restlessly in her sleep and sought the warmth of Ben who lay beside her. As the first fingers of grey lightened the room, she reluctantly opened her eyes. It was six o'clock. She would have to get up soon and face the day. The main thing on her agenda was the staff meeting she'd called for ten o'clock. It was time to tell them what was happening and to allay the rumours she knew were sweeping through the hotel.

Leaning on an elbow, she looked down at the sleeping man beside her. Ben was lying on his back as he always did, and was softly snoring, his broad chest rising and falling under her hand. This was the first time she'd let him share her bed at the hotel, but she was glad she had. She watched him for a moment, needing this small oasis of peace to prepare her for another day of waiting.

His lashes feathered shadows on his cheeks, the stubble was dark and scratchy on his chin, and his hair was a sooty haze on the pillow. Cassandra had called him an ageing hippy, but at thirty-nine, Ben looked vibrant and youthful, and a sad, sweet smile touched her lips as she thought of her daughter's disapproval.

Reap the Whirlwind

Resting her head on his chest she ran her fingers through the fine hair that ran in a curly line down his flat belly. She could hear the steady thud of his heart, and feel the warmth of his sleeping flesh, and they brought her solace.

Ben stirred and his pulse quickened as Laura caressed him. His hand ran along the curve of her ribs and down into the valley of her waist, before following the swell of her hip.

Laura pressed closer to him, breathing in his smell, aching for his warmth as she reacted to his touch. She lifted her head and looked into his eyes.

'Good morning,' she whispered.

'You're asking for trouble, waking a man like this,' he muttered, his eyes glinting as he cupped her bottom and pulled her tightly to him.

'And what kind of trouble would that be?' she murmured as she kissed his chest and ran her hand down beneath the duvet.

Ben moved lazily on the sheet, his long body manipulating her until she was lying beneath him.

'This kind of trouble.' His voice was thick with sleepy desire, his dark eyes luminous as he slipped inside her.

Laura's breath caught and she encircled his waist with her legs, opening up to him, drawing him in, wanting to possess him – to be possessed by him. Each long, sensuous thrust brought her closer to climax. Each soft endearance, each touch of his hands and mouth took away the harshness of reality and took her to a place where there was only pleasure. Flashes of light and velvet thunder filled her head as their bodies moved together. Wave after wave of desire swept over her, until she thought she could bear no more. Then came the final, rapturous release, which left them breathless and spent.

Ben smothered her face in butterfly kisses, then finally eased his weight off her, leaned on his elbow and stroked back the damp tendrils of copper hair.

'Hi.' He grinned and kissed her forehead. 'That was some wake-up call.'

Laura gave a feline stretch. Her skin tingled with a liquid

warmth and the slow, languorous need to love him again began to grow and make her senses swim. For the first time in more than a week, she had been able to put everything else aside. The real world seemed to be a distant, sharp-edged thing which existed only outside the bedroom door. And she wanted to delay the moment she would have to face it again.

Ben cupped his hand over her hip and gave it a gentle squeeze. 'I fancy a shower.' His words were soft, honeyed warmth in her ear.

Without waiting for an answer, he gathered her up and climbed out of bed. Striding across the room, he carried her into the bathroom and turned on the water.

Laura gasped as the water ran icy cold over them, but Ben held her tightly to him and the sound of his booming laughter ricocheted off the tiled walls as she made a pretence of struggling.

The water warmed, then ran in a hot cascade over them as he washed her hair, his fingers strong, but gentle as they massaged her scalp and freed the tangles. Then he picked up the soap and washed every inch of her, kissing one rosy nipple, then the other, before turning his attention to her navel, and the mound of fiery hair between her legs.

They took their time to explore one another, to give pleasure as they took it. Their love-making was slow and erotic, the warmth of the water enhancing the mood, the slipperiness of their flesh sliding against one another heightening their desires. And when it was over, Laura knew she would never find another man to love as much as this one.

*

Malcolm was sitting on the floor of the landing, his head on his knees, his arms wrapped around his legs. The tears had dried long ago, but the voices of the wheels still chattered and whispered in his head.

He listened to them for a while, but his mind was on other things. They were coming to tear down the house. He had to find a hiding place for Lillian.

'Have to leave. Have to go,' mourned the wheels.

'Yes,' he whispered.

The sound of his own voice made him lift his head and he stared into the gathering gloom. Somehow, he realised, he had lost the day, and for just a moment he felt a shaft of fear. He had lost days before. Days he couldn't explain, days that brought confusion and sent him to That Place. He shuddered and hugged his knees tighter to his chest.

'Take you away. Take you away,' sang the wheels.

The voices brought him back from the pit of despair and he lifted his head and shrieked back in defiance. 'They can't make me go. I won't let them.'

The wheels stayed silent, but he could still feel their presence, could still smell the oil and the hot metal.

He sniffed the air and was surprised at the stench that drifted into the landing. Lillian would be angry. The smell was awful, it pervaded the walls and hung like a malevolent cloud from the ceiling.

Malcolm started as he thought he heard her voice.

'Cleanliness is next to godliness. Clean it up, Malcolm. Wash clean in the blood of the Lord.'

'Yes, Mamma,' he whispered. Then he put his hand over his mouth and stifled a giggle. Lillian was dead. Silenced for ever. They would think he was mad if they heard him talking to her. And he wasn't mad. He couldn't be. They'd let him come home from That Place. The mad ones had to stay in there.

Malcolm glanced at the bedroom door, then quickly looked away. Lillian was, of course, right. He would have to scrub and polish and clear away his things before the men came to pull down the house.

But there was still the problem of hiding Lillian's body, and he didn't know if he had the stomach for it. She really did smell awful.

He pushed that worry aside, glad to have something to do. Energy returned and he slowly eased up the wall until he was standing. His legs ached and the muscles in his thighs quivered after having been in one position for so long, but that didn't really matter.

He had a purpose now. A mission which had to be fulfilled before the bulldozers came to smash the house down. Then he would be free to hunt for the presence that watched him so closely. Free to untangle its fingers from his mind and blind those eyes that followed him with such intensity. He was looking forward to the confrontation. It would be a test of his powers, a rite of passage into the world inhabited by others like him.

*

Laura still tingled an hour after Ben had left for the university. She felt warm and sated, and for the first time since Cassandra's disappearance, she experienced a calmness, a certainty that everything would turn out all right.

The staff meeting went smoothly, and although she caught one or two sly glances and whispers, she thought there was sympathy and support from most of them. This was borne out by the soft words of encouragement and the awkward handshakes that were offered as they filed out of the staff sitting-room.

Edward Stone, the chef was the last to leave, and Laura silently hoped he wasn't about to cause trouble.

'We have to get more kitchen staff, Mrs Kingsley,' he said abruptly. 'I'm sorry to bother you at a time like this, but I cannot be expected to prepare banquets if I don't have the staff to support me.' He raised one eloquent brow and waited.

'How many have left in the past week, Edward? What's been going on in that kitchen that I haven't been told about?' Laura dug her hands into her suit pockets and faced him squarely. The kitchen was the heart of the hotel. If it didn't function properly, then it affected everything else. And despite Edward's assumption that he was in charge, this was her hotel and she was sick of his domineering manner towards the staff.

'I had to get rid of that waitress and her boyfriend. Lazy, the pair of them. Then there's the kitchen porter and that mincing coffee shop assistant. Not a brain between them.'

'They don't need to have great depth of brain power, Edward, merely a willingness to earn their wages,' she said pressing down on the exasperation. The coffee shop assistant was as effeminate as Diana Dors, but he was good with customers, especially the old ladies. It would seem strange not having him around, but it also explained the drop in takings for that part of the hotel.

Edward shrugged and smoothed his starched apron. 'I need people who think for themselves. I have to use all my energy in my creations. I can't be chasing KPs to clean up the mess when I have banquets to prepare.'

Really, he was too pompous for words, Laura thought fighting to master the giggle that bubbled too close to the surface. 'I'll telephone the agency immediately. You'll have your staff in the next couple of days.'

She followed him out of the room and made her way through reception. What she saw, made her realise how quickly things could slide when she didn't make her presence felt. The flower displays were wilting, the carpet needed hoovering and the display of local attractions obviously hadn't been tidied or checked for days. The flyer for last week's music and arts festival was still pinned to the board and the leaflets for the coach tours were screwed up and left in a heap.

After sending for her assistant manager, Martin, she made her opinions felt, and left for her own apartment. There was some clearing up of her own to do before Clara came to say goodbye. Tom was leaving for America this afternoon, and Clara was to spend a few days with friends in London. She would be sorry to see her go, but they needed time and space to come to terms with their new-found relationship. And if there was any news of Cassandra, Clara was only a telephone call away.

The tiny kitchen was piled with dirty dishes and she wondered for a moment how so much mess could have been made by so few. Quickly loading the dishwasher, she began to clean the apartment. One of the bedroom staff would have done it for her, most of them needed the extra cash, but this morning she had felt a return of energy and doing this simple chore gave her pleasure. There was a satisfaction in being busy, it didn't leave time for thoughts of anything else.

She began to hum quietly to herself as she cleared the coffee cups and brandy glasses from last night. And as she polished and dusted, her spirits rose and hope flared. Cassandra was alive, she could feel it. Perhaps today she would come home.

She looked out of the window. The sun was shining, and that was always a good omen. It was a beautiful autumn day, with soft white clouds and a crisp east wind that made the gulls swoop and scream over the fishing smacks. Only good things could happen on a day like this, she thought. I have to believe that, have to keep telling myself it will be all right – or I'll go mad.

With a speed born of experience, the kitchen and sitting-room were soon cleared and polished. She dragged the hoover into the bedroom and began to make the big double bed. There was a warmth inside her as she touched the sheets and remembered their love-making, a secret smile tugging at the corners of her mouth as she caught the drift of Ben's aftershave.

She switched off the hoover as a different sound penetrated her thoughts. Was that the apartment doorbell? She listened for a moment and was about to return to her hoovering when it came again.

'Cass. There's news of Cass,' she muttered as she tore off her apron. She caught sight of herself in the mirror above the hall table and ruefully tried to bring some order to her unruly hair before tearing open the door.

'About time. I've been ringing and ringing.'

'David.' Laura clutched the door and felt the euphoria drain away. 'What a surprise.' It wasn't really, but she had to think of something to say. Like the rotten apple in the barrel, she knew he would surface sooner or later.

David kissed the air on either side of her face and stepped into the apartment. He looked just the same, still as handsome, still sleek and fit. Yet as the light caught his face she thought she noticed a cobweb of lines around his eyes, a dissipation to the soft edges of his mouth.

'You're looking well, Laura. But then you take after your mother. How are you?'

Laura followed him into the sitting-room. 'I suppose this visit is about Cassandra?' I might as well get down to basics, she thought. I refuse to play his games any more.

David made himself comfortable on the couch, carefully adjusting the creases in his Armani suit trousers. 'Why didn't you tell me, Laura? It's at times like these we should stand together – forget our differences.'

Laura remained standing, her arms folded around her waist. She would have laughed if that statement hadn't been quite so ludicrous. Since when did David want to be involved in the crises of her life?

'There's nothing to tell, David. Cass is missing, there's nothing anyone can do but wait until she turns up.'

David flicked the thin gold lighter and lit his cigarette. Laura noticed the Patek Philippe watch, the silk tie and hand-stitched shirt. David had expensive tastes, pity he didn't think to spend money on his twins, she thought bitterly.

'I think it's a bit more complex than that, Laura. I understand there's been a murder up in Saxon Woods. You even went to the morgue.' His blue eyes held her for a moment, then released their grasp. 'Why don't you sit down and tell me about it? You've been going through a rough time, and I bet that cow Clara hasn't been near you.'

Laura reached for a cigarette and lit it. It took all her will power to contain the trembling in her hands.

'Clara's been here all the time. She's been wonderful,' she finally managed.

David gave a derisive snort and tweaked his tie. 'My, my, things must have changed.'

Laura looked at him. He was sitting in her sitting-room, on her couch, he had once been her husband, but now he was almost a stranger. Yet, was it possible that he'd changed too? The smile was wide and friendly, the sentiment apparently genuine. She decided, reluctantly, to give him the benefit of the doubt. There was enough drama in her life, it couldn't hurt to be pleasant.

'The one good thing to come out of this is the long talks I've had with Mum. We're getting to know one another again, learning to be able to live together.'

David's eyes shifted away as they examined the room. 'I looked upstairs for you. The place looks good. You've done well.'

Laura felt a jolt of alarm. The hotel had always been a contentious issue between them. 'Thank you. It's much harder than I expected, but I seem to be getting somewhere at last.'

'I never doubted it. You always were ambitious, Laura. Pity the work ethic doesn't stretch to our daughters.' His gaze hardened and he mashed the cigarette into the ashtray.

Laura battled to stay calm. She would not be drawn, would not fall into the same old traps he used to set when they were married. He hadn't changed.

'I see you have no answer to that one. Perhaps you should seriously consider whether you were cut out to have it all. A career and children are two very great responsibilities, and you certainly seem more successful at one than the other.'

His smile was still pleasant, his relaxed demeanour masking whatever was going on in that devious mind. Laura decided to change the subject.

'Would you like coffee? I've just made some.'

'Ever the efficient hostess. Why not?'

Laura had caught the sarcasm, but she chose to ignore it. Pouring the coffee from the percolator, she set it in front of him.

'Will you try to visit Melissa whilst you're in Sussex? She's not been well, and I'm sure she'd benefit from seeing you.' *If she can still remember you.* She bit down on the codicil and it remained silent.

'I'm a busy man, Laura. I expect you to take care of that side of things. You know how that place affects me.'

She faced him, hands deep in the pockets of her suit jacket, chin tilted in defiance. 'I'm surprised it affects you at all. You've been there so rarely,' she snapped.

'Ah! I knew you wouldn't be able to keep that temper of yours under control. I'm surprised it took so long.' His eyes shone in humourless glee.

Laura ignored him. 'I take it you saw the interview I did for the television.'

David carefully placed his coffee cup on the table, then took his time to wipe his mouth on the linen napkin. His eyes were suddenly cold as they regarded her.

'Yes. I got the news second hand.'

His voice was soft, but it held a brittleness which sent alarm bells jangling for Laura. A depth of menace which he'd honed to perfection over the years since Melissa's troubles. David was at his most dangerous when he was like this. She had to diffuse the situation – and quickly.

'I didn't have your number,' she said with a bravado she didn't feel.

David eyed her. 'You have the name and number of my answering service. They would have found me.'

Laura swallowed. 'I didn't think . . .'

'You never do, Laura. Not when it concerns me.' He suddenly got up from the couch, but he didn't approach her.

Laura edged away from him, putting a chair between them. There was a fierceness in that quiet voice. David had always been fiery tempered, but since the troubles with Melissa, it had found a new depth. A depth she couldn't fathom. David's change had been subtle, but then she knew him too well to be fooled by the veneer of harnessed control.

'My dear Laura, you're not afraid of me are you? After all these years apart? I'm merely trying to point out that you show a remarkable knack for negligence. First one daughter, then another.' He shook his head as though in remorse. 'What are we going to do about you?'

Laura was stung into a retort, even though she knew the probable outcome of the dangerous game she was playing.

'You have no right to call me negligent. When was the last time you bothered to write or call? You have two daughters,

David, but you seem to have conveniently forgotten they exist. So don't you dare accuse me of being a bad mother.' The anger brought heat to her face and made her heart thud as she glared at him.

There was a disturbing stillness about David, an icy veneer of nonchalance, which Laura knew hid something far more menacing.

'How like you to turn the blame around and accuse me of forgetting my children. Please remind me of the salient facts,' he said with heavy sarcasm. 'Wasn't it you who began divorce proceedings? Wasn't it you who took out a court order restraining me from coming to the hotel?'

He stayed silent for a moment and the atmosphere in the room became claustrophobic. 'You have a nasty habit of endangering your children, Laura. I would call that negligent. Wouldn't you?'

Laura clenched her fists and tried to keep hold of her temper. 'Cassandra's run away. If any harm had come to her, we'd have heard by now.'

David advanced towards her, but kept the chair between them. 'And why did she do that, Laura?' His voice was mesmerising, and Laura was reminded of a snake charmer she'd seen in India. Only this time, David was the cobra waiting to strike, she was the mongoose.

'I don't know. It was just a teenage tantrum,' she said with as much calm as she could muster.

'Don't lie to me.' His voice was a pistol crack in the silence. 'You had a row, didn't you? You tried to force your will on my daughter and she found it unbearable to stay here. I know how that feels.'

Laura couldn't remain silent, not in the face of such injustice. 'How dare you!' she hissed. 'Our marriage ended because you used your fists to get your own way. It ended because you took my trust and threw it in my face by taking out those extra mortgages and forging my signature. You rubbed my nose in all the dirty little affairs you had locally, and treated me like something you'd brought in on your shoe.'

She snatched a breath. 'You were too weak to face up to

what happened to Melissa and never got over the fact that it was partly because of you that she's in hospital and will probably never come out.'

Laura's breathing was rapid, her voice growing shrill as the anger built into a crescendo. 'Cassandra wanted to go to a rave. I said no. She went and didn't come home. End of story. It's me who's had to pick up the pieces and go on day after day, never knowing if she's still alive. Never really sure if I will see her again. I've been punished enough, so don't you dare come into my home and fling your disgusting accusations.'

'Your home?' he sneered. 'You forget, Laura, I own half of it.'

'You gave up your rights to this place the minute you signed the divorce papers. I hold the mortgage deeds. I'm the one who pays the interest on the loans you so deviously arranged.' Her anger was out of control and she couldn't stop. 'What happened to all that money, David? What was it, women, gambling, expensive suits to hide the cheapness of your real self?'

David's hand shot out. His shove sent her stumbling backwards. He followed her across the room and out into the hallway, his eyes blazing.

Laura felt the nausea and cold dread. It was all starting again. He would beat her until she begged him to stop. Then simply walk away and pretend it never happened. She dodged the second shove and scrambled along the wall until she reached the kitchen door.

'Who do you think you are, to talk to me like that?' His breath was jagged, his eyes bright with malice and what looked suspiciously like excitement as he lifted his hand to strike.

Laura swerved, but the blow caught the side of her head and sent her reeling into the door jamb. It stunned her for an instant, then she was filled with such rage, that she spun to face him, suddenly unafraid and prepared to put up a fight.

'Don't touch me, you bastard,' she snarled. 'I'm not the same Laura you can turn into a snivelling wreck.'

David laughed and the sound of it chilled as he swiftly

closed the gap between them and encircled her throat with powerful fingers.

'I could kill you with one flick of my wrist, and you'd know nothing about it,' he breathed into her face. The vindictive excitement was alight in his eyes at the promise of what was to come. 'But that isn't the answer, is it? Why should I become the victim again, when it was you – always you, behind everything that's happened between us?' He maintained his grip and slipped off his jacket.

Laura's mouth dried and fear was iced droplets on her spine as she felt the breath squeezed from her throat. Yet she knew she had to find the strength to fight back, to stop him from hurting her like he used to.

'Touch me again and I'll stick this in you,' she gasped as she desperately scrabbled behind her and found the bread knife.

David hesitated, his grip loosening a fraction as his eyes flitted between the sharp serrated blade and Laura's face.

'Careful, darling. You might cut yourself,' he drawled with sarcastic bravado as he kept her at arm's length and tightened his grasp.

Laura sliced the air between them and he jumped back as the blade flashed lightning on the walls and across his face.

'One more step, and I cut you,' she said as clearly as she could through her aching throat. 'You don't frighten me any more, David. You beat that out of me before you left.'

David stood in silence for a moment, then he shrugged, his face lit with a radiant smile. 'You should learn not to provoke, Laura. My God, you're sexy when you're roused. You look like an avenging harpy.' He made a tentative gesture with his hands. 'Forgive me?'

'No,' she said coldly as she gripped the knife. This was an old trick of his and the metamorphosis had brought it all back as she watched it. He always wanted sex after beating her. Fast, brutal, unfeeling sex. He would play the reasonable, intelligent charmer for a while, then he would change back again just as quickly. It was a scene they had played many times and she didn't want another performance.

'That might have worked twelve years ago, but you can't fool me now. We have nothing to say to one another. Get out.'

David put his hands in his pockets, but kept a wary eye on the long, cold blade of the knife. 'Remember how you dug your nails into my back when you came? Remember how we ripped off our clothes and had it on the floor, or against a table? We were good together, Laura. Sure you don't want a quick one – just for old times' sake?'

'All I want is for you to go. The thought of you touching me again makes me sick.' The knife point never wavered, but her pulse raced and her knuckles showed white.

The veneer of charm slipped. 'I'm not going until you apologise for the things you said. I have all the time in the world and we can just go on standing here for as long as you like. But sooner or later you will tell me why you didn't think it neccessary to tell me about Cassandra. You made me look a fool. That makes me angry. And you know what happens when I get angry, Laura.'

'The lady wants you to leave, buster. I should do just that if I were you.'

David whirled round and came face to face with Ben.

There was silence for a heartbeat and Laura's gaze flitted between the two men as she kept the knife clasped in front of her.

'Who the hell are you?' David gasped, the colour draining from his handsome face.

'I might ask the same question, but I don't really want to know. Just get your ass outa here.' Ben's powerfully built frame filled the doorway.

Laura lowered the knife and edged towards him. 'This is David. He came to find out about Cassandra,' she said coldly.

'Did you tell him?'

Laura nodded.

Ben put his finger under her chin and turned her face to the light. 'Your neck is bruised, and there's a cut above your eyebrow.'

Laura touched her forehead and winced. 'Just get him out of here. I don't want any more trouble,' she said.

David straightened his tie and smoothed his hair. 'This the new boyfriend, then?' he said with a smirk as he looked Ben up and down. 'I thought you had more taste. No wonder Cassandra wanted to leave home. Looks like you're turning this place into a hippy commune.'

Laura felt Ben tense and put a restraining hand on his arm. 'He's itching for a fight, just ignore him.'

'I bet you haven't told him about Melissa. See how long he sticks around when he finds out how your negligence left your kid in the nuthouse.' David's voice was high-pitched and there was an electricity of excitement in his eyes.

It was Laura's turn to tense. Surely, even David wouldn't stoop so low as to drag up the past. Not now – not while Cassandra was still missing, and the hurt was so raw.

Ben put his arm around her. 'I know about Melissa. I've been to visit her, which is more than you've done. Laura's a fine mom, and I won't have you come in here and beat up on her,' he said softly, his Texan drawl more pronounced than usual.

David pretended not to hear. He advanced on Ben and said in a conspiratorial whisper. 'You see, my dear wife has this nasty habit which she obviously hasn't cured. She's so busy being a bossy, organised career woman, that she has no time for the important things. Like where her children are. And what they're doing. And who with.'

He swung round to face Laura. 'Isn't that right, Laura dear? Come on, bitch. Tell us. We're dying to know.'

'I've heard enough,' said Ben grimly. He grasped David's shirt and dragged him to the apartment door. Unlocking it, he pushed him out into the alleyway and held him up against the wall.

'One more word outa you, buddy, and I cream your face. Understood?'

David paled and nodded, all bravado gone.

Ben let go of his shirt and smoothed the collar and tie, his face inches from David's. 'Now, you be a good ol' boy and clear off, or I'll shove your head so far down your neck, you'll be smelling the roses from up your ass. Do I make myself understood?'

David muttered something incomprehensible, then bent to pick up the jacket Laura had thrown after him. He stumbled down the alleyway, then turned.

'Ask her what happened to Melissa. Get her to tell you why she's in the hospital and will never grow older than six. Ten years isn't so long. I'm sure she remembers.' He gave a victorious laugh and hurried away.

Ben tensed, coiled like a spring to race after him, but Laura put a hand on his arm.

'Don't Ben. He's not worth it.'

'That guy needs to be taught a lesson,' he growled, as he clenched his fists. 'Beating up on women. I'd like to see how he holds out against a man.'

With the door bolted behind her, Laura began to tremble. She would have to tell Ben the truth about Melissa. It was unfair to keep him in the dark any longer.

11

It was cold and wet and three hours until dawn, but Malcolm hardly noticed. The night had sped past in a welter of cleaning and scrubbing and moving furniture.

He pushed through the back door, his arms loaded with Lillian's religious tracts, and the last of her clothes. Stumbling over the litter-strewn garden, he made his way to the bonfire he was building. It was almost ready. Just a few journeys into the house, then he could light it.

He nudged his glasses over the bridge of his nose, then turned and squinted into the half-light, at the row of remaining houses. All was quiet, all was dark and sleeping. He touched the mark on his cheek. His fingers were rough and cold and he shivered as the drizzle misted his glasses. The windows were like blinded eyes staring back at him and he wondered if anyone was watching from behind the sheets of plywood.

Malcolm gave a secret smile which turned into a soft snigger. It didn't matter if they were. They couldn't hurt him, couldn't possibly understand what he was doing. Why should they? They were like all the rest, dull and stupid and intent only on the things which affected them.

He took off his glasses and cleaned them on the hem of his shirt. Station Villas looked better with the sharp edges softened, the colours blurred, the decay masked by myopia.

The thought that perhaps he should also commit his spectacles to the bonfire came to him, then was as swiftly set aside. He was almost blind without them, and he needed to be able to see. Needed to have a sharpness of vision to hunt down the predator who watched him so keenly. Replacing them firmly on his nose, he experienced a thrill of excitement which brought a zest and a purpose to his footsteps as he returned to the house. He was almost finished.

Number 29 Station Villas echoed now it was denuded of furniture, and he took the stairs two at a time, eager to be done with the task ahead.

Lillian's door was open, the light bright and revealing after the gloom outside. The only item of furniture in the room was the bed. It straddled the bare floor like a squatting bullfrog on its bulbous, stubby, oak legs. On its back, it bore the weight of a very dead, odorous Lillian.

Malcolm tugged the handkerchief from his pocket and tied it in a makeshift mask over his mouth and nose. After the crisp cold of the garden, the stench was overpowering. Yet he had to go on. He couldn't stop now.

He approached the bed and looked down at her. She seemed larger than ever, uglier than ever. This was not the Lillian he wanted to remember. This was a travesty of the woman he'd loved when he was small, and she bore no resemblance to his mother. He leaned across the spreading, stinking bulk of her and reached for the wig. It didn't suit her, and she had no right to it.

Grasping the long blonde hair, he tugged. Lillian's head moved on the pillow, but the wig remained where it was.

Malcolm gave a sharp cry of frustration. It was stuck fast to the wound in the back of her head. Lillian was still defying him, even in death. She was laughing at him, enjoying his fear, revelling in his abhorrence. He clenched his fists. She wasn't going to beat him. She had no right to that wig and he wanted it back.

He tugged again, unwilling to touch that marbled face that was shadowed now with darker, more sinister blotches, fearful of the closed eyes and sagging jaw. Her head rolled back and forth as he pulled and sweated. Then, just as he'd thought he would never succeed, the wig tore free.

Fine, grey wisps of hair and slivers of scalp dangled grotesquely from the hand-stitched cap which held it all together. A dark, rusty stain marred the silky perfection of the blonde hair, stiffening it, making it brittle and odious.

Malcolm gasped in disgust and threw the wig into the corner. He would come back for it later.

Spreading the square of tarpaulin on the floor, Malcolm caught hold of the mattress and tipped Lillian off the bed. She landed with a spongy thud and Malcolm giggled as the air was expelled from her body in a rousing fart.

Lillian had always been coy about bodily functions. It served her right that she should be humiliated. Perhaps now, she knew how it felt.

Malcolm quickly covered her, making a parcel of the heavy tarpaulin and tying it with thick string. His breath was sharp and painful as he struggled with heavy limbs and stubborn feet and hands that slipped away from him and made the task almost impossible. The smell of her seeped through the makeshift mask and tainted his nose and throat making him gag as the sweat trickled down his back in icy runnels.

Finally, it was done. He looked down at the bulky parcel and gave a shuddering sigh of revulsion, before dragging it to the door and out onto the landing. With one hefty kick, he sent the whole thing tumbling down the stairs.

'Good riddance,' he whispered as he heard the satisfying snap of bone against wood.

His secret smile played at the corners of his mouth, and he waited until the bundle came to rest in the hall before following it down.

A pain shot through his chest as he hauled Lillian into the kitchen and the muscles on his arms bulged and trembled as the weight of her took all his strength. When he was satisfied that she was out of sight in the shadows beneath the sink, he took a moment to catch his breath and drink some water. This was going to be harder than he'd thought. He would have to hurry if he was to finish what he'd started. This was the last full day left to him before the men came to tear down the house.

It took more than an hour to wrestle the heavy bed through the narrow doorway and down the stairs and into the back garden. He dragged it across the rubble and weeds and finally managed to lean it against the bonfire.

He was exhausted and trembling with the effort, but there was an excitement that urged him on and refused to let him rest. He was almost there, almost finished. Racing back to the house, he collected the last of Lillian's gore-stained bedclothes and flung them on top of the pyre.

He paused for a moment, taking in deep breaths of sweet, rain-drenched air as he waited for his pulse to stop racing. The sweat and the rain had soaked his shirt and trousers, making them cling, and his glasses were once again steamed up, but it didn't matter. One more journey to Lillian's room and he could light the fire.

Malcolm looked at the sticks of furniture he'd been familiar with all his life and felt nothing but elation. There was his bed, the bed Lillian had tied him into when she thought he should be punished. There was the kitchen table, the chairs, the old couch out of the sitting-room. He remembered his father sitting on that couch, but he couldn't quite conjure up what he looked like – it had been so long ago.

He turned his back and ran into the house. Picking up the crucifix, he turned the bloodied face away from him before switching out the light and closing the door for the last time on Lillian's room. Hurrying down the stairs, he felt the adrenalin surge and it made his head swim. The crucifix was the last reminder of Lillian. The last tangible evidence of his torture. He would enjoy watching it burn.

Burying the crucifix up to the knees, so it stood above the pyre like a guy on bonfire night, he glared into the plaster face. It stared back at him, the features masked by a deep red stain.

'Let's see who burns in hell, now,' Malcolm hissed defiantly before turning away and reaching for the petrol can he'd had filled the night before.

When the can was empty, he threw it onto the bonfire. Flicking back the cover on his father's old-fashioned lighter, he ran his thumb over the rough metal wheel and watched the flame dance in the breeze. His concentration on that small, flickering flame was consuming and the excitement made him tremble as the cold and dampness of his surroundings were almost forgotten.

He tossed the lighter towards the bonfire and was thrown back, winded, by the explosive inferno that followed. Then the flames caught, turned red and hungry and began to devour the dry, brittle wood and the ancient upholstery. It ran in rivulets through the nylon sheets and cotton dresses, and licked at the pages of the religious books before gobbling them up and turning them black.

Malcolm watched in awe as the fire spread voraciously through the pile of memories. Plumes of choking smoke drifted up into the damp, grey morning, taking with them the charred remnants of Lillian's religious tracts, making them dance and flutter until they were consumed. He should have done this a long time ago, but there had always been Lillian, and she would have punished him severely over such sacrilege.

The thought of her made him wish he'd put her on the bonfire. It would be so much easier than the plan he had in mind. He watched the fire for a moment, gazing into the dancing, weaving flames, almost mesmerised by them as he speculated on the choices he had. Then he shook his head at his own stupidity. Of course he couldn't do that. They would find her and come looking for him. They would punish him and send him to That Place if he burned Lillian. No. He had a much better plan and he would stick with that.

The flames had reached the crucifix, caressing the plastered legs, climbing silently and inexorably towards the speared chest and thorn-crowned head.

He touched the scar on his face and wet his lips as the painted eyes looked down at him. Those eyes made him uneasy. They seemed to be silently reproaching him, crying out for him to stop before it was too late.

'You don't scare me any more,' he muttered as he took a hesitant step back. 'You're just plaster and paint. Just one of Lillian's nasty habits. You deserve to burn.'

The flames scorched the face and Malcolm stared in horror

as great tears rolled down the blackened cheeks and splashed into the fire, making them hiss and splutter.

Jesus on his cross was crying.

He backed away, mesmerised, yet very afraid. He shouldn't have put the crucifix on the bonfire. He would be punished for the work he'd done today. Punished and sent to hell to burn for ever. Lillian had told him he would. And right now, he believed it.

*

The incident room at Brighton CID Headquarters was buzzing with activity, even though it was only eight thirty in the morning. At last they had something to go on, a needle to find in the haystack of paperwork and false leads.

'What you got for me, Ramona?'

'An ID on this last victim. It came in late last night while I was catching up on some of our other cases.'

The WDS opened the case notes. 'Missing persons had her on file. But it was the piece in the paper that brought results.' She passed a photograph across the desk.

DCI Stonenam looked at the fresh-faced child who smiled back at him. She was in her school uniform and her long blonde hair was tied in two bunches which trailed over her shoulders. The image didn't bear any relation to the mutilated child on the mortuary slab.

'Our victim is Mary Elizabeth Funnell, sixteen years old, a persistent runaway. That photograph was taken three years ago, it was the only one available. Her grandmother reported her missing six months ago. Seems Mary's mother has a new boyfriend, and Mary and he don't get on. The grandmother, Mrs Glover, took Mary in several times, but she's crippled with arthritis and found it difficult to cope with a stroppy teenager. Mary had been missing for a month before anyone realised. The mother thought she was with Mrs Glover and didn't bother to contact her. Mrs Glover thought she'd gone home.'

Stoneham reached for the file and digested the information.

Reap the Whirlwind

'Last reported sighting was with a group of travellers in Brighton,' he muttered almost to himself. 'It fits. Has someone formally identified the body?'

'The mother's coming down from Liverpool sometime today. She didn't seem particularly put out by the news that her only child is in a morgue. In fact, all she seemed interested in was getting a free trip to the south coast.'

Stoneham's colleague slammed the file shut and tipped it into the out tray. 'What have you got?'

'Still nothing.' He began to pace. 'Been going through those files, but unless I've missed something, there isn't a clue to who's doing these murders. Perhaps, once we've interviewed Mrs Funnell, we'll know more. But I think we're grasping at straws.'

His WDS nodded. 'I doubt she'll help much. But you never know, Guv.' She looked at him thoughtfully. 'That other girl still worries you, doesn't she?'

'Cassandra Kingsley, you mean? Yes. Something not right there. All my instincts tell me that Darren "Snake" Smith knows more than he's letting on, but it's out of our hands. No crime suspected. Missing persons will deal with it from now on. They've contacted the usual agencies. All Mrs Kingsley can do is wait for news.'

He approached the vast map on the incident room wall. Coloured pins marked the locations of the bodies. 'There has to be a link between these girls, but I'm darned if I know what it is.'

'What's on your mind, Guv?'

'Not sure. Get me some coloured tape, Ramona. I want to try something,' he muttered.

Stoneham began with Karen Walker in Crawley, the first known victim. He rolled out the tape and connected it to the pins of the next two which were in Southampton and Dover. When he fixed the final pin and the map was complete, they both stood back and surveyed it.

'Looks like a satellite dish,' his DS murmured thoughtfully. Then she gave a sigh and shrugged her shoulders. 'Unless it's the work of aliens, I don't think this helps much.'

'I'm not so sure. What do all these places have in common?'

'Southampton and Dover are ports, so is Saxonbridge. Reigate, Crawley and Finsbury are landlocked. They are all large towns or urban communities, except for Saxonbridge. The only connection I can see is that they are all in the south.' She turned to her superior, a wrinkle threading her brow. 'What are you getting at?'

'What is the single most difficult problem on our city streets today?'

'Runaways.'

'And what else do all large towns have in common?'

'Shopping malls, hospitals, some have airports and docks and all of them have railway stations.'

'Yes.' He jabbed the map. 'Railway stations, where the homeless and the runaways congregate. Each murder site was within a short distance of a mainline station. Someone is killing off these kids who live on the streets.'

'Saxonbridge doesn't have a mainline station, and Mary's body was discovered at least ten miles away. And what about Tanya Van Hauer? She wasn't a runaway, she was happy and settled with her family.'

'I might have the answer to that little problem.' He riffled through Tanya's file.

'The statement made by Mrs Paley-Smythe who employed Tanya didn't say very much. But this one sentence is significant.' He waved the piece of paper at her before reading it aloud. '"Tanya had been to a disco and I had said I would pick her up. But she had bought a season ticket for the train and said she would make her own way home".'

He should have known there were no easy answers, for his DS had other ideas.

'That doesn't answer the question about this latest one. Wolves Farm is about ten miles inland from Saxonbridge and the station. The trains run infrequently and after ten o'clock there is no service. I'm sorry, Guv, but I already checked. The idea of trains came to me last night.'

The bloody woman was just too sharp, but he knew that,

somehow, railways were connected to the killings. He stared up at the map, willing it to tell him something.

'If all the others were connected to mainline stations, then why suddenly change tack? It doesn't make sense. Unless . . . Unless . . .' There was that flash of insight again. Why hadn't he thought of it before? It was so simple and it had been staring him in the face. He began to untangle the green tape.

The DCI didn't notice the expectant hush that had fallen over the incident room as he cut the tape into shorter lengths and replaced them on the map. This time he started from a different location, radiating the tape out to the various murder sites.

'Now what do you see?' he asked as he stepped back.

'I see someone desperate to find answers, Guv,' retorted his partner drily.

'And I thought you were bright. Don't you see, these murder sites are all within three hours of train travel from Brighton. Our man had local knowledge to lead him to Wolves Farm and the rave. He had to be in the area that day when the flyers went out. This was a spur of the moment thing, he was offered the chance and took it. He didn't plan it like the others and there was a carelessness about this last one that pointed to his haste. We are looking for someone from Sussex.'

'That cuts it down to several hundred thousand,' the woman said tartly. 'And what about the possibility of our man driving a car or a lorry? He didn't have to use the trains to find the runaways, he could have picked them up from the streets. God knows, enough of these kids are on the game. It would have been easy enough. Any more good ideas?'

The DCI swung away from the map and began to pace. 'I can live with that idea, but I'm not convinced. Maybe on the last murder, but not with the others. It would explain how he reached the farm though. No-one reported giving a lift to a hitcher, or seeing anyone on the road leading from the farm that didn't fit in with the general pattern of travellers and teenagers.'

He paused for a moment, and stared sightlessly out of the window. 'Maybe you have something there, Ramona. This was a hasty murder, one that wasn't planned. It convinces me our murderer is local, and that he changed his routine to fit it in. He may very well have used a car or some kind of vehicle to reach the farm and make his getaway. But that doesn't mean he didn't make use of the trains for the others.'

'We could be looking for a rep, a taxi driver, a long-distance lorry driver or even someone who works on the railways. The list is endless. I don't see how we can possibly pinpoint one man purely on the assumption that he used the trains.'

'Let's just think about that. I've been in the business of policing for long enough to have learned some common sense. I don't profess to be a trick-cyclist, and wouldn't want to. But we know more about this man than we think.'

The clatter and noise of the incident room was gone. In its place was a silence heavy with expectant concentration.

'Our man has been killing for over ten years. As far as we know, the earliest was in 1985, but the records don't go back any further on the central computer. Men like him don't become murderers overnight. They start out as peeping toms, then go on to expose themselves to women in lonely, out of the way places.'

The silence grew more dense.

'The progression of their crimes are like an addict seeking a greater rush. They lose the kick out of these simple acts of perversion and want the thrill of something more dangerous. Common assault, or rape.'

The policewoman nodded.

'Then he kills his first victim, maybe by accident, maybe not. But the rush he gets from that takes him on a high he's never experienced before. It gives him everything he ever dreamed of – power, excitement, revenge, all in one glorious act of violence. You see our man feels nothing very much most of the time. He's amoral, with no conception of good and evil. He wants, so he takes.'

The Detective Chief Inspector looked over the young, expectant faces that were raised towards him. He suddenly felt like a very old, wise owl whose feathers were greying and tattered, but who still commanded respect. The thought made him hesitate for a moment. If he could impart just one iota of the things he'd learned over the years, then his career had not been wasted. In years to come, these young, bright people would be in charge of their own investigation team, and he was going to do his best to make sure they succeeded.

'Police work isn't just about door-to-door inquiries and the collection of facts and evidence. It's about knowing the type of person we are looking for, and through experience and hard work we come to realise that they all leave clues.'

'We have nothing on these murders, Guv. That's why it's such a bastard to solve. Or have you been hiding something from us?' Detective Constable William Giddings was all of twenty-three and the station wag. He leaned back in his chair, his broad grin sweeping over his colleagues who sniggered in response.

There always has to be one, thought Stoneham ruefully.

'If you shut up long enough Giddings, you might learn something,' he barked. He leaned forward. 'If you prefer to take over, please, feel free. I know how much you like being the centre of attention.'

Giddings had the grace to redden and the older man regretted being sharp with him. God knows, he thought, we need the Giddings of this world to bring a little levity into the job and to keep us sane.

He reached for the files and spread them out on the table before him.

'All our murders, as far as we can gather, were committed on a Tuesday. The only one that breaks the pattern is this last one.' He looked up. 'Tuesday is a strange night, isn't it? Nothing much happens on a Tuesday. It isn't like the weekend, with the pubs and clubs doing a roaring trade, with people out and about having a good time.'

'Yeah, all the Chinese take-aways are closed on Tuesdays.'

Stoneham shot Giddings a look of stern rebuke and carried on. 'Young Giddings has made a very valid point. Tuesdays are slow, people are getting over the weekend and money's tight. Ask any tom on the streets and she'll tell you that

Tuesdays are her slowest night. A lot of places are closed on a Tuesday. It's a good day to have time off.' He stayed silent for a moment to let that sink in.

Giddings thankfully remained quiet, but the detective could see the gleam in his eye.

'I don't think we're looking for a Chinese chef with a meat cleaver, Giddings, that would be too easy,' he remarked drily to forestall any nonsense. He waited for the rustle of laughter to die down. 'But I do think we're looking for someone in the service industry – retail, hotel, transport, entertainment, food outlet of some kind. It's in these areas that staff are given days off mid-week. The weekends are their busiest times.'

'It could be someone who's unemployed, or a freelance rep or driver. Don't forget, this last murder was done on a Friday.'

Stoneham nodded. 'You're right, Ramona. But it was done sometime after two o'clock in the morning. Plenty of time to finish work and get up there.'

The silence in the room was almost tangible. Turning to the blackboard the DCI took down the photographs of the victims and picked up the stump of chalk.

'Let's drop the supposition for a moment and collate the facts. This man has killed six times. The victims were all young, fit girls who put up one hell of a fight. He must have been covered in blood, maybe scratched and bruised. No wife would ignore another woman's scratch marks, or not question her husband about the state of his clothes, or the disappearance of a coat or jacket. Therefore, I think our man is single, or at least living alone for most of the time.'

No-one interrupted him. This was not the time for levity.

'The kind of man who starts out as a peeping tom or a flasher, would find it very difficult to maintain any kind of relationship with a woman. Deep down he's terrified of them, and his acts of perversion are committed solely for the pleasure of watching their fear.'

Jack wrote on the blackboard.

Previous offences before 1985. Peeping, flashing, assault. Single, murders on Tuesdays.

Service industry, unemployed, self-employed, travelling salesman, lorry driver.

He looked out on the sea of faces. 'He was probably quite young when he committed that first murder. There were no attempts at intercourse, no sign that he was aroused. That came later. The reason I think he was young then, is compounded by the fact that he's still strong enough to overcome a struggling, clawing, kicking girl and smash her face in. The tight ring of bruising on their wrists shows a man with hands strong enough and large enough to pin his victims down with one hand whilst he beat them with the other. I would place his age at anything between twenty-five and forty. He has a car, or access to some kind of transport. He also travels by train.'

Stoneham added these facts to the list on the blackboard, shooting his DS a glance of defiance before carrying on.

'There was a gap of three years between the murders of Lesley Moore and Tanya Van Hauer, and another gap between Gina Pirelli and this latest one. This kind of killer doesn't break for a vacation. He could no more stop than fly to the moon. He was hooked on killing, had to do it at least once a year. Where was he between 1987 and 1990? And between 1991 and 1995? Prison, mental institution, hospital? Or were there more murders that we just don't know about?'

He was writing faster now, filling the black space with his looping, slanting script.

'If, as I suspect, he has a history of mental illness, then that compounds the idea that he's a loner. But don't be fooled into thinking that because he's raving mad he isn't clever, because for over ten years he's got away with it. Either by luck or by sheer cunning, he hasn't made a mistake. No fingerprints, no blood, no flesh under his victims' nails. There were no stray fibres found on the victims' clothes, no traces of paint or oil or anything else that could lead to her attacker. He understands only too well that he can be traced through DNA. This man dresses for the occasion, covers himself in something that will leave no trace. He goes prepared.'

He leaned forward, his gaze trawling slowly over each and

every face that looked back at him. 'But there is one thing we know without doubt. He hates women. In particular, he hates very young women with long blonde hair. Perhaps a younger sister made fun of him, or his mother abused him when he was small. Perhaps he was jilted in a humiliating fashion by his first girlfriend – who knows? Some woman somewhere is the key to all'this, because he's been getting his revenge since 1985 and if we don't stop him, he'll just carry on doing it.'

The chalk squeaked as he wrote another line on the board. There was barely any black showing now.

'There had been an attempt at rape on Lesley Moore, but no semen was found, only internal bruising which suggests he managed an erection but not ejaculation. Perhaps he was abused as a child, perhaps the sexual act repulses him. Either way, he feels an uncontrollable rage at his inability to commit the final insult. He's impotent. That's why he's resorted to the stake.'

DCI Stoneham threw down the stub of chalk.

'As I said, we know an awful lot about our man. All we have to do now is find him.'

*

Malcolm waited until the bonfire had collapsed into a smouldering mess of charred wood and ash. The crucifix had finally succumbed to the flames, toppling into the very heart of the fire, where it caught and flared, the tongues of flame spluttering and sparking on the heat-distorted, figure. The unease hadn't left him as he watched it burn. And the voices of the wheels had begun to whisper again, sounding more and more like Lillian as they gathered strength.

'Burn in hell. You will burn in hell. In hell. In hell.'

He turned his back on the fire as the spirals of ethereal smoke twisted up into the dull, gloomy sky. The day was already half gone, and he had things to do.

Returning to the house, he slowly wandered from room to room. The ghosts of the past were still here, despite the lack of furniture, and he thought he could hear their voices echoing in the silence.

'Lillian, I want you to see the doctor. You're not well, duck.' His father's voice was gentle, tinged with weariness, ragged with frustration. Lillian's madness was becoming more evident as the years progressed.

'I don't need to see a doctor,' shrieked Lillian, her face suffused, her eyes bright with fervour. 'The Lord is my Saviour. I don't need those quacks to prod and poke and give me their pills. Servants of Satan, they are.'

'Lillian, stop it.' Stanley Squires took a hesitant step towards her, one hand stretched out to placate. 'The Lord gave the doctors the gift of healing. He wouldn't have done that if he didn't think it right. Now would he?' If Stanley believed in God at all, it certainly wasn't in such a vengeful one, but he used the words he knew Lillian would accept.

Lillian glared back at him, her mouth fixed in a grim line, her eyes feral between the puffy lids. She picked up her Bible from the table and stalked out of the room, her hips jiggling beneath the dowdy grey dress she had taken to wearing every day.

'Eee, lad, I don't know what to do. She's my wife and I feel responsible, but we can't go on like this.' Stanley's voice was ragged with emotion as he ran his hand over his thinning fair hair.

Ten-year-old Malcolm looked at his father and saw the weariness in him, the lost hope, the frustration of not being able to cope with Lillian's illness. He knew his mother was sick, and the violence that had manifested itself lately made him more afraid of her than ever before. But he still loved her, needed to know she loved him, even if it meant a beating, or being locked in his room with no food for days. At least she didn't ignore him.

He watched Stanley, wanting to help, to take away the hurt he could see in his father's eyes, but he didn't know how to express the turmoil of emotions that boiled inside him. The little scene that he'd just witnessed was a replay of so many others. His mother's denial of her madness, his father's gentle pleading, then Mamma's terrible silence, which was more eloquent than all the shouting.

That silence had a way of ending all conversation, all reasonable argument. She was implacable, when she clamped her mouth shut and picked up her Bible like that.

Malcolm slid down the wall and watched himself as that young boy. He saw ten-year-old Malcolm in his school uniform, cross the room and put his arms around his father, needing the warmth of him, the comfort and reassurance of his strength and understanding.

'Don't be soft, and stop that snivelling, lad. You're almost a man. Lillian's turning you into a right sissy.' Stanley shoved the young Malcolm away from him, his mouth twisted in a sneer of disgust as he brushed away the tears from his jacket.

Stanley was a big man, a foreman on a building site, with a burly chest and roughened hands. Brought up in the north of England, he was a man's man, terrified of being thought soft, and unable to express his emotions clearly. And he expected his son to be like him.

Malcolm shivered in that cold, bare room as he remembered the hurt of that rejection. Even his father disliked him. Tears pricked his eyes and he took off his glasses and angrily scrubbed his face. Sitting here was doing him no good at all.

Leaving the sitting-room, he slowly toured the empty house, but the memories kept flooding back, bringing pain and humiliation with them, and those memories would not be denied.

He climbed the stairs and went into his bedroom. It was small, with a sloping ceiling and a window that overlooked the once busy shunting yards. He stood for a moment and watched the scene below him. There were only a few trains now, but he could remember when there had been coal carriers and wood carriers and long lines of rattling, clanking containers of cement and steel.

As a little boy, he'd stood in this same place every day watching the activity in the shunting yards. They had been his lifeline to the world outside and he'd pictured in his mind where those great mounds of deliveries were bound for. Now, with the grey drizzle of the rain of the dirty windows, it was as if time had pulled a gauzy curtain over his memories. The boy who had stood at this window was gone, just like the trains. Only the voices remained.

Malcolm turned away from the window and looked at the room that in his childhood, had been refuge and prison. The bed was gone, so were the cupboards. The shelves were cleared and the thin rug burned. There should have been nothing left to remember in this room, but there was – there were the memories.

It was late evening and twelve-year-old Malcolm was in bed, listening to the trains running over the tracks. They seemed to be talking to him and he tried to make out what they were saying – but the words were indistinct, and the game soon bored him.

He ran his hand over his belly and down to the fuzz of hair which had sprouted there over the past few months. It still surprised him to find it there, but it gave him a nice feeling when he stroked it and played with his thing. He flicked a finger over it and laughed softly when it bounced back, stiff and stubby to stand erect. This had never happened before when he'd had to make pee pee, as Lillian called it, and for an instant, he wondered if there was something wrong.

He touched it again, and decided that he liked the sensations that swirled and spiralled down into the hard little balls of flesh at its base. Such pleasant feelings couldn't possibly be wrong. He snuggled further into the blankets and began to stroke himself.

The door burst open and the room was flooded with light as Lillian thundered into the room.

'I know what you're doing, you filthy little beast!' she yelled as she advanced towards the bed.

Malcolm felt a warm, stickiness in his hand and the stiff little stalk shrivelled to nothing as Lillian flung back the covers.

'Dirty, sinful!' shrieked Lillian as she laid into him with

stinging slaps and thudding punches. 'That's the Devil's game. Touch it and you touch sin.'

'No, Mamma. I wasn't doing anything,' he whimpered as he twisted and turned on the bed to avoid Lillian's ferocious beating. His head buzzed, his ears rang, and fear was a living, squirming thing in the pit of his stomach.

Lillian ignored him and pulled the sheet from beneath him and held it up to the light.

'The Devil has made you spill your seed. Satan has opened up the path to your soul so he can dwell in there and make you his servant. See!' she yelled. 'The stain of evil. The mark of the Devil for all to see.'

She flung the sheet to the floor and leaned over the bed, her face inches away from Malcolm's as she fumbled in her hair. 'Play the Devil's games and you will burn in hell-fire. I must stop this before it is too late.'

Malcolm watched in awful terror as his mother pulled the elastic band from her hair and advanced on him.

'There's only one way to foil the Devil. Cast out the sin. Cut off the evil flesh so he can no longer play his filthy games. Let it turn black and rotten like the Devil's heart. Make it shrivel and die, until it drops off.'

Lillian's voice was rasping now, her breath rapid and uneven as she . . .

Malcolm screamed, and the scream echoed in his head and bounced off the walls, until it brought him back to the present. The sweat was cold on his face, icy down his back, running in rivers down his legs. The pain in his groin was overwhelming. It was as though it was only yesterday.

He waited for the pain to ebb into a throbbing ache, then turned from the room and slammed the door. His father had come soon after that and taken the elastic band away, but the agony had lasted for days. Yet he'd never forgotten his mother's words. Never played with his thing again. It had shrivelled up inside him, as though remembering the fiery torture, wanting to escape it.

Malcolm looked away as he passed Lillian's door. He had

Reap the Whirlwind

no wish to conjure up the memories that particular room evoked.

Hurrying down the stairs he went into the kitchen and picked up the keys to the lock-up. Dangling them over the still, bulky parcel that filled the space beneath the sink, Malcolm sniggered.

'Thought you knew everything, didn't you, Mother? Thought I was stupid and didn't know how to save my money? Well, you're about to get a big surprise.' He gave a harsh cough of laughter and left the kitchen.

The lock-up was two blocks away and Malcolm hurried along the streets, surprised at how quickly the day had disappeared. It was almost dark, but that didn't matter, it served his purpose. Pulling back the mouldering doors with their flaking paint, he breathed a sigh of satisfaction. Everything was as it should be.

The motor-bike and sidecar gleamed in the electric light, and as he switched on the engine and settled himself on the seat, he felt a sigh of pleasure. Lillian had never known about the bike, and yet he'd had it for years. It was the first thing he'd come to check on after That Place, and it had never let him down.

The engine throbbed beneath him, and the petrol gauge showed almost a full tank as he eased the throttle and slowly emerged from the lock-up. Leaving the doors open and the light on, he headed for home. He wouldn't be needing the garage any more.

As he waited for the darkness to settle and the outside sounds to dwindle, Malcolm pulled on the rainproof trousers and jacket. Then he sat down and drank the last of the milk before checking the string on the parcel.

When he was satisfied that no-one could witness what he was about to do, he fastened his suitcase on the luggage rack at the back of the bike, then returned for Lillian.

She seemed heavier and more unwieldy than he remembered, and he wondered for an awful moment whether she would fit. After what seemed like hours, he finally had her squashed in the sidecar, with the rain hood fastened tightly down. He stood back and admired his handiwork. No-one could see inside, least of all guess what his cargo was.

Returning to the house, he picked up the helmet, took a last look at the hallway, then stepped out into the drizzle. There seemed no point in locking the door, so he didn't bother. Station Villas already looked abandoned and the bulldozers were lined up across the street. Tomorrow everything would be gone, even the memories.

He swung his leg over the bike and switched on the engine. The developers were doing him a favour, he decided. This was a new start, and when he'd rid himself of Lillian, he could begin his quest for the unseen presence. Once that was disposed of, he could begin his life again.

He opened the throttle and, without a backward glance, left the street for the last time.

12

Paul Galloway had no idea how long he'd sat in the car, but he was surprised to find the street lights had come on and the day was fast closing in. Returning to the present, he listened to the rain hammering on the roof and watched it sluice down the window.

He was aware suddenly, of being very cold. Memories had the power to chill, to permeate the bones and numb the senses. Yet the past would always be with him, clinging to him with the ethereal tenacity of a shadow. It was those memories which had forged him into the man he had become. Those memories which had lost him a part of the day and imprisoned him on this lonely, country road.

Switching on the engine, he slowly pulled away from the kerb and headed back to London. The day had been a disaster and the rage that he'd felt hadn't diminished. It had merely grown steely and settled in a knot of heat in his groin. The memories of the past had enforced the anger, stoked it into something he could barely contain, and he found his hand was shaking on the steering wheel.

As he drove carefully in the slow lane of the motorway, he let his thoughts twist and turn, seeking a way to escape the situation he'd found himself in. Bill's rejection was only a part of the jigsaw, there were other things to consider. Deeper, darker things that crept into his mind and brought an urgency that he knew he didn't have the strength to ignore.

'Too soon,' he muttered. 'It's much too soon.'

Yet even as his words broke the silence, he knew he wouldn't be able to resist. Not now. Not after what had happened today, and the knowledge that tomorrow would bring its own set of problems merely enhanced his urgency. They were problems which he had little chance of solving – and he needed to feel in control.

Without conscious thought, Paul manoeuvred the BMW through London's one-way system until he reached the quieter, seedier streets that were off the city tourist route. The windscreen wipers hummed and the polluted rain left grimy tracks across the metallic painted bonnet, but he hardly noticed. He was looking for something else.

He slowed the car and inched along the road. Tramps in doorways ignored him and cowered out of the rain in their cardboard boxes and blankets of newspaper. Groups of youths watched him over their cans of lager with predatory eyes that swept enviously over the expensive car. A fat redhead in white stilettos swept back her coat to reveal cold, mottled flesh which had been squeezed into a miniskirt and bra, but she was not what he was looking for.

It was ten minutes later when he saw her. She was huddled in a doorway, her long fair hair wetly plastered to her thin face, her skinny frame encased in a tight, red woollen dress and see-through plastic mac.

Paul drew up, letting the engine idle. The window opened with an electric whine and they stared at one another.

She pushed, almost reluctantly, away from the door and approached the car and Paul felt the excitement grow as she leaned towards him. Her eyes were blue, her hair natural blonde. She had the face and body of a waif and it was difficult to tell her age, but he guessed she was barely seventeen. Just the way he liked them.

'Yeah?'

'Doing business?' Paul felt his stomach muscles tremble with anticipation.

'You ain't the law, are yer?' The vowels were flat, the words punctuated by the circulation of chewing gum as she eyed him speculatively.

'I have fifty quid says I'm not. You doing business or do I

Reap the Whirlwind

drive away?' Paul ran his thumb over the notes in his wallet, giving her just a glimpse of what she could earn. Not that he would pay her, but she didn't know that. He saw the greed flash in her eyes as she reached for the door handle.

'If you're buying, I'm supplying,' she said with false cheerfulness, and got into the car.

Paul swung the BMW away from the kerb as the warmth of the powerful heater brought her smell to him. It was a mixture of cheap perfume, cigarette smoke and damp wool. The knot in his belly tightened as he put his foot down on the accelerator. The erotic stench of fear would come later.

He glanced across at her. The skirt barely covered her snatch and there was a hole in her stockings, but nothing could diminish that air of childish innocence, that fragility which he found both exciting and abhorrent. They were all cunts, all asking for trouble. That innocence was just a veneer they plastered on like their make-up. All women were whores when it came down to basics, even when they called themselves mothers and wives. And they needed to be taught a lesson.

He pulled down the zipper on his trousers and released his cock. 'Suck it, bitch,' he growled, his voice rough with sexual urgency.

Perhaps this time he would find satisfaction. Perhaps this time he wouldn't lose the urge quite so quickly. The time and the place were right – as they had been before. It was dark and secret in the car – yet he knew the real test would come when he could feel the rain on his back, and smell the dank wetness of the earth as she struggled against him.

The girl dipped her head, her long hair fanning over his lap, and Paul gave a gasp of pleasure as her warm, wet mouth encircled him. Then he turned the BMW into a dark sideroad and headed for the river and the derelict warehouses that huddled beneath the railway arches.

As his breath grew ragged, and the whore's head pumped up and down at his groin, he switched off the engine. There was the sound of a train thundering overhead on its way to

Victoria, and his lips drew back over his teeth. This was an ideal place for what he had planned.

No-one would hear her scream.

*

Malcolm looked in the wing-mirror. The night had descended sooty black with a promise of more rain, and his was the only vehicle on the road to Brighton.

He hunched over the handlebars to get as much shelter as he could from the fairing. It was cold tonight, cold enough to give a person a glimpse of the grave-yard and that eternal sleep from which there was no escape. But he had to get as far away as possible from Hastings before the night was over.

Malcolm shivered as he glanced across at the sidecar. The bundle was merely a deeper shadow camouflaged by the weatherbeaten canvas and plastic of the hood. He had to get rid of it – and soon. It no longer represented Lillian, or any human form. It was merely a burden he had to dispose of before daylight. A burden that tied him to the old life – the life where Lillian was in charge. It was the reason why he had to find a special place to hide it. A place where it could moulder and return to the earth, leaving him free to follow the voices and the siren's song of the watching presence.

Peering through the misted visor of his helmet, he drew in his breath with a hiss and brought the old Triumph to a standstill. He had come to an intersection, and leading away from the main arterial road was a slip road which led to what had once been the city dumping ground.

His breath plumed grey in the darkness as he let the engine idle. This was his second visit in the space of a few days and already he could see a change. Soon there would be a massive bypass here, with flyovers and great sweeps of concrete thrusting through the fold in the Downs. The voices had proved correct. It suited his purpose to perfection.

With a snatched glance behind him, he was reassured that the road was still deserted. A bubble of excitement gurgled in his throat and his heart dealt hammer-blows against his ribs as he eased the bike and sidecar down the slip road. It was almost over.

The headlight danced over the ghostly mounds of broken rock and heaped earth as the Triumph jolted over the mud-strewn track. The stench of long forgotten waste permeated the scarf he had tied over his nose and mouth, but it was of little concern. Lillian would be at home here, he thought acidly. She can rot along with all the other garbage.

The powerful beam glittered on the tall wire fence that had been erected since his last visit, and he brought the bike to a slithering halt. This was not part of his plan. It was a deliberate attempt to stop him from disposing of Lillian. And that made him angry. With a sharp exhalation he twisted the throttle and followed the perimeter of the fence.

The bike skidded in the mud and the wheels of the sidecar jolted into a pothole and stuck fast. Malcolm climbed off the bike and heaved the sidecar out of the mud. Lillian was too heavy, she was making the bike unwieldy, and as the minutes passed, his anger grew and he cursed the voices for having led him here.

Then he saw an opening. Another slip road which had been hastily laid away from the main road for the heavy construction machinery. As far as he could tell, it led to the south of the old city dump, onto a minor road behind Brighton University.

The engine idled as he searched for any signs of life. Nothing moved. The heavy plant machinery stood like hump-backed monsters in the darkness, monoliths of a forgotten age, sleeping giants waiting for dawn to awaken them. Piping and concrete culverts were stacked in hectic bundles beside the workmen's huts, and as the winter moon showed its pale face from behind a cloud, the chalk white scars in the voluptuous curves of the plundered Downs shone with an obscenity Malcolm found irresistible.

He edged the bike down the slip road until he reached the most recent site of the land-fill, then he killed the engine and the lights.

Climbing off the bike, he sniffed the air, his breath leaving traces of ghostly vapour. Despite the overriding stench of the rotting garbage, he could smell the richness of the earth, and could almost taste the lushness of the downland grass that had been churned and flattened by the bulldozers.

Was this how it would smell at Station Villas? It was an idle thought and he shrugged it off. It didn't really matter.

With one final, lingering look of reassurance, he turned and walked around the bike to the sidecar. His footsteps crunched on the frost-encrusted mud, and his breath seemed loud and very visible in the silent gloom. The feeling of being watched was strong now and, although he glanced repeatedly over his shoulder, he knew it was no earthly presence.

He began to fumble with the rusted studs that fastened the rain cover. His fingers were clumsy with cold, sliding over the metal, rasping against the canvas.

'Oy! What do yer think yer doin'?'

Malcolm whirled round, the blood draining from his face, his heart thudding so painfully he thought it would choke him. Where had he come from? Why hadn't he heard him?

The security guard was merely a dark silhouette behind a powerful torchlight. The Alsatian danced at the end of a chain, its jaws snapping, a deep growl rumbling in its throat.

Malcolm eyed the dog with terror as he reached behind him and grappled with the studs that seemed to have grown too big for their holes. Realising he couldn't fasten them in time, he edged away from the sidecar, stumbled against the front wheel of the bike and grasped the handlebar.

'I just stopped for a leak,' he stammered. 'No law against that is there?'

The security guard advanced, the Alsatian straining at the chain. The growl had become a snarl and Malcolm could see the gleam of teeth against the dark muzzle of fur.

'This 'ere's private property. Can't you read?' The guard's voice was loud in the silence, rough with the sharp edges of a cockney accent. He advanced another few paces and shone his torch over the bike, then flashed it on Malcolm's terrified face.

'Pissing in yer sidecar, were yer? Could'a done that up on

the main road. Wot you really up to?' He came another step closer.

Malcolm swung his leg over the bike and reached for the keys. He couldn't have answered him if he wanted to. His tongue was cleft to the roof of his mouth and his Adam's apple bobbed spasmodically in his throat.

The dog strained at the chain, its front legs pawing the air, its eyes yellow in the gloom as it snapped and snarled.

Malcolm's terror increased. The keys weren't in the ignition, or in his pocket. The panic was raw-edged, sharp and painful as he searched the ground. He must have dropped them, or knocked them from the ignition in his haste to dispose of the bundle.

His frantic gaze slithered to a halt as he noticed the glint of the guard's torch on something beside the front wheel. It was the bunch of keys.

His gaze hitched between the Alsatian that strained to reach the sidecar, and the keys on the ground. They were out of reach and without the bike he had no other means of escape. He was trapped.

'Down, Sabre,' rapped the guard, tugging on the chain.

The Alsatian whined and snarled, but obeyed instantly, its ferocious gaze never leaving Malcolm as it rested its muzzle on its front paws.

Yellow eyes held Malcolm in a trance and for one crazy instant he thought he could read the animal's mind. It had scented Lillian and the smell of her made it want to kill him. Made it slaver in the desire to sink its teeth in his throat and taste the warm salt of his blood.

Malcolm went cold, immobilised by those hypnotic yellow orbs, powerless to protect himself.

'I bet, that if I opened this hood, I'd find a load of old crap you thought you could dump here.' The guard's voice was tight with menace as he bent to pick up the keys. 'Couldn't you wait for the city dump to open, then? Or are you trying to get rid of something you don't want anyone to know about?' The torch was lifted and the beam shone directly into Malcolm's eyes.

Malcolm's gaze followed the gloved hand as it cupped the bunch of keys, and he licked his lips as he tried to speak. But his throat had closed and he was capable only of an unintelligible croak. He swung back off the bike and took a hesitant step towards the guard.

The Alsatian leaped to its feet and bared its teeth.

Malcolm was transfixed. The full horror of his predicament was shadowed only by his fear of the dog.

'Sabre doesn't like the look of you,' said the guard cheerfully as he flung the keys into the air and caught them again. 'Neither do I. But it's too cold to be standing around arguing the toss, so fuck off before I change me mind and let Sabre 'ave you.' He threw the keys and they landed at Malcolm's feet.

The guard pulled the dog away as it whined in frustration and danced on its toes in an effort to reach Malcolm and the sidecar.

Malcolm scrambled in the dirt, found the keys and hurried back to the bike. Relief washed over him as he jammed the key into the ignition.

But the release of fear was short-lived. The guard had followed Malcolm and was now shining his torch on the sidecar. The Alsatian had found the opening between the studs and thrust its front paws under the rain cover and was whining with excitement as it shuffled its long dark snout towards the tarpaulin parcel that was Lillian.

'Here, wait a minute! Just what you got in there? Sabre's doin' his nut.'

The key turned and Malcolm opened up the throttle. Spinning the Triumph in a tight circle, he sprayed the dog and the guard with earth as he roared back up the slip road and out onto the narrow country lane.

He had to drive for several miles before he could stop and fasten the weather-proof cover, but his hands still shook and the copper taste of fear was bitter in his mouth. The voices had almost betrayed him with their silence. They hadn't warned him, hadn't told him how close he would come to being caught.

It was to be another three hours before he found the perfect hiding place, and by the time dawn sketched a cold white line on the horizon, he knew he had performed his task well.

'You're gonna fly, Mamma,' he whispered.

He stood for a moment and breathed in the wonderful, clean, cold air. The white cliffs shone in the dawn light and the wind carried the salt from the sea to sting his face. He had finished his task, now he could begin to live again.

His pale eyes gleamed behind the thick lenses and he raised his chin as the short hairs bristled on the back of his neck. He was no longer alone.

'I can see you,' whispered the voice in the stillness. 'I know who you are, and what you've done. You have to pay, have to pay, have to pay . . .'

He could almost see a face in the shifting, shimmering vapour that filled his head.

'Follow me. Find me. Come with me and know the truth.' The voice was a soft caress, drawing him towards it, making him look into the face behind the veil of secret malevolence.

What he saw there terrified him, yet he was powerless to look away, to move or have any lucid thought.

He stared into blinded eyes whose depths encompassed the abyss of horrors past and horrors yet to come, and heard the treacherous whisper from lips that were sealed for ever in that opaque visage.

Then the ethereal spirit dissipated like smoke, and he was left only with the whisper of its breath, foul on his cheek.

Malcolm turned and ran, stumbling over the rough terrain, tripping over roots and tearing his coat on barbed wire in his eagerness to reach the bike. He had to find the face behind the voice. Had to track it down and stifle it before it grew too powerful.

As dawn chased the shadows from the Downs, Malcolm raced inland. The fear dissolved as the cold wind blew away the stench of the image's breath and cleared his mind, and in its place came an excitement that made his heart hammer. The presence had revealed one of its secrets already.

It was female and uncertain of its power. Therefore it was vulnerable.

13

The inquiry into the series of murders had gathered momentum, and in the days following the discovery of Mary Funnell, over two thousand statements had been taken, and more than a hundred known offenders pulled in for questioning. All leads ended nowhere and because of this tempers were frayed and the mountain of paperwork was growing.

It had been DCI Stoneham's idea to go back to the beginning. To return to Crawley, to the site of the first murder. If they were to learn anything about the man they were hunting, then it was logical to return to the source. And DCI Williams was just the man to help.

'This is a nasty business, Jack. I got the files out when you called and looked through them. There are one or two things in there that you might find interesting, but on the whole, all leads ended arse upward.' He pushed the stack of files towards the Brighton CID man.

Stoneham read slowly through them and realised they told him almost nothing new. 'He's graduated to more violence since then,' he murmured when he'd finished reading. 'What can you remember about the main suspects for this first case?'

'There were three, and two minor ones. But as you can see, we didn't have enough to hold any of them. These two were brought in as a matter of course. Both were seen in the vicinity, but had confirmed alibis so they couldn't have done the murder. This one's boss came in to make a statement, and this lad was very young, and his mother confirmed his whereabouts. They were fairly slender options, but in a case like this, we had to explore all the possibilities.'

'Yeah, I know what you mean. I get the feeling I'm pissing in the wind on this one.'

Stoneham read the autopsy report, the short statements by the two minor suspects and then went on to the statements made by the other three. 'Where are they now?'

DCI Williams reached for the files.

'Herbert Sidney Lownes is doing fifteen years in Pentonville for two charges of rape and assault with a deadly weapon. I checked, he doesn't come up for parole for another three years, so he couldn't be your man.'

He paused and opened the next file. 'Michael Roberts was arrested three months ago. One of his toms turned him in after he assaulted her six-year-old daughter. He was refused bail, thank God, so he's banged up waiting for trial.'

'And this one?' Stoneham pushed the photograph across the desk. 'Doesn't look familiar.'

Williams leaned back in his chair. 'Magnus Erikson. Came up clean as a whistle, but I still have my doubts. We hauled him in and questioned him for hours, but his story was watertight and we couldn't budge him.'

Williams thrust himself forward and jabbed at the photograph. 'We had to let him go in the end, but all my instinct told me he was hiding something.'

'Why did you bring him in? He doesn't have form.' Stoneham riffled through the thin file, then looked back at Williams.

'I thought you'd ask, so I dug this out. Erikson didn't have form, because we couldn't pin anything on him at the time. Here, read that and tell me what you think.'

Stoneham opened the file and experienced a cold wash of horror. Here were the answers, not to the murder case he was investigating, but to something else. And maybe they were both connected.

'We're going to have to forget about lunch, mate. I need

to know everything there is to know about Erikson, then I've got to get back to Brighton.'

*

Daphne Phillips hitched up her bra strap and got out of the car. She wasn't in the best of moods, and the memory of her previous encounter with one of the tenants of Station Villas and the sight of what awaited her, didn't improve it.

A knot of workmen stood in the road outside number 27 shouting encouragement, and when they saw Daphne they sent up a derisive cheer that was mingled with cat-calls and whistles.

Daphne swept past them, but she was quaking with embarrassment. Someone would pay for this humiliation. And that someone was the skinny string-bean who had called her out to clear up the mess she'd made.

Patricia Jackson was hovering on the doorstep of number 27 and Daphne gave her a piercing look of disdain. Really, she thought, the girl was an incompetent. With that long, drooping skirt and untidy hair she looked a mess. Girls these days didn't know the meaning of grooming, and even less, how to comport themselves in public.

'Thank goodness you've come. I've tried everything, but the old boy won't budge, and the workmen refuse to help.' Patricia Jackson's earnest face was innocent of make-up, her soulful eyes glistening with tears as she hooked back the long brown hair and tucked it behind her ears in a gesture of frustration and helplessness.

'Pull yourself together, girl. Good heavens, you're supposed to be representing the housing department.' Daphne put on her most daunting expression and was gratified to see the girl cringe. Girls like her would never have been employed by government offices in my day, she thought smugly.

'Have you called the police?'

'Oh, no. I didn't want to do that. Mr Hodges is over eighty. I don't want to upset him.' Patricia sniffed and dropped her handbag as she nervously searched for a tissue.

Daphne Phillips gave her a scathing look. 'Upset him? The silly little man has more spunk than you'll ever have. I'll bet you haven't heard language like it. He's as tough as old boots and just likes making trouble. I'll soon sort him out.'

Patricia stood aside as Daphne hammered on the door.

'Mr Hodges? It's Daphne Phillips. Open this door, or I'll call the police. Do you hear me?'

There was silence behind the chipped paintwork and rotten wood. Then came the shuffle of slippers against linoleum and a shadow darkened the frosted glass panel.

'Piss off you old cow. I ain't goin' until I got someone to collect my things.'

Daphne glared at Patricia. 'Didn't you arrange for the removers?'

Patricia scrabbled in her bag and pulled out her notebook. 'He didn't say anything to me about removers,' she muttered as the contents of her bag fell on the step. After finding her notebook and turning endless pages, she looked back at Daphne and bit her lip. 'I forgot to contact them,' she whispered.

'Go and telephone now. Really, Patricia. I'll have to have a word with the director. I do expect some semblance of intelligence in my staff.' She bent down and pushed open the letter box. 'Soon have you organised, Mr Hodges. Miss Jackson has gone to arrange for a carrier. Shouldn't be long now.'

The bolt was drawn back and a pointed, lined face appeared from behind the door. 'Knew you'd sort it out,' Mr Hodges spluttered through his three remaining teeth. 'Dozy tart. Couldn't arrange a piss-up in a brewery.'

'That's enough of that, Mr Hodges. You only had to explain and she would have handled it.' Daphne had her doubts, but loyalty to her staff in front of the public was uppermost on her list of etiquette. 'I'm just going to check on next door, whilst I'm here. I'll be back in a minute.'

He shook his head. 'No-one there. Left last night.'

Daphne peered across the ragged hedge that divided the

houses and noticed that the front door of number 29 was standing ajar.

'But they can't move into their flat until this afternoon. Where on earth could they have gone?'

The irritation was growing, and she gave her bra strap a vicious tug. How on earth was she supposed to help these wretched people if they made up the rules as they went along?

Mr Hodges opened the door a little wider to reveal his ensemble of baggy trousers which were held up by ancient braces and collarless shirt which had definitely seen better days.

'He went on 'is own I think. Burned all his stuff and left late last night. Sounded like a motor-bike to me.'

Daphne stared at him, trying to digest the information and swallow her impatience. 'Burned . . .? What about his mother? He hasn't left her in there, has he?'

Mr Hodges gave a grin that exposed pink gums. 'None of my business, lady. Reckon you'll have to sort that one out as well.' He slammed the door and shot the bolt.

Daphne hauled on her straps, and turned to face the workmen who had advanced to get a better sight and sound of what was happening.

'Have you been into the house next door? Is there anyone there?'

A chorus of mumbled denials and much amused shaking of heads greeted this question. Then one of the men stepped forward and Daphne assumed he was the foreman.

'No point in going in until the old boy's gone. Can't start work with people about. Dangerous. What's the matter, luv? You lost someone?' He turned to share his wit with his mates and Daphne almost lost her control.

She hurried up the path to number 29 and cautiously pushed open the door.

'Hello? Anyone there?' Her voice sounded tremulous, almost girlish, and she despised her timerity, but after the experience the other day, she was wary. That Malcolm Squires had been a queer fish and no mistake.

The silence in the house seemed to close in as she stepped into the hallway. But as she made a swift inspection of the downstairs, she began to feel more confident. It certainly looked deserted and there was no furniture or carpets left behind. She looked up the stairs and hesitated. Did she have the courage to go on with this inspection?

'Don't be such a ninny, Daphne,' she scolded herself gruffly. 'There's no-one here, but it's your duty to check.'

Her sensible brogues rang on the uncarpeted stairs and her hand trembled as she pushed open one of the doors. It was a bedroom, bare of furniture, with no clue as to where the occupant had gone. She walked over to the window and looked down into the garden.

Hodges was right, she thought. That's the remains of a very big bonfire.

Puzzled, she turned from the window and made her way to the second bedroom. Had Mr Squires burned everything and left his mother behind? He'd been so positive the other day that he and his mother would move into the flat. Strange, very strange.

Daphne knocked on the door. 'Mrs Squires? Are you in there? Can you hear me? It's Mrs Phillips from the housing department.'

There was silence from the other side of the door, and it took all of Daphne's courage to turn the handle.

The room was as empty as the rest of the house, but as she stood there puzzled and angry, she noticed the signs of a hasty departure. Deep gouges showed white against the varnished floorboards where a heavy bed had been dragged out of the room. The door frame was also chipped and scratched, and at some point a dirty rag had been hastily wiped over the paintwork. A lighter mark on the wall was in the shape of a vast crucifix and there were stains of something on the skirting board beneath where the bed must have been.

Daphne shivered. Something was very wrong here, she could feel it in her bones and in the way the room seemed to close in on her. There was a smell, too. A strange smell, that drifted above the antiseptic that had been used to wash the floor.

She took a step into the room and switched on the light. The gloom of the winter day was banished and something in the corner of the room caught the outer line of her vision.

Daphne, feeling only slightly better now the light was on and it was obvious the house was empty, crossed the room and touched the thing with the toe of her shoe.

It took several more tentative prods and many moments before she realised what it was. But when recognition hit her frayed senses she backed away, her hands over her mouth, the scream erupting into the silent, claustrophobic room in a hoarse, reverberating wail.

*

Laura had woken early that morning, with an incredible sense of loss. The feeling was so deep, that as she opened her eyes, she realised she had been crying in her sleep.

She touched the throbbing cut above her eye and felt the bruising that ached in her throat. Looking over at Ben, she decided not to wake him. How could she explain the fathomless emptiness that filled her with a darkness that was more pitch than night? Or convey in words how the loss of her children and the destruction of her marriage had come to haunt, to torment her with a yearning to turn back the clock and begin again.

Creeping out of bed, she snatched up her robe and quietly left the room. It was wishful thinking to want to turn back time, but the feeling of emptiness, of abandonment and bereavement was almost tangible and she needed time to weep, time to mourn.

The apartment was still and only the ticking of the clock measured the passage of hours. As dawn turned into grey morning and the outside sounds filtered into the room, she reached out to them for solace. A few solitary gulls screeched above the trees and a lorry rumbled past on its way to the harbour, but despite their presence, they offered no comfort, and she felt more alone than she had ever done.

'Laura? What you doing up so early? You're not sick, are you?' Ben opened the curtains and perched on the arm of her chair.

Laura noticed he'd pulled on jeans and a sweater, but his feet were bare and his hair was tangled. She tried to smile, to hide the evidence of her tears, but she knew she hadn't fooled him.

'C'mon honey. It's time we talked. You've been avoiding the subject of David and Melissa for more than a day. Don't you think you should let it out? It can't be doing you any good at all to bottle it up like this.' Ben's words were soft and coaxing, but Laura could hear the impatience that coloured them.

He was right, she thought. I have been shying away from the truth. Yet, where to begin? David had opened up a Pandora's box and her one wish now was to close the lid firmly on the past. But that was the cowardly way out, she silently admitted. If she and Ben were to have any kind of lasting relationship, then she would have to tell him the truth about Melissa's 'accident'.

She tucked her feet beneath her and huddled in the corner of the couch. The emptiness was still inside, gnawing away at her resolve, but there was no escape, no excuse to delay speaking any longer. She looked over at Ben.

'You do love me, don't you Ben?' She licked her lips and twisted her hands in her lap. 'I mean, do you love me enough to want to stay with me, regardless of what I tell you?'

She watched him, examining every nuance, every shadow of thought that showed itself on his expressive face. She needed reassurance before she could say more.

Ben sat forward, his gaze holding her, a frown creasing his forehead. 'What kind a question's that, honey? You know I love you – will always love you, regardless of what you tell me.' He shrugged his shoulders. 'I've done things I'm ashamed of, but it doesn't make me any different to the man you see now. You will always be my lovely, fiery-headed Laura.'

He made no move to touch her, perhaps realising she needed

space and time to think, and for that she was grateful. Yet she found it hard to look into his eyes, afraid of what she might see there once she began to talk.

'I lied to you, Ben. Lied about what really happened to Melissa.'

'I guessed as much from David's malicious remarks,' Ben replied slowly. His gaze was unwavering as he put his hand over hers. 'Tell me if you want, but it will make no difference as to how I feel. You have my word on that.'

Laura felt the warmth of his hand and it gave her the added courage to face that Pandora's box and fight the demons it had exposed. When she spoke, her voice was calm.

'I have to go back a long way, Ben. Back to the very beginning.'

He nodded, and suddenly the tension lifted and she found it easy to face the past.

'We were living in Crawley,' she began. 'Clara was working in London, so I spent a lot of time on my own. David and I met at college. I was just sixteen and he was seventeen when we started going out together. He lived on the other side of town with his father.'

She took a deep breath and tried to still the drumming of her heart. It was all coming back and she could almost see that street again.

'David's father always frightened me. He was a giant of a man who ran his building company with a tight rein. His temper was legendary amongst the men who worked for him, but there were brains behind the brawn, and the business had done very well.'

She paused and smiled. 'I met his mother for the first time at the wedding. She seemed nice, but she looked defeated, and I suspect life with the giant had been hard and it had taken a great deal of courage to leave him.' She gave a sigh. 'David didn't say much about his mother, and I know he never went to visit her. I often wondered why.'

She fell silent and the only sound in the room was the ticking of the radiators as they heated up.

Ben didn't break that silence, the only move he made was

to light a cigarette and put the spent match in the ash-tray. But his gaze never strayed from her face, his concentration was absolute.

'What I felt for David was different to all the other crushes I'd had. It was as if we'd been waiting for each other. We were very young, but at the time it didn't seem to matter. Our futures were inextricably entwined and neither of us wanted it any other way.'

Laura took a deep breath. 'I suppose we were born looking for the same thing. Love and comfort, the reassurance that someone cared. I was lonely, Clara was never at home and I hated coming back to an empty house. David's father was either working or socialising and I suppose we recognised that need for companionship in each other.'

Laura fell silent as the flash cards of memory paraded before her. Their first date, first kiss. It seemed a lifetime ago.

'I found out I was pregnant three days before my eighteenth birthday. I'd played hookey from college and gone to see the doctor instead. He sat me down and told me I was three months pregnant – with twins.'

She looked up at Ben, trying hard to smile, to take away the pain of that memory.

'I waited days before I plucked up the courage to tell Clara. I expected a terrible row, or at the very least, to be thrown out of the house. But she sat and talked with me all through the night, going over the options, discussing my feelings on abortion and adoption. Never once did she raise her voice or lose her temper.'

Laura gave a cough of regret. 'I thought at the time how cold-blooded she seemed, how unmoved by the traumatic turn of events which were about to ruin my life. But I realise now that she did the sensible thing. My emotions were out of control, and I needed someone steady and reliable to put me back onto an even keel.'

She lit a cigarette and watched the smoke curl to the ceiling. She could remember that night so clearly, that it felt as though time had stood still. Her mother's face, drawn and pale in the electric light, her own fevered tears and dread for the future.

The surprising uncertainty of whether David would still love her, still want her, now she was having his babies.

'I was brought up a Catholic, and although we never really had much to do with the church, I was indoctrinated enough to believe that God was punishing me two-fold. But Clara would have none of it, called it emotional blackmail and said I was overreacting.'

She shot a look at Ben and gave a wry smile. 'Clara is very practical, she doesn't allow emotion to colour her judgement.'

'She sure is some kinda lady,' murmured Ben.

Laura nodded. 'Yes. I just wish I'd known that earlier.'

The silence was companionable and Laura was surprised to find dawn had come and gone, and now the sun was streaming in through the window.

'Clara telephoned David's father. I could hear him shouting and cursing at the other end, but Clara didn't flinch. She merely ordered him to bring David to the house for a conference. She has a way of getting people to obey her without raising her voice. David and I bore the brunt of his father's anger, but Clara managed to quieten him eventually and we spent the rest of that day discussing our future.'

Laura sighed and tugged back the heavy curls from her face.

'They left it up to us in the end. And we decided to get married. David only had another term to finish his A levels, and I could carry on with my hotel management training until the last minute, then complete the course afterwards. David's father offered to support us until David got a full-time job, and Clara said we could live with her.'

'I don't see what you're so worried about, Laura. I've heard lots of stories like this. You weren't unique.'

Laura shrugged. 'I know, silly isn't it? We were just two kids that got in a mess. But it's what happened later that changed everything.' The room seemed colder suddenly, the air around her thick with gloom, and she found it difficult to breathe.

'Come on, honey. Finish it. It won't seem so bad once

you've let it out.' Ben's voice was deep and reassuring and she looked across at him and gave a tremulous smile.

'Maybe,' she murmured. 'Wait until I've finished, then we'll see.'

Ben rested one foot on his knee and leaned back into the chair. 'I'm listening.'

'We got married in the local registry office four weeks after my eighteenth birthday. David moved in with me and Clara and we both carried on with our educations. It felt strange, sleeping with David in the room I'd grown up in. And with Clara only next door.'

'I can see it could have been a problem.' Ben's voice was soft, as though he was afraid to break the train of her thoughts.

Laura shook her head. 'It was fine. Clara didn't interfere and David and I were very happy. I gave birth to Cassandra and Melissa in the early spring. It was too crowded in Mum's house by the time the twins were toddling so we moved into a small flat in Ifield. As we had the twins, we were eligible for council housing.'

She gave a wry smile. 'Clara nearly blew a fuse, but I felt it wouldn't be right to ask her for help. She'd already housed us for more than a year as it was, and she had her own problems by then. Her latest marriage had come to a sticky end and things were rough.'

Laura looked down and realised she was picking at the skin around her nails. Clenching her fists in her lap, she stared towards the window. Here it comes, she thought as her skin turned cold. I don't want to tell him. Don't want to turn back the pages and go over the past again – but I have to. It must be finished once and for all. Put the demons behind me, and begin again.

'David started hitting me when the twins were eighteen months old. I was terrified of him, never having been exposed to domestic violence before, but I couldn't tell Mum.' Her voice faltered as she heard Ben's sharp intake of breath. 'I suppose I was ashamed, and in some way, could almost understand David's frustration. He was barely twenty years old, holding down a job in a factory because his father refused to employ him. "Learn to stand on your own two feet, boy," was what he'd said. His attitude was that we had made our own mess, so it was up to us to clean it up.'

'He had a point, but it seemed a bit tough on you both.' Ben's eyes were fathomless brown beneath his brows.

Laura shrugged. 'David knew he had to knuckle under and get on with it. The job paid well, but gave him little satisfaction, and he was saddled with a wife he regarded as too young and inexperienced to run a house and two small children properly. I gave up college, resorted to a correspondence course and did my best, but it never seemed good enough. Some days, I had to stay indoors and wait for the bruises to fade. I couldn't have faced my mother in that state.'

'Clara would have coped, Laura. It would have broken her heart to see you treated that way, but she'd have taken you and the twins and looked after you. Why the hell did you keep it a secret?'

Laura shrugged. 'Maybe it was pride – stupid, illogical pride. I wasn't going to fail in my marriage, like my mother. I didn't want people to know the humiliation I felt when David hit me. It would merely have confounded the dire warnings we'd been bombarded with at the beginning. Clara and I didn't have a close relationship, and it's only in the past few days that I learned she knew what was happening. Back then I considered myself grown up. I had to learn to take care of myself.'

Laura sighed. 'I was naive, stupid. David could be so sweet, so loving and gentle. So penitent. I always believed him when he said he was sorry.'

Tears dewed her eyelashes as she looked at Ben. 'If only we had the power of hindsight, how much easier life would be.'

As the silence stretched and the minutes ticked by, Laura was taken back to that small council flat on the edge of Ifield. She experienced again the sickening dread in the pit of her stomach as David's key turned in the latch. Remembered once more the hasty glance around the flat to make sure everything was spotless and neat, that her study books were packed away and out of sight. She felt the thud of her pulse as she prayed for the twins to sleep through the night. He was always worse after a bad night's sleep.

'Laura. Honey?' Ben's voice drifted into her thoughts and brought her back. 'You were miles away,' he said softly.

'Was I? It felt too close for comfort.'

'Perhaps I was wrong to make you drag it all up like this. You don't have to go on if you don't want to.'

Laura stubbed out the cigarette. 'No. I want to finish. I can't pretend it's easy, but it has to be done sometime, so why not now? After all, it's almost as if the clock has turned back and I'm faced with the same situation.'

She looked across at Ben and saw the puzzlement in his eyes. Would that puzzlement turn to dismay, or distrust? She would have to risk it, there couldn't be any more barriers to their relationship. Not after what happened with David yesterday.

'David finally managed to get an apprenticeship and we moved to a tiny house in County Oak, and for the next four and a half years we struggled to make ends meet. I went back to evening classes and got my diploma in hotel management. Things were a little better because he liked what he was doing, and with me earning as well, we could see a future.' She paused.

'Then the company he worked for relocated and they laid off most of the men. David had finished his apprenticeship, but now he had no job. There was a recession and even his father's business folded. It wasn't long after that his father committed suicide.'

Laura's voice dropped to a murmur. 'David was shocked by what he saw as the weakness in his father. He'd always been so strong, so forceful. For him to have gassed himself in his car was, to David, an act of cowardice.'

Laura shuddered as she remembered David's anger, his refusal to attend the ceremony at the crematorium. They'd been bitter days, days when she'd deliberately stayed silent and out of the way.

'I was the bread-winner suddenly. The job he'd scorned

in the big hotel was paying the bills and putting food on the table. He didn't like it. Things turned nasty. The day after the twins' sixth birthday, he lost his temper because he found cake crumbs in the carpet. I should have gone to hospital, but I didn't dare leave him alone with the girls. It was my day off, so they hadn't gone to the child-minder as usual.'

'He didn't touch the girls, did he?' Ben was tensed, coiled like a spring, ready to rush out and find the man who'd dared to cause so much pain.

Laura shook her head. 'He never beat them, thank God. I made sure he was never alone with them when he was in a black mood.'

She shrugged as if to make light of what was to come. Yet the darkness was there, the emptiness, the sense of loss and despair. 'As for me, I had a cracked rib, two black eyes and a sprained wrist. I also had a migraine that refused to budge, despite all the pills I took, and my sense of balance had been disrupted because of the punches he threw at my head.'

She tried to give a wan smile, but knew she'd failed dismally. 'I was a mess.'

'In Texas, we have ways of dealing with scum like him. The guy should be horse-whipped,' Ben snarled through gritted teeth as his hands bunched into fists and thudded on his knees.

Laura had a sharp image of Ben standing over David with a whip, and it made her shiver. Violence couldn't be beaten out of a man. It merely made him worse.

'David's father used to beat him and his mother. Another thrashing wouldn't have changed anything,' she said softly.

Ben rammed his hands in his pockets, but Laura could still see the tension in him, and feel the reined-in anger he was having difficulty in harnessing.

'Why the hell did you stay with him? There must have been something you could have done.'

'I wasn't brave enough then,' she murmured. 'I had no money, no place to go. Mother had just married again and was living in America. There was no-one to turn to and I didn't have the courage to just walk away with the girls and try to begin again.'

She paused for a moment. 'Battered wives don't make friends, they keep to themselves. It's a lonely life.'

Ben smouldered in silence, his heavy brows drawn in an angry, perplexed line. 'I wish I'd been around then,' he muttered. 'I'd have taken care of you.'

Laura glanced at him, but said nothing. It was a hypothetical declaration – it served no purpose. She lit another cigarette and stared off into space.

The sound of the doorbell broke the mood and Laura shot Ben a glance of dismay. She had steeled herself to tell him, now fate had intervened and she didn't know if she would ever have the courage to finish.

'I'll go,' said Ben swiftly rising from the couch. 'You get some clothes on before you freeze.'

Laura dragged herself off the couch and turned towards the bedroom. Ben was right, she was cold, and although the central heating was on, the coldness she felt was deep inside her where nothing could touch it.

'Laura.'

There was something in the tone of his voice that filled her with dread, and it took all her will-power to turn and face him. 'Cassandra? Is it . . .'

'It's the police, Laura.' Ben's face was grim as he stood aside and made room for Detective Chief Inspector Jack Stoneham to enter.

*

Daphne came to, and found herself lying on the floor of the landing surrounded by concerned faces. Rough faces that looked strangely out of place in the order of things. She tried to lift her head, but her senses swam and she fell back.

'There, there, missus. You've had a nasty turn. Lie still for a minute and you'll feel better.'

She looked up and realised with shame that she was being held in a burly pair of arms that were covered in coarse

Reap the Whirlwind

dark hair. The warmth of him, the strength and smell of him reminded her of Henry. He'd been a hirsute man, a man she'd loved with a passion until the day he passed away. Now she felt only embarrassment as she looked up into those concerned eyes of the foreman. 'Did you see?' she managed to gasp.

'Aye. I called the coppers. Should be here in a minute. Now you just lay still until you feel a bit more steady on yer pins. Reckon you had a nasty do there.'

Daphne struggled out of his arms. It was just too comfortable, too reminiscent of Henry, and she was afraid that if she remained there, she would disgrace herself further.

Pulling down her skirt and hitching at her straps, she patted her hair and made sure everything was in its place and respectable.

'Thank you,' she said primly. 'I'm quite all right now.' She caught the amused glint in the man's eyes and hurriedly looked away. She had made a fool of herself and no mistake. Now she just wanted to leave this dreadful house and get into the fresh air.

She made her unsteady way down the stairs and gulped in the cold winter air as she reached the doorstep. Mr Hodges was looking over the fence at her and she gave him a shaky smile. 'Soon have you sorted out, Mr Hodges.'

The police car turned the corner and ground to a halt outside the house. The two policemen looked barely old enough to have left school and Daphne wondered what the world was coming to when they sent boys to do a man's job.

The foreman came up behind her and put his hand on her shoulder. 'I think you'd better come upstairs. This lady found something horrible in one of the bedrooms. Me and the lads went round the house and there are one or two things you should look at. Something odd's been going on here and we don't like the look of it.'

14

Paul Galloway drove the BMW straight from the carwash and valet service to the rental office. Once he'd paid his bill, he picked up his bags and headed for the street. All the evidence of last night's events had been cleaned away and forgotten. It was time to get out of London. Time to make a deal with the people who would pay big bucks to get their hands on the Arab's plans.

'Good morning, Mr Galloway. Were you thinking of leaving us?' The voice was soft and tinged with the rhythm of the Middle East.

Paul clutched the handle of the case as he turned to face Hussein. At that moment he would have given anything to escape those piercing eyes which seemed to know his deepest, darkest secrets.

'Just returning the car,' he muttered unnecessarily. 'I was about to call you.'

The Arab smiled, but there was little humour in it and his gaze remained as penetrating as ever. 'Really? Now why do I not believe you?'

Paul straightened his shoulders and tried to look as coldly disinterested as he could, but his stomach churned and his mouth had dried. 'You have my word on it. My word as an Englishman and a gentleman.'

The Arab's lips twitched. 'An Englishman's word means nothing if he is not a gentleman, Galloway. And knowing what I do, I would not class you as a gentleman.'

Paul felt his courage drain beneath the other man's unwavering stare. 'What do you want?' he croaked.

'We need to talk. But we cannot do it here. Come, I have a car waiting.' Hussein gripped Paul's arm and led him across the pavement to the sleek limousine that waited there.

Paul darted an anxious look over his shoulder. The street was deserted. He had no choice but to obey.

The interior of the car was dark, shadowed by the tinted windows and black leather upholstery. The chauffeur was a muted figure behind a wall of glass, and Paul guessed that the rear of the car was sound-proof.

Hussein adjusted his suit jacket and lit a cigar. He offered one to Paul, but his throat was so constricted, he had to refuse. He would have choked if he'd tried to smoke now.

'So. Paul. You were not successful with Mr Boniface. What are your plans for completing our little assignment?'

Paul sat on the edge of the seat, the luggage wedged between his feet. 'How . . .?' Cold sweat beaded his forehead as he thought about the things that had happened in the last twelve hours. 'You've been following me.' It was a dull acceptance.

'Of course. We have to make sure those plans do not fall into the wrong hands.'

'How long . . .?' Paul wet his lips.

Hussein regarded the cigar smoke, a wry twist to his thin mouth. 'The girl was an unnecessary diversion. So careless – and messy.' He shuddered delicately. 'We don't appreciate you taking such risks, Mr Galloway.'

Paul nodded as he surreptitiously wiped sweaty palms on his trouser leg. 'It won't happen again,' he said quickly.

'No. It won't.' The Arab's voice was whip thin, sharp as a scimitar in the confines of the car. 'Because the next time we will inform the police and your career as the negotiator will come to an end.'

The silence was awkward, tinged with apprehension and menace. Paul broke it before his nerve gave out. 'I have had an idea about the plans, Mr Hussein,' he said defensively.

Hussein's hooded eyes revealing nothing of his thoughts.

'I will divide the drawings. It can be done with ease because of the size.' He pulled out the plans and laid them on top of his suitcase.

As he pointed out the way it could be done, he was amazed to find that his hand was steady and his voice sounded confident. He was thinking on his feet, talking, planning, making decisions an instant before he articulated them. Yet he knew he appeared calm and in control, and that gave him a sense of power.

The Arab nodded as he digested Paul's suggestions. 'It is good. You will organise the redrafting?'

'I'll see to it personally. It may take a little time, but by the end of the week I should be able to guarantee confirmation.'

'It is settled. But first I would like to show you something. It is a little reminder, a keepsake for you when the contracts are accomplished.' He pressed a button and the television screen flickered into life.

Paul stared at the grainy video recording. It had been taken the night before and although it was not of the best quality, there was no doubt about the contents.

'This is my guarantee you will do nothing hasty. There will be someone following you at all times until our business is completed. You would be wise to remember it. The police, I think would be most interested in your little . . . hobby.'

*

'I have no news of your daughter, Mrs Kingsley, and I'm sorry to call so early. But there are questions I need to ask you.'

The policeman seemed to fill the room and as Laura searched for some sign of what those questions could be, a cold certainty settled over her.

'It's about David, isn't it?' she whispered.

Stoneham nodded solemnly. 'We need to talk, Mrs Kingsley. And this time, I want the truth – all of it – without any hedging or prevaricating, however nasty it might be.'

'Hey buster. Where do you get off talking to her like that? She's the victim here.'

The detective whirled round to face Ben, his face grim, his mouth set in a line of white anger. 'You're free to leave if you don't like it, or Mrs Kingsley can make a statement down at the station. Either way, I want you to shut up and her to talk. Get my drift?'

Laura watched as the two men glared at each other. The day had taken on a sense of the surreal. This wasn't happening, not again.

'Well, Mrs Kingsley? Or should I say, Mrs Magnus Erikson?'

Laura slumped onto the couch and held up a hand to silence Ben's sharp exclamation. 'How much do you know, Detective?' Her voice had the timbre of surrender.

'Enough. But I'd like you to tell me anyway.'

His voice had lost the harshness and there was an understanding in his eyes that told her he wouldn't condemn. After all, she reasoned, he was a copper, there couldn't be much left in life to shock him.

'You don't have to tell him anything, Laura. Call your lawyer. Better still, I'll call mine.' Ben reached for the telephone, but Laura stilled him.

'Sit down Ben. I might as well finish the story I was telling you. I have nothing to hide. Not now.'

She turned back to the detective and gave a weary smile. 'It's a terrible story, isn't it? Are you sure you want to hear it?'

Stoneham nodded. 'Take your time, love. We've got all day.'

Laura looked up at Ben. 'David's real name was Magnus, but he hated it. He told me that when he was six he made his father an ultimatum. He would change his name to David or move in with his mother.'

Ben shot a look of malevolence towards the policeman and took her hands. 'You shouldn't say any more without a lawyer, honey. The cop will twist everything you say.'

'This isn't New York, or *Hill Street Blues*. I think

Reap the Whirlwind

Detective Chief Inspector Stoneham deserves to hear the truth. Although I doubt it will help find Cassandra.'

She turned to Stoneham and gave him a shortened version of what she'd already told Ben. Then she gathered the remains of her strength and carried on.

'David left the house about lunch-time that day. I told the girls to go into the garden to play while I tried to sort myself out. I kept an eye on them through the window, but by now, my headache was so bad, I could hardly see. I thought if I laid down for a while, I could get rid of it.'

She licked her lips. Her throat was dry and the air felt like syrup in her lungs. 'I must have fallen asleep on the couch.'

She lapsed into silence, remembering how Cassandra had wakened her, tugging with her small hands, crying because Melissa had gone to play without her.

'I woke up feeling worse than before, but Cassandra was almost hysterical with fury. Melissa had gone off, and she couldn't find her.'

Laura was transported back to that house in County Oak. Time went into reverse, but it did nothing to lessen the clarity of the images it brought.

The cold, bright sunlight of a crisp spring day flooded into the small sitting-room and sparkled on Cassandra's tears. Laura's head felt fuzzy, her eyes ached in their sockets and there was a knifing pain in her side. Swinging her feet to the floor, she sat up and tried to calm the child.

'Who has Melissa gone to play with? Did you see her go?' The sharp pain in her side had shifted. Fear was tangible, a living thing that grasped her heart and began to squeeze.

Cassandra shook her head, making her blonde curls dance. 'I was drawing you a picture and she went into the garden.'

Laura tried to keep the panic out of her voice, the fear out of her grip as she pulled the child towards her.

'How long ago, Cassandra? Can you tell Mummy on the big clock over there?' The children were learning to tell the time at school, but Cassandra found it difficult to grasp.

She shook her head. 'I was drawing for ever such a long time. Then I went to look for her and she was gone.' Her high, childish voice was interspersed with sobbing hiccups. 'She's a bad girl. She promised to play with me.' The mouth puckered as she stamped her foot.

Laura's mouth dried as panic set in. 'Do you know where she could have gone, Cassandra? Is there a special place she could be hiding? A friend she could have gone to see without telling you?' She tried to keep her voice low, the panic hidden behind a soft façade of gentle words.

Cassandra shrugged, her blue eyes suddenly unfocused, her words slurred as though they'd been dragged from the very depths of her conscience.

'Gone to see the rabbits,' she muttered. 'But they all gone. Nasty doggy ate them.'

Laura felt a shiver touch her shoulders and thread through her spine. What was it that Cassandra knew? When she was like this it was frightening. It was as if she was in a trance. But that couldn't be possible, she was only six.

'Cassie, darling. Where are these rabbits?' Fear was riding on her back, his spurs digging in, his hands tight on the reins of her crumbling composure.

Cassandra looked at her, her eyes clear as a summer day, innocent and wide as she popped her thumb in her mouth. 'Don't know, but I drawed you a picture,' she mumbled.

Laura snatched up the drawing. The page was filled with the figure of a dog. A brown dog, with yellow eyes and snarling teeth. At its feet lay a dead rabbit.

She gathered up the child and rushed into the garden. The back gate was open, Melissa's bike was lying on the pavement. There was no sign of the six-year-old.

Laura dragged herself back to the present, only dimly aware of the two men who sat so still as they listened.

'I spent the rest of the afternoon hammering on doors and looking in garages, sheds and gardens. I stopped people in the street and asked them if they'd seen a child who looked like Cassandra, but no-one had. I asked teenage boys if they had rabbits, or knew of someone who did. But to no avail. It was as if she had simply vanished.'

Laura felt the awful void of darkness begin to fill her.

Ben grasped her hands. 'Christ, honey, I didn't realise. No wonder . . .'

Laura barely heard him, was hardly aware of his presence. She was being dragged back to the past. Back to the worst thirty-six hours she had ever spent – until now.

'The police were very kind. They sent a young policewoman to sit with me and she took over. I was incapable of doing anything, except pace the floor and run to the window every time someone went past on the pavement.'

Laura stared across the room, seeing nothing but the images from that awful day. 'David came home very late and in a filthy mood.'

She could see him now, as clearly as if he was in the room with her. His hair was dishevelled, his collar undone, his tie askew.

'What the hell's going on here? Why are all the lights on and whose is that car outside. You got a man in there?' David's voice was slurred, he'd been drinking and was itching for a fight.

'I tried to warn him about what had happened, but the policewoman emerged from the kitchen before I had time to speak.'

Laura looked down at her hands, which were lifeless in her lap. 'His dark mood seemed to vanish immediately, but as the policewoman told him what had happened, I realised it was only a mask. Every time he looked at me I could see the accusation, the contempt and rage he really felt.'

Ben's hands were warm over her cold fingers, but she couldn't look into his eyes. Not until she'd finished.

'At midnight, they had to call off the search. Fog had rolled in and there was nothing they could do until morning. They took me and David to the police station for questioning.' Her voice faltered as she remembered the cold bare room and the stern faces of the CID officers as they questioned her.

'They asked me the same questions over and over again, until I was so confused and upset they hardly made sense any more. They asked about my injuries, about how I coped with motherhood and a job. But all the time I knew they suspected me of having done something to my own child.'

She lifted a pinched, tearless face to Ben. 'They thought I'd hurt Melissa.'

Ben's grip tightened on her hands. 'Then they didn't know you at all,' he said softly, shooting a fierce look of reproach at Stoneham.

Laura looked away. 'They had to ask, it was all a part of their job. But it made me feel dirty, guilty by association. After all, if I had been a proper mother, I would have kept an eye on Melissa, wouldn't I?'

Ben shifted beside her, and the detective chewed on his lip. But neither of them spoke.

'They let me go early the next morning, but David was still in custody for another twenty-four hours. They had reconstructed the day's events and David didn't have an alibi for the hours he was away from the house. They had found blood on his shirt cuff, and his knuckles were bruised. After seeing my injuries and confirming with my medical records that I was either very clumsy, or the victim of a sadistic husband, they decided David was the most likely suspect.'

Her voice dropped to a whisper. 'They even had me believing he could have hurt Melissa. He was perfectly capable of it, and he was in such a rage that day.'

'Had he?' Ben's Texan drawl was a whip-crack in the silent room.

Laura cowered in the chair, dragging her hands from Ben's clasp, closing her eyes on the images behind her eye-lids.

'If I even suspected he had, I would never have stayed with him. He was a violent man, but not a pervert. He couldn't have done those awful things to Melissa,' she said coldly.

She took a shuddering breath, but as she began to speak again, there was a strength in her voice and she felt the anger return.

'They found Melissa thirty-six hours later. She was lying in a copse of trees on the outskirts of the town recreation ground. Half buried beneath thick shrubbery, she'd been tracked down by a sniffer dog. She'd been beaten senseless and sexually abused, but was still alive. I made them tell me what had happened. I needed to know what that animal had done to her. Needed to experience some of the pain my little girl had gone through. It was the rage against the bastard who had done those things that carried me through the next few months.'

Ben dropped his head and she felt the tears warm on her hands. 'Oh, my God. Laura,' he groaned. 'Poor little Melissa. You should have told me.'

Laura cupped his face for a moment, then absently stroked his hair as she returned to that day when her life changed irrevocably. 'It was my fault she was snatched by some pervert. My fault she's suffering Post Traumatic Stress Disorder. If I'd not been so taken up with my own problems, I would have kept an eye on her.'

Ben's head snapped up. 'That's crap and you know it. If that bastard had been a proper husband to you, it would never have happened. It wasn't your fault he beat up on you.'

Laura's eyes were hazy with thought. 'Maybe,' she muttered. 'We'll never really know, will we?'

'Did they catch the pervert? Is he behind bars?' Ben turned to the silent, watching detective, but it was Laura who answered.

'The file remains open, but as the years pass, it becomes more and more certain they won't catch him. David was their chief suspect for a while and Cassandra was put on the "at risk" register. Over the next few weeks they questioned him repeatedly, making him go over his statement, trying to needle him into a confession. Every time a child was molested or a girl was raped and beaten, they would drag him in and hold him for hours.'

Laura leaned back into the cushions. She was feeling the pain of those weeks, remembering the cold anger in David's eyes as he struggled to contain the need to use her as a punch-bag. His punishments grew more insidious. Instead of using his fists, he began to question her every move, to criticise her clothes, her work, her ability to raise her children. He accused her of spying on him for the police, of making secret telephone calls and visits to the police station, often waking her in the middle of the night to interrogate her. It reached the point where Laura almost wished he'd resort to his fists again, because the damage he was inflicting was far more serious than bruises which could be healed.

'Are you all right, Mrs Kingsley? We could stop for a while if you like.' Stoneham's voice had a concerned edge to it.

Laura shook her head and gave a wintry grimace. 'If I stop now, I'll never finish.' She took a deep breath. It was almost over, and she could feel the weight of those memories lifting from her shoulders. It had helped to share them, been a kind of therapy, in a way.

'Melissa was in a coma for nearly a month. The doctors said her brain had been damaged by a particularly nasty blow to the head. Coupled with the PTSD she would never fully recover even if she did come round. My Melissa's a tough little cookie,' she said with a ghostly smile. 'She defied them by waking up. But she was lost in her own world and hardly ever spoke again. Her body healed, but her mind was impaired, and the epilepsy is only one of the ghastly manifestations of the evil he left her with.'

'Go on Mrs Kingsley. What happened next?' The detective's voice broke into her thoughts and pulled her back to the present.

'There was a murder. A particularly nasty one, which involved a very young girl, and coming so soon after Melissa's abduction they hauled David in for questioning. It was an impossible situation. The publicity was awful, and when it leaked out that David was under suspicion, we were hounded day and night by the press and the locals. We knew we had to move, so when the police dropped all charges, we changed our name to Kingsley, sold up and with the help of a large mortgage, bought this place. It was to be a fresh start, but of course no-one can walk away from that kind of trauma without being scarred. We had to see a social worker every month. Cassandra was on the "at risk" register until David and I were divorced.'

Laura looked away as she hugged her waist. 'David never got over the humiliation of being questioned and suspected of such heinous crimes. He never forgave me for letting Melissa's abduction happen in the first place, and he was a changed man – more bitter – more devious. If I had been older and wiser, less scarred by what had happened, I would have acknowledgd that our marriage was over.' She pushed back the heavy curls. She was feeling unspeakably weary.

She looked at Ben, then over at Stoneham. 'Is that why you've come today? Because Cassandra is missing and there's been another murder?'

The detective's eyes revealed the depths of pity he held for Laura, and his mouth was set in a grim line. 'Have you seen your husband recently, Mrs Kingsley?'

'He was here yesterday,' interrupted Ben. 'Can't you see what he did to her?'

'Mrs Kingsley?'

Laura lifted her chin. 'He was here. He'd been told about Cassandra and came to taunt me.'

'Do you know where he's living? Is he staying locally?' Stoneham had pulled out his notebook.

Laura shook her head. 'He didn't say. I have no idea what he's doing now, or where he's working. I'm sorry.'

'He was carrying a briefcase, so maybe he was doing business in the area,' said Ben grimly. 'If I'd had my way, he'd be sporting a bloody nose as well.'

'Do you have a recent photograph of him, Mrs Kingsley?'

'No. We only stayed together for a year after Melissa's abduction. I burned everything he left behind. I didn't want him tainting our future as well as our past.'

'Do you think he had anything to do with either Melissa or the murders, Mrs Kingsley? Any suspicions, or doubts?'

Laura shook her head. 'He didn't hurt Melissa, I'm positive of that. He was protective of the girls, and too enraged over Melissa's injuries. The blood on his cuff and the bruising on his knuckles was because of his punching me. The doctor proved that with a blood test.'

She paused. 'As for these murdered girls. I don't honestly

know. He's a violent man who enjoys using his fists against women. But I don't believe he has the courage to commit murder, let alone withstand the hours of questioning by the police without breaking down and confessing.'

Laura regarded him, her gaze steady. 'You see he was more of a coward than his father, and that's what made him violent towards me; I couldn't fight back, didn't have the physical strength. Against a man, against life, he was nothing.'

Ben took her in his arms and Laura knew in that moment, she had finally learned to come to terms with the devastation that had haunted her.

*

Malcolm screwed up the paper bag and dropped it in the wire basket nailed to the wall of the shelter. The sandwich was the first thing he'd eaten for hours and now he wished he'd bought a coffee as well. Despite the waterproof jacket and trousers, and the thick sweater and jeans, the cold and tension of the past twenty-four hours had seeped into his bones, making his hands shake and his spine rigid.

As he rested his forearms on his knees and looked out at the bright, sparkling sea, he was able to push the discomfort away. There were other, more pressing needs to see to. He had little money, and couldn't risk returning to Hastings. The fat woman from the housing department was too nosy, she would suspect something had happened to Lillian when they didn't turn up at the flat. Women like her didn't let things slip, they worried at it like a terrier until they had all the answers.

The brightness of the sun on the water hurt his eyes and he took off his glasses and pinched the bridge of his nose, pressing down hard, his eyes squeezed shut. When he opened them, he realised he was being watched by a small boy of about four or five.

They stared at one another for a long moment, then the child smiled at him, his face lighting up beneath the halo of fair hair, his eyes glittering with curiosity.

Malcolm smiled back, warmed by the child's innocent appraisal, his offered friendship that held no prejudice.

A shadow blocked out the sun and the warmth of the smile. He looked up.

A woman was standing beside the boy, her hand tugging at his arm. 'Come away, Sean. You shouldn't talk to tramps.'

'I'm not . . . I didn't mean . . .' Malcolm flustered.

The mother snatched the child's hand in a tighter grip and pulled him away. 'I don't know what Brighton's coming to when they let these people doss in the shelters. How many times have I told you not to go near them,' she said crossly as her high heels rang on the promenade. 'They should be locked away from decent, hard-working people.'

Malcolm watched the way her coat swung against her legs, and the indignant set of her shoulders as she pulled the child along with her. The little boy threw a bewildered glance over his shoulder, then he was gone.

His hands curled into fists and he stared out towards the water. That was how it started. A mother's influence, hasty words spoken without thought, prejudice seeded in the fertile mind that would blossom and grow over the years. The memory of Lillian drifted into his mind. Her influence had made him what he was, but he'd punished her and that was good. The innocent had to be protected.

He closed his eyes and leaned back against the graffiti covered wall. The weariness and tension had suddenly left him, and in its place was a strength, a certainty that it would all soon be over. The voices were talking to him again, drawing him in, showing him what he had to do.

'Follow the eyes. Follow the voice. Seek her out, seek her out, seek her out.'

Malcolm listened for a while, lulled into a sense of security, distanced from the events of the past forty-eight hours. The voices would help him find the presence behind the eyes that watched him. The voices were his only friend, the only thing in his life that he could depend upon.

'Come to me. Find me. I'm here, here, here . . .'

The sound of her siren song was compelling and Malcolm knew the wheels had brought her to him.

Snatching up his helmet, he walked back to his motorbike. She was close, very close. And she wanted him to find her. Pulling down the visor, he turned the key and adjusted the throttle. He had to head east, along the coast.

She was there, waiting for him in a big white house.

*

Chief Superintendent Chapman and DCI Stoneham faced one another across Stoneham's desk. It was late and although both men were tired and on edge, there was a sense of exhilaration in the detective that was caught by his superior.

'Why go to Crawley? They could have sent the files down by courier. What are you playing at, Stoneham?'

The DCI flipped back the pages of the file he'd brought back with him. 'Remember the missing teenager we thought was the victim?'

Chapman nodded.

'I thought I recognised the mother, and when I visited the hotel that first time I saw this photograph.' He picked up the glossy six by four snapshot and waved it in Chapman's direction.

'So? What's this got to do with the murders? I thought missing persons were dealing with her now.'

'They are. But you see this isn't the snapshot from the hotel. This is the one from the Crawley files.'

Chapman stilled, his torso rigid with anticipation.

'Go on.'

'This was taken ten years ago. Melissa and Cassandra were about to celebrate their sixth birthday. Two days later, Melissa disappeared. It was over thirty-six hours before she was found. She was alive, but only just.'

Chapman picked up the snapshot and looked at it. 'I seem to remember something of the case. It wasn't on my patch, but I know feelings were running high. Didn't the father have something to do with it?' He dropped the photograph. 'I still don't see what this has to do with the current murder.'

Stoneham grunted. 'The father was questioned, but there wasn't enough evidence to hold him. It was what happened four weeks later, that I'm interested in.'

'What are you getting at, Jack? Does this have a bearing on the case in hand, or is this just pie in the sky?'

'Let's put it this way, sir. Magnus Erikson never proved his innocence, and the file is still open on Melissa Erikson's abduction and assault. Four weeks later he was pulled in for questioning on the murder of twelve-year-old Karen Walker, but again there wasn't enough to hold him.' Stoneham took a breath. 'I've just been to see the mother and she can confirm that her ex-husband is in the area.'

The late evening silence in the building seemed to stretch and settle into an ominous cloud around them.

'Doesn't it seem a strange coincidence that he should be around at the time of his other daughter's disappearance, and the murder of Karen Walker? Now Cassandra is missing and Mary Funnell turns up dead in Saxon Woods. Karen and Mary were killed by the same man, I would bet a month's pay on it.'

'I thought their name was Kingsley.'

'It is. They changed it by deed poll after they left Crawley to come here.'

'Do we know where he is now?'

'No. But he's all steamed up about Cassandra, even went as far as turning up at the mother's yesterday and giving her a hiding. I reckon he's not too far away.'

Chapman let out a long, deep sigh. 'That doesn't mean he was in the vicinity two weeks ago.'

Stoneham leaned forward. 'We have a series of murders that have never been solved, and two children that disappeared at the same time. The one thing linking both these events is Magnus Erikson. I need to get his photograph and description in every police car, police station and beat copper's pocket. He has to be tracked down and brought in. I suspect Magnus–David–Erikson could answer a lot of questions. He's the first real lead we have and we dare not let him go.'

The silence settle round them as the senior officer's mind sifted the information.

'What do we know about this man, Jack? Can he be tied into the other murders?'

'He's a wife-beater, although Laura Kingsley never pressed charges. The day his daughter went missing, the MO had a look at her and diagnosed a cracked rib and concussion. She also had a black eye and bruising all over her body. Her medical records confirmed this was a regular event.'

The DCI had his superior's full attention.

'He's a nasty piece of work. There is evidence he forged Mrs Kingsley's signature on mortgage documents and after looking through the local files, I've found several complaints against him by women who claim he charmed money out of them and beat them up. None of the cases were pursued as the women were too afraid of their husbands finding out, or too ashamed to have been such fools. All in all, David Erikson is a ponce and a woman-hater.'

'That doesn't make him a murderer, Jack.'

'He's young enough, fit enough, violent enough. He's been in the right place at the right time for at least two of the murders and both of the abductions. I want to know where he was at the time of the other murders. After the marriage break-up he could have been anywhere. What work was he doing, who employed him, where did he live? There are too many unanswered questions. I need to speak to him. Give me the authorisation to follow this up, sir.'

Chapman pushed back his chair. 'You have the authorisation. But go carefully, Jack. We have to be sure on this one. Can't afford to make any more mistakes. Not after the débâcle of Miller. Any progress is to be reported immediately. We need to get this thing wrapped up.'

He left the room.

Stoneham leaned back in his chair and swivelled it to face the window. A lone sky-rocket hurtled into the darkening sky and burst into a blossom of colour. The bonfire-night festivities were starting early as usual. There were another two days before the fifth.

He picked up the file on David Erikson and left the office. Brighton CID officers could forget about sleep for the next few days.

15

The night had been a restless one, the dreams so vivid, they clung to her, colouring the dawn with shadows and voices from the past. Yet Laura knew the memories would fade, knew she had finally found the strength to push them away and look to the future.

She shrugged into her comfortable old dressing-gown and drew back the curtains. The sun winked at her through the bare branches of the wind-swept trees, giving her glimpses of its light, its warmth, its promise of the new day.

'Laura? You okay?' Ben drew her back against his chest, shielding her from the cold.

She nodded. 'I suppose you think I was wrong to stay married to such a bastard?'

Ben dipped his chin until it rested in the crook of her neck. 'I think you were wrong not to confide in Clara. But you did what you thought was right and you can't be blamed for that,' he said softly.

Laura turned within the circle of his arms and leaned her cheek against his chest. 'I was afraid you'd be appalled at the terrible things that happened. Afraid you'd think me weak. Thank you for still loving me,' she mumbled.

Ben tipped her chin with his fingers and looked deep into her eyes. 'You're one gutsy little lady, and I'm proud to have you love me. I'm not David, Laura. I'll never let you down, never knowingly hurt you or keep secrets from you.'

Laura drew back and studied his face. 'We all have secrets, Ben. Why don't you tell me the truth about your father? He's not quite what you led me to believe, is he?' She spoke softly, not wanting to break the moment, but needing to know the true history of this man.

Ben's expression hardened, then he turned away and pulled on his clothes. Tugging his dark hair into a loose ponytail, he avoided eye contact.

Laura crossed the room and grasped his hands. Looking up at him she could see the struggle of mixed emotions flit across his face. 'The truth can't be worse than I experienced. Let's clear the air, Ben. Start afresh,' she coaxed.

Ben hugged her fiercely, planted a kiss on her forehead, then just as rapidly moved away into the other room. He busied himself with making coffee.

Laura waited, but she could feel the tension surrounding him. It hung over him like a pall.

'Who told you about my father?' he said finally as he stared out of the window onto the carpark at the rear of the hotel.

'Clara. She ran into your parents on one of her interminable cruises. When she found out who he was, I suspect she gave him the third degree.' Laura kept the tone of her voice light, the last thing she wanted to do was make him withdraw into silence. She could see he'd been hurt, and she understood the courage it took to face it, to talk about it and allow the wounds to heal.

Ben grunted and smoked his cigarette. 'My father's gotten the tightest mouth in the whole of Texas. I doubt she learned much.'

Laura sat in the chair, feet curled beneath her. 'You don't know Clara. His reticence probably honed her curiosity and she began to dig. She knows about his business dealings and the property he owns worldwide. You forget, Clara has many fingers in many pies, there's not much escapes her. Especially a self-made man, rich from the Texan oil fields.'

Ben nodded, but he didn't turn from the window.

Laura wondered what was going through his mind. Doubt nagged her. Perhaps it would have been better to leave things as they were. If Ben was hurting from something his father had done to him, then it wasn't fair to pry and make things worse.

There had been enough soul-searching in the last twelve hours to satisfy the most voracious appetite.

She was about to break the uncomfortable silence, when Ben began to speak.

'Yeah. Black gold. My father's one of the richest men in the States.' His tone was scathing.

Laura was intrigued. 'Why are you so ashamed of his fortune, Ben? Why the radical, man-of-the-people politics and the downright disapproval of wealth regardless of whose it is?'

'Because money turns a man into something he's no right to be.'

Laura digested this morsel of invective, but remained silent. There was obviously more to come – and by the sound of it, the pain cut deep.

'My father came back from the Korean war with more money in his pockets than he'd ever had. He and Momma were married just before he was shipped out to the Far East, so when he came home, they were almost strangers. My eldest brother, Mikey, refused to go near him by all accounts, and it took a whole lot of persuading before he'd have much to do with him.'

Laura watched the expressions flit across his face as the sunlight caught him and held him, but she said nothing.

'Well, my father told Momma he'd met this good ol' boy in a bar in Laredo who had a plot of land to sell. Momma wasn't too pleased about that. She was a city girl, born and raised in Dallas, and now I was on the way and she didn't take too kindly to moving out into the boonies.' Ben gave a wry snigger, turned from the window and began to pace.

'He got the land dirt cheap, because no self-respecting cattle baron would have looked at it twice. It had little water, and only Joshua trees and scrub to give it any character. He settled down to raise his family and make his fortune. Seems this old guy in the bar back in Laredo had had a testing done for oil, but had run out of money and couldn't find anyone, apart from my father, who'd take him seriously.'

Ben gave her a wintry smile, before resuming his pacing.

'Seems he was prone to telling a tale or two when he'd been drinking. And that was most of the time. Jimmy Beam was his closest buddy by all accounts.'

Laura watched him. There was a restlessness in him, a tautness she'd never witnessed before. His Texan drawl was thickening, becoming more pronounced as the memories flooded back. She suddenly wished she hadn't probed into his past, but it was done now – too late to back away.

Ben seemed lost in his own world, his eyes misty with memory as he stared into those years of his boyhood.

'Momma thought my father had lost his mind, buying into such a hare-brained scheme, but she was not the kind'a woman to make a fuss. So she raised us as best she could and it couldn't have been easy. I was the baby, the runt of the litter, born long after the others, when she was already worn out. There were five of us in all, and she buried another three.'

Laura tried to lighten the mood, deliberately sounding cheerful. 'She seems to be reaping the rewards now. Clara said she was very elegant and beautifully dressed.'

Ben whipped round, his eyes dark with anger in his drawn face. 'That woman's not my momma. She's just some old gal my father married to make him look good. A Houston harlot half his age with dollar signs for brains.'

'Sorry. I didn't realise . . .' Laura tailed off, uncertain of how to react in the face of this uncharacteristic anger. When he resumed his pacing and the silence grew unbearable, she tentatively asked, 'What happened to your mother?'

Ben ground the cigarette into the ashtray, paused for a moment and gave a great sigh, as though the burden of memory was too great. His eyes were dull, and his hands shook as he jammed them into the pockets of his jeans.

'My father worked the land for twenty years before he struck oil. By this time, Momma was already an old woman, although in years she couldn't have been more than forty. She looked so thin and tired that we young 'uns helped when we could to put things straight around the homestead. It was a poor place, with unforgiving dust over everything, a roof that leaked and not enough room to swing a racoon. Water had to be brought from the stream that ran across the land, and it was only after five or six more years that he could afford the time and money to have a well dug.'

Laura tried to imagine what life had been for Ben all those years ago, but it was impossible. It jolted her to think how different they were, made her realise how lucky she'd been, and how ungrateful.

'Father struck oil and we thought it would be the beginning of a better life, especially for Momma. But apart from a few new gadgets in the kitchen, all his money went into digging more wells and buying more land. He was in the grip of oil fever and there was nothing we could do about it. By the time I was seventeen, he'd found oil in one hundred and forty-five diggings.'

Ben slumped against the wall, his shoulders hunched as if to protect himself from the memories. 'But he still wasn't satisfied. He left us to run the homestead and travelled to Houston where he built himself a sky-scraper to house his fancy offices.'

'Why didn't he take you with him? Surely he could have afforded to leave the homestead to a manager?'

'His mind doesn't work that way, Laura. He looked at us and it made him uncomfortable. We reminded him of his roots. Momma didn't scrub up too well after all those years of dust and heat and work, and besides she's sick by now, coughing up blood. The women in Houston turned his head and he decided Momma would be better off staying put. She could have someone to do the chores in the house and she need never worry about money or the medical bills. But he wanted his own life and that life was in Houston – without us.'

Ben hooked his thumbs behind the silver belt buckle and stared off into space. 'Momma died shortly after he left, and that was the end of our family. My two sisters got married and moved away. They never write. Mikey joined up and was killed on his second tour in Vietnam. My other brother, Jimmy joined the Marines and he was killed during a parachute drop over Phnom Penh. If Momma had still been alive they wouldn't have gone to fight. My father was the cause of their deaths just as surely as if he'd pulled the trigger.'

Ben gave another enormous sigh and shrugged his shoulders. 'Either way, I never forgave him.'

'So how did you manage to get a doctorate in fine art and art history? It seems such a strange thing for someone to do when they've had such a rough start in life. Didn't you ever want to follow in your father's footsteps?'

'I was good in school, top of the class, especially at art, and my mother encouraged me. We had to be careful though, my father thought painting was for sissies. After she died, I took the money she'd kept for our college fees and enrolled into UCLA.'

Ben gave a soft laugh, the tension seemed to have left him, and the restlessness was over. 'My father was so busy making money he never noticed I wasn't at home. I finished University and finally went to visit him in Houston. We didn't have much to say to one another, but I guess he thought I was just another hayseed looking for a job. He started to make plans to bring me into the oil business, but I told him I wanted nothing to do with it. I planned to go to Europe, to paint for a while in Paris and visit the museums and galleries in London before taking my PhD.'

'I bet that didn't go down too well.' Laura smiled.

Ben grinned back, suddenly looking young and handsome despite having almost reached his fortieth birthday.

'He was fit enough to be tied. Boy, you should have seen him jumping and swearing and carrying on. It was the best vengeance I could have wrought on the old bastard. He tried to make me feel guilty by saying I was his only living son, therefore I had a duty to follow him into the business. He even accused me of being gay – probably because I'd gone to art college and lived in California. But I wasn't having any of that. He'd killed our mother, and as far as I was concerned he was welcome to his life as long as he left me out of it. The upshot was, he cut me off without a red cent. But I was happy with that. I wanted nothing to do with his blood money.'

He turned to Laura and pulled her from the couch and

Reap the Whirlwind

into his arms. 'What you see is what you get, honey. I'm no rich boy with Texas millions. Just a poor guy from the boondocks who got himself an education. Still want me?'

Laura leaned into him. 'Yes,' she said simply. 'Just promise you won't dig for oil in the hotel carpark.'

They held each other and began to laugh. It grew until the tears ran and their sides ached. It was cleansing, that laughter, fulfilling and promising for the future.

*

Malcolm let the motor-bike idle as he looked at the hotel. The voices had drawn him to this place, had taken his mind and tugged until he'd obeyed. Now he was here, he didn't know what to do. What significance did it have in the course of things? Who would he find behind that grand façade and elegant gardens?

The voices were murmuring, cajoling, urging him to walk up that path and find the source of the watching eyes. Yet he was suddenly afraid. How much power did the watcher have? Did she know the secrets of his mind, could she draw his energy and will from him without his knowing?

The wind was bitter and salt-laden as it swept in from the sea and the gulls mournful cries made him uneasy. It was as if the souls of the dead had come to join in the chorus of voices that filled his head.

Pulling down the visor, Malcolm opened up the throttle and moved away from the kerb. He followed the road and turned off down the lane which led to the carpark at the back of the hotel. All was quiet, the place appeared to be deserted.

He sat for a while and regarded the empty windows that seemed to be watching him. Was she inside, could she see him, or was she just in his mind, taunting him, drawing him into her web of deceit like Lillian?

'Can I help you?'

Malcolm started as the voice bellowed above the growl of the bike.

'Have you come about the job?'

Malcolm looked up at the enormous man in the chef's whites and nodded. The voices had led him to her. The voices had known he was needed here. It was an omen. He switched off the bike and took off his helmet.

'You'd better come in. Did the agency send you?'

Malcolm shook his head, he would have to think fast, but the voices were making it difficult to concentrate through their chattering.

'I saw it advertised in the job centre, so I thought I'd just come up and see if it was still vacant,' he stammered.

'Kitchen or coffee lounge?' The chef had closed the door behind them and was now leading him into the familiar chaos of the vast kitchen.

Malcolm swallowed. 'Kitchen.' He was lost if the job entailed any kind of cooking, but it was a good chance to get inside the place where she was hiding and he knew he had to make the most of it.

'I am Mr Edward and I run my kitchen the same as I did in the London Savoy. No spitting, no swearing, punctuality is vital and I don't hold with gossiping on duty.' He raised one heavy eyebrow and glared down at Malcolm. 'What experience have you had?'

'I've worked in kitchens for the last five years. Various hotels, all over the south coast.' Malcolm could feel the perspiration trickle down his ribs. Things were going too fast for him to control them.

'References?'

'I can get them,' Malcolm lied.

The chef nodded. 'What's your name, by the way? You didn't tell me.'

'John Smith,' said Malcolm hastily and regretted it the minute it was out. What a stupid name to come up with. If only the voices would shut up for a minute and let him think.

'When can you start, John Smith?' The chef's eyebrows had shot up and his piercing glower rooted Malcolm to the floor.

'Straight away. I have everything with me.'

'Where did you say you saw the vacancy advertised?'

Malcolm swallowed. 'At the job centre. This is the hotel that wants a kitchen porter, isn't it?'

The chef nodded slowly, his gaze unwavering, then turning away, he reached for the notice-board and slapped a sheet of paper into Malcolm's hand.

'This is the kitchen rota. Stick to it and give me no trouble and the job's yours. Miss one morning without a damn good reason and you'll be sacked immediately. Tardiness is punished with fines, and sloppy work is dealt with swiftly. It's amazing how quickly you people learn by having to do the same thing over and over until it's right.'

Malcolm stuffed his hands in his pockets to stop them shaking. He was in the same house as the presence. He could feel her in the walls and in the air. The voices had brought him here, they would tell him when it was right to make his move.

'We have only limited facilities for staff accommodation, so you will have to find somewhere for yourself. There are plenty of bed-sits in Saxonbridge. Find something today and come into work first thing in the morning.' The chef turned on his heel and began to oversee the preparation of vegetables.

Malcolm hovered for a moment, then realising the chef had probably forgotten his existence, scuttled out of the kitchen and returned to the bike. As he manoeuvred the bike in a wide arc around the carpark, he glanced into one of the windows and saw a face.

It was a face he'd have recognised anywhere. A face from the past that brought back the memory of something that had happened a long time ago, and with that memory came the sound of the wind moaning in the trees.

The surprise and fear made him tremble. The voices had to be mistaken. This couldn't be the face behind the presence. Couldn't possibly be the power that had drawn him to this place. Yet, if it was, then it would take him full circle.

*

The wonders of modern technology had taken the original photograph of Magnus Erikson and with the aid of computer enhancement, aged it. The handsome face had been softened at the edges, shadows added around the eyes, the jaw line less defined. Laura Kingsley had approved the changes and now it was winging its way to every police station in the country. Someone somewhere would recognise him, but the DCI in charge of the investigation still held the belief that his quarry remained in Sussex. If he hadn't abducted his daughter then he would stick around until she turned up. The other possibility was unlikely, but they were dealing with the unknown, and if Erikson had killed his daughter, then he could be anywhere. That was a scenario none of them wished to consider. The case was tangled enough, without any more complications.

Things had taken a different turn that afternoon, but one that was unexpected and could have caused more problems than it was perhaps worth. Yet, as strange as it was, it still had to be considered.

PC Giddings, the station house wag had been doing the usual rounds of psychiatric hospitals and sheltered accommodation for the dispossessed mental patients that flooded the already overworked local council. As an after-thought, he had called into the private nursing home which nestled in a fold of the South Downs and had had a long and interesting chat with a rather attractive student nurse. Giddings was good at getting information from pretty girls.

He faced his superior, uncertain how his information would be received. Stoneham was not a man to mess with.

'Student Nurse Ling said one of the patients has been drawing strange pictures which all show rows of eyes. She also said that sometimes, this patient talks about a fox chasing her and dead rabbits.' He stuttered to a halt when he saw the look in his boss's eye.

Stoneham leaned forward, his fingers steepled to his mouth. 'So this Student Nurse Ling thinks one of her patients is psychic, does she? Now I've heard it all. And how did this lovely Miss Ling find out about the fox? It couldn't have been from a young, besotted policeman, could it?' His voice became sharp, his back rigid.

Giddings shuffled from one foot to the other and had the grace to blush a deeper red. 'It sort of slipped out, Guv. But it got her to talk, and she would be in trouble if anyone found out, so I don't think she could have been lying.'

Stoneham's voice was loud in the ensuing silence. 'When I want to bring in a medium, Giddings, I will do so from the hundreds that are supposedly sane. When I resort to talking to the mentally sick, then it really will be time for me to hang up my truncheon. There's a vast difference between psychiatric and psychic. If you didn't know that, go and look it up in a dictionary.'

Giddings shut his notebook and pocketed it. 'Just thought you'd like to know,' he muttered. 'Can I go home now, I've been on my feet for over twenty-four hours.'

'Yeah. Push off, young Giddings. And don't get too downhearted. We can all get carried away by a pair of flashing eyes and a short skirt.'

Stoneham was a man who believed in plain thinking and plain speaking. He knew that other sections of the force had called in mediums to help with a particularly baffling case, and whether by luck or judgement had managed to get a good result. But as far as he was concerned it was all a lot of eye-wash. He'd solved hundreds of cases without the help of a raving lunatic who thought they could see things in the ether. He'd do this the old-fashioned way. Mediums and seers and those that see things in the shadows were all right for the television. This was real life. It was sordid and violent and not very pleasant to live with, but it was all he had.

*

Paul had chosen the location of the hotel deliberately. It was only a short taxi ride away from Heathrow Airport. The man following him would have to make only one mistake and Paul would be on the next plane out of here. Things were closing in, becoming too charged with danger for it to be worth his while any more.

Tamara Lee

The day was drawing to a close and Paul heaved a sigh of relief as he finally shut the door to his room. It had been a long, tiresome day, one in which he'd been made very aware of his follower, and after the lack of sleep the night before, he should have been ready for bed. Yet the adrenalin surged and his mind ticked over the possibilities for escape. His shadow had made no attempt to hide, in fact the man was in the bedroom opposite, the door ajar, watching and waiting for Paul to make a move. It merely added spice to an already exciting, frightening scenario.

'You can't go without sleep for very long, you bastard,' he hissed as he pulled off his tie and loosened his collar. 'Sooner or later you're going to slip up – then I'm out of here.'

He gave a feral grin and changed into a pair of slacks and a loose sweater. His quick thinking had saved the day earlier on, and he was confident his luck would hold.

The best part of the day had been spent in taxis. Paul had gone from one porno cinema to another, taking great delight in seeing the Arab's discomfort. He made a pretence of telephoning factory owners and making bogus appointments, but in reality, he was ringing the speaking clock.

Paul sniggered as he thought of the plans in his briefcase. He had no intention of changing them, they were worth far too much to the right people. When he made his escape, they would go with him. They were his collateral.

Feeling confident and very pleased with himself, he tugged the pillows away from the bedspread and rested back on them as he reached for the telephone. Before he switched to the adult channel, he would watch the news and call room service. He could have asked for a girl to be sent to his room, but he didn't really feel like it – not after last night.

His hand stilled, and his confidence plummeted as the telephone rang. It had to be Hussein. No-one else knew he was here.

'Yes?'

'Have you seen the news, Mr Galloway?' The Arab's voice was distorted and Paul realised he must be calling from his limousine.

Reap the Whirlwind

'No. I haven't got time for television. There are plans to be redesigned, remember?' Paul realised his tone was abrasive, but it was the only way to camouflage his nervousness.

'Do you have a television in your room?'

Paul gave a nervous laugh. 'Of course.'

'Then I suggest you turn it on. There is something in the local London area news that should interest you.'

Paul scrabbled for the remote control and made several attempts at pressing the button before he was successful. His breath caught, and when he recovered enough to speak, his words were rasping and hesitant.

'You promised . . . You said . . .'

'This is not my doing, Mr Galloway. We did all we could to hide your little indiscretion, but obviously something must have gone wrong. I thought you should know that Hussein does not break his word. The contracts are very important to us, and we do not wish to jeopardise them, that is why our little keepsake will remain a secret until your work is finished. Take care, Mr Galloway, for we can no longer guarantee your safety.'

Paul stared at the television screen, only vaguely aware of the Arab breaking the connection. As the newsreader finished the item and the screen was filled with weather charts, he dropped the receiver and pushed his way up the pillows.

When he tried to light a cheroot, his hand shook so badly it took a while before he could draw the smoke into his lungs. Hussein had no reason to lie, and Paul knew the Arab had been telling the truth when he said things had been taken care of. Yet moments ago there had been graphic colour photographs of the girl filling the television screen.

There could be only one explanation. Someone else had been under those arches last night. Someone else had hidden in the shadows, their movements muffled by the roar of the overhead trains as they witnessed the events which had brought him to this room. And that someone had gone to the police.

Paul chewed on the cheroot, his heart hammering, his palms slick. He had to find a way out. Had to slip past his minder and somehow reach Heathrow. But before that, he would need to change his appearance, for whoever had gone to the police about the girl might have seen him, and he couldn't risk the danger of arrest.

He climbed off the bed and began to move restlessly around the room. There were things from his past that were best buried. Things which could send him to prison for a long time if they caught up with him. The smoke from his cheroot burned his throat as the thoughts whirled in his head. The events of the past few weeks were closing in and soon there would be no escape. There was no more time to waste.

*

Malcolm was restless. He'd found a room easily enough in one of the tall Victorian houses that lined the back streets of Saxonbridge, but the urge to prowl in the darkness and to return to the hotel was too great for him to control.

Letting himself out of his room, he pocketed the key and hurried downstairs. Once out in the open he breathed in great gulps of the salty air and felt instantly better. The atmosphere in the room had closed in on him, bringing with it the reminders of years of its inhabitants. Ancient rings scoured into the table from an endless succession of hot mugs, damp in the walls, unsavoury stains in the carpet and burns from cigarettes in the furniture. The mattress was worn and lumpy and there were marks on it that Malcolm found repellent. He'd taken the mattress off the bed and rolled it up and stuffed it in a cupboard. He couldn't possibly have slept on such a disgusting thing, not knowing what those stains represented.

As he moved slowly along the pavement, he looked up at the buildings that towered above the road. Nothing moved, and no lights shone from those windows, but then, it was very late. It was as if he was the only person awake. The only person left in this small seaside town to witness the silence and the stillness.

The pleasure in his freedom made his step lighter. He couldn't have walked the streets like this when Lillian was waiting for him at home. There would be no more pills, no more ranting and raving and endless questions when he returned to his room. He was free to do what he wanted, when he wanted and the power that thought gave him made him feel invincible.

Reaching the bottom of the hill, he realised he had a good view of the harbour. The tall lights that illuminated the docks were surrounded by the silvery flutter of birds that had been fooled into thinking it was daytime. They looked magical, flitting against the dark sky, their wings dusted with silver as they caught the light beams.

He stood entranced, watching them wheel in and out of the darkness. He thought back to the dust motes in the rays of sunlight on the kitchen floor at Station Villas. Perhaps there was magic after all. These birds seemed to prove it.

'Come to me. Find me. Catch me if you can. I can see you. See you. See you.'

Malcolm sniffed the air, his senses honed to the slightest of sounds, his hackles rising as the voice sang its lullaby. He closed his eyes, willing the voice to continue, almost daring it to grow louder and to reveal itself.

'Almost there.' It was a whisper in his head.

Malcolm began to sway as the hypnotic voice recited its mantra. 'Show me,' he murmured.

'Chase you down, turn you in. Lock you away. Lock you away. Run, Malcolm, run.' The wheels began to chatter, quickening their pace, smothering the sibilance of the presence's voice until it was lost in the rattle of iron rolling on iron.

Malcolm put his hands over his ears and turned away from the harbour. The voices of the wheels were constant now, chattering, whispering, confusing him with their distorted logic, and conflicting instructions. Drowning the gentle whisper that lured him to the answers. Driving him, for ever driving him to . . . what?

He stumbled into the shrubbery that surrounded the rear entrance to the hotel. He had to make them stop.

'Put you away. Put you away. They're coming to get

you. Coming to get you. Run away. Run away. Run away.'

The darkness closed in as the voices screamed in the tunnels of his mind and roared over their ghostly tracks.

He trembled in the thick cover of the greenery and cowered from them. There was menace in the voices of the wheels, their comfort and constancy had turned malicious and greedy. Eating away at him, pecking at the tender, raw edges of his sanity. Yet he mustn't let that be. He knew what happened when he lost control. Knew what they did to him when they locked him away. He had to find a way to block them out. A way to escape from their torment and reach the soft sibilance of the temptress whose voice drew him ever onward.

A light went on in the annexe window and he cowered into the shelter of the shrubbery, his heart hammering against his ribs, his eyes blinking rapidly behind the thick lenses of his glasses.

'Danger, danger,' screamed the wheels.

'Come and find me. You're getting cold. Seek me out, look towards the north.' The other voice was soft and insistent, compelling in its gentleness. 'Follow me, follow me, follow me . . .'

Malcolm's myopic gaze was drawn to the woman who closed the curtains and shut out the square of light. The voices mumbled and grumbled, hissed and whined, but he refused to listen and they subsided enough for him to think clearly. He was near the end of his quest. But this woman was not the one who whispered in his mind and watched from the ether, she was merely the guide, the sign post.

He squatted in the soft, damp earth beneath the rhododendrons, his gaze pinned to those drawn curtains and the light that glistened where they didn't quite meet. The voices had led him here and he would have to follow her until she took him to the one that murmured such beguiling words in his head.

*

Reap the Whirlwind

Dudley Furminger leaned back in the chair and rested his feet on the shelf beneath the reception desk. He was tired and he was bored, this was no way for a man of twenty-two to spend a Friday night. He should be out with the lads sinking a few pints and screwing the arse off that little brunette from social sciences that he'd had his eye on for the past three weeks. She'd been giving off all the right signals, and if he played his cards right, he reckoned he'd cracked it.

The eight-hour shift stretched out in front of him in a procession of empty hours that should be filled with study, yet he knew it wouldn't happen. The night portering job at the Wilton House Hotel had seemed like a good idea at the time, but now he wasn't so sure. Burning the candle at both ends like this was beginning to tell, and things were catching up on him.

He grimaced as he thought of his tutor's angry face that morning when he'd been caught asleep in the University library. One more warning and he could kiss goodbye to the degree he'd worked so hard for over the last two years. Doctor Rice hadn't minced words, he'd be out on his ear if he missed one more lecture.

He sighed and flicked open the electronics text book. The tightly printed page danced in front of his bleary eyes and he had to make a conscious effort to concentrate. It was all right for Rice to go ballistic, but in his day students probably got decent grants and could afford to spend their time studying or screwing.

'I bet the old bastard didn't have to sit around hotel lobbies to earn a crust,' he muttered as he picked up a pen and began to work out an equation for an electrical power source.

Dudley was deep into the mathematical problem when he heard the whine of the lift motor. He looked up at the clock and was surprised that anyone was about at this unearthly time of the morning. The weariness and the boredom were washed away by the thought that perhaps someone was trying to leave without paying. It would make a change to even speak to anyone during his long night shift, but if it meant a bit of aggro, well, he was in the right mood for it.

He watched the numbers descend and waited for the

doors to open, the electronics book forgotten on his lap, the mathematical problem set aside.

When the man stepped out of the lift, Dudley was on his feet. It was the guy from room 405. The one that had booked in late last night, a few moments before the Arab who'd asked all the questions and insisted on a room opposite 405. He hadn't liked the look of either of them and he was sure something was going on between them. Still, the man wasn't carrying any luggage so it didn't look as if he was doing a runner. What he and the Arab got up to was none of his business.

'Can I help you, sir?' His voice sounded loud in the stillness of the hotel lobby and he squared his shoulders to give off the impression that he wouldn't stand any nonsense. If the bloke was a poof, and the Arab had made him suspicious, then he wanted none of it.

'Is there an all-night chemist close by?'

Dudley gave him a quick once-over. Tall, blonde, with a good tan that didn't quite mask the faded scars on his cheek, he guessed he was about forty. The suit was expensive, the gold watch on his wrist the real McCoy, yet there was something in his demeanour, something shifty in his eyes that Dudley couldn't quite pin-point.

'Turn right out of the doors, then left at the next crossroads. There's a corner shop that's open all night, but I don't know if they do chemist stuff,' he said quickly as his gaze returned to those cold blue eyes, Probably run out of condoms or after another jar of vaseline, he thought disgustedly.

Without a word of acknowledgement, the man turned away and headed for the front door.

Dudley followed him and found the appropriate key to unlock it. The owner of the hotel had been very definite about keeping the doors locked at night. He'd been caught once too often by the chancers who used the hotel as their private knocking shop.

The man from room 405 pushed past him and strode off down the road. Dudley watched him for a moment, lost in thought, and was startled when the soft voice behind him said, 'Excuse me.'

Dudley whirled round, his heart banging a rapid tattoo against his ribs. The bastard must have moved quietly for him not to have heard anything, he thought as he stepped aside and let the Arab pass. He watched the Arab follow the man from room 405 until he disappeared around the corner.

'Curiouser and curiouser,' he muttered. 'Whatever those two are up to has got to be dodgy. Perhaps I'd better tell the day porter, he'll know what to do. I'm glad the shift's almost over.'

16

Various, seemingly unrelated items of news had been relayed to Brighton CID Headquarters during the past twenty-four hours. Two of them had possibilities of a tie-in with the current murder inquiry, whilst another was merely bizarre.

The first was the discovery of someone's scalp in a condemned house in Hastings – unusual enough to cause comment amongst the case-hardened world-weary police detectives, but not high on their list of gruesome discoveries to remain a talking point for very long. Forensics were making the usual DNA tests and the results were expected within hours. So far there had been no sign of a victim, but it was a certainty they would find a body before too long. No-one could have survived such a vicious attack.

The second was more interesting. An elderly woman's bloated, partly decomposed body had been found buried in the base of a bonfire. If it hadn't been for a retired brigadier, she'd have gone up with the fireworks, and the work of the Forensics Team would have been increased two-fold.

Yet the third item was the one DCI Stoneham was most interested in, and that was the reason he was sitting in an interview room in London at nine in the morning after precious little sleep. A tom had been attacked under the railway arches behind Victoria. The MO was similar to the Brighton murder, and the ones before, but this time there had been a witness. The Met had thought he'd appreciate sitting in on the questioning.

The DCI and his woman police sergeant listened as DCI Gregson filled them in about how they'd heard a whisper on the street that Loretta had seen something, and had pulled her in for questioning about midnight.

Stoneham looked at the woman who sat chain-smoking on the other side of the desk. Her profession was as obvious as the cheap auburn wig and heavy make-up.

'We'd like you to tell us what you saw, Loretta,' DCI Gregson said briskly.

'Blimey, I said it all once. You ain't got no right keeping me in here like this. I been up all bleedin' night. I need me kip.' The tom crossed one pale, meaty thigh over the other and her scrap of skirt rode even further towards her stomach as she tapped the air impatiently with the toe of her white stiletto shoe.

DCI Gregson leaned back in his chair with a sigh. 'Loretta, you and me go way back, girl. Now, we both know where we picked you up last night and what you were doing at the time. So I suggest we get on with things and you can go back home and get your beauty sleep.'

Loretta favoured the Brighton detectives with a belligerent glare and lit another cigarette from the stub of the last.

Stoneham noted the bitten nails, the cheap clothes and the desperate attempt of the tom to make herself look younger. The wig and the make-up merely made her look like a man in drag, and she had to be at least fifty. He felt a surge of pity, and it wasn't an alien emotion. He felt the same for all the girls who made their living on their backs. There had to be a better way, if only the poor cows had the sense to realise it.

'So, Loretta. What did you see the other night, then?' He kept his voice soft and maintained eye contact.

Loretta eyed him thoughtfully, as though weighing him up. She must have liked what she saw, because she gave a ghost of a smile before dragging deeply on the cigarette.

'Like I told 'im. I was waiting for my friend to pick me up when this geezer comes by in this fancy car. I seen him look at me, like he was searching for a particular fancy, but he drove off up the street and I didn't think no more of it.

Reap the Whirlwind

In this game you lose some, you win some. There's always another one along in a minute.' She gave a harsh cough of laughter at her own humour.

'What kind of car was it, Loretta? Can you remember?'

Loretta shrugged beneath the matted weight of her fake fur coat. 'Foreign. BMW I think.'

'Loretta knows her cars,' interrupted Gregson. 'She's been in the business long enough to recognise a punter with money.'

'So what happened next?' Stoneham was getting impatient. If this turned out to be a wind-up, he'd let Gregson have the full force of his frustration.

'Well,' Loretta puffed the last of the cigarette and stubbed it out. 'It were raining, so I decided to call it a night. No sense in standing about when the punters 'ave all gorn 'ome. So I walks up the road and sees this car again. Only this time it's pulled up to the kerb and the punter's talking to Claire.'

'Who's Claire?' Stoneham was making notes, even though he'd have a transcript of the interview when it was over.

'Silly young cow who don't know what she's about,' Loretta said scornfully. 'She's only been in the business a few weeks and I kept on telling her to watch it, but of course they don't listen to me. Oh, no. Think they know it all. They think pimps ain't no use, but let me tell you, my bloke's always around somewhere. He's worth the dosh just to make sure I'm okay.'

She leaned forward, her cleavage in danger of spilling over in the tight blouse. 'I always carry a can of hairspray. Never know when you need to get out fast, and a quick squirt in the eyes gives me time if Duane ain't near enough.'

'Get on with it, Loretta.' Gregson gave a mighty yawn. 'You aren't the only one that's been up all bleeding night.'

'Keep yer 'air on. Nearly there. Blimey, you that impatient between the sheets as well? Got a lightning trigger on yer tool?'

Gregson glared at her and Stoneham attempted to hide the smile he couldn't quite control.

'I seen Claire getting into 'is car and he drives off down

the road. Well, I was going that way meself, so I keeps on walking. It's really pissing down now and I'm bloody well soaking and in a filthy temper. Duane shoulda met me, and there's no bleedin' sign of 'im. Anyway, I turns the corner, 'cos it's a short cut to the flat, and blow me, but the car's parked under the arches. I didn't think nothing of it of course, been there meself a few times.'

She gave a grin and exposed a row of surprisingly good teeth. 'Then the door opened and the punter got out. Fair shook me up it did, when I saw what he was doing.'

Silence fell and Loretta waited just long enough to irritate everyone before speaking again.

'He'd got her tied up, hadn't he? Feet and hands, like. He pulled her out of the car and slung her over his shoulder and carted her off under the arches to where it's really dark. She was alive, 'cos I could see her wriggling, but she weren't screaming or nothing.'

Stoneham watched the prostitute's face. There was a world of experience and sadness in there behind the paint and tough façade, and her eyes were as old as time itself.

'I didn't know what to do, so I hid behind one of them pillars and sort of peeked round it. You see, I didn't know if the punter had paid for that sort of rough stuff. 'Cos Claire does do that kinda thing. But it looked like it was gettin' a bit outa hand, and I thought it best to 'ang around, seein' as how she's only sixteen and still green.'

Cigarettes were passed round, and Stoneham leaned across to give Loretta a light. 'Why, what was he doing to Claire?'

Loretta took a deep drag of the cigarette and closed her eyes. 'He dumped her on the ground and went back to the car. I thought he'd finished, so I was about to go and untie the poor little cow when he comes back.'

She opened her eyes and they were wide with horror. 'He was all dressed in this overall thing like the bin men wear, only plastic, and when I saw the look on 'is face I knew he was going to give her real grief.'

'How did you see him, Loretta? I thought you said it was dark under the arches.'

'A train went over and sparked electricity as he left his car. It were only for a second, but I'll never forget that face.' She shuddered.

'Go on,' said Gregson, his expression grim.

'He walks over to Claire and makes her kneel on the ground in front of him. He undoes his flies and makes her gobble him for a while. Her head's going up and down like a good 'un and I'm about to go when I hears 'im swear. It was soft like, but in the silence between the trains, it sort of echoed. Gave me the shivers, I can tell you.'

She fell silent for a moment and Jack could see she was reliving the experience.

'He pulls Claire away from him by the hair, rough like, and gets 'er in the jaw with 'is fist. She must have bitten him or something, anyway, he didn't like it. He says something to her and she's crying and pleading and trying to get his dick in her mouth again. I reckon he couldn't get it up and he was blamin' her.'

She looked sagely at the two men. 'Blokes always do.'

The WDS shifted in the chair and tried to hide the fact she was smiling.

'Anyways,' Loretta sighed. 'He picks her up by the hair like she don't weigh nothing. Then he starts punching her. He hit her so hard her 'ead bounced off her shoulders, but she ain't making much noise, just little whimpers. Fair turned my stomach. I wish Duane had been around, he'd have sorted the bastard out. Then he pins her up against the wall and starts using her like a punch-bag. I could hear 'is breath like, as 'is fists sunk into her belly.' She bowed her head. 'It was 'orrible. I ain't seen nothing like it.'

Stoneham looked at Gregson. 'I don't see that this has any bearing on . . .'

Gregson held up his hand. 'Wait, Jack. There's more.'

'If this is a wasted journey, Gregson, I'll have your balls,' Stoneham muttered.

'If you two want a punch up, I'm off.' Loretta uncrossed her legs and revealed a scrap of red, transparent underwear.

'Just get on with it,' growled Gregson.

'All right, but it's you what keeps interrupting,' she retorted belligerently. 'By this time, Claire's about done in, but he ain't finished. He lets her fall to the ground like, then puts something around her neck. Can't see what it is, but it's shiny, 'cos I seen it glitter when the train come over and the electric sparks jumped off the rails. Then he starts to pull her all over the ground, kicking her and bashing her head against the wall. She's done in, had to be, 'cos she's not even trying to fight 'im off now.'

The silence was tangible as they all pictured the scene. Stoneham felt the despair deep in his gut. It would always be like this, he thought, until the law is changed and prostitution is made legal and safe.

He turned to Gregson. 'Any ideas on what he had round her neck?'

Gregson shook his head. 'Something thin, and metallic, but forensics haven't finished their tests yet.'

The detective from Brighton slumped in the chair. This was turning into a farce. There seemed to be no connection between the case he was on and this brutal attack, so why the hell had he been dragged out of bed at six in the bloody morning?

Loretta's voice broke into his thoughts. 'He must have wore himself out, 'cos he suddenly takes the thing from around her neck and unties her hands and feet, then gets back in his car. He didn't even check to see if she was still alive,' she added bitterly. 'Just drove away. Men like that always get away with it. Smart clothes, smart money, smart lawyers.'

'I don't suppose you thought to take the licence plate number, did you?' Stoneham had heard enough, thought the entire morning a waste of time, but you never knew.

'Yeah.' Loretta pushed a grubby scrap of paper across the table. 'I only had a lipstick on me, but it's right, I checked it twice.'

Stoneham looked down at the bright red notation. Was this the first clue to the murderer? 'What about Claire?'

'She was alive, but only just. I did what I could, but she was too far gone for me to move her, so I run down the road to the phone box and called an ambulance. Duane turned up

Reap the Whirlwind

and weren't too happy, that's why I weren't there when they arrived. But what else could I do?'

'You did the right thing, Loretta. Claire's seriously ill, but because you called them quickly enough, the doctors think she'll pull through, and her mother's come down from Liverpool and is going to take her home when she can be moved.'

Loretta nodded solemnly. 'Good. The streets are no place for kids like that. Trouble is, they're getting younger and younger. I seen a kid of twelve out the other night, but it's the punters who should be arrested, it's them what wants the kids. Supply and demand, it's always the same.'

Gregson nodded. 'We do our best. But we can't be everywhere. Now I want you to look at these pictures and tell me if you recognise the man you saw the other night. I know you've done it once before, but humour me.'

'He weren't the only one, you know. There was another bloke watching and all.'

The three police officers sat in stunned silence.

'You never said anything about another man,' roared Gregson.

Loretta shrugged. 'You didn't ask.'

'Can you describe him?' DCI Stoneham was on the edge of his seat. This put paid to the idea that the killer was responsible for this last attack. He was a loner, everything pointed to that.

'Arab. But he weren't with this bloke. Could have been a private detective. I reckon he was tailing him, 'cos he stayed out of sight and I had to be real careful he didn't see me.'

'Did he leave when the punter got in his car?'

'Yeah. He didn't hang about, but I didn't see what he was driving, must have left it around the corner. Anyway, I was doing me best to keep out of sight and when the coast was clear I got to Claire as quick as I could.'

Gregson laid out a series of photographs.

'That's 'im.' Loretta's stubby, nicotine-stained finger prodded the photograph of Paul Galloway.

*

Cassandra turned uneasily in her sleep as the sound of muted voices intruded into her dream. Jed was leaving for the day and Tabitha was helping him with his heavy coat. A blast of cold air swept into the confined space, then was swiftly dammed as Tabitha slammed the caravan door.

She opened her eyes, saw the rain streaming down the windows and felt the bite of cold nip at her bare shoulders. Condensation sweated on the walls and there was a warm, earthy smell of people and cooking and unwashed clothes. She closed her eyes again and snuggled back down into the warmth of the sleeping bag. There was no need to get up, no rush to be somewhere, she was free to do as she pleased.

Yet sleep evaded her, and it wasn't because of the pain in her ribs or the bruises which seemed to cover most of her body. A sharp, poignant picture of her mother and sister came to haunt her and she felt a stab of guilt. Laura would be frantic by now, it was two weeks since she'd left home. Perhaps she should telephone?

She thought of Laura's reaction, of the recriminations for having disobeyed her, and her own inability to explain why she'd not bothered to make contact. As each day passed it was becoming more difficult to find the courage to face the music. In a jolt of awareness, she knew she couldn't go home. But there was Melissa, it would be impossible to stay away for ever.

The thought of her family made the knife of guilt twist in a searing plunge. To return home now wouldn't heal the hurt she'd inflicted on Laura. Couldn't possibly make up for the way she had brought the past back to punish her mother. Perhaps it was better just to disappear. To see the bewilderment and hurt in Laura's eyes would be too painful, and she knew she didn't have the courage to face it – not yet, anyway.

Cassandra turned away from the wall and stared up at the caravan roof. It was stained with tobacco and cooking, and there were hairline cracks in the paint. No answers there, she decided.

Reap the Whirlwind

'You're awake then. Want a cuppa?' Tabitha's cheerful face swam into view, surrounded by a drift of long dark hair which was prematurely streaked with grey.

Cassandra struggled painfully to sit up on the makeshift bed, and poked one arm out of the warmth of the sleeping bag to take the mug of steaming tea.

'Thanks,' she said, then grinned. 'Cold this morning, isn't it?'

Tabitha shrugged. 'You get used to it, duck. I hardly notice any more.' She plumped herself down on the other side of the table and began to roll a cigarette.

Cassandra watched the nimble fingers shred the tobacco and roll a perfect smoke. Tabitha could have been anything between thirty and fifty. She was dressed, as usual, in layers of baggy sweaters and tattered shirts, which hung over a long, brightly coloured skirt. Doc Martens and thick socks completed the ensemble. Cheap jewellery studded her ears and nose, and rings and bracelets glittered on her hands and arms. Her nails were cut square and bare of polish and tobacco stained her fingers.

Tabitha must have been aware of her gaze, for she looked up and smiled. 'Want one?'

Cassandra shook her head. 'You know I don't smoke.'

Tabitha lit her cigarette, held it in the corner of her mouth, then plaited her long hair into a rope that hung over her shoulder and reached her waist. Tying it with a length of scarlet ribbon, she never once took her gaze from Cassandra.

'You take Es. What's the difference? Both will kill you in the end.'

Cassandra gripped the mug. 'I only did it the once.'

'Yeah. Heard that before.' Tabitha's mouth turned down in disbelief. 'You was out of your head when we found you. Your clothes all torn, your face a mess. You must have taken some beating, but you wasn't in no pain as far as I could see.'

Tabitha's eyes were screwed up against the cigarette smoke as she held Cassandra's gaze. 'It was me what cleaned you up.

You was in a fair old state, girl. Don't you think it's about time you told me what happened?'

Cassandra took a sip of tea, then slowly put the mug on the table between them. She was playing for time, hoping that if she didn't answer, Tabitha wouldn't persist. It had worked all the other times the subject had been broached.

'I seen it all, darlin'. Ain't nothing shocks me any more. Me and Jed's been travellers for twenty years, and we seen all sorts.' She shook her head, making her long earrings jingle musically. 'The kids what drop out today is different to when me and Jed took to the road. They ain't got no pride, no rhyme or reason in their lives, they just drift from place to place living off the social. Most of them is on something, and would sell their souls or their babies for the next fix. The rest are just losers who think life on the road is easy.' She gave a snort of derision. 'They soon end up in a squat. November sorts out the wheat from the chaff, sends them back to the cities. Only the tough survive an English winter.'

Tabitha rested the cigarette in the ashtray and fell silent, her dark gaze skimming over Cassandra's face.

'You don't fit into the frame, luv. You speak nice, your jewellery's real silver and you have the complexion of someone who eats regular. What happened to you before we found you? Why do you stay with us? It's been a long time. Ain't you got a home to go to?'

Cassandra looked into the older woman's face, and realised she wanted to talk. Needed to let out all the hurt and rage and confusion that had led her to this caravan.

Tabitha seemed to sense this and gave a gentle smile.

'Take your time, duck. We got all day. Jed's out looking for a bit of work to buy a crank shaft for the Land Rover. Could be gone for hours.' She folded her arms across her chest and waited.

Cassandra swallowed another mouthful of tea. Tabitha's encouraging smile seemed to make it easier to talk, and once she started, she found she couldn't stop. She told her about her parents' break-up, about the hotel and something of Melissa and the hospital, and finally, about the night of the rave.

'My boyfriend tried to rape me,' she said quietly. 'I managed to fight him off, and headed for shelter in Saxon Woods.' She felt the heat of tears in her eyes and the thud of her heart as she remembered back. 'I didn't hear him come after me. One moment I was alone and stumbling about in the dark. The next, he was grabbing me by the hair and punching me.'

She was once more in that dark, drizzly night with the sound of the rave acting as a backdrop to the strangely silent, frantic struggle against Snake.

One of his hands was snared in her hair, his fingers tugging, twisting and painful. The other was lashing out, punching with such force that it took her breath away. His rings cut her face, his knuckles bruised her cheekbone and split her lip. But still she fought in the only way she knew how. With her feet and her teeth and her nails.

'You don't turn your back on me, cunt!' he hissed as his fist caught a glancing blow on the side of her head. 'What you think I give you the tab for? Nothing's free in this life, bitch. You're gonna pay.'

Cassandra fought the waves of nausea and the flashing neon effects of the tab. Fear had given her strength to overcome the heaviness of her limbs, the lethargy in her body. She kicked out and caught him in the knee cap. Then she bunched her fist and sank it with all her strength into his stomach.

She heard him gasp as the air exploded from his lungs, and felt his grip in her hair weaken. Pulling away from him, she tried to run, but he caught her arm and threw her to the ground.

He began to kick her. The toe of his heavy boots thudding into her side, jarring on bone, bruising flesh, tearing into the thin fabric of her clothes.

'I'll teach you,' he gasped as his breath became ragged with the energy he was expending. 'I'll teach you a lesson you'll never forget.'

'Snake. Stop it. You'll have the pigs crawling all over us in a minute. Come on, she ain't worth it.'

Cassandra heard Lennie's voice drift beneath the thunder of pain which roared in her head. She lay in the grass, her head buried in her arms, her knees up to her chest, making herself as small as possible, sinking into the ground, disappearing into the darkness. Anything to escape the kicks.

'I must have passed out,' she said quietly. 'All I can remember is opening my eyes and wondering where I was. When I tried to stand there was a pain in my side and my face felt swollen and there was blood everywhere.'

Cassandra looked out of the window and watched the trickle of rain running down the glass. She could see her reflection, see the bruises and cuts that disfigured her mouth and eyes with their rainbow colours.

'The E must have still been working, because although I knew I was hurt, it was as though it had happened to someone else. It was as if I was an onlooker . . .'

She drifted into silence and looked past her reflection and out at the collection of caravans and trucks and battered cars which filled the temporary camp-site of the travellers. No-one was moving around outside this morning, apart from a couple of half-starved dogs which were foraging in the long grass.

'I began to walk. I didn't know where I was going, or what direction I was heading, I just knew I had to get as far away from Snake as possible.'

Tabitha reached out and took Cassandra's hand. She held it for a moment, then turned it over and gazed into the palm.

'We found you up on Telscombe Hill. You must have been walking all night to get so far,' she murmured. 'I reckon you got a couple of cracked ribs, should have seen a doctor by rights.'

Cassandra shook her head. 'No. I don't want anyone to know where I am. I'm not ready to go home yet.'

'What about your mum? She'll be out of her mind with worry.'

Cassandra fell silent. The warmth of Tabitha's hand seemed to be working up her arm. It was strangely healing, and the hurt in her ribs had definitely lessened. 'There are things she doesn't understand . . .'

Reap the Whirlwind

Tabitha lifted her dark gaze from Cassandra's palm and caught the younger girl's eyes. Her pupils were wide and unfocused, and there was a strange, knowing expression on her face.

Cassandra felt a pang of fear, and tried to pull her hand from Tabitha's grasp. But the older woman was stronger and her gaze held Cassandra, stilling her, pinning her to the bench.

'Your name suits you, girl. You have the gift. Beware of using it lightly. It can bring evil as well as good, as I've learned to me cost.'

'Wh – what do you mean?'

Tabitha folded Cassandra's fingers over her palm, and gently released her grip.

'You know what I mean, girl. You've got the gift of foresight. The same gift as yer namesake, Cassandra.'

'Who was she?' This was something new, and although Tabitha's gaze was mesmerising, and her pronouncement unsettling, Cassandra was fascinated. It also turned the conversation away from Laura and Melissa and she was grateful for the reprieve.

Tabitha leaned back against the cushions and folded her arms. Her gaze still held the younger girl in her thrall.

'It's from a Greek legend. Priam and Hecuba had twins. A boy called Helenus and a girl called Cassandra. After a day of too much wine, and probably an orgy or two thrown in, the infant twins were left in the temple by their drunken parents. When Hecuba returned to fetch 'em, she saw the sacred serpents of the temple licking the twins' ears. From that day on, both children were gifted with prophetic powers.'

Tabitha's eyes darkened, and the only sound in the caravan was her voice.

'Years later, Cassandra was courted by Apollo. She rejected 'im, and just like all men, it 'urt 'is pride, so he cursed her power of foresight by spitting into her mouth. From that day on, her prophecies were never believed, even though she saw the death of her lover, Agamemnon, and warned of the treachery of the Trojan Horse.'

'How do you know all this?' Cassandra hitched up the

sleeping bag and leaned across the table. She was aware of the patronising challenge in her voice, and was ashamed of it.

Tabitha's eyes lost their dreamy lustre and grew sharp and intelligent.

'Jus 'cos I choose to live like this, darlin', don't mean I 'ad no education.' She sighed and shrugged. 'Me dad ran a second 'and book stall in Petticoat Lane. I used to sit under that stall every Sunday when I was a nipper, and read everything I could get me 'ands on. They was an escape, you see, from the day-to-day grind of the real world and life in the two-room flat in the Isle of Dogs. My one adventure that didn't cost no money. I knew most of the legends before I finished primary school.'

Cassandra digested this information, and tried to picture Tabitha as a small child huddled beneath a coster's barrow. It was quite easy, there was still something of the urchin in her face.

'What happened to Cassandra?' she asked finally, eager to hear the rest of the story, and in some way at ease now that someone else knew of the powers she possessed.

Tabitha shrugged. 'Who knows?'

'That's not fair. You can't start a story and not finish it.' Cassandra was bitterly disappointed and couldn't disguise the petulance in her voice.

Tabitha got up and began to busily tidy the caravan. 'Cassandra 'ad her head chopped off by Clytemnestra, Agamemnon's wife. It's only a legend. It shouldn't concern you, duck.'

She swung round and leaned over Cassandra. 'But you watch out – guard your gift well. I see trouble in your 'and, trouble for you and your twin. Listen to the voices that come to you. Take notice of the things you see. They'll protect you.'

'How do you know all this, Tabitha?' Cassandra was shivering, but it wasn't from the cold. It was from the certainty that Tabitha had seen the visions in her hand and was right.

Tabitha's smile was enigmatic. 'I got the gift too, ain't I? You don't have to be no Romany to 'ave it – as you should know, not being one yerself. I go to the fairs and read the future in palms and in the crystals. I do a bit of healing and can tell what's troubling the poor souls what comes to me. Your path of destiny was chosen over ten years ago, and you can't avoid it.'

Cassandra looked into those dark, lustrous eyes that held such a depth of knowledge and accepted the truth.

Tabitha's voice was a sigh, barely audible above the sound of the rain.

'The circle of time is almost complete, darlin'. You have to face the past and bring it to justice. For as it says in the Bible, "They have sown the wind, and they shall reap the whirlwind."'

17

Laura walked slowly back up the hill to the carpark. The three snatched hours of the morning had been wasted in yet another fruitless search for Cassandra. The clubs and bars beneath the Brighton promenade were closed, the seafront deserted.

She'd tried the back-street pubs, but when she roused the landlords and showed them Cassandra's photograph, there had been little curiosity, merely the shaking of a head or the nonchalant shrug. Laura knew that to them, Cassandra was just one more statistic, just another teenage girl who'd left home. And there were so many – she hadn't realised until now – now that she was thrown into this twilight world of street children and the new generation of the abandoned and forgotten.

The frustration made her want to weep, yet she knew she had to be strong, strong enough to go on searching. Strong enough to ask questions and enter places that were alien to her, like the dingy bars and clubs, where she was eyed with suspicion and the customers were tight-lipped. No-one seemed to care or want to listen. No-one shared the gut-wrenching fear she had learned to live with, or understood the void Cassandra's disappearance had left in her life. Only another mother would understand that sickly fear, that torment when her child was missing and therefore in danger.

The searching and heartache had got her nowhere, but she couldn't accept defeat, couldn't rest until someone somewhere gave her a glimmer of hope, a word, a sign, that Cassandra was still alive.

The telephone was ringing as she slotted the key into the lock and she slammed through the apartment door and ran to snatch it up before the connection was broken.

'Where the fuck have you been? I've been ringing all morning.'

'David.' Laura swallowed. She didn't want this now, her defences were at their lowest and she couldn't handle any more trouble.

'Is she back?' His voice was bullish, tight with anger.

'No. I was out looking for her, but there's no news and the police know as much as I do, which is very little.'

Laura tried to catch her breath, to sound calm and in control, but she knew David had heard the edginess in her voice. His next words were evidence of that.

'How does it feel to be guilty, Laura? How does it feel when things slip and slide away from you, and there's no-one to help, no-one who will listen? This is your punishment for all the things you let them do to me when Melissa disappeared.'

Laura gripped the receiver. 'That's unfair and you know it. I stood by you, believed you when you said you had nothing to do with what happened to Melissa. I'm still doing that, even after your behaviour the other day.' Her pulse raced as the weeks of frustration and anger simmered to a rapid boil.

'What did you say?' David's voice had quietened, softened, grown wary and touched with menace.

'I said I'm still defending you with the police, though why . . .'

'What the fuck have you been saying to the police?'

His shout made her flinch and she almost dropped the receiver.

'They came and asked me about Melissa, and when they saw the bruises on my neck they began to ask questions about you.' She heard the iciness in her voice as she gained control. She felt nothing for him, he could think what he liked.

'And I suppose you were only too keen to spill the dirt. Never could keep your fucking mouth shut. You're just like my mother, whining and crying and always pleading for pity when you're too stupid to think for yourself.'

His voice dropped several degrees as he hissed the malevolence down the telephone wires. 'What exactly did you say to them?'

Laura was tempted to slam down the receiver, to break contact with the bully at the other end. Yet she knew she couldn't do that. It would only make him more furious, more inclined to turn up on her doorstep again. She felt the anger make her legs tremble, but she held on to her temper and maintained an icy remoteness as she told him what had happened at Stoneham's last visit.

'I didn't tell them any more than they already knew,' she finished.

There was silence for a tense moment. 'I wondered how long it would take them to make the connection. Still, they don't know everything.'

'What do you mean?' A shaft of fear stabbed her as the doubts flooded in. Had Stoneham been right to assume David had something to do with Melissa's disappearance?

His voice was lighter suddenly, and he even managed a cough of laughter. 'I mean, my darling wife, they don't know where I am. You see, unlike you, I have the ability to think fast, to know when to keep my mouth shut and my options open. It will take a very clever Mr Plod to find me.'

Laura gripped the receiver, alert and on guard. 'Why should they want to find you?' She was amazed at how calm she sounded, because inside, she was trembling. 'Why the need for secrecy, David? What the hell are you up to?'

'You really are stupid, aren't you? You and my mother have a lot in common.'

Laura heard the impatient exhalation at the other end of the line.

'The plods have put two and two together and as usual come up with five. They'll connect me with both twins' disappearances and the two murders. I won't go through all that again, Laura. Not for you or anyone else. You leave me to mind my own affairs while you take care of yours. And Laura . . .'

'Yes?' The doubts were pressing in, the image of the girl in the mortuary crystal bright.

'If you know what's good for you, you won't go running off at the mouth every time I get in touch. I'll ring again in a few days. Hopefully, by then you will have news of Cassandra.' He broke the connection.

Laura dropped the receiver into its cradle and buried her face in her hands. She didn't cry, couldn't dredge up the energy it would need, for she had done with crying over David. Done with expending any effort into trying to understand what made the man tick. She was drained of all emotion, bankrupt of tears.

The sharp rap on the door made her start and she whirled round as the footsteps approached from the hall.

'Mrs Kingsley? Is it not convenient? I can come back later.'

Laura shook her head, making her autumn curls bounce in the sunlight that poured through the window. 'It's all right, Edward. Just taking a minute to recharge the batteries.'

The chef stood uncertainly before her, pristine in his kitchen whites, enormous in the tall hat. He was sober and upright, and it took Laura a moment to recognise the unaccustomed expression on his face. It was compassion.

'Still no news of Cassandra?'

She shook her head, she didn't want to discuss her problems, didn't want to think about anything but hotel business at the moment.

'Are those the menus for tonight?' Her voice was deliberately light, but she knew it sounded brittle.

Edward handed them over. 'I've engaged a girl for the coffee shop. She seems quite bright and is very attractive, so it should pull the customers in. And I've got someone to fill in as KP.' His forehead knotted in a frown.

Laura looked up from the menus. 'Is there a problem?'

Edward stayed silent for a moment as though planning what to say and how to say it. When he did speak, his words came slowly.

'I'm not sure. I found him prowling about outside yesterday and automatically took him as an applicant. But after thinking about it, I realised there was something odd about him.'

Laura handed back the menus, her thoughts flitting to the other things she had to see to upstairs. 'Does it matter, Edward? After all, he won't get anywhere near the guests and he's only employed to do the dishes and clean up. If you were so unsure, why did you take him on?'

Edward raised a shrug. 'I'm short-staffed and there was no-one else. He seems to know his way around a kitchen, but there's something . . .'

Laura's patience waned. 'If you don't want him, get rid of him. Really, Edward, I've never known you to be so dithery.'

Edward drew himself up to his full height in pompous indignation. 'I cannot run my kitchen properly without the correct number of staff. I took the man on and I will keep an eye on him. But you should know he said he'd seen the job advertised in the job centre and that was why he'd turned up for an interview.'

Laura moved away from him. There was a lot to be done before the conference dinner tonight, and time was wasting.

'So? What's unusual about that?'

'We didn't place the post with the job centre. We used the agency, just like always.'

Laura shrugged as she read through the guest list. They would have to put two extra tables into the dining hall.

'He must have heard about the job from someone else. Have you seen references?'

'No, but he said he can get them. That's another thing, when I asked him this morning he was very cagey about where he'd worked before. There's something not right, but I can't put my finger on it.'

Laura led the way to the connecting door that divided the apartment from the hotel.

'I shouldn't worry too much, Edward. Keep the post advertised with the agency and use this man until you find a replacement. I doubt he'll cause any trouble. After all, what harm can a kitchen porter do?'

*

One telephone call to DVLC Headquarters had traced the car at the scene of Claire's attack to a hire company. By the time DCI Stoneham had returned to Brighton, he knew it had been leased to a certain Paul Galloway, who was staying at the Hyde Park Hilton. Unfortunately, Mr Galloway had since moved on.

Stoneham executed a peremptory rap on Chapman's door and strode into the office without waiting for a reply. It was past midday, and after such little sleep, he should have been exhausted. Yet the adrenalin buzzed and he looked forward eagerly to the rest of the day.

Chapman looked up from the scatter of paperwork that covered his desk. 'About time. What's going on in London that has anything to do with the case in hand?'

His DCI filled him in on the details of the interview with the tom, then pushed the open file across the desk.

Chapman looked at the photograph of the man identified by the prostitute. His puzzled expression cleared and he nodded.

'Go on.'

'His description has been circulated to all the hotels in a thirty-mile radius of London, but it will take time to do a blanket coverage. They're as short on man-power as we are.'

'How do you know he's still in London? The press have already got hold of this one. He could be anywhere by now.'

'Tell me about it. Just another little problem to make our job more difficult than it already is. And we don't really know if he's the one involved in our murders. We could be chasing our own tails.'

Chapman remained silent for a moment, his gaze steady on his DCI's face. 'You wouldn't have your dander up if you didn't think there was a connection, Jack. Stick with it.'

Stoneham swept one jaundiced eye over Chapman. 'Of course the Met will want their piece of the action before we can question him. But they promised to let me know the minute he's pulled in so we can sit in on the interview.'

Chapman grunted. 'If you believe that, you'll believe anything. The Met will tie him up neater than a gnat's arsehole. We'll be lucky to have much left by the time they're finished with him.'

'Don't be so cynical, sir. They want this bastard caught as much as we do. They'll play the game. It's not in their interest to do otherwise. Remember, Gina was killed on their patch, and this latest attack was right under their noses. They're involved as much as we are.'

The adrenalin was still coursing as Stoneham riffled though his briefcase, then dropped a thin folder on the desk.

'This is the reason I have to believe we're after the right man, sir.'

Chapman glanced through the paperwork. 'Nasty. Similar MO. You could have something here.'

'The tom had a Coke bottle jammed up her jacksie. It's about as close as we come. There was bruising on her neck as well as most of the rest of her. Poor cow was lucky to survive, but at least we got a good description.'

'Got a face and a name to fit the frame as well, if this is anything to go by. Could be the break you're after, Jack.'

The DCI nodded, his thoughts sifting through the information he'd gleaned this bright, sunny morning. Chapman's next words brought his attention sharply back to his superior.

'This came while you were out. I put DI Felling on to it for now, but I'd prefer you to take over the investigation.'

Stoneham remained silent as his superior pushed a buff folder towards him. His case-load was already mountainous, but that was police work. It was just frustrating not to be able to concentrate on one thing at a time. Especially when the pieces of the puzzle were finally beginning to make sense.

Chapman must have noticed Stoneham's reluctance to read the file, because after a moment's hesitation, he related the contents to his DCI.

'As you probably know, a body was found hidden in a

bonfire at Cathedral Gap. The victim is an elderly caucasian of about sixty. She had been dead for approximately a week to ten days and there were signs of rapid deterioration. There was a deep head wound and some evidence of damage to the surrounding areas of scalp. No other signs of violence before death, but her legs and arms had been broken sometime after rigor mortis set in. The pathologist promises more details when he's finished the PM but it could be a while, he's been busy with the RTA on the M23 last night.'

Stoneham absorbed the information in silence.

'So far, we have no name, and although forensics have fingerprinted her, it was impossible to do much more. Dental records are out, because she had no teeth. Must have had a full set of dentures, but as yet, there's no sign of them. The victim was wrapped in a tarpaulin. She was grossly overweight and wearing only a nightgown which had been recently washed and ironed. There was a wedding ring on her finger and no distinguishing marks. The Police Surgeon reckons death was instantaneous, caused by the head wound. Christ, Stoneham, half her brains were gone.'

DCI Stoneham nodded thoughtfully. It couldn't have been a pretty sight. Murder never was – you just had to learn to blank it out, to treat each ghastly manifestation of man's inhumanity to man with as little emotion as possible.

'Any signs of how she got there?'

Chapman shook his head. 'I've got the team working out there, but there's been a lot of traffic in that area. It's right near the carpark to the pub and what with ramblers and sightseers it's difficult to isolate one set of tyre tracks or footprints from another.'

'Statements?'

'The body was found by a retired Brigadier Blacksmith. He and the landlord of the pub were very helpful.' Chapman edged the folder closer to his DCI.

'I don't see why Felling can't handle it. I've got enough on my plate with this other thing about to break.'

Chapman gave a wintry smile. 'Then you'll have to deal with two murders at once, Stoneham. Our lady of the bonfire didn't die of natural causes. It appears she'd been scalped.'

Stoneham remembered the seemingly isolated reports he'd seen the previous day and the excitement of the chase made him instantly alert. Reaching for the folder, he eagerly scanned the statements. It could take a long time to catch the maniac who was killing the young girls, but there was a chance of nailing this one – and quick – if his hunch was right.

Stoneham swept up the report and headed for the door. 'Leave it with me,' he said tersely.

The Crown and Anchor was perched on the edge of the cliffs and over a century of history would soon be lost for ever as the chalk face crumbled nearer each year, but as long as it was there, it was open for business. And tonight would be one of the busiest. Stoneham took a deep, refreshing breath of the salt-laden breeze that caressed the ramshackle building and watched the gulls swooping over the seven cathedral arches of chalk cliffs. It was good to get out of the station, it was just unfortunate about the circumstances.

Brigadier Harvey Blacksmith, DSO and bar, was obviously not the sort of man to lie in bed when there was work to be done, thought Stoneham as he listened to the old boy recount his tale. Yet he could see the glint in his eye and the heightened colour in his sun-creased cheeks and realised the old bugger probably hadn't had so much fun since the Khyber Pass Incident.

The Brigadier tugged his handlebar moustache and took a sip of brandy the landlord had kindly placed in front of him. Then he lined up the beer mats with military precision and placed his glass squarely in the centre. All present and correct and on parade. In his plus-fours, woollen shirt, shooting socks and heavy brogues, he sat ram-rod straight on the wooden settle, and Stoneham could just picture him striding out over the Downs as the sun rose. He was of the old school heroes, Stoneham thought, principled and at odds with the modern world. Only England could produce a man like the Brigadier.

'Been retired over fifteen years, don't you know. But old habits die hard – order is the thing – efficiency. When things need doing around here they need to be done properly. I see to it that the locals are whipped into line. Terribly lax, most of 'em.'

Stoneham dipped his chin to hide his amusement as the Brigadier pontificated. It was going to be difficult to keep the old boy on track.

'I understand you were in charge of the building of the bonfire, sir? How did this particular addition escape your notice until this morning?'

The retired Brigadier rapped his walking stick sharply against the brogues, his expression embarrassed. 'Spot of sick leave. Damn malaria, don't you know. Blasted nuisance. Try to ignore it, but now and again it puts me off me stroke.'

Stoneham could see that Blacksmith's years in India had left their mark and the proud old man was impatient with what he saw as an imposition, a weakness in his make-up. 'So you came down this morning . . .' he coaxed.

'The success of the festivities is down to me this time, and after the débâcle last year – should never trust an estate agent to do anything right – I wanted to make sure the villagers had followed my instructions. Does them no harm to have their weekends filled with useful occupation, and they'll regret the passing of the traditional bonfire when this place finally goes into the sea.'

He took another swig of brandy. 'Give me a bunch of squaddies any time,' he muttered through his moustache. 'At least one can throw them in the glasshouse if they don't do as they're told.'

Stoneham smiled at this and had to turn away, and as he did, he caught sight of the bonfire through the salt crusted window. It had been built well away from the cliff edge and the pub, its girth broad, its height well over twelve feet. As yet, the guy had not been placed on the top. That would come tonight after the torch-light procession from the village green.

Brigadier Blacksmith's voice made Stoneham turn back.

'Seem to have done what I told 'em, but thought I'd better check.'

Stoneham listened, the pictures conjured up as the Brigadier talked. He could see the proud stance, the critical eye as the old boy circled the heap of wood and old mattresses, prodding the edifice with his walking stick to tidy away an errant timber or fluttering newspaper that dared fall out of line.

'It wasn't as good as the funeral pyres one saw in India, but one could hardly expect the civilians of Sussex to know how to build fires that burn properly, and in the absence of my Indian Riflemen, this would have to suffice.' The Brigadier paused and tugged his moustache. 'Then I realised something was wrong. I'd told them to put the more combustible items on the top, and it looked as if someone had been poking about at the base, stuffing black bin liners in there. There was also the most appalling smell of something rotting.'

Stoneham waited patiently as the old boy eyed the landlord.

'Infernal nuisance,' Blacksmith muttered. 'Thought some blighter had been using my bonfire as a rubbish tip. Sorry Stanley.' This was a gruff apology, his gaze not quite reaching the landlord. 'Poked it with me walking stick, don't you know, but that proved worse than useless, so I got down to have a better look.' He massaged his knees, as though remembering the arthritic pain this manoeuvre had brought.

'So it was you who actually found the body?' Stoneham was making notes.

Blacksmith shook his head. 'I could smell something ghastly, but I was intent on trying to reach the rubbish bag to hook it out, so didn't take much notice.' He nodded in the landlord's direction. 'Stanley here was the one who realised what the smell was and where it was coming from. Should have had me wits about me. Saw a lot of dead in India during the cholera epidemics.'

Stanley Windsor, the landlord of the Crown and Anchor, smeared the remains of his hair across his bald pate, his eyes glinting with humour. Then he seemed to remember the seriousness of the situation and looked grim. 'Easier for me to have a look-see, and when I realised what was buried under there I called you lot in.'

'What kind of security have you got here? All seems rather isolated and open to the elements.'

The landlord shrugged and took another sip of brandy. 'What's there to secure? There's the carpark of course and I suppose I could have those security lights that turn on if anyone comes too near the pub. But as you can see, the place is about to tumble down the cliff any minute. Not much point in doing anything but lock the doors and set the bar alarms.'

Stoneham turned back to the Brigadier. 'You say you didn't inspect the bonfire during the past two days, sir. So it could have been there for some time?'

The Brigadier shifted uncomfortably on the hard wooden settle and shot the Brighton man a belligerent glare. 'Damn nuisance, but can't be helped. Malaria makes a chap too groggy to leave his bed. I didn't manage to inspect it at all until this morning.'

'So the body could have been there for a couple of days without you noticing anything?'

'It wasn't there the first day, because I inspected the site before building began. Then I returned that evening to make sure it was secure.' The Brigadier was blustering.

Stoneham checked Felling's notes. The man had remembered to get names and addresses of all those involved in the building of the bonfire, and various local coppers were calling on them today. He turned his attention to Stanley Windsor.

'Do you remember hearing or seeing anything out of the ordinary over the past two nights? The body had to be carried here, so we can assume it was probably by car.'

Windsor shook his head. 'Kids use the carpark late at night for getting up to the kind of things their parents wouldn't let them do in their own homes. There's always two or three parked out there once the pub's shut. I used to go out and move them on, but now I don't bother. If they want to freeze their bums off by screwing in the back seats, who am I to stop them?'

'Quite. So there was no unusual noise, or suspicious

characters hanging about in the last two nights then? Nothing out of the ordinary?'

'It's a disgrace,' interrupted the Brigadier. 'Should bring back the birch and National Service. The youth of today have no back-bone, no discipline.'

'Nothing really.' Stanley Windsor pursed his lips and folded his hands over his beer belly. He seemed unfazed by the Brigadier's outburst. Probably used to him banging on about the youth of today, thought Stoneham.

'Mind you, there was that motor-bike I heard about four o'clock the other morning. I'd had a bad night's sleep because of the storm and I was just dozing when I heard it revving up. Sounded like it was stuck in the mud or something. I was about to get out of bed and see what the hell was going on when the bike drove off. Didn't think much of it at the time. It was just a bloody nuisance after a bad night.'

Stoneham relaxed and a fleeting smile touched his eyes.

'A motor-bike? I don't think our victim was in any state to be carried on the back of a bike, Mr Windsor. By all accounts she was a very large lady.'

Stanley Windsor's jaw drooped at the memory. 'She certainly was. I only saw a leg and an arm, but even trussed up like that, she couldn't have been carried on a bike.'

The notebook was closed. 'Thank you, gentlemen. I shouldn't have to bother you again.' He got up to leave.

'Can we go ahead with the bonfire arrangements? It could be the last Guy Fawkes Night in this place after nearly fifty years. It's rather become a tradition.'

'I'll have a word with the team outside. But the bonfire will have to be demolished. There could be vital evidence still buried in it. If this is done and the team are satisfied, then I don't see why not.'

Stoneham eyed the Brigadier, aware of the twinkle he couldn't quite disguise. 'I'm sure that with you in charge, sir, it will soon be built again ready for tonight.'

'Nasty business,' muttered the Brigadier. 'Things like this were unheard of in my day.' He straightened to a rigid, parade-ground attention. 'But once you give the all clear, I'll soon have things organised. You can count on me.'

Stoneham left the Crown and Anchor. It had turned into a lovely day and he stared wistfully out to sea. The sunlight sparkled on the calm water and there was a salt-laden breeze feathering the tufted downland grass. Gulls squabbled and screamed overhead as they circled in their never-ending search for food and the policeman watched them enviously before returning to his gruesome task.

The bonfire had now been dismantled, each piece carefully checked before being piled in a heap some distance away. Stoneham approached the leader of the team who was standing having a quiet cigarette in the lee of a tree.

'Found anything?'

The man nodded and picked up a plastic evidence bag. 'One set of false teeth. They must have been put in separate to the body, 'cos we found them in another section of the fire. Apart from that, nothing.'

The DCI thought for a moment, his eyes raking the remains of the bonfire before returning to the long grass and spiny hillocks of thistles. 'Has the area been searched for tyre tracks or footprints?'

The policeman stamped on the butt of his cigarette. 'It's been pissing down for days. The earth's as soft as shit. We eliminated the Brigadier's and the landlord's footprints and those of the kids that must have been helping to build the thing. But people have been tramping over this bit of ground for three days. It's an impossible task to identify just one set of footprints.'

'The landlord said something about a motorbike getting stuck in the mud a couple of nights ago.' Stoneham's mind was running over the statements he'd just taken, sifting, sorting, looking for answers.

The policeman nodded. 'Over there.' He pointed to a grassy area about fifty feet away.

Stoneham raised an enquiring eyebrow, then followed the policeman across the quagmire.

'Looks like someone got stuck in here and had the Devil's

own job getting out. But it wasn't a motor-bike, too many wheels.'

The earth was churned, globules of dried mud flung in a wide arc behind where the rear wheel of the bike must have been.

'It was a motor-bike. But it had a sidecar. Look.'

The imprint of three tyres formed a triangle, and from the direction of the wheels and the mud splatters it was obvious to the detective that it wasn't a Robin Reliant that had got stuck in the mud.

'Anyone taken a casting of these?'

'Yeah. It was the last thing the forensic team did before they left.'

Stoneham was deep in thought, and when he spoke, it was almost casually, as if to himself.

'He couldn't have put her on the back of a bike because she was too big for that. But he could have squashed her into a sidecar. Perhaps that explains the broken arm and leg. He had to bend her to fit.'

He and the team leader exchanged a look of agreement.

'Right. I'd better get back to the morgue and see what's been happening.' Stoneham picked his way over the coarse, sweet smelling grass to the car. If they could find out what kind of bike it was, it would help. But he'd given his WDS a task before he'd left Brighton, and if she'd managed to get hold of the right people in Hastings, they might not even need that.

True to form, Ramona Knight had the information he needed, and her voice came over the radio receiver before he'd driven more than a mile from Cathedral Gap.

'I've spoken to Hastings, Guv. Looks like we can ID the body. But we have a problem.'

'Spit it out, Ramona.' The adrenalin buzz was ebbing. Stoneham was tired and cold and hungry. He didn't need any more complications today.

'The victim is a Mrs Lillian Squires.' The WDS went on with the domestic details. 'Seems she wasn't scalped. Doc Harding's rushed through the p.m. and has confirmed that death was caused by a heavy object caving in the back of her head. The so-called scalp, was in fact a home-made wig.'

'So what's the complication?' Stoneham had parked the car and was only half listening as he watched a seagull hover, motionless, in the wind.

'She's got a son. He was released back into the community five years ago when Hellingly Mental Hospital closed down. He's a certified paranoid schizophrenic and has to take regular medication to control his illness.'

The DCI sighed. 'So, what's new? I could give you a list as long as your arm of people released back into the community who have no business being there.'

'Malcolm Squires had a job as a kitchen porter in a Hastings Hotel. He hasn't turned up for work the last few days. No-one's seen him since the day before they repossessed the house. And the forensics team have found the discarded medicine bottles he threw onto the bonfire he had before leaving.'

The WDS paused for effect just long enough to irritate her superior, then went on.

'They were full, Guv. I checked with his doctor, and it doesn't look as if he's taken any medication for days. That means we've got a dangerous man out there. A man who has probably already murdered his mother and is quite capable of murdering again.'

'Shit.' Stoneham chewed his bottom lip as he thought of the remains of the Brigadier's funeral pyre. 'He likes bloody bonfires too, Ramona. Might be sick in the head, but he wasn't daft enough to do the dirty deed on his own doorstep.'

There was no reply at the other end of the two-way radio as he thought things over.

'He's gone to ground somewhere, and we have to find him. Get the lads to ring round all the hotels between Brighton and Hastings. If there's no response, spread the net inland. Kitchen porter is probably the only work he's capable of, and he has to eat, so he'll stick to what he knows. Check with the DSS and his social worker as well. Then send the lads to do the rounds of the doss houses.'

Reap the Whirlwind

DS Knight's reply was crisp. 'Already started, Guv.'

'I'm off to the morgue. Ring me if you find anything new. You'll go far, DS Knight,' he finished tartly as he broke the connection. It was at times like this he looked forward to retirement. Women were taking over the world.

*

Malcolm worked quickly in the heat of the kitchen, and made sure he was as inconspicuous as possible. He'd caught the chef eyeing him with suspicion and knew it would only be a matter of time before he was found out.

It was a pity really, he mused as he pulled a heavy load of dishes out of the washer. The hotel ran a tight kitchen, but the staff seemed friendly enough and at least they didn't take the mickey out of him. He could have worked here, could have settled in quite nicely. But he knew he would have to be ready to move on. Ready to follow the woman he'd seen at the window. For it was she who would show him the way to the person behind the voice.

He knew who she was, he'd asked, but the name meant nothing. Yet there was something familiar about her, something which tugged at the corners of his memory and made him feel uneasy.

The lunch-time rush was finally over and as he finished the last of the plates and stacked them on the shelves, he wondered how he was going to manage to keep an eye on her. The hours were long, the breaks taken in rota. There would be little time to follow her, but the hotel was a good hiding place. They wouldn't think of looking for him here when they discovered what he'd done with Lillian.

He thought of her for an instant, then dismissed her. By tonight she would be gone for ever. Consumed in the hell-fire and damnation she was always preaching. Ashes to ashes, dust to dust. He smiled to himself at the thought.

'Don't you have a home to go to?' It was Mr Edward.

Malcolm nodded and hurried to remove the long apron that was tied around his waist.

'Be back here by five.'

Malcolm scurried out of the door to his motor-bike, very aware the chef was watching him, arms akimbo in the doorway.

He kick-started the bike, cursing beneath his breath. It wouldn't do to make the man more suspicious. He would have to ride away, leave the bike somewhere close, then walk back. It was imperative he followed the woman if she left the apartment.

'Run Malcolm, run. Take you away, take you away. I see you, see you, see you.'

Malcolm drove out of the back entrance and turned the corner. The chant of the train wheels was haunting him, drowning out the soft enticing whispers of her voice.

He parked the bike behind a BT junction box that was shielded from the road by overhanging trees and a rough hedge. Then he hurried back to the hotel and cowered in the shrubbery. He could see into the apartment. Could make out the furniture and the pictures on the walls. Her car was parked outside.

He breathed a sigh of relief. He hadn't missed her.

*

The convoy of trucks and caravans had pulled off the road sometime after five o'clock and set up camp in a field outside Salisbury. It was a long journey to the west coast of Wales and it would be several days before they reached their winter camping ground. Jed's Land Rover was still playing up, and several of the other travellers had had trouble with their ancient buses and vans.

It was Cassandra's fifteenth day away from home.

Night had come early, dark and eerily silent on the hills that overlooked the ancient town with its slender, Gothic spire. A sprinkling of stars glimmered high above them and a pale sliver of moon hung against the velvet black of the sky.

It was cold, the grass brittle with frost beneath their feet, yet Cassandra wasn't touched by it. She was warmed by the fire that had been built in the centre of the encampment, her face glowing, her outstretched hands toasted as she watched the sparks fly into the night for their final, glorious dance before they died.

There was the soft strum of a guitar, the occasional rustle of laughter and the whine of a fretful child. Subdued lights glowed in the windows of the caravans, making the dancing shadows of the inhabitants move with a liquid beauty that would fade with the sun. The dogs lay contented beneath the trucks and buses, their ears alert for any sound of intrusion. No-one seemed to care that the field was muddy, the night was cold and it promised to rain before morning. They were free to live as they wanted.

Cassandra was aware of the others as the joints were passed round and a contented peace enfolded the travellers, but the sound of them and the sight of them was lost in a haze of foreboding.

It was as though she was surrounded by darkness, and only the fire existed. The flames leaped and danced, sending sparks flying, wood crackling and ashes shifting. Each minute sound was clear and precise, imprinted in her mind. The tongues of flame were bright and mesmerising as she hugged her knees and watched them devour the wood and rubbish.

The warmth touched her face, but suddenly she was cold. The light of the flames brightened the night, but deep inside her it was dark – so dark, it made her shiver.

It was on its way, closing in, drawing her down, prying into the very depths of her soul until she was merely a husk, a vessel for its power.

That special gift, that demonic blessing of awareness touched her and brought images of things she could no longer understand. It was more powerful than before – closer – demanding. As she felt the force of its arrival, she knew she would have to open her mind to it. Will it to show itself regardless of how fearsome it might be.

Yet the part of her which could still reason knew the dangers, forcing her to hold back, to protect and guard against the evil that was about to ensnare her. If she opened up her consciousness too willingly, she might never escape.

The heat shimmered in a halo above the fire, and smoke drifted in a hazy veil up into the sky. And as she watched, she saw a woman, grotesque in a flowing nightgown that was stained with blood. Her hands reached out as if imploring for mercy as her face crumpled and grew hideous with fear.

Her mind asked the question. 'What does this mean?'

'Watch and remember,' whispered the voice in her head that sounded so unnervingly familiar.

Cassandra followed the woman as she struggled to claw her way off the rumpled, filthy bed. There was someone with her, his shadow dark across the whiteness of her gown. Somewhere, in the distance, she thought she could hear the rumble of trains.

Her limbs grew heavy and her pulse-rate slowed until it was almost non-existent. The flames of the fire filled her vision, touched the fifth dimension of her awareness and drew her in. The clarity was at its zenith. The fear stifled in a cloak of numbed emotion.

Nothing was being left to chance this time. Now she would see him. Now she would know who haunted her dreams and gave her waking nightmares. It was too late to pull back. Too late to think of her own safety.

The woman lay beneath the vast crucifix, pinned in death to the blood-soaked sheets as viscid grey matter seeped from the wound in her head.

Cassandra moaned as the woman's eyes sought her out and held her attention. She dug her fingers into her knees and trembled as the visions filled her mind, her eyes, her very core.

The figure which bent over the bed in that austere room was in the shadows – still anonymous, still a mystery. She watched helplessly as the last breath sighed between the flaccid mouth – and tasted blood in her throat, copper on her tongue.

Cassandra sensed she was drifting closer in that world of visions. Hovering above him, willing him to turn and face her.

Yet she was afraid, more afraid than she had ever been. For the protective shield she had thrown up as armour against this evil had been torn away. Leaving her exposed, and at his mercy. What would she see? What terrible secrets did he hide?

The scene changed in the time it took for a beat of her heart. Now it was dark, and the shadowed figure was moving across rough grass. He was carrying something. Something heavy and unwieldy.

She drifted unwillingly closer.

The figure stilled and lifted his head to scan his surroundings. He sniffed the air like a predator. He knew she was there. Could feel her watchfulness. Scent the sourness of her fear as he probed her mind.

Cassandra battled to draw back from those rasping, taunting fingers of curiosity. She needed the sanctuary of darkness to sweep her into oblivion – to take her back to the reality of the camp-site and away from his malevolence.

Yet it was not to be.

The figure turned slowly to face her and the scream was silent in her head, racing through the deserted hallways and corridors of her mind, filling her senses, turning night into day, then back to night.

His eyes searched for her and in their fathomless depths she could see the abyss of hell.

He began to laugh, to howl with delight as she trembled on the brink of sanity. He was the predator and she was the prey. There would be no escape.

'I know who you are,' whispered a voice behind her. 'I know what you've done and you will have to pay. Have to pay. Have to pay . . .'

Cassandra whirled towards the voice, recognising it, yet disbelieving it was possible. An ethereal face hovered in the mist, then was gone in a vapour trail of gauzy clouds.

'Melissssssssaaaa?' Her voice was a whisper, never uttered, merely a thought, echoing in the canyons of her mind.

'Come with me, Cassandra. Follow me, follow me, follow me . . .'

In that instant of bewildered terror, Cassandra knew she

and her twin were in mortal danger. Melissa had brought her the visions – had shown her the evil. Her uncommunicative twin had found the only way of showing her how to find the messenger of her nightmares and silence him for ever.

But who was he? And why had Melissa broken her silence to bring him to her?

18

Laura tugged at her hair, then wound one of the auburn curls around her finger. Round and round, tighter and tighter, only to release it and begin again. It was a childish gesture, one made almost without thought. Yet it gave her a kind of comfort, a return to a time when life was less complicated, less fraught.

'Honey, it's time we went home. You look bushed.'

Laura slowly came out of the trance at the sound of Ben's voice. She looked across at him and gave a smile. 'You go. I'm staying here in case Melissa needs me.'

Ben reached for her hand and held it, stilling her fingers, making her release her hair.

'There's nothing more anyone can do, honey. Melissa's had a rough few hours, but she's sleeping now. Come on. Time you had something to eat.'

Laura shook her head and looked down at the silent wraith who lay so still beneath the white sheets. Melissa's hysterical outbursts had stopped as abruptly as they had begun. Now she seemed at peace, her limbs soft and relaxed, her eyes closed on the reality of the world. It was as if she had accepted her fate and was content.

In Laura's deepest, darkest part of her mind, she wondered if Melissa was preparing to die.

'I'm going to lose her too, aren't I?' she whispered. The tears were bringing a lump to her throat. 'Where is Cassandra? What did I do that was so bad . . .?'

Ben moved around the bed and pulled her to her feet.

'You've done nothing, hon. This isn't a punishment, even though it may seem like it. Melissa's in the best place, you have nothing to blame yourself for.'

Laura clung to him. He was her rock, her lifeline in all this madness, and she was weary with having to stay strong.

'You must rest, Laura. All this frantic activity and late-night prowling has got to come to an end. The hotel will run itself for a while, and Melissa's not had an epileptic fit for days. As for running yourself ragged trying to find Cassandra, let the cops do their job. They're better equipped.'

She drew back sharply. 'I have to do something, Ben. I can't just sit around here or at the hotel waiting for things to happen. I have to be out there. Looking, asking questions, making a nuisance of myself at the police station. If I don't, they'll just forget Cassandra. She'll be put in a file somewhere and become a statistic.'

'That's bullshit and you know it. Stoneham's involved now, he'll make sure she isn't forgotten.'

Laura returned to the chair and took Melissa's limp hand and held it against her cheek. Ben could say what he liked. Her opinion held.

'Stoneham's not working in missing persons. He might appear sympathetic, but I don't believe he'll do anything to find her. He was more interested in David the last time I saw him.'

Ben sighed and rammed his hands into his pockets as he looked down at her.

'Personally, I hope they catch the bastard and lock him up for a very long time.'

She kissed Melissa and gathered her things together. Ben was right. She was at the end of her tether, and if she didn't get some sleep soon, she would crack up. Then she'd be no use to either of her children should they need her again.

'Well, they should have an idea where he is after that call this morning,' she said brusquely. 'I thought about it for a while after Stoneham's last visit and finally agreed to a phone tap. David has a lot of questions to answer and it's time he faced the music.'

*

Malcolm shivered in the darkness as he hunkered down in the bushes and leaned against the ancient brickwork. This place made him afraid.

The walls loomed over him, darker shadows against the night sky. The barricaded windows stared down at him like sightless eyes. He knew what this place was, had been in one that had the same ominous feel about it. Yet his memories seemed confused, for there the similarities ended. The place he'd been sent to didn't have pictures on the walls, or soft music playing in the entrance hall. He could remember only the smell of human waste and that sharp, pungent aroma of bleach. Could hear only the screams of the ones they kept in that special part of the building. The part where they'd threatened to take him if he didn't do as they said.

'Why did you bring me here?' he asked the voice that filled his mind with whispers.

He sank his head into his arms and made himself small in the darkness, cowering from the memories and the endless parade of voices.

'Got to pay, got to pay, got to pay,' they whispered.

Malcolm lifted his head, searching for the face and the eyes he knew were watching him. Yet there was only a moonless sky and the creak of ancient tree limbs to accompany him.

The sound of footsteps alerted him, and he turned away from the voices, forcing them back into the void, spurning their persistence. She was coming.

Laura Kingsley emerged from the building, her bright hair catching the light from the porch, making it glitter and spark against the whiteness of her face. She was looking up at the man who had come with her, smiling as she fastened the belt on her coat.

Malcolm drew back his lips and hissed a sigh through his clenched teeth. She had brought him here, led him away from the hotel and through the South Downs to this place of torment just as surely as the voices. He had no need to follow her any more, for this was where he would stay. His journey had reached the end. The certainty of that knowledge sent a thrill of anticipation winging through him.

This was where he would find the source of the voice and silence it for ever.

*

'Cassandra? You all right, duck?'

She drifted in the twilight world between trance and awareness and the pain in her head blotted out all coherent thought. Dry, autumnal leaves rustled in the cold wind of the vision's aftermath, heralding the onset of the migraine, bringing sunlight and shadow to dapple behind her eyelids. The vision had gone, the voice faded into the mist of distant horizons, but the images were still imprinted like negatives on her mind.

'Get her in the van, Jed. She's not right.'

Cassandra was vaguely aware of being lifted, of being carried against a broad chest that smelled of diesel fumes and wood smoke. The rough cloth of his coat prickled her face and his hands encompassed her frame as easily as if she weighed no more than a feather.

There was no energy to struggle, no will to leave that comforting breadth of chest, or those strong, capable arms.

'I have to go,' she murmured. Her lips felt numb, her tongue was cleft to the roof of her mouth, dry and enlarged, threatening to smother her.

Now the autumnal leaves had changed, had drawn back and enticed the tidal wave of migraine. Crashing rollers of it, breaking and retreating on the shores of her sanity, stifling all thought, blurring her sight and sending sparks of light to dazzle as though the ocean of pain had been touched by fire.

'You ain't going nowhere, darlin'. Put her in our bed for now, Jed. The visions have drained her, she needs to replenish her energy.'

The bed was soft beneath her back, the pillow downy

at her head, the covers scented with lavender and wild thyme. Cassandra felt her life-force spark weakly beneath the darkness of oblivion. She had to leave, had to find Melissa.

A gentle hand was lifting her head. A cup brought to her lips.

'Drink, darlin'. It's only herbs. They'll help bring back the strength to fight the demons.'

Cassandra flinched at the strangeness of the warm liquid that trickled down her throat, but she didn't have the strength to push Tabitha's hand away, so she meekly obeyed.

The pain diminished within moments of draining the cup, the high tide and crashing waves ebbed to a gentle whisper and the spark of life glowed more brightly.

Cassandra drifted in the twilight world between reality and fantasy, floating in a cocoon of soft, embracing clouds. She would sleep for a while, then she would find her twin.

*

The incident room was quieter than usual, and colder than it was outside, but it was still early, and hopefully the sun would take off some of the chill, though it was doubtful. The DCI's office faced north.

Stoneham flopped into his chair, keeping his coat on for warmth. The heating was off again.

DI Felling came into the room, heading straight for Stoneham. 'Pulled in a Lennie Bates last night, Guv. Possession and suspicion of dealing.'

'Drug Squad, Felling. Nothing to do with me.' Stoneham opened a file and pretended to be engrossed.

'Wants to do a deal. Says he's got information about that missing teenager of yours.'

He suddenly had Stonenam's full attention. 'Cassandra Kingsley?'

Felling nodded. 'But if you're not interested . . .'

'Don't be so bloody daft.' The DCI shoved back his chair and pulled off his coat. 'Where is he?'

'Downstairs.'

'Put him in interview room 1. I'm coming down. By the way, any more on the Squires thing?'

'Not much. We traced the bike and sidecar, and there was a sighting of it on the coast road late last night, so we know he's in the area. Couple of patrol officers going off duty. We hadn't sent out the notice, so they didn't pull him up.'

Stoneham's mind was working. There was something about that name, Squires. He was sure he'd seen it before, but he was darned if he knew where.

Felling was still talking, interrupting his sluggish thought waves.

'Do you know how many hotels there are between Hastings and Brighton, Guv? Could take a month of Sundays to find him. And there's no guarantee he's even working.'

Stoneham nodded tersely and both men left the room.

'Have someone ring the social and see if he's claiming. Then get on to the local hospitals and doctors. See if he's tried to get his medication. He can't just vanish into thin air, especially if he's off his pills. His behaviour would make him too noticeable.'

The two police officers thudded down the stairs to the ground floor. 'We need a collar soon on one of these murders, and Squires looks to be the most straightforward. Can't afford to balls it up.'

Lennie Bates was not the most thrilling sight first thing in the morning, but what he had to say about Cassandra Kingsley made it worth while.

'So after Darren beat her up, what happened next?'

'We had things to do, so we left her there.' Lennie was his usual morose self and the acne showed no sign of improvement.

Stoneham leaned back in his chair and studied him coldly. 'So you stop him from beating her up, and just walk away?'

Lennie nodded. 'She were all right, though. Still breathing, like.'

'Pleased to hear it. What happened next? If you're giving me the run around, boy, you'll find yourself locked up for a long time. I don't take kindly to little shits like you disturbing my morning's work for nothing.'

'Didn't see her again 'til much later. Just before your lot picked us up. She were walking across the fields, sorta staggering. I reckoned she knew what she were doing, so I didn't think nothing more of it.'

Lennie came to a sullen halt, but he must have seen the steely warning in the detective's eyes, because after a moment, he carried on.

'Bumped into a mate of mine yesterday. He seen her only the day before. Shacked up with some old travelling woman by all accounts.'

'How come he knew who she was?' Stoneham was motionless, his voice soft.

Lennie shrugged. 'Her bleedin' face were all over the papers weren't it? My mate reckoned there might be a reward in it if I told you lot.' He eyed the two detectives speculatively.

'Well, your mate was wrong. I tell you what, Lennie. You tell me everything you know about Cassandra Kingsley and I'll have a word with the arresting officer. Maybe he won't throw the book at you this time.'

'So we got a deal then?' Lennie's hopeful smile reddened the acne.

'Depends. Where were these travellers heading, Lennie?' Neither Stoneham or Felling were stupid enough to do deals with the little scrote, but it wouldn't hurt to string him along.

'West. The stone circle or something.'

'You mean Stonehenge, Salisbury?'

'Yeah, that's it. Now do we have a deal?'

Stoneham turned to Felling. 'Take him back to the cells. I've got some phone calls to make.' He left the room and shut the door on Lennie's outraged bellows.

Hurrying back to the incident room, he snatched up the phone and contacted the Salisbury police.

They already knew about the travellers and were about to go in and move them on. The owner of the field they were camping in had rounded up a few hundred outraged locals and they suspected there would be trouble before long if nothing was done.

'I'm faxing her details and photograph through to you now. Let me know when you pick her up.'

'Good news?' WDS Knight was standing beside him.

'Hopefully. We seem to have found Mrs Kingsley's missing daughter.' Stoneham tilted his chair back to get nearer the warming radiator.

His WDS bit her lip and looked down at the piece of paper in her hand.

The chair was slammed back to the floor. He didn't like the expression on his partner's face. 'What?'

'Looks like Mrs Kingsley's in for quite a day. Her husband phoned her yesterday and we got a trace. It was from a payphone.'

'And?' It was so very infuriating when Ramona paused for effect.

'No sign. But he's been seen in that area over the past few days and the local coppers are doing a thorough blitz. They hope to have him by tonight.'

*

Cassandra emerged from sleep as the cold, bright sunlight of a winter dawn penetrated the thin curtains. She lay for a moment, confused and disorientated, warm within the downy covers. Then memory returned, and with it came the cold certainty that Melissa needed her. There was no time to waste.

'You're leaving, ain't yer?' Tabitha's voice was soft, but underlying that softness was the edge of accepted truth.

Cassandra nodded as she struggled to dress beneath the heavy covers. 'I must get to Melissa.'

Tabitha nodded thoughtfully, her dark eyes unfocused as they gazed into the ether. 'There's danger ahead, luv. The ring of time's almost come full circle. You 'ave to make 'em believe yer. Show 'em the way.'

Reap the Whirlwind

Cassandra emerged from the thick sweater and swept back her long hair from her face.

'Can you see him too?' she whispered.

Tabitha reached out and stroked the glossy hair that fell in a sheet of pale silk down Cassandra's back. 'The one who stays in the shadows, hides his face in darkness. Only you have the power to remove that darkness.'

Cassandra felt the strength in Tabitha's fingers as she plaited her hair into a single rope and tied it with ribbon. The strength brought a warmth, and a soothing, healing contentment that chased away the fears and brought her courage.

The older woman cupped Cassandra's face with her gentle fingers, and for a moment of silence they regarded one another.

'You've got a battle before you, girl. Just remember, your sword is knowledge, your shield is strength. The banner you carry is truth. Rub out the curse of your namesake, Cassandra. Shred the veils that blind 'em and make 'em see.'

Cassandra closed her eyes and gave a trembling sigh. The weight of responsibilty was a heavy burden, but one she carried willingly for her sister.

'I must go,' she whispered finally, and regretfully.

Tabitha pressed something into her palm, and when Cassandra looked down she gave a cry of anguish. 'I can't take this.'

Her fingers were folded over the grubby notes and her hands were clasped in Tabitha's strong, warm grasp.

'Take it with our blessing, Cassandra. Jed'll drive you to the station. Now you must get outa here. There'll be trouble soon.'

The caravan door was thrust open and Jed's dark, cheerful face appeared.

'Time for the off. You ready, girl? Best if we can get away before the fighting breaks out.'

Cassandra blinked back the tears and struggled to contain the pain of parting as she gave Tabitha a hug. They had known each other for such a short time, yet Cassandra felt as though they had been a part of one another for ever.

'You'll be all right, won't you?' she murmured. 'That lot out there sound nasty.'

Tabitha squeezed her arms. 'We're used to it, duck. They'll move us on, that's all.' She smiled and was suddenly transformed into a beauty. 'We'll meet again, Cassandra. There's no need for them tears, 'cos the next time I sees yer, it'll be for a celebration.'

Cassandra followed Jed across the muddy field and climbed into the Land Rover. As the tyres bit into the tarmac and scattered the crowd of angry demonstrators, she looked over her shoulder.

Tabitha was merely a blur of colour set in the framework of an ancient caravan. Then she was gone.

*

Paul Galloway had spent the best part of the last twelve hours flicking through the television channels. He was bored, but at least they helped to pass the time.

He rolled off the bed, stretched and eased the stiffness in his neck and back. The drawings were scattered over the coffee table. If Hussein or his minder came to check on him it would appear he was keeping his side of the bargain.

Easing the joints in his knees, he strolled around the room and absently picked up the remains of the club sandwich he'd had delivered by room-service. The bread was dry, the meat not as fresh as he would have liked, but it was a form of sustenance, a boost to his flagging energy. His nocturnal jaunt to the all-night supermarket had been his only departure from the room, one which he knew he couldn't repeat once the young night porter had come back on duty, so there was no chance of eating in a nearby restaurant.

Paul chewed on the sandwich and stared at his reflection in the mirror tiles that covered one wall. It still gave him a jolt, seeing himself like this, but the more he looked, the better he felt about it. His tanned face didn't look out of place beneath the dark hair, and the scars were almost gone.

It had been an absolute bastard getting the dye into his hair. He'd stood around for what seemed like for ever waiting for it to take, then he'd had to repeat the process all over again when he discovered the fair patches he'd missed.

'Thank God I thought to buy more than one bottle of the stuff,' he muttered through the last of the sandwich.

Tossing the crust onto the plate, he strode over to the door. Time to check on his minder.

The keyhole was large enough for him to see the room opposite. To witness the door that stood ajar and the Arab who sat patiently watching room 405.

Paul flinched as the Arab's eyes seemed to find his. Felt the cold tremor of fear as those eyes relayed the message that he was trapped, imprisoned in this hateful room until he'd performed the tasks he'd been allocated.

He moved away from the door and began to pace, his fingers nervously plucking at the thin strand of gold that encircled his neck.

'You can't stay awake for ever, you bastard,' he muttered. 'I've kept an eye on you too. You work alone, you must be very tired by now.'

His watch told him it was almost five. It would soon be dark, and time to make his move.

He returned to the table and carefully packed away the plans. They were his security, his lifeline to provide the cash that would ease his escape. Someone, somewhere would pay handsomely for these documents.

Checking his wallet, he counted out the notes. There was enough to buy a plane ticket, enough to hire a cab. He disregarded the credit cards, they would be too easily traced. And this time his disappearance would have to be total. Hussein was not a man to be crossed, neither was Hussein's master.

Paul shivered and his hand shook as he folded his shirts and underwear into the briefcase. The death squads came in the night, silent, deadly and highly skilled. They lived in the shadows, behind closed doors, around street corners, making themselves visible only for the time it took to silence the traitors to the cause. There were never any witnesses.

He lit a cigarette and crushed the empty packet. Living in the Middle East had educated him in the vengeful ways of his Arab masters, but none was as evil, as omnipotent as the man he was about to betray.

Paul's mind whirled with conflicting thoughts, his skin prickling with fear. Perhaps he should stay. Perhaps it would be better to risk the course of British justice than the corruption of justice meted out by the henchmen who asked no questions and gave no mercy.

Paul left the briefcase on the bed and paced the room as his fevered thoughts raged. Stay, or run?

If he ran, then he would spend the rest of his life in hiding. A new face, new name, new occupation. The risk of being recognised, the slip of the tongue, the chance encounter with someone from his past. Was he courageous enough to go through with it? Did he have the strength to survive such a life?

He looked at his watch again. The minutes ticked by, the seconds raced. Yet he still could not come to a decision.

It would be nothing new to live in the shadows. His life had been changed before and he'd survived. But this was far more dangerous. There was just too much at stake, too many unknown factors. Even if he stayed, and used the plans to barter his way out of the mess, there was the awful prospect of prison. British justice wasn't as harsh, but the other prisoners would mete out cruel punishment when they found out who he was.

Paul leaned against the door, the cigarette nervously hitched between hand and mouth. He had to summon up the courage to make a move one way or the other.

His heart lost a beat, stumbled and trapped his breath in his throat.

The sound in the hallway had been soft, almost inaudible, and he would have missed it if he hadn't been pressed so closely to the door. There was someone moving furtively along the hallway. Someone whose footsteps had come to a halt outside his room.

He eased down and looked through the key-hole. The door opposite was shut, the Arab out of sight. Paul chewed his lip. Something was wrong. The man had never left his post before except to follow him. And it was too quiet, too empty out there.

Sweat broke cold on his face and trickled an icy runnels down his ribs. Was this a trick? Another gambit in the Arab's game of chess? Or was he merely convinced Paul would never dare to cross the man in the Middle East?

The memory of those furtive footsteps made him falter as the confusion swept through him. The need to make an instant decision was electric. If he was going to make a break it would have to be now. Once he'd left the sanctuary of his hotel room there would be no turning back. He would cease to exist as Paul Galloway.

Snatching up the brief case, he returned to the door, the decision still not fully formed, his actions robotic.

His hand shook as he again checked the hallway through the key-hole. There didn't seem to be anyone outside and the door to the Arab's room was still firmly shut.

Was he waiting out of sight somewhere in another doorway, knowing Paul would try to escape? Would he come, as silent as a shadow, to punish? And would he be alone?

His heart was hammering, the sweat stinging his eyes. He could still turn back, still choose to stay and see it through. And yet – and yet . . .

His hand moved on the knob, the door swung open. He had made the decision. It was now or never.

The thunder of voices deafened him. The clutch of fingers on his arms, on his shoulders, around his waist, made him writhe in terror.

They knew. They'd waited. It was the end.

He began to struggle, to kick and bellow his terror, to plead for his life, to swear allegiance and obedience if only they would let him go. He'd seen what they were capable of, heard the stories. He didn't want to die like that.

There were too many of them, and they were strong. Stronger than he would have ever thought possible.

He was falling, down, down, down. The briefcase torn from his grasp, the air expelled from his lungs beneath the weight of the men who pinned him to the floor.

Breath lost, terror complete, face rammed against the carpet.

It was over.

Paul Galloway closed his eyes in surrender, yearned for the strength to hide his cowardice and waited for the final plunge of a knife. At least it would be quick.

'David Magnus Erikson, I am arresting you on suspicion of five counts of murder and one count of attempted murder.'

19

Laura woke slowly, dragging herself from the heavy sleep that seemed so reluctant to leave her. She lay, eyes still closed, wanting to delay the moment when she would have to face the new day. Then the sound of muted voices from the sittingroom brought her eyes open and hope flaring. With one liquid movement, she swung her legs off the bed and swiped the dressing-gown over her shoulders. Tying the belt as she went, Laura headed for the door.

'Good morning, darling.'

'Mother.' Laura swallowed the fleeting disappointment. 'I heard voices, I thought it was someone with news of Cassandra,' she finished lamely.

Clara flashed her a look of resignation. 'I know I should have called first, but I wanted to surprise you.' She tugged at the hem of her Chanel suit. 'Sorry you were disappointed.'

Laura swiftly crossed the room and kissed the scented cheek, then sat next to her and held her hand.

'It's lovely to see you, and of course I'm not disappointed.'

They regarded one another for a moment and Laura acknowledged silently that she was glad Clara had come home. They had spent too long apart, the family was disintegrating before her eyes and after their talk at the clinic all those days ago, it was time to mend the fences and begin again.

'I thought you were in New York?'

Clara shrugged elegant shoulders. 'Your stepfather's tied

up with business meetings and I really couldn't face the endless round of lunches and benefits. It all seems so trivial when I think of what you're going through. I couldn't get you and the twins out of my mind.'

'I'm glad you're back. A lot's been happening.'

Clara returned the pressure on Laura's hand. 'I know, Ben's been filling me in.' She leaned closer and added in a low murmur. 'He's a gem, darling. Hold on to him. You won't do any better.'

Laura relaxed and leaned back into the cushions with a laugh. 'I do recognise a good thing when I see it, Mother. I've no intentions of letting him slip through my fingers.'

'Glad to hear it. Now if y'all have finished talking about me, I suggest we have breakfast and get back to Melissa.' Ben's eyes were bright with humour as he put down the tray and poured out the strong black coffee and added sweetener for Clara.

'How is she?' Clara sipped the coffee and looked at Laura over the rim of her cup.

'Strangely enough, she seems a little better,' said Laura carefully. She didn't want to give Clara false hope, but there had definitely been signs that Melissa was coming out of her crisis. 'She seems more relaxed and is sleeping without medication. The last fit she had was over a week ago and Dr Baines says the drawing therapy has really helped. She's finding a way to communicate at last.'

There was silence in the room as her voice tailed off. Laura and Ben looked at one another.

'What are you keeping from me?' Clara put her cup and saucer firmly on the table and her gaze trawled back and forth between them.

'Melissa's been doing strange kinda drawin's. I saw something like that in Alabama when I was working there one semester as part of my degree.'

Clara leaned foreward. 'And?'

Ben looked at Laura, then studied the pattern on the coffee cup.

'The kids I was teaching had problems and the only way

into their minds was through their drawings. It was all there in gruesome detail, Clara. Abuse, despair, hatred, anger. Melissa's drawings have the same darkness about them, but so far none of us can make out what she's trying to tell us.'

'Probably something to do with what happened to her,' retorted Clara.

'I'm certain it is, and so are the doctors. But none of it makes sense. She seems to have this fixation about foxes or dogs. And rows and rows of eyes.'

Laura shivered and drew the dressing-gown closer. 'Cassandra drew something very like that the afternoon Melissa disappeared, but I didn't take much notice of it at the time. Now I wish I had.'

Clara twisted the expensive rings on her fingers, her gaze distant as she looked into space. 'Cassandra's a special child, Laura. Always has been.'

'I know. I find it disconcerting at times. She would always know when the telephone was about to ring, and who was at the other end. And do you remember when she dreamed about that awful plane crash hours before it happened?'

'I'll never forget it, and she was so young. Seven, eight years old, yet so insistent.' Clara seemed to be making an enormous effort to drag herself back to the present. 'It was too late for us to do anything that time. But I get the feeling that Cassandra's disappearance and Melissa's drawings could be linked. Perhaps we should take these strange events as a warning.'

'Come on! You don't seriously believe in all that voodoo, hoodoo nonsense, do you?' Ben eyed them both with amazed disbelief. 'We're living in the twentieth century. Witches and soothsayers went out with the Ark.'

Laura looked across at her mother. 'You don't know the girls as well as we do, Ben. There are things in the past that would defy all argument. I think Mother's right. There's something about to happen and only the girls have the key.'

*

After watching the woman drive away into the night, Malcolm had spent several hours prowling the grounds of the private hospital. Security was lax and he'd found it easy to evade the night-watchman, yet he could find no way of entering the building without arousing suspicion.

The problem nagged at him as the voices grew more insistent. They whispered and cajoled, taunted and enticed. The train wheels rumbled over their ghostly tracks and the smell of hot oil and smoke was strong. She was inside this place. Waiting for him, calling him. He had to find a way to reach her.

He rounded the corner and leaned against the wall. The sun would soon be up and he would have to leave. Pushing his glasses over the bridge of his nose, he squinted into the lightening sky and shivered. He was cold and hungry and the voices were hurting his head. If she wanted him to obey, then why didn't she give him a sign?

The first rays of the sun sketched a cold white line on the horizon. The blinding, reflected glare caught the edge of his glasses and made his eyes water. He turned his head and looked through the window pane that had caused this temporary blindness.

It was the hospital laundry, built as an annexe to the main building, its ugly, utilitarian bulk hidden at the back away from the grand façade. Malcolm trembled and his stomach executed a slow roll. Maybe she was giving him a sign after all. Was this her way of showing him how to find her?

He stood for a moment in an agony of indecision. The voices were louder now, their whispers echoing in his head, making it difficult to think. The low rumble of the wheels was growing in intensity, drawing nearer, bringing their voices to join the maddening chorus.

A bewildering parade of emotions swept through him as he hesitated. There was danger here. This place held secrets, secrets he didn't want to acknowledge. Yet he had to find her. Had to see the person behind the voice that tormented him. Had to face that person and understand why she watched him, why she probed his mind so fiercely and refused to free him.

Malcolm looked back at the window. Someone had forgotten to close it completely. It was a sign that he was doing the right thing.

He pushed up the latch, and with a final, hasty look over his shoulder, he climbed into the laundry room.

*

Laura brushed back the fine, pale hair from Melissa's forehead and smiled. 'Hello, darling. Look who's come to see you.'

Melissa's expression didn't change, but Laura thought she saw an answering glint of something in her eyes as Clara came to sit beside her.

'I think she knows you're here, Mother,' she said with awe.

Clara took Melissa's hand and kissed it. 'I think you're imagining things, darling.' She pressed the pale, limp hand against her cheek. 'If only . . .'

'What is it? Mother?' Laura sat rigid as the expression on Clara's face changed.

'Look.' Clara tipped her head towards the door.

Laura turned, gasped and put her hands over her mouth. She remained rooted to the chair, incapable of speech, bereft of cohesive thought.

'Mum? Granny C?'

Cassandra was framed in the doorway. The well-worn Doc Martens peeped out from beneath the long, colourful skirt. A ragged purple sweater reached almost to her knees beneath the leather coat and her fair hair was plaited in a rope over her shoulder. She looked like a gypsy waif.

'Cassie!'

Laura was on the move, the chair knocked to the floor behind her as she rushed to embrace the child she thought she'd lost. She felt the trembling thinness of her, drank in the sight of her beautiful blue eyes and pale, freckled skin. There were no words invented that could express how she was feeling. She was replete with happiness, overflowing with the joy of holding her, touching her, renewing the sight and the scent of her. Yet at the same time there were so many questions. So much she wanted to say, so many bridges that had to be crossed to heal the rift of their parting.

'I'm sorry, Mum. I didn't mean to run away. I didn't want to hurt you. It just happened. Please say you'll forgive me.'

The tears were warm and damp on Laura's cheek as they clutched one another, but she made no move to wipe them away. They were a part of her child, a reminder of the torment she must have gone through in their days apart.

'There's nothing to forgive,' crooned Laura as she drew back and cupped Cassandra's face in her hands. Her hungry gaze devouring that much loved face and her heart aching at the sight of the fading bruises and cuts.

'I thought I'd never see you again. What happened, Cass? Why didn't you ring? I wouldn't have been cross.'

Cassandra's eyes dipped to the floor as she pulled at a loose thread in her sweater.

'I was going to ring, but I didn't know what to say. Then as the days went by I lost my nerve and it just became impossible to pick up a phone. I knew you'd be worried out of your mind, knew how angry you would be.'

She lifted bewildered eyes. 'There were some weird things going on, Mum. And I wanted space and time to think things over and get them straight in my head.'

Laura stroked back the wisps of hair that strayed from the plait, noticing the frayed scarlet ribbon that held it together.

'I'm not angry, Cass. Never was. Just going crazy with not knowing where you were or what had happened to you.'

She sighed as she retied the ribbon. It was as if time had stood still and Cassandra was once more five years old and having her hair plaited for school. The memory made the pain in her heart more real, more burdensome. It enforced the protectiveness she yearned to give this troubled child. Underlined the responsibility of mothering and found her wanting.

'They pulled that Snake person in for questioning you

know. I was convinced he'd done away with you.' She feathered the bruise on Cassandra's cheekbone and felt her wince. 'Did he do this?'

Cassandra nodded, her gaze evading Laura's. 'Don't hassle me about it, Mum. It's over.'

'Can't a grandmother get a look in around here? What about a kiss and a hug?'

Laura watched as Cassandra flung herself into Clara's arms and held her. The titian red and the pale blond silk came together in the shaft of sunlight and seemed to bring summer and autumn into the silent hospital room. An unwanted spark of jealousy speared her and she pushed it away. It was time to let Cassandra live her own life. She would have to learn to let go.

Cassandra withdrew from Clara's embrace and approached the silent, watching Melissa. Without a word, she climbed onto the bed, laid down and took her twin into her arms. Then, with a sigh, she closed her eyes.

'I came back because Melissa called me. We have to protect her, watch over her. There's danger in this place.'

Laura looked at her twins, then back to her mother. A shaft of fear speared the silence between them. This child of hers was changed, grown in confidence, with an air of quiet capability about her. She'd seen things and been places that Laura might never fully understand, and if there was a grain of truth in what she said, then they would fight it together. At least she had come home.

*

The location was a London police station. The time was two thirty in the afternoon of Erikson's first full day of questioning.

DCI Stoneham eyed David Erikson with disgust. Everything he'd come to know about the man was being underlined by his behaviour. Laura Kingsley's ex-husband was a snivelling, ingratiating coward. A weak man who preyed on women for his own perverted satisfaction because they were, in his eyes, the weaker sex. Now he was sheltering behind a lawyer, refusing to talk.

The door opened and a young PC nodded to the bald, bull-necked Met officer in charge. Stoneham watched DCI Anderson converse in a low monotone, then take charge of a package before shutting the door. Curiosity, and impatience were making him restless. He had questions to ask this bastard, but as usual, the Met was having it all its own way.

Anderson settled his bulk on the uncomfortable wooden chair. 'Now then, Mr Erikson. Perhaps you'd like to watch a little something that was handed in to my detective sergeant about six hours after your arrest.'

It was a rhetorical question, as Anderson didn't wait for a reply. Instead, he finished rigging up the television and video that had been brought in earlier and slotted the cassette into the machine.

Erikson blanched and his solicitor bent his head to listen to the hasty whisper.

Anderson's meaty hand hovered over the start button.

'I have to insist that my client and I see this video before any more questions are put to him. I demand time alone with my client to do just that.'

'Fair enough. Perhaps when he's watched it, he'll be more forthcoming,' snapped Anderson. He scraped back his chair. 'Don't even consider trying to tamper with it, either. It won't do you any good. We already made a copy.'

Stoneham followed Anderson's lumbering figure out of the interview room. He gave a vast yawn and headed for the coffee machine down the hall. The night had been a long one after receiving the call from the Met at midnight. He'd driven straight up, but because of restrictions and the presence of Erikson's solicitor, they'd had to wait until the afternoon to begin questioning him again.

'Any further news on the courier?' Stoneham grimaced. The coffee was foul.

Anderson shook his head. 'The package was picked up by the courier service from an hotel in Victoria. The receptionist couldn't give much of a description, merely said she thought the girl that left it looked like she slept on the streets, but as she had the money, she didn't take much notice.'

Their makeshift breakfast was interrupted half an hour later as Erikson's solicitor tapped on the door.

'My client is ready to make a statement,' he said solemnly. 'I don't wish to hurry you, but I do have to be in court in an hour.'

Anderson rose like a human monolith from his chair. 'Then you'd better get your client to spill his guts, and fast. The video tape is only the beginning.'

Stoneham hurried after them, his mind returning to Brighton and his DS. She should have the test results from the path lab some time today.

Erikson's face was drawn and pale beneath the tan and the hair dye. His eyes refused to meet theirs as they entered the room and sat down.

'I want to make a deal,' he said quietly.

Anderson's bulk shifted in the chair. 'I don't think you realise what serious charges you're facing. You're in no position to make deals, Erikson.'

'I have proof that one of the most unstable regimes is trying to build nuclear weapons. I can give you names and places, factory sites here in England that are willing to supply the necessary engineering.'

The room stilled and all Stoneham could hear was the stentorian breathing of his colleague.

'Bullshit. Don't waste my time, Erikson. Get on with the statement.' Anderson's voice was a growl which echoed through the room and out into the hallway.

David Erikson sat forward and rested his arms on the table between them. 'Get my briefcase. The plans are all in there. Then we'll see who's talking bullshit.'

Anderson looked at Stoneham, his eyes blank with confusion. 'We don't have a briefcase,' he said shortly.

Erikson clenched his fists on the table, his eyes were wild and staring. 'I had it when you manhandled me in the hotel. You must have it. I felt it pulled out of my hand.'

Anderson spoke into the tape recorder and left the room, only to return minutes later.

'No briefcase, Erikson. We searched the room and brought everything back here.'

Erikson slumped across the table, his head buried in his arms. 'The bastard must have made off with it in the confusion,' he mumbled. 'Jesus Christ, what a mess.'

'I don't know what you're on about, Erikson, but you're wasting my time. Are you making a statement, or do I put you back in the cells?'

David Erikson finally lifted his head. Defeat lay heavy in his eyes and in the slope of his shoulders. 'I'll make the statement. They've stitched me up. First the video, now the missing plans. I don't have any real choice, do I?'

The day wore on and the police officers became more restless. The statement had taken over two hours, then Erikson was escorted back to his cell for the obligatory rest between interviews. The whole thing was getting on their tits and there was still no word from Brighton.

Stoneham was in Anderson's office. He looked at his watch. Perhaps he should call and find out if the Salisbury police had managed to catch up with Cassandra Kingsley. She'd already slipped through their fingers once, but she couldn't have got very far.

He was eyeing the telephone on Anderson's desk when the door burst open.

'Right. Your turn, Stoneham. Let's see if we can't wrap this up nice and tight and waterproof.'

'Let's just hope he has the right bloody answers, or I'll have Chapman to contend with when I get back.'

Erikson had had a shower and a shave and was looking fresh and confident after his rest. His solicitor had gone, and now there was a younger man from the same firm in his place.

The Brighton detective slammed the pile of buff folders on the desk and sat down. The last few hours had been used profitably, now he would see if this cocky bastard could wriggle out of this one.

Reap the Whirlwind

'Your daughter's been spotted by the way. Alive and well, and living with a group of travellers. We should be sending her home to her mother soon.'

He waited for Erikson's reaction, but was disappointed. The man revealed nothing.

'Why have you brought me back here? I told you everything.'

'Not quite everything, Erikson.' He opened the first of the buff folders. 'I want you to go back to the spring of 1985. You should remember it. It was the spring your daughter Melissa was abducted and assaulted.'

He caught the fear in Erikson's eyes and noticed the tightening of that mean little mouth.

'You had no alibi for the time that Karen Walker was murdered. Perhaps you'd like to explain where you were and what you were doing on the afternoon of the 16th of March.'

Erikson shot a look of panic at the young lawyer. 'Do I have to answer him? I was released with no charges. They had nothing to go on. No proof that I had anything to do with Karen's murder.'

'I fail to see what this line of questioning has to do with the current charge against my client, Chief Inspector. Mr Erikson was cleared of all charges pertaining to the Walker murder.'

The Brighton detective held the younger man's attention. 'He's just confessed to brutally attacking two young prostitutes. Your client has owned up to being a misogynist and a pervert. I have six dead girls who were beaten and strangled with a wire noose before they were defiled by a wooden stake. I can place him in the area of at least two of those murders, and I want some answers.'

Erikson and his lawyer conferred for some minutes, then the lawyer nodded. 'My client is willing to tell you everything he knows. But he wishes to make it clear that he had nothing to do with these girl's deaths.'

'We'll see about that,' Stoneham mumbled. 'Where were you on the afternoon Karen Walker died?'

'I was out looking for a job. I was made redundant and

because of the police harassment after Melissa's abduction, it wasn't easy to persuade an employer to take me on.' Erikson's manner was sullen, and his pale blue eyes flickered over the room in evasion of Stoneham's penetrating glare.

'Names, addresses of these prospective employers.'

'I can't remember now. Christ Almighty, man. It was over ten years ago.'

'What exactly is your line of employment, Erikson?'

The man looked startled, unsettled by the change. 'Engineer. I did my apprenticeship when I left school and stayed with the same company until it folded.'

'But you aren't an engineer any more, are you? What exactly do you do to earn a crust, Erikson? By the looks of that suit, whatever it is, it must be either highly profitable, or very illegal.'

'I'm a fixer. I take on clients who want something manufactured and arrange for the machinery and the men to do the job.'

'It's a bit more than that, isn't it? What you really do is brown nose to the people with more money than morals and fix them up a nice little private arsenal. An engineering factory here, a warehouse there, men and machinery transported across the world, all camouflage for the real business of omnipotent power and destruction for your megalomaniac masters.'

Erikson shrugged. 'If that's what you want to believe.'

'Oh, I believe it. There's a couple of men from the Home Office who were very informative once they knew you'd been arrested. You should have kept quiet about these missing plans, you were so keen to find.' Stoneham paused, noting the sharp look in Erikson's eyes. 'Why did you change your name?'

'No law against it.'

'What were you hiding, Erikson? Your shady past, or your predilection for violence against young girls? That's a dodgy game in the Middle East. They cut your balls off for things like that over there.'

Erikson studied the ceiling.

'What were you doing in Brighton on the night of October 28th?' The detective's voice was hard-edged as the words shot like machine-gun fire across the table.

Erikson flinched. 'I wasn't in Brighton,' he snapped.

'Don't lie to me, Erikson. You were seen.'

David Erikson's hand shook as he lit a cigarette. All bravado was sinking fast. 'Then they were mistaken,' he mumbled.

Stoneham threw down a photograph. 'Remember her?'

The glance was fleeting before Erikson shook his head.

'Her name was Mary Funnell. She was sixteen. She died sometime on the night of October 28th this year.'

'I told you, I don't know her. Never seen her before.'

'What about this one? Remember her?' Another photograph was placed on the table.

Erikson didn't reply.

'You probably never knew her name, but Charmaine Roberts remembers you. Has cause to. She was badly beaten, and if it hadn't been for her pimp, she would have died.'

'Okay, so I was in Brighton,' Erikson shouted. 'But you can't pin murder on me for that. The bitch turned nasty and I slapped her round a bit. She was fine when I left her. How the hell do you know it wasn't the pimp that beat her up?'

'It's not something that particular pimp has ever resorted to,' retorted Stoneham tartly. 'What was the reason for the altercation with Charmaine, Erikson? Could it have had something to do with the fact that you're impotent?'

'There's nothing wrong with me,' growled Erikson. 'The bitch wasn't very good at her job, that's all.'

'I have a report here from a doctor in Harley Street. Apparently, you've been seeing him on your visits to this country over the past five years. What does this doctor specialise in, Erikson?'

'Stress,' blustered the man opposite.

'I've spoken to him, and although stress may be the underlying reason for your impotency, it doesn't alter the fact that you can't get it up. It was the reason you lost your temper under the railway arches the other night. The reason you beat up Charmaine Roberts and the tom in Soho. Wasn't it?'

'I obviously can't change your mind, so I won't bother to sink to your level, Stoneham. You haven't said anything yet to tie me in with these murders. Don't you think it's about time to admit you were wrong, and let me go?'

The DCI ignored him as the tension built.

'So after leaving Charmaine in such an unsatisfactory manner, what did you do next, eh? Go off to the rave looking for another target? Bump into Mary? Finish what you started?'

Erikson's face was suffused with rage. 'Rave? What bloody rave? The pimp you so endearingly believe can do no wrong, beat the shit out of me. I was in no fit state to go anywhere.'

'So you knew nothing about the rave on Saxon Hill? You never went there?'

'I've already told you.'

'Then how come you dropped this in Charmaine's bedroom?' He pushed the brightly coloured flyer across the table. 'How come the landlord of the Stag's Head remembers you being handed this earlier on? How come it's covered in your fingerprints?'

The silence was heavy as Erikson slumped back into his chair, but the detective wasn't finished.

'The overalls we found in your room. The ones you were wearing in the video. Are they a part of the ritual when you beat up women?'

The plastic evidence bag was dumped onto the table. The black vinyl coveralls gleamed dully in the electric light.

'Do they turn you on?' persisted Stoneham.

'Obviously not, seeing as how you believe I'm impotent,' snarled Erikson.

'But they're the perfect cover if someone's clawing and scratching to get away from you. They leave no trace on the victim, carry no fibres, can be washed and put in their plastic bag nice and neat until the next time.'

Erikson lifted his frightened gaze to Jack. 'I like the

feel of plastic. It isn't against the law,' he whispered weakly.

'It's my duty to warn you David, Magnus Erikson, that you can be placed in the same area as that of two victims. You have been video taped in the act of violating a young woman in a brutal manner, dressed in clothes that would hide all forensic evidence. In each case of murder there was no attempt at sexual intercourse and no semen. It is the expert opinion of the police psychiatrist that the murderer is impotent. What do you have to say?'

Erikson was shaking, and there was a blue tinge to his lips. 'I want time to speak to my lawyer. Alone.'

20

Malcolm's hurried search through the clean laundry had borne fruit. Now, with the olive green shirt and trousers and the tiny white name tag, he would be able to move through the hospital without suspicion.

He slid his tongue over his top lip as he concentrated on writing 'John Smith' on the tag. The name had worked for him once, why not again? With one last careful check that he'd made no spelling mistakes, he pinned it on and reached for the door.

It was locked.

He pulled and twisted and searched for a key, but there was no mistake. He was shut in here until the workforce arrived. The sweat beaded his forehead and his heart thudded against his ribs.

'Shut you away. Lock the door. Lose the key. Close you in, close you in, close you in . . .' The voices rose in unison to fill his head and make him wither.

'Stop it. Stop it. It's not my fault. Don't do this to me,' he moaned as he covered his ears and cowered against the locked door.

The room closed in on him and the ceiling loomed nearer to the floor. Malcolm slid down the wall and buried his head in his arms. It was like before. A locked room that gleamed white and surgically shining. There was nowhere to run and nowhere to hide. They were waiting for him outside that door which had no key. Waiting with their white coats and their sharp needles.

He sobbed as he thought of the rough hands and the rougher voices, of the pills shoved down his throat and the straps that held him while they put electricity into his head.

'Run, Malcolm, run. Coming to get you, coming to get you, coming to get you.'

Malcolm jerked up his head. He could hear footsteps in the hall. Voices that didn't belong with the ones in his mind. They were coming.

The window rattled in the wind, reminding him of how he'd got into this place. It offered a chance to escape, to hide before they opened the door and found him there.

Malcolm crossed the room at a run. He climbed up onto the sink and plunged head-first out of the window, leaving it to clatter behind him.

The air was punched from his lungs as he landed on the ground, but he knew he couldn't stay there. Rolling away from the building, he sought the shelter of the bushes and lay gasping in the damp undergrowth.

'Some silly bugger left the window open last night, Stan. And look at the state of my nice clean sink.'

Malcolm sank further into the cover of greenery.

'Better check nothing's missing, Ruby. Though I can't say I'd want a load of old hospital bedding.'

'Let's have a coffee first, I . . .'

The window was slammed shut and the sound of the latch dropping made Malcolm sigh with relief. It would be all right, and he was sure that no-one would miss a pair of porter's trousers and a shirt.

He caught his breath and smothered the chuckle. I've been very clever, he thought. And they wanted to shut me away. Said I was sick, crazy in the head.

The elation turned to calculating slyness and his pale eyes glittered behind the thick lenses. 'I'll show them,' he whispered.

Minutes later he was away from the laundry and rounding another corner. Crouching beneath a window, he listened and realised he'd come to the kitchens. The sound of rattling dishes and the smell of cooking meat made his mouth water.

He was very hungry and he couldn't remember when he'd last eaten.

He hesitated for a moment as something strange occurred to him. There were a lot of things he couldn't remember. Things he knew were important. Yet they slithered away from him just as he thought he'd got a firm grip on them.

Malcolm shook his head as though to clear it. The voices were to blame of course. The voices and the rumble of the wheels. They were no longer his friends. That was why he was here. To silence them. To make them go away and stop their tormenting.

Leaving the enticing aroma of the kitchen area, he carried on round the building until he came to a narrow door set back in the wall. It swung back at the touch of a finger, and revealed steep concrete steps that appeared to meander to the next floor.

Malcolm darted an anxious look behind him, and warily stepped into the gloom. With his senses alerted to every sound and smell that surrounded him, he clutched the iron railing and began to climb.

The stairwell was bare of paint or plaster and as the steps progressed on their seemingly endless journey upwards, Malcolm's nerve almost left him. He had no idea where they were leading, or what he would find at the end. He knew only that he had come too far to back away now. She was in here somewhere and he had to find her.

His footsteps echoed in the silence and his breath was painfully shallow as he reached the final step. He paused and regarded the door in front of him, not quite ready to face whatever was behind it. He listened, and hearing nothing that enlightened him, steeled himself to push it open.

The room he'd entered was vast and eerily empty. The walls were white, the floor covered in highly polished green linoleum. Light came from a long narrow window, and he could see into the hallway through the open door. Bundles of refuse sacks were stacked against two of the walls and by the third was a collection of cardboard boxes marked 'SHARPS'.

Yet Malcolm's attention was on the great furnace which was set in the fourth wall. It hummed and flickered like a sleeping giant, waiting patiently for the next meal.

Malcolm watched the somnolent flames, drawn to their beauty, mesmerised by their lazy brightness. He'd always liked fire – it reminded him of ... The memory skidded away, lost beneath the jangling taunts in his mind.

The slam of a door and the sound of running feet brought him sharply back to the present. He had to get out of here – and quick.

The open door revealed a long, empty hallway. Empty but for a trolley. Malcolm dusted down his borrowed clothes and stepped out confidently. This was something he recognised, something that didn't need to be dragged from hazy memory. He grasped the handles of the trolley and began to push it down the hall.

'I see you, see you, see you.'

Malcolm's footsteps faltered as the soft, lullaby of her voice drifted in his head like mist. 'Where are you?' he answered her silently.

'See you. See you. See you.' The voice was taunting him, wavering in that veil of secrecy she always hid behind, before slithering away.

Malcolm pushed the trolley down the endless corridors, turning left and right, past shuttered rooms and open waiting lounges. The tide of humanity eddying past him, eyes averted, set on a distant goal as they hurried on their way. He began to wonder if he was invisible. Perhaps the voices were shielding him, hiding him from those who were incapable of understanding the power in his head.

'Where are you going with that? We need it in room 26.'

Malcolm's heart stumbled out of sequence. 'I'm new here,' he mumbled.

The nurse barely looked at him. Her starched cap and neat uniform bristled with importance as she gave an impatient sigh and rustled the papers on her clip-board.

'Follow me,' she ordered. 'You people certainly take your time, and there should be two of you to help with the lifting.'

Malcolm hurried after her neat, angular figure as she strode down the corridor, his eyes flickering back and forth into the rooms they were passing. The purveyor of the whispers was close, he could feel her presence, almost the scent of her.

'Come on then. I haven't got all day.'

Malcolm tried to concentrate, but it was getting harder. The voices were persistent, growing in number, pushing the soft tissue in his head until he thought it would tear and spill the contents of his mind onto the floor.

The nurse was looking at him now. The full heat of her dark gaze was centred on him, impaling him, making him clumsy as he helped transfer the white shrouded figure from the bed.

'Ops 3.'

Malcolm chewed his lip. The rage against her was building, the fear escalating. If I don't get out of here she'll see what's happening in my head. Nurses can do things like that. They have pills and needles and things to turn off the sun and make it endlessly dark. If only she'd turn away and stop staring at me.

'I'll show you the way. But really, you'll have to move quicker if you want to keep your job here.'

Malcolm saw her examine the name tag on his shirt. His hands were sweaty on the handles of the trolley and his legs had somehow lost their ability to hold him up.

'Don't I know you?' The dark eyes were burning into him, the frown drawing the heavy eyebrows into a line of puzzlement.

Malcolm shook his head, afraid to speak, mesmerised by her frank, all-encompassing stare. His head ached and his ears buzzed. The wheels were roaring over the points, the black tunnel looming fast.

She shook her head. 'I never forget a face. It'll come to me. I know I've seen you somewhere before.'

*

Cassandra was suddenly awake and alert. 'He's here,' she whispered.

'Who? Darling, what are you talking about?'

The sound of Laura's voice was distant, muffled, and the autumnal leaves were fluttering in her head again, catching the sun in bright needles of light.

'He's here,' she repeated softly. 'The circle of time is closing fast. He must be stopped.' Ochre and yellow, red and gold, fluttering, dancing, sighing as they rustled and whispered in that fifth dimension.

Melissa stirred beside her, reaching for her, grasping her hand, becoming the conduit for the visions that flashed in her head.

'Cassandra stop it. You're frightening me.' Laura's voice seemed ethereal, a part of another world. A world that had no flashes of colour, or shadowed figures.

Cassandra felt the power ebb, the veil of mist draw back from her eyes. Yet she knew it was gathering strength and would return. She had to make them listen, to make them believe before it was too late. Had to harness the power she and Melissa had been given for the time when it would be needed most.

She looked at the three people sitting around the bed. There was Granny C, as lovely and as elegant as ever, her wide green eyes filled with acceptance. We are alike, you and I, she thought. You know about the things in my head. Understand what I see when the autumn leaves begin their dance.

Her gaze shifted to Laura. Poor Mum. The elfin face was nude of make-up and her fiery hair was scraped back to reveal the anguish she'd suffered over the last weeks. Cassandra felt a plunge of regret, but knew she would have to blank it out, forget it. There was no time to make amends. Not now.

Cassandra turned finally to Ben. His long legs were stretched out before him, the cowboy boots scuffed and worn. His hands were deep in the pockets of his jeans and in his eyes she saw disbelief, scorn.

'There's a man,' she began hesitantly, looking deeply into one pair of eyes before going to the next. 'Melissa can see him clearly and she's trying to use me as a vessel for her knowledge.

Reap the Whirlwind

He knows we can see him. Knows we can speak to him. We have heard him, watched him, sensed his presence. He brings evil intentions with him.'

'Come on, honey. Don't frighten your Momma with all that spooky talk.' Ben stood up, the chair scraping the floor.

Cassandra held him still, locked into him with the power of her mind. She could feel the strength coming from Melissa, as if it were an electric charge.

'I have a gift,' she said solemnly. 'The gift of the fifth dimension. Melissa and I have always shared this gift, but now I am the only one who can convey the messages she is receiving.'

'Listen to her, Ben. Don't be too hasty in your judgement.' Clara's voice was low, and she reached out to grasp his hand. 'There are stranger things between heaven and earth than we could ever imagine.'

Cassandra felt Melissa's arm snake around her waist. She looked into her twin's eyes and there, where there was once an endless vacuum, was life. A restless, yearning life that struggled to be born, that screamed for release in that silent world of torment.

'I understand.' Cassandra transmitted the thought as she held Melissa close. 'I'm here now. We'll face him together and unlock the door to your silence.'

She turned to the three people she trusted, but as she spoke, she realised the words were not her own. They were her twin's.

'Our paths of destiny were drawn ten years ago. This man brings the key that will unlock the chains that bind. He must be found, for although he carries the key of freedom, he also carries the scythe of death. We are about to reap the whirlwind.'

'For Christ's sake, Laura. Are you going to listen to this nonsense? The kid's freakin' out!'

Cassandra watched as Laura's gaze hitched between them. She could see the confusion, the hesitancy, the eagerness to believe and the doubts that made her falter.

'This man,' mumbled Laura, her hands twisting in her

lap. 'Who is he? And why should he mean harm to you both?'

Cassandra looked at her twin. The veil of darkness had descended once more in her eyes.

'Melissa isn't ready to tell us yet.'

'I don't believe what I'm hearing,' groaned Ben as he shifted impatiently in his chair. He threw bewildered glances at the women and gave a great sigh of frustration.

'Stop it, Ben.' Laura's voice was sharp. 'If Cassandra says Melissa's in danger, than I believe her. I'm not going to make the same mistake again. I'm calling the police.'

Ben turned to Clara. 'Can't you make her see sense? What the hell are the cops going to make of this? They'll think Laura's going nuts!'

Clara looked up at him and shook her head. 'Out of my hands, I'm afraid. Do sit still, Ben. I think it's time I told you all about the strange things my granny could see. And about the times when we thought she'd completely fallen off her perch.' She smiled. 'But it was surprising how many things she knew. She even saw the twins before they were conceived, and knew they would be blessed, as she was.'

Cassandra watched the disbelief flit across Ben's handsome face as he ran his fingers through his shaggy hair. She closed her eyes and felt comforted by the familiar tales of her great-great-grandmother. At that moment, the inherited gift which had missed three generations made her seem very close.

*

It was four o'clock in the afternoon and David Erikson was talking. His nervous fingers clung to the cigarette in his mouth as if it offered a lifeline. The interview room was thick with smoke and they had already used three cassette tapes to take his statement.

'I had nothing to do with any of this. Okay,' he held up his hands, then let them fall. 'I was in the area for two of the murders, but I swear to God I knew nothing about them.'

'Religious, are you?' Stoneham remarked drily.

Erikson lifted his head and eyed him. 'No. That doesn't mean I don't believe in justice. But what you're doing is trying to pin these murders on me. I wasn't the only one pulled in when Karen whatsername got killed. Why don't you get them in here and brow-beat them?'

'Because one of them is a guest of Her Majesty and the other was only fourteen at the time and had an alibi,' snarled the detective from Brighton.

'How the hell do you expect me to convince you I'm not lying?'

A passport was tossed onto the table. 'This shows you were in the country each time a murder was committed. You give me an alibi for the times when you were in this country and then I might begin to believe you.'

Erikson slumped across the table. 'I've already told you. I was here on business, I had people to see, deals to close. These people won't talk. I have no alibi.'

'Like 'em young, don't you?' snapped Stoneham as he changed tack once again. 'Charmaine was eighteen, but her punters thought they were getting fourteen-year-old meat. Dress up for you, did she? Put on the gym slip so you could get into character before you beat her up?'

'So bloody what? She's a whore, they do things like that! I went to her because I needed sex. If you'd lived in the Middle East, you'd understand.' Erikson's fists came down hard on the table, making the ashtray judder.

'Karen Walker wasn't a tom. Neither were Patricia Riley, Lesley Moore, Tanya, Gina, or Mary. They were kids, Erikson. Just poor, lonely, lost kids.' He leaned across the table until he was inches away from Erikson's face. 'Perverts like you make me sick.'

'That's enough, Stoneham,' warned the solicitor. 'Unless you change this line of questioning, I'm afraid I'll have to put a stop to the interview.'

'What did you use to strangle them with, Erikson?' Stoneham hadn't moved out of Erikson's face, his gaze never releasing the hold on the man in front of him. 'What was it? Come on, you might as well tell me.'

Erikson shook his head, his fists knotted on the table between them.

'Piano wire, cheese cutter, guitar string? What?'

'I didn't do it,' David whispered.

'I suggest you used this.' The thin loop of gold glittered beneath the bright lamp.

Erikson stilled, his eyes blinking rapidly as the breath hissed through his teeth. 'You've got no proof,' he whispered.

Stoneham opened the small plastic bag and pulled out the gold wire necklace that had been taken from Erikson at his arrest. It was finely crafted, and as thin as a cat's whisker. He let it dangle from his finger, careful not to destroy any evidence.

'Forensics say otherwise. Still sticking to your story, Erikson?'

'I had that made in Iran last year,' Erikson was shouting, pushing away from the table and glaring down at the police officer. 'I couldn't possibly have killed those girls with it, and I've got the receipt to prove it. You're fitting me up with this and I refuse to answer any more of your questions.'

Stoneham had heard enough. The video tape would prove beyond doubt that Erikson had used it on the young tom. Now it was up to forensics to see if they could nail him for any of the others, but the odds were long and the man in front of him made him nauseous.

'How can you sleep at night, Erikson? What goes on in that twisted mind that blanks out all the horror? Take him back to the cells. There's a nasty smell in here.'

'Bit rough, weren't you, Jack?' Anderson's bulk rose from the chair and threw a vast shadow against the wall.

'It's creeps like him that makes me glad I'm retiring,' replied Stoneham wearily. 'If I was rough on him, then I hate to think what sort of treatment he'll get in prison.'

'He'll get sectioned. All the nonces do,' replied Anderson gruffly as they went out into the hall. 'By the way, your DS phoned. Can you ring her back?'

Stoneham nodded, but he was deep in thought. Although he disliked Erikson intensely and knew that there was enough evidence to get him into court, there was something not right about the whole thing. Something that made him uneasy, hesitant to push him further. Erikson might be perverted and too quick with his fists, but he didn't really fit the profile. He was too visible, too urbane, too confident. And that wasn't all that nagged him.

'What's up, Jack?'

He looked back at Anderson, hardly seeing him as the elusive grain of clarity once more evaded cohesive thought.

'I don't know,' he said slowly. His tired mind sifted through the interview that had just finished. 'I've got the feeling I've missed something vital. Something that slipped away before I could grab hold of it. But I'm so tired, the last few hours are just a blur.'

'Call your DS and meet me at the King's Head for a pint.'

Stoneham mumbled assent, the interview going round and round in a confusing jumble in his head as he reached for the telephone. Perhaps he'd think better after a good night's kip.

*

Malcolm finally managed to get away from the nurse who asked too many questions and who looked so probingly into his face. He shivered as he closed the door behind him and hurried away. How could she have known him? What was it she saw in his eyes? Could she hear the voices too?

He exchanged the trolley for a wheel-chair. It was easier to push and made it look as though he was busy. They were always busy in places like this, he thought. Taking people away, bringing them back, an endless parade of locked doors and white uniforms.

The antiseptic smell that was so horribly familiar was strong in his nostrils, invading his senses. This place was closing in on him, bringing the voices to scream and claw as they fought to free themselves from his head. The train was bearing down on him, looming out of the darkness of the tunnel, the sound of its wheels burning fire through the tracks of his mind.

She was here, close, closer. Calling him, drawing him in, showing him the way to silence the turmoil he could no longer control.

'The time is right, right, right. Do it now, now, now. Find her, find her, find her.'

Malcolm's plimsolls squeaked on the highly polished floor as he hurried down corridors. His eyes blinked rapidly as he tried to read the confusing signs on the walls. She had to be here – had to – the voices had told him. She had told him. But where, where?

He thrust open doors, and eyed each passer-by with intensity as his footsteps quickened. It would be dark soon. The time was coming for the circle to be joined.

Malcolm hesitated and leaned against a wall to catch his breath. He was suddenly afraid. Where had that thought come from? It was alien, nothing to do with his intentions.

He took off his glasses and rubbed his hand over his eyes. If only the voices would still. If only his head didn't hurt so much. He couldn't think, couldn't concentrate.

A voice down the hall brought his head up and he sniffed the air. He'd caught a scent, a presence that was stronger than those around it. It was her. He'd found the source.

The door was open just enough for him to see into the room. Yet as he edged forward and saw the occupants of that room, his courage left him.

He felt the shifting, sighing weight of the voices still. In their place came a silence, a void more terrible than he'd ever experienced. And in the darkness of that void came a glimmer of white that brought back memories. Memories he'd pushed to the furthest recesses of his mind, never to take out and examine. Memories that had the power to bring back the agony of the wheels on the tracks.

Now he understood the significance of the ring of time.

*

'Ramona? Jack Stoneham.'

'At last. What you doing up there, Guv? Having an all-nighter?' Her voice was jovial, but edged with something else.

'Looking that way,' he replied through a yawn. 'What's going on your end?'

'Mrs Kingsley's phoned. The daughter's turned up.'

Stoneham felt a pleasurable lightening of spirit, at last something was resolved.

'There's been a couple of developments though, both bad news, and I don't quite know how you're going to take it.'

The pleasure died instantly at the sound of her wary voice. 'What now?'

'Mrs Kingsley seems to believe her daughter can see things.' She hesitated. 'You know, visions, voices, things that are going to happen in the future.'

'Hold it right there, Ramona. I told you before, all that nonsense is for the birds. Just what the hell are you playing at, disturbing me with such drivel?'

WDS Knight sighed at the other end of the line and her superior officer shuffled his feet impatiently. He'd hoped for more sense from the level-headed Ramona Knight. Today was not turning out to be a good one.

'She says Cassandra's convinced there's a man stalking her and Melissa. Seems the kid can see him in her mind, and is putting the wind up everyone by saying he's out to kill her and her twin.'

Stoneham gave a snort of derisive laughter. He'd considered Laura Kingsley intelligent – odd how appearances could deceive.

'Mrs Kingsley's most insistent we take this seriously, Guv. She's been on the phone demanding police protection twice today already.'

DS Knight's voice was firm as it came down the line, but Stoneham thought he could hear a tremor of humour lacing through it.

'She says Cassandra knows he's hiding somewhere in the clinic and is just waiting to pounce. Seems this man has something to do with the past, though God alone knows what that's supposed to mean, and she's frightened for the twins' safety.'

'Sounds like the strain's been getting to her. If she phones again tell her we don't really have much to do with the occult. All our customers are, unfortunately for us, very much of this world. I suggest you advise her to see one of the doctors at that fancy clinic, and get some nice little white tablets.'

'Thanks for nothing, Guv. Knew you'd be a tower of strength in a moment of crisis.' The sarcasm was grade one, gold-plated purity.

'Send Giddings then. Do him good to see how the other half live. Tell him to have a quick shufty round, then get back double quick to his desk.' He sighed. 'If that's it, I'm off for a pint and a kip.'

'Wait!' DS Knight's voice stopped him from slamming down the receiver.

'Not more good news, I hope,' he drawled matching her sarcasm. 'I don't know how I'll stand all the excitement.'

'How are you getting on with Erikson?'

'I'm not. Something's bugging me and I don't know what it is.' Stoneham was suddenly serious as he tugged at his ear lobe. Mrs Kingsley's problems were minute compared to his at the moment.

'I think we could have been mistaken on this one, Guv.'

'Why?' he said carefully.

'Because forensics have just sent their report on the wig they found at Station Villas.'

'Ramona don't piss about. If you've got something to tell me then get on with it!' The anger was Stoneham's way of coping with the dread that was washing great icy waves through his head.

'Looks like we've got the wrong bloke again, Guv.

The wig was made up with human hair. The hair of eight different women, six of which match our victims. It's Malcolm Squires we have to find before he kills again.'

21

'Right, Felling. You've been doing all the donkey-work on the Squires murder. What you got?'

Stoneham threw off his coat and tossed it in the vague direction of the filing cabinet. He'd broken the speed limit on the M23 and had made the journey back to Brighton in record time.

'Malcolm Squires, twenty-four, kitchen porter. Missing for five days, didn't turn up for work and isn't claiming the dole. His supplementary benefit hasn't been collected this week either. Diagnosed as schizophrenic at nineteen and sent to Hellingly Hospital. A string of minor charges when he was a boy. Peeping into the women's changing rooms at the health centre, and on the new housing estate, stealing dirty books from the porno shop outside Victoria Station, and touching up some old trout who was walking her dog. He graduated to watching lovers in their cars, and following prostitutes to see what they got up to with their punters. Because of his youth he was given community service, then spent a brief spell in borstal.'

'No prison record, then?' Stoneham bit into the rather stale sandwich from the canteen, and wiped the mayonnaise off his chin.

Felling shook his head. 'There was some trouble with a tom over Ashford way. Seems she made fun of his inexperience and his inability to get it up. He saw red, went totally ballistic and attempted to strangle her with his bare hands.' He grinned. 'Picked the wrong one there.

Turns out the tom was built like a tank, with a right hook to match.'

Stoneham allowed himself to smile sadly. 'Poor bugger didn't have much luck, did he?'

'The police were only called in because a neighbour complained about the noise. The tom wasn't hurt, and she didn't want to press charges. But because of his previous record, the arresting officer decided to call in the shrink. Turned out Squires had this thing about trains.'

Stoneham looked up at Felling, his eyes wide with astonishment. 'I knew it,' he breathed.

Felling shook his head. 'Not that way, Guv. He reckoned they talked to him. Told him what to do. The shrink's report is all here, but what it comes down to is, Squires believed he had to obey the voices of the train wheels or they would come in the night when he was asleep and crush him on the rail.'

Felling smirked. 'A grade "A" nut, by all accounts.'

'What's his background? Anyone talked to his welfare officer?'

DS Knight perched on the corner of his desk. 'I did. She gave me access to his report. His father left when he was about fourteen. He's now living in Scotland with his second wife. There's been no contact with Malcolm since. The mother was a religious nut, preaching hell-fire to anyone that cared to listen, and when she realised that the rest of the world was on a course to damnation, she became somewhat of a recluse. Evidently she rarely left her bedroom.'

The three police officers exchanged world-weary sighs.

'The kid was always a loner, regarded as a prime target for bullying at school. He was classed as a failure, played truant regularly and left school with no qualifications. He was on the "at risk" register until he was fifteen, but as there was no sign of abuse, it was thought best to leave him with his mother.'

'No wonder he's gone the way he has,' muttered Stoneham. 'How come he went back to her when they let him out of Hellingly? Surely they could have found him sheltered accommodation?'

DS Knight shook her head. 'Not with the social services the way they are at the moment, Guv. They were only too pleased when the mother managed to convince the authorities that he was better off at home. It was about the only time in the last six years that she left the house. So, despite the fact that she herself should have been under medical supervision, Malcolm was released into her custody.'

Stoneham was making rapid notes. 'There's the five-year gap. He must have started killing when he was very young.'

His hand stilled. 'Shit,' he groaned. 'Now I know what it was that was bugging me.'

He ploughed through the envelope folders on his desk and pulled out Karen Walker's. It was incomplete. Snatching up the phone he dialled and waited. After a brief conversation with the DCI at Crawley, he slammed it back down.

'Shit, shit and shit. It was there all the time and I missed it.'

'What?' DS Knight swung off the desk.

'When Karen Walker's body was found, they rounded up three suspects. One of them was a fourteen-year-old boy who was seen coming away from the common at about the time Karen must have been killed. He was given an alibi by his mother and as the witness couldn't identify him from the line-up, they let him go and thought no more about it. I skipped over the report because it didn't seem to have any bearing at the time, but I should have been more careful.'

He plunged his face into his hands and expelled a great breath of regret. 'Lillian Squires said her son Malcolm was at home with her all day.'

He felt the sympathy she was trying to convey in the silence that followed his outburst. Yet it didn't make the carelessness any more bearable. He should have read the damn report more thoroughly, gone through it line by line and checked every tiny detail. Instead of that, he'd done a Chapman. Got the bit between his teeth and gone haring after the wrong suspect. Everything about Squires fitted the profile of the man he'd been seeking. The loner with a history of mental illness, the low intelligence, and the petty crimes that had begun to escalate. Now he had all the information at his finger-tips, but was he too late to stop it from happening again?

'Any more sightings of that bike,' he said finally as he scrubbed at his face and tried to get his brain into gear.

There was silence in the incident room.

The sound of the telephone made him start, and he snatched it up. 'Stoneham,' he barked.

'This is Laura Kingsley. I demand to know why you've sent a copper that's still wet behind the ears. My girls are in danger and I expect you to do something about it.'

Stoneham ran his hand through his hair and stifled the exasperation. This was the last thing he needed.

'Detective Constable Giddings might be young, Mrs Kingsley, but I assure you, he does know his job,' he said with all the tact he could muster.

'I know this sounds crazy to you, and I don't blame you for not believing me, but you have to promise to come out to the clinic and see me tonight. I'll explain everything when you get here.'

'I have a murder inquiry to deal with Mrs Kingsley, I just don't have the time or the man-power to go rushing around the countryside at the whim of someone who's been under a terrible strain. Why don't you just enjoy having your daughter home again, and get a good night's sleep.'

'Does this inquiry have something to do with a very large woman in a nightdress, Stoneham?'

The DCI gripped the receiver. 'I cannot discuss . . .'

'A woman with a wig?' Laura Kingsley interrupted.

He threw a surprised glance at his DS who was listening on the extension.

'What do you know about that, Mrs Kingsley?'

'More than you think,' said Laura grimly. 'I'll expect you within the next half hour.' The line was disconnected.

Stoneham slowly dropped the receiver into its niche as his gaze held Ramona Knight's.

She shrugged. 'Giddings running off at the mouth again?'

Stoneham chewed his thumb. 'I don't think so. Why should he need to tell her anything about the Squires inquiry? He was only there to find out what was making the woman so jumpy, not to regale them with murder hunts.'

A rather nasty, weasel thought was squirming through his mind and, try as he might, he couldn't dismiss it.

'What was it Giddings said about one of the patients at that fancy clinic? Something about strange drawings, foxes, eyes.'

DS Knight picked up her coat and put it on. 'You dismissed it as hocus-pocus. Don't tell me you're turning into a believer of the occult, Guv?'

Her amused expression irritated the hell out of him and he leaped from his chair and headed for the door. 'You know, Ramona. There are times when you really piss me off.'

'Likewise,' she retorted without rancour.

*

Malcolm pressed back into the shadow of the pillar as the door was swung open and the man stood, silhouetted in its frame.

'I won't be long, honey. You sure you're okay?'

'Just hurry back, Ben,' came the woman's voice from inside the room.

Malcolm watched as the tall American passed him and went out the door. The journey back to the hotel would take at least half an hour. He should be gone for quite a while if he had to pack a case. It was the two women that frustrated him. They never left the room together, and it looked as if they were planning to stay the night.

The hallway lights dimmed as the darkness outside became total. Malcolm remembered how they had done the same thing at That Place. It was the signal for the nightly round of pills and the final slamming of the doors before the long hours of loneliness. He would have to hurry.

He eased out from behind the pillar and felt the comforting presence of the things he'd fetched from the bike. They nestled in his pocket, ready for when he would need them. It was a part of the ritual he always played out before he went hunting, but his mind couldn't quite grasp what the rest of that ritual was. He seemed to remember long fine hair and the taste of something sticky on his mouth, but the memory slipped away from him, leaving only a trace of candle smoke to taunt him.

'The time is right. Do it now. Silence her.' The wheels were whispering, gathering speed as they approached.

'I'm going to phone Stoneham again.' The woman's voice came from the room and Malcolm could hear the tap, tap, tap of her heels on the polished floor.

He scuttled back into the shadows and finding one of the doors ajar, pressed into the room. It was empty. From his vantage point, he watched the woman hurry purposefully down the long corridor and disappear around the corner.

Malcolm drew back his lips in a feral grin, and his heart began to drum to the beat of the train wheels. He knew the telephone box was at the other end of this floor because he'd followed her the first time. She would be gone long enough for him to carry out the ritual.

'Seek her out,' hissed the wheels as they emerged from the vapour of steam and bore down on him with malevolence. 'Seek her out and destroy.'

Malcolm felt the strength that their whispers brought him. They drowned the insistent murmur of her voice and gave him confidence. If he did as they said, then she would leave him alone, and he could go back to the comfort of what he knew and understood. The soothing sound of well-oiled wheels on a track and the siren song of their lullaby.

The door to their room was closed, but Malcolm suddenly felt confident about what he must do next. But he had to hurry, there was no time to waste.

'Telephone call for Mrs Kingsley,' he called as he rapped firmly on the door.

The older woman opened it a crack and looked up at him. 'She's not here. Who would call her?'

Malcolm shook his head as he kept the door between himself and the two evil females that he knew were on the bed.

'They just said it was urgent,' he said, giving her a beaming

Reap the Whirlwind

smile. Women always said he had a nice smile. It was how he got them talking. How he fooled them into thinking he meant no harm.

The woman threw a hesitant look over her shoulder, then stepped out and shut the door firmly behind her. 'I suppose it'll be all right if it's urgent,' she murmured to herself. 'Where's the phone?'

'In the doctor's office,' replied Malcolm, still smiling, still maintaining eye contact. He could feel the excitement churning in his stomach and the slick coldness of the sweat on his palms.

'Dr Baines' office? Why should anyone be calling my daughter there?'

'They did say it was urgent,' he persisted, feeling the smile slip a little as the frustration mounted. Why didn't she just go? The other one would be back soon and then there would be trouble.

'Are you sure it was for Mrs Kingsley? No-one else knows we're here except for the police, and she's talking to Stoneham right now.'

Malcolm nodded, his hand slipping into his pocket, his fingers caressing the shiny, sharp smoothness of the thing he had hidden in there. If she didn't shut up right now, he would have to silence her.

The woman gave him a piercing glance, then turned and hurried away.

Malcolm exhaled and released his grip on the worn, wooden handles of the weapon in his pocket. At last.

He watched her hurry down the corridor, then listened as her footsteps rattled down the stairs. He was alone, and the only thing between him and the source of the troublesome, probing voice, was the thickness of a plywood door.

With a steady hand, he reached out and turned the handle.

*

'If this is a wild goose chase, then I'm going to arrest Mrs Kingsley for wasting police time,' muttered Stoneham as he swung the car round the tortuous bends of the downland road. 'I've got better things to do than play nursemaid to a couple of hysterical teenagers.'

'We're all tired, Guv. It's been a long couple of weeks. But if you don't slow down, neither of us will live to be nursemaid to anyone.'

The DCI eased his foot off the accelerator, but his fingers still gripped the steering wheel. The headlights picked up the ragged hedges on either side of the road, and the trees dipped threateningly close overhead. The countryside was all right most of the time, but at this moment he wished he was back on the streets of London. At least you could drive from A to B in a reasonably straight line.

The imposing gates were standing open and the headlights picked up the long gravel drive. He drove straight to the front steps and slammed on the brakes, the tyres spitting gravel onto the neat bordering flower beds.

'Remind me to drive next time,' the WDS said drily as she clambered out of the car. 'I forgot what a maniac you are when you get behind a wheel.'

'Where the hell's Giddings? I told him to meet me here.' Stoneham glanced around him, then saw the young policeman sheltering in the dimly lit porch. He was having a crafty fag.

'Sorry about this, Guv. She wasn't having any, it was you or the Chief Constable.' The cigarette was hastily crushed beneath his boot.

'Did you put the idea of Lillian Squires into her head, Giddings?'

The bright, blond head shook vigorously. 'There's a couple of things I think you should know before you go in there, Guv. Mrs Kingsley's not as daft as you might think.'

Stoneham stuffed his hands in his anorak pocket and swayed on his heels. 'And why is that, young Giddings?'

'That girl of hers, the one who went missing – well she's been saying all kinds of things. Don't mind telling you, Guv, it shook me up a bit. Can't really blame the mother for losing it. Not after what she's been through.'

'Hmph. Cassandra's probably high on something if she's been with the travellers.'

'No, Guv. The doctor's seen her.' He put a restraining hand on his superior's arm. 'There's another thing. I was about to come out to meet you when this nurse stopped me and asked me why I was here. Turns out she saw a man in the hospital today that she thought she recognised. It was only as she was coming off duty that she remembered where she'd seen him before.'

The Brighton detective stilled. 'So?' His flesh was beginning to creep and there was a dull nausea in the pit of his stomach.

'She was about to tell the doctor in charge when she saw me. The porter was once a patient in Hellingly.'

Stoneham was on the move. 'Call for back-up at once, Ramona. Come on, Giddings, show me the way, then get the person in charge of this place to meet me there.'

The sound of their running feet brought people into the hallways, but Stoneham ignored them in his haste. The corridors seemed endless and the flights of stairs steep, but finally he was on the right floor. He skidded to a halt as he saw Laura Kingsley come towards him.

'About time. I was just . . .'

'Where're your daughters,' he rasped, grabbing her arms to silence her.

Laura's eyes widened in horror, then she seemed to gather her strength and was running beside him. 'What's happened?' she gasped as they sped along the corridor.

Stoneham didn't answer her. As they reached the door, he pulled Laura to one side and slowly pushed it open.

*

Cassandra could see only the man in front of her. The man who had haunted her dreams and come to her in the visions. At last she could see his face from behind that mask of anonymity.

'I knew you would come,' she whispered.

'I'm here to silence you. To put an end to the whispering in my head.'

Cassandra saw him reach into his pocket. Saw the rubber mask in his hand and knew fear.

'You have to pay for what you did.' Melissa's voice was in her head, urging the forces to gather, so they could fight this final battle of wills. She tightened her grip on Melissa's hand and gave herself up to that force.

'I have the power of the wheels to guide me,' shouted Malcolm as they faced him. 'You can't punish me.' Yet he didn't move towards them, he merely slipped the mask over his face and glared wildly through the narrow slits of the foxy face.

Cassandra felt the energy surge through her, growing in strength, radiating from her and her sister to the man that stood before them. She saw him falter, watched as the pale blue eyes blinked behind the mask, and the hands fumbled with the worn handles of the cheese cutter.

The autumn leaves were rustling now, flickering in the sunlight, chattering in the cold wind that blew through the hills and valleys of her mind. Melissa was with her, she too could see the leaves, could hear their dry, crackling rasp as they blew to the four corners of the earth.

'I see a boy,' Cassandra murmured. 'A boy not yet fully grown. There's a child with him. A little girl. It's my sister.' The pain shot through her as the scene unfurled, but, like the man before her, she was incapable of pulling away, of blanking out the horror that lay in wait for her.

Malcolm could also see the park which was distanced from the housing estate by the main road. At the top of the hill, sheltered by a stand of oak trees, the panorama of the town sprawled before him. Yet his focus wasn't on the lines of roofs, or the arteries of tarmac which fed the heart of that town, it was on the child that stood trustingly beside him.

She was a pretty little thing, he acknowledged, as his gaze swept over her blonde curls and baby face with its blue eyes and soft mouth. At six, she was several years younger than him, but he could see how she would look in ten years time. It was the reason he'd persuaded her to come with him to the park. The reason why he hated her.

'Want to go home now,' she whispered, her thumb creeping slowly to her mouth, her eyes bright with tears. 'Want my mummy.'

He tightened his grip on her hand as the impatience mingled with the excitement. Yet he didn't want to frighten her, so he hunkered down and pulled her close. She was soft and warm and he could smell the sweetness of her. It was right that he should end it today. End it before the years turned the sweetness sour, and the softness, tensile.

'I've got something to show you,' he murmured. 'There's rabbits. Don't you want to see them?'

She shook her head, making the curls bounce and glitter in the last of the sun. 'Want to go home,' she mumbled around her thumb.

He took a deep breath and pulled her into the lengthening shadows of the copse. 'Let's play a game,' he said, the gathering maelstrom of emotions cracking his pre-pubescent voice.

'Don't want to play.' She was crying now, tugging her hand to release his grip. 'Want to go home. Want my mummy.'

He came to an abrupt halt. They were in a small clearing. The traffic on the main road was muted, and the only sound that came with the dusk was the rustle of birds in the tree tops. The shadows were deeper now, cloaking the trees with ebony fingers.

The power was on him. The need surging out of control. It was time – the wheels had told him so.

'Go on then. Find your mum,' he said harshly as he pushed her away, his gaze pinned to the tear-streaked face that looked up at him. Tears couldn't sway him. He'd witnessed too many with Lillian, and they had lost their power. Now he had to be strong, purposeful. Play out the game he'd imagined repeatedly over the last year when Lillian thought he was sleeping.

She looked round fearfully, her cotton dress a glimmer of white in the pool of gathering darkness. Her sobs were louder now, dimpled hands rubbing at her eyes as she sidled back to him.

'I'm frightened,' she hiccupped through the tears. 'Don't like it here.'

Malcolm took the rubber mask out of his pocket. His hands were steady, but he could feel the damp expectation on his skin.

'Play a game with me,' he said quietly, his gaze never leaving her face. 'Then you can go home to your mum.'

'Promise?' she whispered, as the thumb crept back into her mouth.

The boy nodded, then slipped the mask over his face. He watched the growing terror in her eyes and his mouth dried. The smell of the rubber mask mingled with his breath and the knowledge of what was to come thrilled in his blood. He took a pace and loomed over her. He had her full attention.

'I am the Fox,' he growled. 'And you are the rabbit. You have to run. Run as fast as you can. 'Cos if I catch you. I'll kill you.'

The trance was broken for Cassandra by an alien sound in the room. It was the sound of plimsolls squeaking on a tiled floor.

Malcolm was slowly advancing, the cheese wire stretched between his hands. His eyes were wild and staring behind the mask, his breath a rasp.

'I only wanted to play. I didn't mean to hurt her, but she fell and bumped her head, and she wouldn't stop screaming. It was the voices that made me kill her. The voices of the wheels.'

'I'm the voice of all the others, Malcolm. And my voice is stronger and more powerful than that of your wheels. Why, Malcolm? Why did you kill all those innocent girls?'

'They were all Lilllan. Lillian before she grew fat and old and disgusting. I had to do it, had to stop it before they changed. She took away my sex, made it dirty. I had to do the same with hers.' He advanced another step. They were inches away from each other.

Cassandra reached behind and felt for the chair. She

gripped it as she and Melissa held Malcolm's gaze. Her fingers tightened around it. She was lifting it, swinging it, plunging it into his face, knocking him off balance. Now she was advancing, smashing the chair over his body as he cowered on the floor.

'You have to pay for what you've done, Malcolm Squires. You have to pay,' she grunted as her arm rose and fell and the chair thudded into him.

'Cassie, stop it!'

Laura's voice came from some distant place that had no meaning in the world she was lost in. She lifted the chair, ready to strike again. Strong hands pinned her arms and took it away.

'C'mon, luv. It's over,' said a gruff, but kindly voice very close to her ear.

Cassandra looked around in dazed confusion. Why were Mum, and Granny C, and Ben looking at her in such a strange way? Why were there so many people crowding into the room?

She suddenly felt deadly tired. The rustling leaves were returning to flicker behind her eyelids, and the first crashing waves were breaking over the rocky landscape of her strength.

'Melissa?' Her voice sounded odd, distant and not really a part of her.

She felt her sister's hand creep into her own and grasped it. Then as she looked into Melissa's eyes, she realised the visions were gone for ever. Justice was done – the circle completed.